RAVE REVIEWS FOR THE WORK OF
SHANNON DRAKE

"Drake is an expert storyteller who keeps the reader
enthralled with a fast-paced story peopled with
wonderful characters."
—*Romantic Times BOOKreviews* on *Reckless*

"Shannon Drake lures [readers] into a spellbinding
romance tinged with a gothic twist."
—*Romantic Times BOOKreviews* on *Wicked*

"Drake weaves an intricate plot into a delicious romance,
which makes for captivating, adventurous
and wonderfully wicked reading."
—*Romantic Times BOOKreviews* on *When We Touch*

"Bringing back the terrific heroes and heroines from
her previous titles, Drake gives *The Awakening* an extra-
special touch. Her expert craftsmanship and true
mastery of the eerie shine through!"
—*Romantic Times BOOKreviews*

"Well-researched and thoroughly entertaining."
—*Publishers Weekly* on *Knight Triumphant*

"Captures readers' hearts with her own
special brand of magic."
—*Affaire de Coeur* on *No Other Woman*

"Shannon Drake continues to produce
addicting romances."
—*Publishers Weekly* on *No Other Woman*

SHANNON DRAKE

Beguiled

HQN™

ISBN-13: 978-0-373-77131-8
ISBN-10:   0-373-77131-2

BEGUILED

For Linda Haywood, Alice Dean and Paula Mayeaux—
and morning coffee on the Carnival Pride.

PROLOGUE

God, do not save the queen!

THE PEN WAS INDEED MIGHTIER than the sword. His fingers might work upon a typewriter, but the sentiment was the same.

Giles Brandon felt his power as he worked in blessed silence. And thank the Lord, he was just coming to the end.

By God, he was good.

Giles pulled the final draft of his article from his typewriter, a self-satisfied smile on his lips. It might be said he was smirking, he thought, amused, but this was probably the best and most inflammatory piece he had done yet.

He set the paper down, leaned back in his chair and

folded his hands over his chest for a moment, basking in his achievement and this moment of silence in which to savor his own talents. His London town house was one of the few set back from the busy street, so he didn't have to deal with the sounds of the common man hurrying about on business, the clatter of hooves on the pavement that came with horse-drawn vehicles, or, by God, the growl and heave and obnoxious horn-tooting of the new-fangled automobiles now becoming more and more popular among the monied classes—and even those not quite so monied, as well. Thick damask drapes covered the windows, adding to the insulation. Indeed, he could hear nothing from the street.

He lifted a hand whimsically. "Indeed," he said aloud. "The pen *is* truly a far more lethal weapon than the sword."

Of course, there was no one to answer. He'd sent his wife—God bless her, the fortune she had brought him, and the fact that she was easily browbeaten by his genius—to her sister's. Talent such as his demanded total concentration. He'd also given the skinny old bag of a housekeeper the night off. He was in his element now. Alone.

He laughed and spoke aloud again. "Alone with my favorite companions, sheer intelligence and cunning—and myself."

Reverently, he picked up the typed sheet of his own brilliance. "This will have them all riled up in the streets." He made a chortling sound. He wasn't so sure he wanted to be in the midst of such upset himself, but he certainly enjoyed the concept of bringing it about. He had been mocked one time too many, his name had been left off one too many invitation lists when it had certainly deserved to be there.

So now…those in power would pay.

He read his headline out loud with dramatic intonation.

"'Has the Monarchy Resorted to Cold-blooded Murder?'"

Yes, people would be grumbling in the streets. There was already suspicion brewing. Well, naturally. It was those who were campaigning to rid the country of the monarchy who had met such a sorry demise.

If he weren't so well mannered, he would certainly have rubbed his hands together in glee.

He stood back from his chair and looked around, reveling in what he had accomplished. This incredible house—of course, it had come through his wife's family, but no matter. His desk was the finest cherrywood. The lamp on his desk was a Tiffany. His carpet was rich and thick and from the Middle East. Yes, he had done well, and all because of the brilliance of his written word.

Tomorrow, the article would run.

And by mid-afternoon…

"By George, I am…" For all of his dexterity with the English language, he could think of no other word. "Brilliant!"

The sudden sound of clapping from just behind him startled him so badly that his heart skipped a beat. He swung around, stunned. He had been alone for hours, so who…?

A figure stood at the rear of the room, right in the corner where the rows of bookshelves met, clapping not with enthusiasm but slowly, rhythmically, with…mockery.

"You!" Giles said, his eyes narrowing with fury. He glanced at his office door. It remained closed, as it had been. The house was locked up; of that he was certain. The housekeeper knew he would have her ears if she ever dared leave without locking up.

So…?

"Brilliant, Giles, oh, yes, just brilliant," the intruder said.

"What are you doing here? How the hell did you get in?"

The visitor shrugged, walking from the shadows into the pool of light cast by the lamp on the desk.

Though Giles could now see his unwelcome caller—and could see no weapon—he felt a sudden sense of acute terror. It was impossible that anyone had gotten in. Impossible that they were alone in a vast world of shadow.

He could not hear the world inside this haven of his…

And no one could hear *him*.

"I serve the greatest good of this country, and I do it well," Giles flared.

"You serve yourself, and you are an egotist," replied the figure. A slow, wry smile touched cruel lips. "But you are about to perform a far greater service. After all, as you have written, we must all be willing to sacrifice."

Giles Brandon's eyes widened.

Only now did he see the weapon.

"No!" he roared.

"You will serve your country, and I promise you, your eulogy will be...brilliant."

Fight! he told himself.

He was a big man.

But, sadly, not an agile one.

He was barely aware when his feeble attempts at defense were thwarted. He didn't even feel the pain.

He *was* aware of his own terrible scream...

Thoughts, madly, insanely, rushed through his head.

The pen *was* mightier than the sword. But a well-honed knife in the hands of a madman...

He felt the hot spill of his own blood; the darkness that had encircled the little haven of light surrounding his desk began to encroach. It flooded his eyes with gray and shadow. And then...

He reached for the paper on his desk. His article. Brilliant. Oh, yes, he was brilliant. His hands spasmed; his fingers shook.

He touched the paper.

He heard his own scream growing fainter, fading....

Scream, he ordered his mouth, his throat, but his body disobeyed.

He choked and gurgled, a horrible gasping sound.

That, too, went unheard beyond the walls of his office, isolated so that a mind such as his would go undisturbed by the annoying clatter of humanity.

Outside the world went on, the sound of hoofbeats on cobblestones and pavement loud. An automobile horn blasted. Music blared from one of the restaurants. A horse whinnied....

And behind the heavy draperies, in the office far from the street, all was finally silent.

Giles Brandon's blood seeped into the fine Middle Eastern carpet as he stared with unseeing eyes.

He heard his heartbeat slowing.

Thump, thump...thump...

And then no more.

He died in quiet, in the silence he had craved, his last thought still an insistence that he was all powerful, the pen, mightier than the sword....

But flesh was weak and a knife sharp.

CHAPTER ONE

"DOWN WITH THE MONARCHY!"

Ally Grayson could hear the shouting as the carriage slowed. They were passing along the main street of the small village of Sutton, and she had suspected, even as they neared the town, that there might be trouble. Both saddened by the mood of the country and curious, she drew back the curtain of the carriage window.

People were milling about in an angry mood bearing placards that read "End the Reign of Thieves!" and "Royal Murder!" Some trudged the street in silence; others shouted angrily before the fine redbrick building that housed the sheriff's office.

Sour stares met the carriage, but no one moved against it. Ally was on her way to see her godfather, Brian Stirling, Earl of Carlyle, an admired and beloved figure despite the fact he was an ardent supporter of sad and aging Victoria. No one would wield a finger against him, his property or those beneath his protection, as his carriage proclaimed her to be.

Still, the tension in the streets was ugly.

Ally saw several people she recognized. Just outside one of the decaying Tudor houses that were so common in the area, she could see the journalist Thane Grier, not taking part in any way but observing avidly. She took time to observe him herself. He was a tall, handsome man, eager to move up in the world and be recognized as a writer of note. She wasn't at all certain what his opinion on the matter at hand might be, nor would he himself think it mattered. She thought—having read many of his articles—he would report objectively. He was not so determined to be an essayist as he was to be known for his acute eye and sound evaluation of the facts.

"See here!" came a shout from the sheriff himself as he emerged onto the steps in front of his office. "You will all stop this nonsense and go about your business!" he roared. "By God, what have we come to? Circus shows?"

Ally felt sore that the sheriff, Sir Angus Cunningham, would have the power to quiet the crowd. He was a war hero who had been knighted for his service in India. A big man, tall, broad-shouldered—and in the process of acquiring an ample girth—he had a head full of snow-white hair, muttonchops and a distinguished mustache.

Even so, there were a few more rumblings, despite the

sheriff's words. "Murder," a woman cried out weakly. "Two men murdered—and them men who spoke out against the waste in Her Majesty's court. Something must be done about a queen who condones—no, orders—such heinous and foul deeds."

Ally couldn't see the woman's face. She was clad in black, a veil observing her features. She was wearing widow's weeds. She did recognize the woman standing next to her, who tried to hush her and draw her into her arms. It was Elizabeth Harrington Prine, widow of Jack Prine, a valiant soldier who had died in South Africa. Through her husband, she owned thousands of acres just west of the forest surrounding the village.

"Murder!" the woman in black shouted again.

Sir Angus didn't get a chance to reply. He was joined on the steps by an ally in the cause of justice, the elderly Lord Lionel Wittburg. Wittburg was taller but thinner, and his hair was pale silver rather than solid white. His reputation, however, reached back almost as long as the queen's reign, and the country had always loved him as a stalwart soldier. He echoed the words that were in Ally's own mind. "How dare you?"

But though he spoke the words full force, Ally sensed he was about to start crying, and she knew why. Hudson Porter—a man with whom he had little in common but who had been a dear comrade from his days in India—was one of the anti-monarchists who had so recently been slain.

A third man joined them. He was far younger, very attractive, a gentleman often seen on the society pages—

a man who had the ability to charm those around him. "Please, this is unseemly behavior for good Englishmen. And women," he added with a roguish smile. "There is no call for this, no need for this." He was Sir Andrew Harrington, cousin of the widow trying to give solace to the woman in black. Hudson Porter had not been married, Ally knew, so the woman could not be his widow. A sister, cousin...lover? The other activist who had been slain, Dirk Dunswoody, had been eighty years old if a day at the time of his murder, and in all those years he had remained a bachelor, studying law and medicine, traveling abroad with the queen's army for much of that time. Why he had turned so violently against the monarchy, no one knew, unless it was because he had felt he should have been knighted for his service. Ally knew there had been a strange scandal associated with his name, and in its wake he had been passed over.

"Please, please, everyone. Go about your business. We will solve nothing here, and all of you know that," Sir Angus told the crowd.

There were continued murmurings, but there was movement, as well.

The crowd was apparently dispersing enough for Shelby, Lord Stirling's coachman, valet, assistant and man of all work to drive the carriage through the streets. As he carefully wended his way, Ally saw that Thane Grier, still keeping his silence and his distance, was busy scribbling notes on a pad he pulled from his vest pocket.

She dropped the curtain as they left the small village

square behind and headed along the road through the forest.

She didn't notice at first when the carriage began to pick up speed. She had dropped deep into thought, worrying about the state of the realm, then about her own situation. She couldn't help but wonder about the summons that was bringing her to the castle. It undoubtedly had something to do with the fact that her birthday was fast approaching. Though she had considered herself an adult for quite some time, her guardians had wanted to protect her from the world as long as possible, and it was only on this birthday that she would finally be considered an adult in their eyes. She loved those who had raised her and cared for her, but she was eager to have a say in her own life. Though her upbringing had been sheltered, she thrived on newspapers and books, and had savored each of her few excursions into the city, to a world of theaters and museums. She certainly considered herself intelligent and well educated, even if most of that education had taken place in a small school in the country or from the private tutors who had been sent to her humble home deep in the woods.

She had managed a bit of a peek at the real world. Though she had grown up in the care of her three "aunties," she'd also had the benefit of her three sets of godparents. How she had been so blessed, she couldn't even imagine. Three wonderful, sweet women to actually raise her, and as an incredible addition to her life, three couples numbered among the peers of the realm to see that she received the best education and many benefits. Those latter three ladies—Maggie, Kat and Camille—were amazing, unique, and had once been hellions, she dared say to herself, even if not to them. She was glad of their wild past, because if they were to become angry when they discovered she had been taking her future into her own hands, she could remind them they were rather modern women themselves. Lady Maggie had defied all convention to minister to the prostitutes in the East End, Camille had met her Lord husband through her work in the Egyptology department at the museum; and Kat had already ventured out on several expeditions to the pyramids of Egypt and even into the Valley of the Kings. They could hardly expect her to be meek and mild and *not* want to make her own way in the world.

As she brooded, the carriage began to go faster and faster, and finally it began to career madly down the road.

Ally was roused from her meditations when she was slammed from one side to the other. She struggled to find her seat once again, and then held on for dear life. She wasn't afraid, just puzzled.

Was Shelby worried that the protesters who had filled the village square might be coming after them? That couldn't be. Surely he knew that frightened farmers and country shopkeepers would offer no real threat. Especially not when there were such illustrious men as Sir Harrington, Sir Cunningham and Lord Wittburg there to assure them.

So why was Shelby suddenly driving like a maniac?

She frowned, scrambling for balance, and realized that the deaths that had brought on the fear and frenzy in the village were certainly frightening enough. Two men murdered, public figures whose views opposed the Crown and who had pushed for an end to the monarchy. The deaths were terrible, and the times in general were hard. The poor queen, Victoria, aging and still so sad; Prince Edward taking on more and more duties; the threat of war in South Africa again...naturally, people were distraught. For many, poverty and ignorance superceded the amazing progress that Victoria's reign had brought in the fields of education and medicine. Workers were protected now, as they had never been before. There were those who protested the allowance given the Royal House. Those who felt that the royals did not do enough to warrant the money spent on the upkeep of their many properties and lavish lifestyle. England had a prime minister and a Parliament, and many felt that should be enough.

With a sharp thunk, a wheel went into a pothole, and she nearly hit the ceiling. What was going on? Shelby wasn't the type to be easily alarmed. He wouldn't be frightened by law-abiding protesters. Then again, the protesters were not the ones actually causing the tremendous unease in the streets and the press at the moment. That unease could be laid at the feet of those trying to inflame the crowd by making people believe that the monarchy was behind the murders of those politicians who were speaking out against them. There were far too many people willing to believe that the Crown was silently behind the murders.

She knew from her studies that anti-monarchists were not new to English politics, and she even understood, at least to some degree, why such a movement had come to the forefront again now. Despite Queen Victoria's determination to bring abstinence and goodness back to the Crown, her children, including her heir, had behaved scandalously. Back in the days of Jack the Ripper, there had even been a theory that her grandson, Prince Albert Victor, was the murderer. Since that day, a very vocal faction of anti-monarchists had not hesitated to step forward. These current murders, said by many to be the monarchy's attempt to quell that faction, had brought the political fever to such a rabid pitch that many of the country's sanest politicians were warning that there must be compromise and temperance, or there would be civil war.

Ally had never met the queen, but from all she had seen and heard, she couldn't believe that the woman who had brought such progress to her empire and still mourned a husband lost decades ago could be guilty of such horror.

But for all her knowledge of history and politics, she realized, she still had no idea why the carriage was racing so terrifyingly fast.

Suddenly, with a jerk, the carriage began to slow.

Surely, she thought, this could have nothing to do with the furor going on because two men, two politicians and writers who had viciously slandered the queen, had been found dead, their throats slit. Or with the distraught people in the streets, bearing their signs to protest the queen and Prince Edward. No, the cause of this had to be quite different, and if so...

If so, she knew the answer.

They moved slower, the horses walking now, not galloping. She heard the sound of a gunshot, and froze. There was shouting from nearby; then she heard Shelby calling hoarsely in return, but she couldn't understand his words.

"Stop the carriage!" a deep, authoritative voice thundered.

Tense, knowing that they were nowhere near the castle, Ally leaned toward the window, pulled back the drapery and looked out.

Her eyes widened in surprise, and it was then that icy rivulets of fear at last snaked through her system.

She had been right.

There was a rider right by her side, a man seated upon a great black stallion, clad in a black coat, hat and mask. Other riders shifted restlessly behind him.

The highwayman!

She had never dreamed that such a thing could happen in her humdrum life. As a devotee to several newspapers, she'd read about this man and his accomplices. In an age when more and more automobiles were finding their way onto the roads, they were being threatened by a highwayman on horseback.

He hadn't killed anyone, she reminded herself. In fact, some were comparing him to Robin Hood. No one seemed quite able to say just which poor people he was giving to, although shortly after the Earl of Warren had been held up, churches in the East End had suddenly been offered large sums to feed and clothe their flocks.

The highwayman had been stopping carriages for the past several months, and had stolen several things here and there, items of sentimental value, that had mysteriously made their way back to their owners. A thief, but not a murderer....

In fact, he had begun his depredations just after the first murder had taken place. As if the country had not had enough to worry about.

The wheels ground to a halt; she heard the whinnying protest of the horses, drawn up so short. And then she heard the coachman's words.

"My man, you'll not be harming the lass. You'll be shooting me first."

Dear Shelby. Her bulky champion and guardian for as long as she could remember. He would protect her to his dying breath.

And because of Shelby, she found courage.

She threw open the carriage door and called out to him. "Shelby, we'll risk no lives for the likes of this thief and his brigands. Whatever the fellow wants, we will give it to him and be on our way."

The highwayman reined in his great black steed and dismounted in an agile leap. His accomplices remained seated upon their horses.

"Who else is in that carriage?" he demanded.

"No one," she said.

He clearly didn't believe her. Striding to the open door, he reached in, seeking no permission. His hands landed upon her waist, and she was lifted unceremoniously from the elegant carriage and set upon the ground. The man apparently believed there must be some hidden compartment within, for he disappeared into the carriage, then jumped out to stand beside her.

"Who are you, and what are you doing, traveling alone on the road?" he demanded. His face was hidden by a black satin eye mask, but he had dark hair, pulled back in a queue at his nape. He wore a wool cape, and his riding boots reached his knees.

At first she was shaking, but she was not going to be cowed. If he meant to change his methods and kill her, he would do so one way or the other. Therefore, she would go down fighting. She would not grovel. He was a thief, a brigand, a wretched excuse for a human being.

"You are nothing but riffraff," she informed him, "and I don't see why my travel arrangements should be any of your business."

"Miss!" Shelby protested, afraid for her.

The highwayman nodded toward one of his men—also masked and dressed in black, a color that meant camouflage in the night—who approached Shelby as the coachman tried to ease a hand toward his pistol.

"Don't do it," the first man warned softly. "No harm will come to you—or the lass."

Ally wondered if it was the word "lass," coming from a man who had no idea of her accomplishments, that both irritated her and gave her such great courage. She was always dismissed as "the lass." Everyone was always doing what they considered best for her. Her accomplishments were applauded, yet her future seemed to belong to everyone but her. Thanks to her privileged upbringing, she knew Latin, French and Italian, geography, history and literature. She could play the piano much more than competently, sing due to the tutelage of Madame D'Arpe, dance because of Monsieur Lonville, and ride as well as any woman living, she was certain, despite an effort to remain humble. She was also very aware that women were beginning to take their places in many previously forbidden arenas; helping to form society and, indeed, the world. She was going to make her mark on the world. Somehow.

She was also the most guarded orphan in the empire, she was quite sure.

"You'll not touch that girl—" Shelby began angrily. But he did not finish. The highwayman had cracked the whip he carried, a long and lethal-looking thing that snapped through the air with the sharpness of a shot. The pistol Shelby had reached for went flying through the air as he cried out, not so much in pain as in surprise.

"My dear fellow," the highwayman said. "We've no wish to harm you *or* the girl. You'll step down, please."

Stiff, angry, wary, Shelby did so. Ally heard a soft expulsion of breath, and when she looked, he was no longer standing. He had sunk easily to the ground, as if he had simply been so tired he had gone to sleep standing.

She started to run toward him, crying out in alarm.

She did not reach him. The highwayman caught her by the shoulders. When she kicked and fought and tried to bite him, he swore softly.

"What is the matter with you, girl? You are playing with your life here."

"What have you done to him?"

"He will awake soon enough, none the worse for wear," he assured her.

"What did you do to him? You've killed him!"

"He isn't dead, I assure you."

She tried again to bite the hand that held her. "This is ridiculous," he hissed, and before she knew it, she was thrown over his shoulder and he was striding quickly off the open road and along a forest trail.

What had she done?

A trickle of fear slipped along her spine, despite her resolve.

"If you think you're going to slit my throat in the woods, you'll be truly sorry," she warned him. "They'll come after you. You are already wanted for your crimes. They'll revive public executions—indeed, they'll bring back drawing and quartering. I'm warning you—"

"You should start *begging* me," he warned.

"Where are you taking me?" she demanded. "You don't even know who I am!"

They had apparently reached his destination. She was quickly and unceremoniously set down on a tree stump next to a small stream through the woods. Oddly, the water bubbled melodiously. The sun was almost gone for the day, just disappearing into the horizon, so they were surrounded by pale glimmers through the canopy of the trees and the coming shadows of the night. He set a foot on the log and leaned close to her. "Seriously, lass, I don't know who you are. Had you answered that question for me at the start, you might well be on your way again already."

"Don't call me 'lass.'"

"I should be calling you an idiot."

"*I*? An idiot? Because I protest a wretched criminal who will surely end his days at the end of a rope?"

"If I'm to hang, anyway, what would it matter if I were to add your body to the list of my trespasses?" he demanded.

"You *will* hang," she said icily.

"Perhaps, but not today. Today, *you* will answer to *me*."

She fell silent, staring at him, once again forcing down any sense of fear. She would not go easily.

She stared at him, eyes burning, head high. "You are young and able-bodied. You might have found legitimate work easily enough. Instead, you have chosen a life of crime."

He laughed softly, truly amused now. "Indeed, lass, of all the young women I have encountered, you are definitely the most brazen. Or the most stupid. I haven't decided yet."

"I told you not to call me 'lass.'"

"You *are* a lass."

"Then you are nothing but a boy, playing at being a man."

He seemed to take no offense; indeed, he smiled slightly.

"Have you a title, then?" he inquired.

She stared at him coldly. "You may call me Miss."

"Miss. So who are you and where are—*were*—you going?"

"Are you an idiot, that you don't recognize a carriage belonging to the Earl of Carlyle?"

She couldn't tell whether he had recognized the carriage or not, for his next question was not an answer.

"What are you doing in his carriage?"

"I haven't stolen it," she retorted.

"That is not an answer."

"It's the only answer you're getting."

He leaned closer. "But it is not the answer I am seeking."

"I'm ever so sorry."

"Pray, don't be sorry—yet. Simply provide me with the information I seek."

"You are a bully and a thief. I owe you nothing."

"I am a highwayman. And your life and safekeeping are in my hands."

"Shoot me, then."

He shook his head, irritated. She lifted her chin. She was afraid, true, but she was oddly excited, as well. The blood was rushing through her veins. Ridiculous as it might seem, she felt up to the challenge.

Strangely, she didn't believe he would really harm her. There was something too…decent?…about his manner.

Perhaps this was simply what she had wanted: something had finally happened in her life. She felt as if she were really living, perhaps for the first time. How sad if it were all about to end.

He laughed aloud and the sound was easy and pleasant. "Let me start over. Dear *mademoiselle,* pray, please, tell me what you're doing in the earl's carriage?"

"Obviously I am going to see the earl."

"Ah. You're good friends, then?"

"He is something of a godfather to me," she explained.

"Indeed?"

"Yes, so you had best take care, lest you truly offend me."

"I'm afraid it matters not at all to me whom I offend."

"The earl will see you skewered through."

"The earl will have to catch me for that, don't you think?"

"Don't underestimate him."

"I never would."

"Pray, tell, exactly what do you want from me? I'm afraid I'm not carrying any riches."

He was still smiling, and his foot continued to rest on the log as he leaned close. She found herself wondering how such a man, well spoken, well dressed, smelling clean but with a hint of musk and leather, could have come to such a pass in life.

"Riches may be attained in any number of ways. If you're beloved of the earl, you're worth a pretty penny."

"I'm not that well loved," she said sharply.

His smile deepened. She wished she could see more of his face.

"Tell me more about yourself," he commanded.

She folded her hands in her lap. "Tell me more about *your*self."

"I asked first."

"But you already know more about me than I know about you," she reminded him primly.

"Ah, but I am the highwayman, and you are the victim," he said.

"Precisely. Victims are not required by any social standard to be cooperative," she informed him.

He leaned closer. "Victims are supposed to be frightened."

"Do you know what I think?"

"Pray, tell me."

"You are not at all dangerous."

"Really?"

"It appears to me that you have at least a modicum of intelligence, and that someone raised you properly. And that, if you chose, you could certainly do well enough without resorting to highway robbery and accosting random victims."

"I'm afraid," he murmured, "that you weren't a random victim."

She was startled, and a trickle of fear began to ice her blood.

"I have nothing. Why would you choose me?"

"You were in the earl's coach."

"Again, I tell you, I have nothing worth stealing," she assured him, more determined now than ever that he believe her.

"You might be quite valuable as a hostage," he informed her.

"Oh!" she cried in frustration. "You are a fool. What

is the matter with you? There are grave things going on in the world. We may well find ourselves in a state of anarchy. Men have been murdered. People are in an uproar. And you are worried about nothing but yourself."

"Hmm."

"Hmm? That's all you have to say?" she demanded.

"Are you going to challenge all the evil in the world?" he asked her softly.

"Are you willing to do nothing about all the evil in the world?" she countered.

He shrugged. "Let's see…can I change the world at this moment? Probably not. Can I change my own situation? I think so. Because I have you, whoever you are, a passenger in the Earl of Carlyle's carriage."

"Please, I have already informed you, I am not worth anything."

"Come, come. You cannot be that naïve. Not a woman of your obvious…worldliness."

She flushed, looking away. She felt as if fire were rushing through her. How could she be so ridiculous as to feel such a tide of emotion because of a highwayman? Good God, how pathetic. She would not allow it.

"I'm telling you, whatever you may wish to think, there is no threat you can make that will change me into a rich swan. I live in the company of several widows, gentle and kind and sheltered. They have little. I seldom leave the woods."

"But when you do, it seems, you leave in style."

"I am lucky to have landed friends who took interest in me as a child."

"Do you work for the earl?"

"No."

"Do you...?" He looked her up and down meaningfully.

"What are you implying?" she demanded indignantly, so angry that she rose, pushing him aside. "The lord's lady is one of the kindest and most beautiful women I have ever met, and I do assure you, he feels the same. How dare you...? Ah, you are but a highwayman, and anything of gentility I've sensed in you is nothing but a mask, far more concealing than the one upon your face. I believe I've quite finished with this ridiculous tête-à-tête, and I would sincerely appreciate it if you would return me to the carriage now."

At first she was afraid he would respond with violence—she had shoved him hard enough to send him reeling backward. For a moment she stood still, very still, regretting her action and wondering, as well, if she dared to run. She was unfamiliar with her surroundings, but running anywhere would have to be preferable to being his prisoner.

But he didn't respond with violence; he didn't even touch her. Laughing, he took a seat upon the fallen log himself.

"Bravo!"

"Bravo?"

"The earl is a lucky man to have such a staunch defender."

"The earl is known for his strength, ethics and honesty, something you would know and appreciate—if you weren't a rogue."

"Ah, that I were only such a man."

"Any man might strive to initiate his attributes."

"Might any man have such a castle?" he asked with amusement.

"A castle does not make a man," she told him primly.

"Nor riches?" he inquired.

She wasn't sure what it was in his tone—a certain bitterness perhaps—but it suddenly made her realize that she might well be in serious peril after all.

She had managed to put some distance between them when she had pushed by him, and now that he was seated, cocky, comfortable, quite certain he was the one in charge, it seemed like the right time to run.

There were many advantages to growing up in a cottage in the woods. She had spent endless days exploring the trails close to her house, playing with imaginary friends, running from place to place. She had often played with the children of the woodsman down the lane, and there had been a time when she was young when the son thought she was quite a hellion. So she was strong, fit and fleet. She thought that she could leave him in the dust.

At first, she did.

Heedless of the water, she bounded across the little rivulet and tore down one of the forest trails. There was a moment when she dared to take pleasure in the sound of his startled oath as she disappeared.

Then she realized not only that she was being followed but followed swiftly.

She tore under a canopy of trees, dexterously flying

over roots, rocks and fallen branches in her way. She kept running and running, following what appeared to be a path, then turning to crash through thicker foliage, hoping to lose her pursuer.

As she ran, the sound of pursuit diminished. Or perhaps it was the thundering of her heart that made all else silent in comparison.

Eventually, she had to stop. Her lungs were burning, her heart pounding in revolt, and her calves cramping. Her delicate boots were far from the perfect footwear for running through the forest.

She gripped a tree, inhaling, exhaling, trying to ease the pain in her chest and limbs. Her hair had come loose, and a wayward strand now teased her nose. She puffed at it, then drew it back, thinking she must look an incredible mess, and yet, at the same time, realizing with pride that she had done it.

She had eluded the highwayman.

Just as that pleasure began to sink in, she heard a soft chuckle.

She spun around.

He was leaning against a tree, arms crossed, as relaxed as if he had not a care in the world. Not a strand of hair had escaped his queue. He wasn't breathing hard. He didn't appear as if he had exerted himself at all.

She straightened, staring at him defiantly.

"You can't escape, you know."

"Actually, I did."

"No, you didn't."

She considered her position. Yes, she could run again. But how had he done it? Caught her in this place so easily?

Her heart sank as she realized her mistake. She had been so determined not to follow a clear trail that she had run in circles. He had realized her error and simply waited until she had come around through the trees.

She wouldn't make that mistake again.

"Don't do it. Such a waste of time and energy," he told her.

"I'm so sorry. Am I being inconvenient?" she asked sarcastically.

He shrugged. "Actually, I had no other pressing engagements for the day."

"You do realize that when the Earl of Carlyle realizes his carriage hasn't arrived, he'll begin searching?"

"Certainly…but not for a while yet, I don't believe."

"And why is that?"

"I suspect he's in the city. There's a celebration at Buckingham Palace today. Someone's birthday. I don't think he'll be home until the evening."

"You know so much about the Earl of Carlyle?" she asked, playing for time. She needed to catch her breath. She was certainly not going to tell him that he was mistaken as to the earl's whereabouts.

"I read the newspapers, Miss…ah, yes, that's right. You've not yet furnished me with your name."

"I don't remember you furnishing me with yours."

"You don't really want to know my name. That would make you dangerous to me, wouldn't it?"

"Then I shan't give you mine."

He smiled. "Caught your breath yet?"

"I'm quite fine, thank you."

"Don't do it."

"Do what?"

"Run again."

"What else would you have me do?"

"I've told you that I don't intend to hurt you."

"And I should trust you?"

"If you run, I'll merely have to catch you again."

"But perhaps you cannot."

He sighed, shaking his head. "I can. And you won't like it when I do."

"I don't like being told what to do, I don't like being held up, and I most certainly don't like conversing with a bandit."

He lifted his hands in a fatalistic gesture. "You must do what you must. And I must do the same."

She lifted her chin again, trying to bring some semblance of order to the streams of tangled blond hair now falling down her back and into her face, impairing her vision. "You could abandon your life of crime. Walk away now. Become a legend. Find gainful employment. Turn over a new leaf."

"I could…."

"Then you must do so," she insisted urgently.

"I'm sorry. I think not."

"Oh…" She let out a sigh of irritation. She saw his muscles beginning to tense, realized that in seconds he would be coming for her.

And so, with little other recourse, she ran again.

This time he caught her quickly.

She felt him behind her before he touched her. Felt the wind, the heat and the power of him.

Then his arms were around her.

The momentum of her desperate flight carried them both forward and down, onto the ground, into the dirt and pine-needle carpet of the forest floor. Her mouth seemed to fill with pine needles and the rich earth. Coughing, sputtering, she tried to turn, but he was on top of her. She managed to get faceup, but no further. He straddled her, still breathing easily and, the greatest insult, still merely amused.

She coughed, staring at him furiously. A greater fear seeped into her, for now she was truly caught.

She didn't try to argue with him; didn't urge him to get up. She simply slammed her fists against his chest with the greatest strength she could summon, twisting frantically at the same time. That managed only to bring forth his own temper at last. He caught her wrists and pinned them high above her head, leaning close as he did so.

His amused smile was gone at last, she was pleased to note.

Yet in that small victory, she realized, she herself was even more the loser.

"Would you stop?" he demanded.

She didn't answer him, only lay perfectly still, looking to one side.

He eased up, still straddling her but no longer pinning her so tightly to the ground.

"I told you that you wouldn't like it if I had to catch you," he said softly.

"You truly are a cad," she whispered.

"I'm a highwayman," he said impatiently. "Hardly a proper escort."

She became aware of his touch, the pressure of his thighs, the way he sat atop her without causing her pain.

Then he touched her.

He reached down, sweeping a wild strand of her hair from her face. His fingers seemed to linger ever so slightly on her cheek.

The touch was gentle, yet he had seized her with real power and did not intend to let up.

She didn't look at him. "What now?" she demanded. "Where do we go from here?"

"You tell me your name and purpose, all I have wanted from the beginning," he said.

She stared at him suddenly, brows knitting in a frown, fear seeping deeply into her again. She knew she should keep her mouth shut, but she could not.

"You're not...one of the anti-monarchists?" she breathed.

She was startled when he smiled, his knuckles brushing her chin with an almost tender assurance.

"No, I'm not. God save the queen. I'm a good, traditional English rogue," he swore softly.

She believed him. Flat on her back, totally his prisoner,

completely at his mercy, she believed him. She let out a soft breath.

"And you've no intention of killing me…or anyone?"

"Never, lass."

"Please stop calling me 'lass.'"

"You won't give me your name."

She stared hard at him. Their position was intimate, and the thought brought a swift flush to her cheeks. He was a complete blackguard, and she loathed herself for thinking his voice was husky, alluring, his touch the most tender she had ever known.

"If you would be so kind as to get off me…?" she suggested.

He rose and reached a hand down to her, lifting her to her feet with no effort. His hand lingered, then dropped from hers.

"My name is Alexandra Grayson."

"What?" he demanded sharply, frowning with such quick tension that she was momentarily taken aback, frightened once again.

Why?

There was nothing about her name, or herself, that should mean anything to anyone.

"I'm Alexandra Grayson, a nobody, I assure you. I have told you. I live in a cottage in the woods with several aunts. The Earl of Carlyle and his lady are like godparents to me. They, and others, have seen to my welfare for as long as I can remember."

"You—you are Alexandra Grayson?" He still sounded as if he were choking.

"What does my name mean to you?" she demanded uneasily, afraid that he had lost his sanity. His hands had tightened into fists at his sides.

He shook his head, easing his hands open. A second later, he was smiling again, amused once more.

"Nothing...it means nothing to me."

"Then—"

"I had thought you were someone else."

He was lying, she thought.

But she had no time to ponder his reasons, for he reached out a hand to her. She stared at it, swallowing hard, uneasy. He was very tall and strong in the green darkness of the forest. She felt the vibrancy and fire of him, though he was still. She had the strangest feeling that if she moved, leaned against him...

It would be good...sweet. Exciting.

So alive.

She stiffened, lowering her head, clenching her teeth. He was nothing but a common criminal!

She looked up. He was still staring intently at her.

"Come," he said at last. "I'll take you back to the carriage and send you on your way."

CHAPTER TWO

THE CARRIAGE SENT ON ITS WAY, Mark Farrow remained in the road, staring after it.

"Mark," Patrick MacIver said, removing his black silk mask, "we must move, and move quickly. That was the Earl of Carlyle's carriage. The minute they reach the castle, the earl will be out like a bloodhound."

The three friends who rode with him as the highwayman's band—Patrick MacIver, Geoff Brennan and Thomas Howell—were all staring at him. Mark nodded.

"We'll split up," he agreed. "Geoff, Thomas, take to the western woods. Patrick and I will travel the eastern route. Make sure you stop at the checkpoint and change horses. We'll do the same. We'll meet up at O'Flannery's, as planned."

They nodded but didn't move immediately. "Well," Thomas said at last, "who was she?"

"Alexandra Grayson," Mark replied.

Patrick let out a gasp. "That was *her*?"

"Quite attractive," Thomas said.

"Stunning," Geoff noted.

"Um...rather self-assured," Patrick noted. Minus his mask—sewn to cover most of his head beneath a hat, Patrick was a blazing and all-too-noticeable redhead.

"Interesting," Geoff said lightly. The son of Henry Brennan, an esteemed member of the House of Commons, Geoff was hailed among their foursome as a thinking man. Tall and lean, with a surprising amount of strength for his build, he was dark-eyed, dark-haired and often grave.

Thomas was the opposite. Sandy-haired, hazel-eyed and possessed of a mercurial sense of humor, he was serious only when necessary. At that moment, he burst into laughter. "You, Sir Farrow, are in trouble, I imagine."

"Shall we get out of here, and laugh at whatever situation I might find myself in later?" Mark suggested dryly.

"O'Flannery's," Geoff said, and by tacit agreement, they all turned their horses and started on their assigned routes for the City of London.

Mark and Patrick moved swiftly until they reached the clearing known as Ennisfarn, where the Farrow family had long maintained a hunting lodge. Though the only one guarding the stable there would be Old Walt, the men entered from the rear, quickly dismounted, stowed their cloaks, found their waistcoats and jackets, and unsaddled the horses. New tack was taken from the racks as they readied new mounts, all in haste and silence.

At last, remounted and on the trail again, their outlaw gear stowed in their saddlebags, Patrick spoke again. "I must say, having seen the girl, I believe I would jump at such a chance as yours, but...well, we are moving into a new world. It's quite archaic that your father insists upon arranging your marriage."

"He made the agreement with Brian Stirling when I was just a lad and the girl a babe," Mark said with a shrug. "I don't know why. She's not Lord Stirling's child, rather his ward. I've always assumed there must be a skeleton in the closet somewhere."

"Ah, yes. Illegitimacy, no doubt," Patrick murmured.

Mark scowled at him. "Don't think of starting such a rumor."

Patrick laughed. "I promise to do nothing of the kind." He grew serious. "Your impending marriage aside, I daresay we're not going to have much of a reputation left soon. We didn't even steal a piece of the girl's jewelry."

"Don't worry. We're going to O'Flannery's."

"And...?" Patrick inquired.

Mark grinned. "Why do you think I warned you against rumor? I intend to start one myself. Trust me—by nightfall, we shall be the most dangerous figures since the days of Jack the Ripper."

THERE WAS NOTHING WRONG with her, Alexandra thought, but from the moment the carriage arrived at the castle, Shelby created such a stir that she was treated like fragile glass. At the gates, before they set off along the long winding drive to the castle, Shelby started shouting for help. Several members of the earl's household rushed out, the countess among them, as they neared the front door.

"The police, my lady!" Shelby cried to the countess. "We must inform the police! We were held up by that despicable creature all the newspapers write of—the highwayman. I was knocked unconscious, and he kidnapped Miss Grayson. He is on the loose but cannot be far. The earl must be informed immediately. This is an outrage. And the poor girl! The gall. The utter gall. How dare he? Anyone in England should recognize the coat of arms on Lord Stirling's carriage."

The countess, Lady Camille, was instantly concerned, but thankfully, she had always been wise and levelheaded and not one to give in to the vapors. Before her marriage to the earl, she had been a commoner and had worked for a living, and she still gave time to the Egyptian department of the museum. She frowned, looking at Ally as Shelby distractedly helped her from the carriage.

"Shelby, please, calm down so we can ascertain all the facts. Ally, were you injured? Are you all right?"

"I'm fine, perfectly fine."

The earl, tall and exceedingly handsome, came up beside his wife. "You're quite sure?" he asked, reaching out to touch her hair. "You're wearing leaves."

"I swear to you, I'm absolutely fine," Ally said.

"I shall call the police," Camille said, turning to head back up the steps to the main entrance to the castle. "Ally, come along. Fine or not, it must have been quite an ordeal. Brian, please, make her come in quickly."

"Yes, in just a moment. Shelby, see that my horse is saddled and ready. If this fellow is on the roads now, I am going after him."

"Oh, but you must not!" Ally protested. "He is—he is armed and dangerous."

Brian Stirling watched Ally with an arched brow and a look that caused her to flush. As if the concept of danger would so much as make him hesitate when a member of his circle had been threatened.

"Come in. While my horse is being saddled, you must give me what details you can." He offered her his arm and called over his shoulder, "Shelby—call three of the men to ride with me."

She accepted his arm, and followed him into the castle. In the foyer, he called for his housekeeper, then led Ally on into the massive kitchen. It was a place she loved dearly. When she had come here as a child, she had often played in the kitchen. There was a huge hearth, and something was always cooking in a pot over the fire. These days it was something dreamed up by Theodore, the "new" cook, as he was called, despite the fact that he had been at the castle for ten years. He was a big man, with cheery red cheeks, and he always had something special and delicious waiting for her when she arrived.

"Theodore, if you please, a brandy for our young miss," the earl requested.

Theodore, who was standing at the great chopping block, his large hands mincing herbs into amazingly small pieces, frowned, wiped his hands off on his apron and hurried to the cabinet.

In a moment, Ally found herself seated by the fire, the earl before her, taking her hands, staring into her eyes. "Now, slowly and completely. What happened?"

"Well, as Shelby said, we were waylaid by the highwayman."

"And what did he want?"

Ally shook her head. "Actually…he took nothing. All he wanted was to search the carriage—and then to know who I was and where I was going."

The earl looked very anxious for a moment. "And he didn't hurt you in any way?"

"Not at all," she murmured.

The earl stood, running his fingers through his hair. He was a tall man, well built, and though his title might well have brought him anything he desired without the least effort on his part, he was a scholar, a patron of antiquities and ready to delve into the day's social issues. He had done his duty in the army, as well. Ally adored him, as she did Camille, and wondered how she had come by such amazing luck as to have them choose to take her beneath their wings. She wasn't being as forthright as he deserved, and she knew it. Had the highwayman hurt her? Indeed, he had wounded both her pride and her ego. But…

She was loathe to say too much.

She realized that she did not want the man caught. She

could not bear to imagine such a gallant thief hanging by the neck until dead.

"Honestly, my lord, there was not much to it. After the first few seconds, I knew I was in no danger."

"The man is a criminal," he said sternly.

"Yes, of course. But I wasn't harmed in any way, and nothing was taken." She hesitated. "I'm afraid that poor Shelby prides himself on his courage and ability, and he is truly a wonderful man and an expert guardian. He was ready to die for me. But the highwayman carries a long whip, and he used it to disarm Shelby. I imagine that he is as much embarrassed as anything else," Ally said.

The countess came into the kitchen. "I have reached the police, and Inspector Turner is on his way. Sadly, he spoke quite honestly to me. There's little he can do now. The ruffian and his fellows have surely long fled the scene. But, Ally, the inspector will be anxious to learn what he can from you about the man's look and manner. So, now, please, tell me what happened."

Ally looked at the earl. He gave her a slight smile. "I'm afraid that you'll be repeating your adventure over and over, my dear."

"Adventure?" Camille protested.

"Well, indeed, it seems that she is none the worse for it," Brian said.

"That does not in the least alleviate what she must have endured," Camille protested. A stray lock of hair fell across her forehead, and she looked at her husband indignantly, hands on her hips. "Well, the police will do what they can. It's quite frightening, though."

"Ally!"

"Ally!"

Two little voices called out to her. Brent and William, six and five, respectively, came running into the kitchen, skirting around their mother to throw themselves at Ally.

"Boys!" Camille protested.

"They're fine," Ally assured her, hugging the children, delighted with their cheerful smiles. They weren't worried or asking her to repeat herself; they were just happy to see her, and she adored them. Brent, the future earl, was continually full of mischief, and William was delighted to follow along, a worthy companion for all his brother's exploits. At the tender age of five, William had already announced that when the time was right, he would be heading off to the Americas to make his own fortune.

"Brian," Camille implored. "Please tell our young gentlemen that they must not crawl all over Ally right now."

"They're fine," Ally insisted. She wanted the boys there to distract her questioners.

"Boys, Ally will be along to play with you after you are bathed and settled for the evening," Brian said, picking up the children, one beneath each arm. They giggled as he walked them to the hallway. "Up to the playroom, my loves," he commanded. "And no dismantling the new telephone today, eh?"

"No, Father," William swore. He was still laughing.

"Really, this is not insignificant," Camille said softly. "What if the children had been in the carriage? What if...if they had tried to run? Or fight?" she asked worriedly.

"The children weren't in the carriage, Ally was, and she apparently handled herself quite well," Brian said, releasing the children and turning back. "My dear, we'll see that two men ride with the carriage at all times now," he told Camille. "Will that make you feel better?"

Camille nodded. "Yes, it will. Until the rogue is stopped. Anyway, Lucy has run a bath for you, Ally, and taken out your clothing for the party tonight. I do wish your aunts would have agreed to come...well, I can't make those darlings do a thing they don't want to do. But it's disturbing that this should happen on such a day, when we've guests arriving so soon." She smiled at her husband. "But then, I suppose people would be quite disappointed to come here without some excitement going on."

"Ally must go up right now and refresh herself," Brian said. "I'll ride out, and, Camille, you must speak with the inspector first when he comes, and by then, perhaps Ally will have remembered more about what happened."

"What exactly is going on tonight?" Ally asked, glad that they seemed to be putting her "adventure" into some sort of perspective. "Your summons was quite mysterious."

"Something terribly exciting," Camille assured her. "So, as Brian suggests, perhaps we should start preparing while we await our policeman."

"Yes, a bath would be lovely," Ally agreed. She didn't add that she would also dearly love a few minutes of privacy. The earl's eyes had seemed to look into her soul, and she was very afraid that she was giving away the fact that she felt as if she'd had an adventure. She was stunned by the way she had felt, talking to the man. The *thief.*

Was her life so truly sheltered and dull that she could be so easily swept away by such an encounter?

Sadly, that answer was yes.

"Come, Ally. Brian, perhaps she should have another brandy in the bath, a bit more to steady her nerves?"

"I rather think her nerves are quite steady already," Brian said. "But she's more than welcome to another."

He turned, shaking his head over the fact that highwaymen could be terrorizing the countryside in this modern age. Theodore was already pouring out a new measure of brandy.

Ally murmured "Thank you" as she hurried after Camille, lowering her eyes to keep the earl from seeing so much.

"I'm off in search of this brigard. I've read that he rides with three companions, Ally. Is this true?"

She nodded. Shelby would tell him anything she didn't, anyway. He would no doubt be riding out with the earl, as well. "Yes, there are four in all," she said.

"And you can tell me nothing else?" he pressed.

She shrugged. "They wore cloaks, hats and masks. I'm afraid there's very little I could say that would help."

"Could say? Or *would* say?" Brian murmured very softly.

"Brian! The men are criminals," Camille said.

"Yes, they are," Brian said firmly, staring at Ally.

"I'm sorry, my lord. I can't even tell you their height or hair color. I'm sorry."

"When this fellow took you off…what happened?" Brian demanded.

"I was angry. We walked and talked in circles until I gave him my name."

"And then?" Brian demanded.

"He returned me to Shelby, and we drove straight here," she said.

The earl nodded and headed toward the door as Camille took her by the arm. "Come along, your bath will grow cold."

"THERE'S FLORENCE," PATRICK said cheerfully as they entered the smoky miasma of O'Flannery's Pub.

Florence Carter, the barmaid, was busy at work behind the taps. She was in her mid-thirties, a woman who had fallen on hard times but found her calling at O'Flannery's. Here she worked very hard for hours a day, but never found herself reduced to prostitution, a common fate for poor and uneducated women in the East End. She was attractive, with red hair and bright green eyes, and a fierce attitude that warned her customers to have fun but behave. Robert O'Flannery, the big Irishman who owned the place, knew that he had found a gem in Flo. She could move like lightning and easily handle the university students who habituated the pub after classes. Florence could tease, she could jest—but she could also stop a brawl before it ever got started, though she was slim and appeared somewhat delicate. She was possessed of a fierce and wiry strength that had taken many a man by surprise.

"What will it be, boys? A pint apiece?" she called out to them.

"Aye, Flo," Mark called. "And have you seen—"

"Your partners in crime are in the booth," she teased back lightly, pointing.

"A bit too close to home, eh?" Patrick murmured.

"Not at all. She merely jests," Mark said.

The pub was crowded, with most men grouped around the bar. Mark and Patrick wove their way through people—workers, fresh from their jobs in the city; students, some laden with books; soldiers; and a few young members of society, sons who would one day claim their fathers' titles—and found Geoff and Thomas.

"Any problems?" Geoff asked.

"Not a one," Mark said, waving at Flo, who was already on her way over, balancing a tray of pints. She dropped off a few en route, easily avoiding the pats that would have fallen upon her posterior, and came to their booth. As she set their pints down, Mark said, "Did you hear? We passed a fellow on the road who heard that the highwayman has been busy again. Apparently he had the audacity to hold up a carriage belonging to the Earl of Carlyle. Luckily, he let the lass within it go her way, unscathed and unrobbed."

"I heard," Patrick said, leaning closer, "that he isn't usually so merciful."

"The newspapers downplay his exploits. The people are up in arms as it is," Geoff whispered.

"They can downplay it all they like," Flo said, whispering as well. "But I've heard he's murdered a victim or two and hidden the bodies, weighted down with bricks, in the lakes and streams."

"Yes, I've heard that, too," Mark said. "If the people in the carriages give him no trouble, he robs them and sends them on their way. But if they protest, fight back... It must be true. You've heard it...we've heard it. He is savage in response to those who fight back. Flo, you must take care."

"Well, now, O'Flannery can be a hard taskmaster, but I have the room above the taproom, you know." Flo shivered. "I need not travel the roads."

"You should be drinking up and heading home," Patrick reminded Mark. "Don't you have a soiree to attend this evening?"

"I do," Mark murmured. "But with Flo here, I've no desire to be heading anywhere."

"You're a flatterer, Sir Mark Farrow, you are. And an earl you'll be one day. You'll be having your way all the time, so it's a good thing for you to be learning a bit of humility now. So, you'll be attending the gala at the Earl of Carlyle's castle, then, will you?"

He smiled and pressed a sizable coin into Flo's hand. "It is where I'm supposed to be. But, Flo, be careful, with that highwayman on the loose. Make sure you travel safely. And warn your fellows at the bar."

"You're a kind man," she told him, fingers closing around the coin. "You'll make a fine earl one day. And yes," she said, changing her tone, "I will warn them all."

As she started to turn away, a man burst through the entry. "Murder!" he roared. "There's been another murder!"

"Who?" someone shouted from the bar area.

"Giles Brandon. The police just found the body. Word is just out on the street. Throat slit, just like the others."

A roar arose in the room, one voice trying to outshout another.

Finally the newcomer's voice rose above the rest. "He had it in his hand, he did. His last fine bit of writing. A blast aimed at the monarchy."

"It will still make the papers," someone predicted.

"Aye, words covered in blood," shouted another man.

"A pox upon Queen Victoria" came another hoarse cry.

Mark started to rise in anger.

Patrick set a hand on his arm. "Let me. I'm a commoner through and through, remember?" he said quietly.

Mark fought to control his temper, lowered his head and nodded.

Patrick rose. "God bless Victoria. The queen will find out who is at this wickedness."

There was silence. Then someone said from the bar, "She'd have no part in this, God save her."

And with that the cry of "God save the queen" went up, and the grumbling turned to whispers....

Mark rose then, looking at the others. "It doesn't appear as if I will be attending that gala this evening after all, gents. We'll talk soon," he said.

The others nodded.

With some men grumbling about the murders and others defending Queen Victoria, the pub was alive with conversation as Mark hurried for the door.

ALLY WAS GRATEFUL FOR THE hot bath, in which she spent all the time she could, indulging herself in the warmth—and privacy. At last she emerged, wrapped herself in the soft linen towel Lucy had left for her and stepped back into the bedroom. A large figure of Isis sat on one side of the dressing table, a canopic jar on the other. In between was a set of silver combs and brushes. Reliefs and statues decorated the room, and papyrusi lined the walls, handsomely framed. It was her room; it had always been so, as long as she could remember. Like the rest of the castle, it was stunningly decorated with both ancient and modern Egyptian art and artifacts. The earl's parents had been explorers, beginning the family fascination, and he had met a passionate proponent in Camille. He knew that the treasures of a poor country could too easily be spirited away by foreigners, and he was a firm proponent of leaving the most valuable in their native land. He was willing, however, to take some of the less valuable pieces for his own pleasure, but he always paid handsomely for his finds. He had told Ally once that for every ancient treasure he purchased, he also looked to the present, hiring artists and artisans to create new pieces for his collection. She remembered when she had been here with the daughter of Lord Wittburg, now a princess in Eastern Europe. Poor Lucinda had been terrified of the mummy cases, and at first Ally had teased her. She had actually hidden in one and jumped out, then been horrified to see how she had frightened the girl. It had taken her hours to calm her down, and she'd been worried that she was going to be barred from the castle forever if her prank was discovered. But Lucinda was kind at heart and never told on her. The episode had made Ally realize that perhaps she was the one who was a bit odd, but she'd grown up around the mummy cases and other artifacts and thought nothing of them. She even knew that in Egypt, mummies were so common they were used for kindling at times, and many people there used the massive stone sarcophagi for planters. Still, she was aware that a passion for all things Egyptian was definitely an acquired taste.

She realized she was feeling a sudden sense of loss, of nostalgia, as if something were about to change forever, but she didn't know what.

She slipped quickly into a silk shift, bloomers and stockings. She was still only half dressed when there came a knock at the door. It was Molly, one of the upstairs maids, and she had come to help Ally complete her ensemble for the evening.

"Have you seen the gown?" Molly asked, her blue eyes bright.

Ally's attention was drawn to the dress that had been laid out on the big four-poster bed. It was an elegant shade of yellow, almost gold, and it was glorious with subtle nips and tucks to emphasize her youthful figure. The embroidered handwork was exquisite.

"The aunties made this?" she asked softly.

Molly nodded. "They giggled like girls when they brought it."

Ally touched the fabric, shaking her head. "And still they would not come tonight," she said sadly.

"Ah, you can't change them," Molly told her.

"I pleaded," Ally said. "You know, if there is such an occasion here again, I will tell them that I will not come if they don't. I know that the earl and his wife argued and wheedled, as well, but those old dears are so stubborn. Still, I swear, next time I will out-stubborn them."

Molly sighed. "Well, there will not be a next time such as this," she said softly, carefully lifting the gown to slip it over Ally's head.

At first Ally couldn't reply—she was muffled by the elegant length of the dress going over her head. When at last she could speak, she demanded, "Molly, just what *is* this occasion? Why was I summoned here tonight?"

Molly flushed, then shrugged. "That is for your godparents to explain."

"Molly…"

"Come, come, they will be here any minute," Molly said, twirling her around to tie her into the gown. "You know, of course, that it was Lady Maggie, one of your own dear grandmothers, who came up with the design, and she took the aunties shopping for the fabric. Of course, there was never any question of hiring a designer for this. Lady Maggie has the most exquisite taste in clothing, and she said there were no finer seamstresses in the land than the aunties."

Ally smiled, proud of her dear aunties in their little cottage in the woods. They loved their simple life. She knew that they could have done very well, out in the world of high fashion. Instead, they chose to remain as they were, living their quiet and happy lives. "Lady Kat's sister is gaining quite a name in the fashion industry. She had a showing in Paris, you know, and even she comes to the aunties for her most important work."

"I know."

"Molly," Ally tried again, thinking to take the woman off guard, "what is going on tonight? Is it an early birthday celebration?"

"You could say so, I suppose. Now, sit and let me fix your hair."

Ally sat, ready to try again, taking another tack.

"The kitchen is overflowing with caterers," she said.

"When Lord Stirling decides to throw a private party," Molly said with pride, "there's no one who would not toss all other offers, business and pleasure, to the wind in order to attend. Of course there are caterers everywhere. Now, sit still. People are beginning to arrive. We need to get you ready."

Another tap sounded at the door, and Lady Camille looked in. She was dressed for the evening in a midnight-blue gown that hugged her body and sported a very small bustle that made it look as if she were gliding when she walked. As always, she was stunningly beautiful and regal. Camille had been born to poverty, then rescued from the streets, and in Ally's mind, she was proof that nobility lived with the heart and soul, and did not spring from a title. She was truly the perfect mate for the earl, since both were strong-willed and also compassionate to the extreme.

"Oh," Camille said, standing by Molly and surveying Ally. "It is perfect. I am so angry at the aunties. They should be here this evening. But I have to commend Maggie the minute she arrives—she chose the color and the fabric. Ally, your eyes look golden and your hair, just a shade darker. My dear girl, you have grown up."

"Thank you," Ally said. "Camille, is this a birthday celebration? Or is there something more going on tonight? I thank God that I am important in your eyes, but—"

The older woman was silent for a moment, then said, "Brian has returned and is downstairs already. He's in quite a state. He and Shelby retraced the carriage route, and he tried a dozen forest trails but was unable to find any sign of that wretched highwayman. Still, we must get on with the evening. And Theodore is feeding the inspector from the Metropolitan Police in the kitchen. We must speak with him at some point. And Angus Cunningham will be here later, so he must be informed about this new development."

"One last touch," Molly said, setting a studded pin into place in Ally's hair. She stepped back and clasped her hands. "Like a princess!" she exclaimed.

Ally kissed Molly's cheeks. "Not a princess, a commoner, Molly, and one who loves you and thanks you."

Molly sniffed suddenly and reached into her pocket for a handkerchief.

"Molly, stop that," Ally said. "I'll stay up here with you, shall I?"

"Nonsense, you're going downstairs," Camille said, laughing. "Come along, lass."

There it was again. That word. *Lass.* She would probably remain a lass in the eyes of those who had helped raise her until she dropped dead of old age.

"There's something I must speak to you about this evening, as well," Ally told the duchess.

"Is there?"

"Yes. I should tell you all at once, I suppose," Ally said. "Because you'll all be here tonight, all of you who have been so kind, taking me in almost as your own child. Sir Hunter and Lady Kat, Lord James and Lady Maggie, and you and Lord Stirling."

"Let us hope," Camille said, glancing at the delicate gold watch pendant she wore around her neck, "we will have a few minutes together before the castle begins to fill, but first, to the kitchen. Inspector Turner is waiting."

"MARK, YOU'RE JUST COMING IN?"

Joseph Farrow was standing by the fire. He was a tall, dignified man, and, Mark thought proudly, he still appeared handsomely fit.

Mark was an only child. His mother had died of fever when he had been but a boy, and though he remembered her gentle smile, the feeling of love with which she had enveloped him, and the scent of her perfume, it was his father who had guided his life.

It was because Joseph was so fine a man that Mark had always allowed this bargain. He would break his father's heart if he were to be the cause of Joseph Farrow breaking his word. Still...

"Father, I cannot attend tonight," Mark said.

He saw the frown that instantly began to furrow his father's brow.

"Mark, this event has been planned for years—"

"I know."

"There was good reason for me to give my word."

"I have no intention of doing any less than promised, Father. But—"

The phone began to ring. Though theirs had been one of the first townhomes in London to have a phone, it seemed that Joseph Farrow still could not accustom himself to the sound of it. He winced at the shrill clang.

Jeeter, Joseph's valet and butler, hurried into the drawing room to lift the receiver off the cradle. He answered with complete dignity, announcing that the caller had reached the home of Lord Farrow. Then he was silent as he held the receiver and looked toward Joseph.

"Detective Douglas," he said quietly.

Joseph looked at his son as he walked over to speak. "Lord Farrow here."

He listened, his eyes still upon Mark.

"Indeed," he said at last.

Jeeter took the receiver from Joseph to return it to the hook.

"Well, son," he said softly, "it will be awkward to express your regrets, but... Giles Brandon, dash it all," he said sadly. "Jeeter, please see that my coach is ready."

When Jeeter had left the room, Joseph looked at his son.

"Go, then. There is a dead man calling your name."

CHAPTER THREE

THE KITCHEN REMAINED ALIVE with movement. Theodore called out directions, and at least two dozen workers and servers were scurrying about.

All movement stopped when Camille first walked in, Ally in tow. Heads bowed in acknowledgment to the lady of the castle.

"Please," Camille murmured, a tinge of color in her cheeks. "Don't let me disturb your hard work." She steered Ally quickly toward a large butcher-block table, where Inspector Turner was waiting.

He'd been well fed. Theodore would have seen to that.

He stood as the women approached. "I'm sorry to be a nuisance on such an evening," he apologized.

He had the look of a sad old basset hound, Ally thought. He had dark eyes that had seen too much, and

a heavily lined face. But his bearing was tall and dignified, and he spoke softly. She believed he took his work
to heart.

"How do you do," she murmured.

"Inspector, my ward, Alexandra Grayson."

"Miss Grayson...I have spoken to Lord Stirling, but
you are the one who can really help me. I need a description of this man, the highwayman."

"I wish that I could help you more, Inspector," Ally
said. "But as to a description...it's quite difficult."

"All right, let me ask you questions, then. Was he
tall or short?"

"Tall."

"And his build?" the inspector queried.

She hesitated.

"Certainly not a skinny chap? Though it's true that a
gun can make a small man seem more powerful than he
really is," he said.

"No, not skinny," she said. They were both staring at
her. She had to give them more than this. "He was built
something like Lord Stirling, I suppose...."

"Rides well?" the inspector asked.

"Very."

"Perhaps someone who has served with the queen's
forces," the inspector said, more to himself than to Ally
or Camille. "Now, what about his face? His coloring?"

She frowned. "Inspector, I wish that I could be more
helpful. All of them wore masks, hats and cloaks."

"But according to Lord Stirling's man, Shelby, the
highwayman himself took off with you."

She shook her head. "He wanted only to know my name, and I was perhaps being a bit stubborn. He took nothing from me."

"And...he did not hurt you in any way?"

If she weren't feeling so uncomfortable herself, she would have felt sorry for the inspector. He was trying to ask the question so delicately.

"I was not harmed in any way at all," she assured him quickly, wondering if she was flushing.

"And nothing was stolen?"

"Nothing." Ally hesitated. "Perhaps it occurred to him that he had stopped a carriage belonging to Lord Stirling, and that Lord Stirling is a man who would come after him himself, and with a vengeance."

"Perhaps," the inspector mused.

He stared at her hard again, and Ally felt even more acutely uncomfortable. This was a man whose job was to question people. It was as if he read her every movement and nuance as he listened to her words.

"So...you can't tell me his eye color?"

"I wish I could. They were dark, I believe, though the mask caused shadows, you know."

"And you must have been very frightened," Camille murmured, loading another layer of guilt upon Ally's shoulders.

"Surely you've had other descriptions," Ally murmured.

"Always the same," Inspector Turner said with a sigh. "Even in broad daylight. People remember the mask, and a cape or a cloak...riding boots. Who in England does not possess a pair of riding boots? But don't fear, Miss Grayson. We will apprehend this culprit."

"I believe we have guests arriving," Camille said as she noted waiters, clad in tuxedos, heading out of the kitchen with trays bearing crystal flutes of champagne.

"Then by all means attend to your company. I believe that Miss Grayson has told me all that she can—all her mind will allow—for the time being," Inspector Turner said.

And what exactly did that mean? Ally wondered.

"It's amazing," Inspector Turner said, shaking his head sadly. "At least, Miss Grayson, you do not sound addled, as do some of the ladies who have been stopped by the highwayman. One would almost think they found the loss of a diamond trinket or the like to be well worth the price of an encounter with the man."

"What?" Camille exclaimed, astonished.

Inspector Turner shrugged. "They tell me he is polite and charming as he robs them."

"Ally is no silly child to have her head turned by such a brigand, no matter how courteous," Camille said.

"Of course," the inspector agreed. "Well, I thank you for your assistance. And I beg you, please, enjoy your soiree."

"Inspector, you are most welcome to join us," Camille said.

"Duty calls, Lady Stirling, but I thank you. I have already partaken of your hospitality. Your cook has seen to it that I've had the best meal I've enjoyed in…ah, well, maybe forever. I will bid you good evening."

"I thank you for coming, Inspector," Camille said.

"Yes, thank you," Ally murmured.

Camille had her arm. Ally smiled uneasily at the inspector as Camille led her from the kitchen. In the hallway to the foyer, Camille shook her head, saying, "All this, on such a night."

"Camille, please, why is tonight such an occasion?" Ally implored.

Camille opened her mouth to answer, but Brian had disengaged himself from a portly gentleman to come toward them. "Camille, my dear, I need you for a moment. Ally, come along and meet Lord Wittburg."

Ally didn't make it across the great hall. There was a mischievous tap on her shoulder, and she spun around.

It was Hunter MacDonald, another of her self-proclaimed guardians. She loved Hunter dearly. He was, in his way, a total rogue—or had been until he had fallen head over heels in love with his wife, Kat. They were a reckless couple, daring and a bit outrageous, ever ready to head out on an adventure.

"My dear, look at you!" Hunter exclaimed, eyes brilliant and teasing. "All grown up. Why, you will leave a horde of swains languishing wherever you walk."

"That's quite kind, Sir Hunter," she said. "But I've been all grown up for some time, you all have simply not noticed."

"I'm wounded."

She laughed. "I'm so glad you're here. I had thought you might be off on another adventure in Egypt."

"Ally, Ally, has all my teaching been in vain? Way too

hot in Egypt at the moment. Perhaps you can join us this year. It may be your one chance."

"My one chance?" she inquired.

But he didn't answer her. Kat had swept past him to give Ally a fierce hug. "Incredible," she said with delight. "I must paint you in this gown."

"Indeed, what a lovely picture," Hunter agreed.

"Perhaps my father should have the honor," Kat said.

"Your father is a great artist, but never doubt that his talent lies in you, as well, my love," Hunter told her.

Ally felt a flash of longing, watching them. She felt a sudden deep craving to know the kind of love they shared. To know someone who would look at her as Hunter looked at Kat.

"Ally," Kat said, drawing back, "whether you are captured in oil by me or my father, it must be done."

"Thank you." And then, before either of them could bring up some other subject, she asked, "Just what is going on tonight?"

Once again, her hopes for an answer were dashed.

"There she is!" cried a voice.

They were joined in a moment by Lady Lavinia Rogers. The widow of the earl who had owned half the lands in the northeast corner of the country, Lavinia was allowed to be bold and curious and quite outspoken. "Did you hear?" she demanded, after pecking cheeks all around with little kisses. "Our Ally was attacked by the highwayman."

Ally could have groaned aloud.

"Good God!" Hunter said angrily, looking ready to

stalk out of the house that very moment and comb heaven and earth to find the culprit.

"I wasn't attacked," Ally protested.

"Not attacked?" Kat said.

"He waylaid the carriage, and that is all. I am fine."

"Ah, that I believe," Lady Lavinia said. She was short, a bit stout and possessed bright blue eyes and hair that seemed to be a true silver. She was clad in a mauve ball gown and adorned with jewels. Some might have said that her couture was too much, but Ally thought that being a bit over-jeweled was perfect for the woman.

Lavinia, she knew, couldn't care less what was said about her. She knew who she was. She loved people and life, and she let it be known.

"I was quite taken by the rogue, too," Lavinia announced with a wink.

"You were waylaid by this man, as well?" Hunter demanded, frowning fiercely.

"I was. But here's the thing. The police are after him, but I don't believe they should be seeking him at all. They need to find the horrendous fellow who is going about murdering people. There has been a third murder. You do know that, don't you?"

Hunter and Kat nodded grimly. Ally frowned. "A third murder?"

"Giles Brandon. His throat was slit. The police have nothing. *Nothing*. Or so I've heard," Lavinia said.

"Lavinia, please. Give them a chance," Hunter said.

Lavinia sniffed. "Give them a chance? By the time they have hunted down this murderer, the country will have collapsed. You do know who Giles Brandon was, don't you, my dear?" she asked Ally.

"Yes, of course. I've read his columns. They are quite incendiary," Ally said.

Lavinia nodded gravely. "I find it quite amazing that we—those who support dear Queen Victoria and her family—must always be so noble, despite the way we are baited. He was found with his last article clutched in his bloody fingers. That article will run in tomorrow's paper—along with the news of his murder. The anti-monarchists are in a howl as it is, can you imagine the damage that will come by tomorrow?"

"Ally!"

This time, her name was being called by Lady Maggie, who was threading her way through the crowd, graciously nodding to those she passed, with Lord Jamie behind her.

Maggie, mindless of all around her, gave Ally a hug, and Jamie did the same. There was confusion again as they greeted Hunter and Kat, and Lady Lavinia, and then Maggie was assessing Ally's gown with pleasure. "The color is just perfect."

"Perfect for tonight," Jamie said, tilting her chin, and giving her a kiss on the cheek.

"*What* is happening tonight?" Ally asked again.

"Did you hear about the third murder? We were just discussing it," Lady Lavinia said.

"Did you know that Ally was waylaid by the highwayman?" Hunter asked Jamie, his voice angry.

"I have just heard," Jamie said.

"About the murder or the highwayman?" Lavinia demanded.

"I was called about the murder, and we just heard about Ally being stopped by the wretched thief," Jamie said.

"He's not wretched, dear," Lavinia said. "He's quite charming, really. Now, as to the murders…"

"Atrocious. Of course, there will be a greater outcry against the monarchy now—as if the queen could be behind such heinous brutality," Jamie said indignantly. "But, Lavinia, you may rest assured. The fellow *will* be apprehended."

Lavinia sniffed. "As if the bobbies ever caught that Jack the Ripper fellow."

"Lavinia," Jamie said quietly, looking oddly uncomfortable, "the Ripper murders are long past, and no one ever really believed that the monarchy was involved then."

"Jamie, don't be so naïve. That theory will go down in the history books, along with others. But we all know—" Lavina began.

"The murders stopped. I think it's obvious the police knew more than they could say," Maggie told Lavinia.

"Silence only enrages people all the more."

Camille swept suddenly up to their group, linking arms with Lavinia. "Shall we move into the great hall? Dinner is being served, and then, after the dancing begins, the announcement will be made. I must move all these people into the dining hall…. Hunter, Jamie, would one of you be so good as to escort Lady Lavinia?"

"What announcement?" Ally inquired.

"Oh," Camille said, "there is Lord Farrow, Earl of Warren. Ally, you must come with me for a minute. Strange, he is alone, it seems. Come, dear."

"Camille," Ally begged. "What announcement?" She spoke seriously, her voice full of determination.

Camille stared at Ally, her lovely cheeks reddening. "One we should have told you about long ago, I'm afraid. We meant to. It's just that we all wanted to be together, and one thing came up after another...." She lifted her hands. "Life, you know," she murmured softly. "I suppose one of us should simply have spoken. This came about years ago, before you were old enough to understand, and then you were old enough, but it always seemed as if the right time had not yet come."

"Lady Camille, what is the announcement?"

But they were interrupted by the arrival of a gentleman. "Dearest Camille," he murmured. Tall, white-haired, and with a fascinating, lined face, he seemed to be one of those men who needed no title to command respect. Ally recognized him as Lord Farrow, the man Camille had indicated only moments before. He sat in the House of Lords, and was continually fighting for shorter hours and better pay for laborers. He was, if she recollected all she had read properly, a peer of the realm, an avid supporter of the queen, and a very good friend to the common folk, as well.

She was pleased to meet him.

"Lord Farrow, may I present our ward, Miss Alexandra Grayson?" Camille said.

He bowed courteously and took her hand, studying her curiously with dark, gentle eyes. She felt the warmth of his touch and also a strange sensation, as if he saw her as an exceptional artifact someone had brought back from an archeological dig, as if he found every aspect of her fascinating.

"How do you do?" she murmured.

"Quite well, and quite pleased to meet you," he said. He smiled at her, then glanced at Camille. "Miss Grayson is indeed a rare beauty." He looked pained for a moment. "I'm terribly sorry that Mark could not be here. He is on the queen's business. Nothing else could have taken him away, I do solemnly swear. You'll have to forgive him." He addressed his final words to Ally.

I don't even know him, Ally thought, but she answered politely, anyway. "Naturally the queen's business takes precedence over any party, my lord."

"Horrid, isn't it?" he said to Camille. "Giles Brandon was a braggart and an oaf, but I fear his death will but inflame the masses."

"So do we all," Camille said.

"Well, I will not dwell on such things in the midst of such beauty," Lord Farrow said.

"Would you escort Ally into the dining room?" Camille asked. "You are seated together, of course," she said, and then she was gone with a whirl.

Of course?

"Giles Brandon was a braggart but a powerful writer," Ally said gravely to Lord Farrow.

"You have read his work?" Lord Farrow demanded, frowning.

"I read everything, my lord. To dispute an argument, one must know what it is."

He arched a brow. "Intriguing. I am fascinated to get to know you, my dear. Let's move in, shall we? I see that Camille is anxious to have her guests seated."

She accepted his arm. The party slowly moved into the great dining hall. They were seated at the north end, surrounded by Brian and Camille, Maggie and Jamie, and Hunter and Kat. As the meal was served and consumed, the conversation covered the next season's expedition to Egypt, the state of museums in London, art and literature, and even the weather.

Ally smiled, replied and offered a comment or two. She longed to stand up and shout. She knew she had the strength of will to demand an answer to the question she had been asking all night.

What was going on? What announcement?

But as she looked around at those near her at the table, she knew she would not. Lady Maggie and Jamie had been the ones who had taken her in when she had been abandoned to the care of a local priest. Maggie's butler, a dear man, now gone several years, had been a relation of her "aunties," so she had been given into their care in the forest, where she could be raised with no stigma because of her orphan beginning. The property where the cottage lay belonged to Lord Stirling. Kat and Hunter, as very good friends of the Stirlings, had adopted her as a godchild, as well, out of sheer love. She owed them all so much. They were all anyone could ever want in a set of guardians—even if it was difficult at times to have quite so many de facto parents. They were all beautiful, powerful and compassionate. They felt a keen sense of responsibility because of the positions life had granted them.

She would never dishonor any of them, and therefore, she would not be rude at Camille's dinner table.

Still, as she looked around, pretending to chat lightly, to smile, to enjoy the evening, the question still raged inside her.

What was going on?

A sense of dread filled her.

She had intended to make her own announcement that night, to confess she had taken her life into her own hands, and done so with a passion. Something told her she would not get the chance.

THE MORGUE SMELLED SHARPLY of antiseptic, which did not, however, mask the underlying stench of death and decomposition.

Mark stood next to the operating table that held the earthly remains of Giles Brandon. Despite the naked lightbulbs above the corpse, the room seemed shadowed. He was there with two men, Dr. Evan Tiel, the coroner, and Detective Ian Douglas.

Detective Douglas was one of the finest men Mark had ever had the pleasure to meet. Big and gruff, he could handle himself against any man. The fifth son of a minor Scottish landowner, he had spent time dabbling in the law at Eton, then returned to his native land to study medicine in Edinburgh. By the end of his studies he'd realized he was most interested in bringing killers to justice and seeing that the innocent were never mistakenly convicted. He was a handsome man, strong and broad-shouldered, but showing the telltale stress of a man who fought a losing battle—defending the innocent and seeking to uproot evil. It might well be a grand and glorious age in which they were living, but poverty was rampant in London, and poverty was a sure breeder of crime.

Dr. Evan Tiel was an equally laudable man. Shorter, slim, wiry, he had the energy of a hummingbird. He was fascinated with the growing field of using science and medicine in the search for justice. He and Douglas had both attended classes in Edinburgh taught by Dr. Bell, the surgeon and teacher who had been Arthur Conan Doyle's inspiration for the character of Sherlock Holmes. While some men might mock the idea of paying heed to a writer of fiction when seeking truth, both Tiel and Douglas saw the wisdom in the methods Holmes propounded. While Bell devoted his observations to ascertaining the causes of disease, such methods were equally applicable in other matters.

"He was found slumped across his desk, his fingers clutching his last article," Ian Douglas said.

"Indeed," Tiel added, "from the way the blood set, it appears that his head was drawn back as his throat was slit, then the body cast forward onto the desk as he bled to death."

"But he fought?" Mark asked, indicating slashes on the arms.

"I surmise," Dr. Tiel said, "that he saw his attacker and fought, but the killer got behind him in the end. He must have stood thus." Tiel demonstrated, using Douglas as the victim. He mimed holding a knife in his hand, showing how it had been drawn against the throat.

"All right," Mark theorized aloud. "Giles Brandon was at his desk, typing. He finished his piece. The killer came into the room, and there was a scuffle, but the killer managed to get behind him and slit his throat."

Ian Douglas cleared his throat. "Here's the problem. The door to the yard was bolted from the inside. The entry gate to the yard was locked. And Giles Brandon kept his office locked. I don't believe the killer simply entered by the door and took Brandon by surprise. I believe he was waiting there for Brandon's return."

"Then it would seem that the killer stood in the back of the room, in the shadows, for a long time," Mark said.

"Yes, that could be so," Ian agreed.

"It's...almost more like an assassination than a simple murder," Mark mused.

Ian Douglas stared at him. "Yes, maybe."

Mark stared down at the sad remains of Giles Brandon. Many had hated the man, but few would wish anyone, even their worst enemy, such an ending.

He studied the slashes on the arms, looked at the deep gash on the neck.

"There are no other injuries to the body? No damage done after death?"

"None," Dr. Tiel assured him.

Mark stood back. "So if the killer was in the room all the time, he—or she—must have had a key," Mark said.

Ian Douglas shook his head. "His wife adored him. He was by all reports a bellowing wretch who abused her verbally, even in public, upon occasion. But she adored him. She thought he was a genius."

"Something he probably told her himself," Mark said sardonically.

Douglas nodded. "No doubt. But there is simply no way she could have done this, nor that she would have allowed it to happen."

"Who else had a key?" Mark asked.

"Only Brandon himself, and the housekeeper, Tilly. And when you meet Tilly, you'll know she didn't do this, either. She is a frail bag of bones, hardworking, but hardly capable of overpowering a man such as Brandon. In addition, she needed the income she received from him, and despite his temper, there was an element of prestige for Tilly in being the housekeeper of such a man."

"If the wife is not guilty and the housekeeper is not guilty, then one or the other was used by the killer. I would say that one of them had her key stolen, then replaced. This was not a random act of violence, obviously, and the killer took his time planning it," Mark said.

"It's another attack on the anti-monarchists," Douglas said, shaking his head. "Doesn't this fool zealot realize he is only making matters worse for the queen?"

Mark was quiet for a minute. "I believe," he said, "that the killer is an anti-monarchist."

"What?" Douglas demanded. "Then why kill…?" His voice trailed off as he realized Mark's point.

"Precisely," Mark murmured. "The idea is to make the populace believe the monarchists are killing these men because they are speaking out. What better way to win a cause then to create an army of martyrs?"

"Then…?" Douglas said, eyes narrowing.

"I think we need to look at Giles Brandon's friends and contemporaries. Because I'm certain of one thing," Mark said.

"And what is that?"

"Giles Brandon knew his killer. I'd say he knew him very well."

WITH DINNER OVER, IT SEEMED that the long table disappeared in an instant. New tables were set against the walls, with elegant little demitasses of coffee, small dessert plates and aperitifs. As the dancing began, Ally began to recognize more and more guests she either knew or knew *about*.

The first to whisk her out on the floor was Brian Stirling. She danced very well with him, since, as a child, she had learned her first dances by standing on his toes, laughing as he swept her around the room.

As they moved across the floor, she whispered, "That journalist is here—Thane Grier."

"Yes."

Brian didn't sound pleased.

"You invited him?"

"Of course. Had I not… Well, it's best to befriend the enemy."

"He's the enemy?"

"Anyone who rules the press can be a dangerous enemy," Brian said. "So of course I asked him here tonight. Especially tonight."

"Brian, I beg of you—"

Brian halted. She realized he'd been tapped on the shoulder. "Lord Stirling, if I may?"

It was Sir Andrew Harrington. She remembered seeing him only that morning, on the steps along with Sir Angus Cunningham and Lord Lionel Wittburg. They had crossed paths a few times through the years, once at a fund-raiser for the antiquities department, and once at one of Maggie's parties to draw attention to the plight of the poor in the East End.

Brian bowed courteously, though he seemed stiff as he graciously ceded her to Sir Harrington.

The man smiled charmingly at her as he took her hand and slipped an arm around her, easily sliding back into the waltz. "You have certainly come of age most beautifully, Miss Grayson," he said.

"Thank you. And you, sir? How are you doing? I saw you this morning."

"You did?"

"In the village."

"Ah, yes…. It seemed Angus could use all the help he could get."

"Military men stand together," she murmured.

He smiled, then looked grave. "I heard you were accosted by that monster, the highwayman."

"I'm quite all right."

"Would that I had been there," he said, sounding angry. "Someone needs to skewer that fellow through."

"Thank you. I am fairly capable, however."

He shook his head and said softly, "You underestimate your beauty and your allure, my dear, and the wickedness in the minds of some men. I tell you now—and I say this passionately, and even knowing that you have strong guardians—if you are ever in need of assistance, I would be there willingly."

He was very good-looking, with rich brown hair and topaz eyes. Strong, tall, not heavily muscled, but still...she could feel the steely power in his hold.

She smiled, inclining her head. "Thank you."

"So...what is the mysterious announcement to be made tonight?" he asked.

She didn't get a chance to tell him that she didn't know herself, for, as if aware that he had just been discussed, Sir Angus Cunningham was the next to cut in.

For such a large man, he danced very well. His voice was gruff when he said, "My dear sweet lass, I am ashamed by what befell you. As sheriff of the village and the surrounding forests, I failed you. Forgive me."

"Angus!" She had known him since she'd been quite young. "You had your hands full this morning. The highwayman is no real threat. An ugly mob *is*."

"You saw that," he murmured.

"And I was very proud of you—you and Lord Wittburg and Sir Harrington. You quelled that crowd quite nicely."

Angus glanced across the room, his expression brooding. "Yes, well…Thane Grier was there, as well. We'll see what rubbish he puts in the paper tomorrow. Of course tomorrow may well be worse…another murder, perhaps." He seemed to catch himself. "Forgive me. We'll not speak of it tonight."

"It is of dire importance," she said softly. Then, her mind suddenly taking a new direction, she frowned.

She had noticed several women there that night in black. Since Queen Victoria had mourned her dear Albert for so long, wearing black had become a trend. Even now, women wore black long after losing someone beloved. There was nothing odd about seeing a woman in black.

And yet…

Staring past Sir Angus's massive shoulder, she caught sight of someone who gave her pause. She didn't know why, but she was suddenly reminded of the woman in the village who had been crying out against the queen.

"Sir Angus?" she said suddenly.

"What, dear?"

"Who was that woman this morning?"

"What woman?"

"In the crowd, shouting so angrily about the monarchy."

"Who wasn't shouting angrily?" he asked rhetorically. "I swear, someone riled up that crowd. There were placards everywhere. Our citizens are normally peaceful and law-abiding, other than that wretched highwayman. Though I believe he hails from London and merely uses my roads for his despicable deeds."

"There was one woman in particular, don't you remember? She was next to Sir Andrew's cousin, who was trying to calm her, I believe."

He opened his mouth to reply, but again the dance was halted. This time it was Lord Joseph Farrow, Earl of Warren, cutting in. Angus relinquished his position.

"You dance beautifully," the earl informed her.

"Thank you."

"I understand that you also have the voice of a lark and play the piano beautifully."

She smiled. "I play the piano—whether beautifully or not is in the ears of those who are listening."

"I am well pleased," he murmured, his eyes bright, and he seemed amused.

She smiled, wondering whether or not it mattered if he was or wasn't pleased.

The music came to an end and did not start up again. She turned around. Lord and Lady Stirling, Sir Hunter and Lady Kat, and Maggie and Lord James were gathered in front of the musicians. Brian, holding Camille's hand, began to speak.

"Friends, we thank you so much for coming. As you know, we have all been privileged to play a part in raising a beautiful young woman. Tonight, we are privileged to announce the engagement of our ward, Miss Alexandra Grayson."

She was certain that her mouth simply gaped open. She shut it swiftly.

"Come, dear," Joseph Farrow said, taking her arm.

She stared at him, but she was so stunned that she

didn't protest when he walked with her toward Brian and the others.

Him? she thought. They're marrying me off to *Lord Farrow?*

Luckily, she realized that Lord Farrow intended to speak. He held her hand, turning her to face the crowd. "I am delighted to come here tonight, to stand in for my son, Mark, who is not able to be here. This is an event long planned by Lord Stirling and myself. Tonight, we announce the engagement of my son, Mark, to Miss Alexandra Grayson."

The round of applause that rose was thunderous.

But no louder than the pounding of Ally's heart.

She felt as if she had been struck by a train.

Engaged? And not to a man who could easily be her father, but to a man who could not even be bothered to attend his own engagement party!

Of course, it did not matter who the man was. It was…archaic. She had her own plans, dreams, aspirations. She had already set those plans into motion….

She was numb. Barely aware that her godparents were hugging her, kissing her cheek.

Barely aware that Lord Farrow had taken a ring from his pocket, that somehow it fit her finger perfectly. Suddenly there was a diamond flashing brilliantly on her hand.

"And," Camille announced loudly over the flurry in the room, "here is our first gift to the newly engaged couple. My goddaughter sings like an angel, and her fingers are pure magic on the keyboard, so…"

Shelby and several of the servants rolled in a glorious piano.

Ally's mouth moved; she tried to thank Camille.

"There is no woman in all of England who looks so lovely in a gown," Maggie announced next. "Lord Jamie and I have arranged a trousseau."

Ally blinked as Molly, smiling broadly, came in bearing an array of stunning materials. Again, the room filled with applause, and Ally found herself hugging Jamie and Maggie, all the while feeling like the worst hypocrite in the world.

It was Kat's turn to speak. She walked forward, eyes dancing. "Hunter and I—"

A horrendous scream cut across her words.

The whole room seemed to freeze.

Another scream, followed by an unintelligible spatter of hysterical words, echoed from the entry hall.

"Excuse me," Brian murmured, starting in the direction of the uproar.

As a body, the guests followed.

Ally, still stunned, found herself swept along in the sea of people.

In the entry, Shelby was trying to hold and calm a woman. She appeared to be perhaps forty and was dressed totally in black. Her hair was silver-gray, and her eyes seemed to be a matching color, burning with insanity.

"He's dead!" she screeched. And, with madness lending her strength, she broke free from Shelby.

Brian lifted a hand, telling Shelby it was all right, to let the woman be.

"Eleanor," he said softly, reaching out to her.

She looked at him; then her eyes narrowed and she let out another terrible scream. Her black mourning attire sailing around her, she spun, looking at the gathered crowd. "He's dead! And you, all of you, supporting the queen. Damn you! You will kill and kill again for your own aims. He is dead. My husband is dead. Giles Brandon, worth dozens of the likes of you. He is dead!"

"Eleanor," Brian said again, but when Shelby would have moved, he silently shook his head, once more allowing the woman her moment of pain and fury.

Again she spun, as if looking for someone in particular.

Ally was startled when the woman's wild eyes suddenly settled upon her and she stretched out a bony, black-clad arm. "You!" she shrieked. "You would-be child of the elite. Curse you! May you die a thousand deaths. So this is your birthday? And you are newly betrothed? Then again I say, curse you! May you die a wretched death before your wedding day ever falls."

CHAPTER FOUR

GILES BRANDON'S TOWN HOUSE was heavily guarded, barricaded by a score of policemen. As he entered the home with Ian Douglas, Mark asked, "How many people were in here after the body was discovered?"

Ian lifted his brows and shrugged unhappily. "The housekeeper and the first officer she found patrolling the street, then another three or four officers. After them, the coroner and several of his assistants."

Mark nodded. Nothing to be done.

He carried a lantern and began his search on the walkway outside the heavy wrought-iron gates. He could see no traces of blood, nor, in the finely manicured grounds, any sign of disturbance. Reaching the front door, he and Ian again made a scrupulous search of the marble, tile and brick that made up the entry.

The entryway was clean, as well.

"Please tell me the housekeeper wasn't allowed to wash the floors or straighten anything once the body was discovered," Mark said.

"As soon as I was called, I saw to it that nothing was touched. I asked her about the floors, and she said she hadn't washed them. She had been working in the kitchen, thinking that would be where she could accomplish the most without making noise. When she first arrived, she believed Giles was still working."

A thorough search of the floors, walls and furniture in the front of the house gave no hint of blood or disturbance.

But as they mounted the stairs, Ian just a few steps in front of Mark, the detective gave a little cry. "A smudge!"

Mark shone the lantern on the spot. Indeed, it looked like a smudge of blood, left behind by a shoe. It was small, however, and suggested only that the killer must have left by the front stairs.

"The man must have gushed blood like a volcano spilling lava," Ian said. "Yet it appears his killer escaped the flow."

"He was in back, no doubt behind his victim, and the blood would have spurted forward."

"Still, it must have been a bloodbath," Ian said.

"But we believe this killer has slain two other victims in like fashion. That would mean he learned how much blood would flow when the throat was slit."

"Kill a man—and know enough to stay clear as he died," Ian said with disgust.

"May I see the room?" Mark asked.

"Indeed, that's why we are here," Ian said.

Upstairs, in Giles Brandon's office, it became even more evident that the killer had known what he was doing. Brandon had been killed when he had been standing behind his desk. The killer had seen to it that he had faced forward and fallen forward as he died. There was a pool of congealed blood on the desk.

The man's typewriter, his own weapon, was caked with it.

"He was gripping his last work as he died?" Mark asked softly.

Ian nodded. "And we handed the article over to the paper—though it bashed the government, as usual. The chief thought that holding back such a piece, when word of it was sure to leak out, would be far more dangerous than allowing it in to print."

"Quite right, I imagine. Still…the pages must have been smudged with blood."

"The article will run in the morning's paper," Ian said. "Along with the news of the man's death."

Mark nodded. "Let's hope there's some sanity out there to counter it."

In his mind, he then began to try to imagine what had happened. There was one corner in the room where someone might have stood unnoticed. Far left, behind the desk. Two bookshelves met there, filled with dark volumes. If someone stood very still…

He went to the corner, watched the desk.

"I'll be Brandon," Ian said quietly.

And so, together, they played out the scene.

"I believe that Brandon stood first, then heard his killer and turned," Ian said.

"Right. Then the killer came forward," Mark said.

"Brandon lifted his arms, so, as he realized the killer was wielding a knife…" Ian continued.

"The killer came forward…and slashed."

"He gashed Brandon's arms, the blood dripped down."

"While Brandon reeled from the assault, the killer grabbed him by the shoulder and shoved him back around."

"His throat," Mark said, "was then slit, left to right."

"Brandon fell forward, reaching for his article."

"The killer stepped back instantly. The blood spewed forward. The knife, however, would have been dripping."

"So," Ian mused, "he must have stashed the knife quickly to keep it from dripping as he exited the room."

"Stairway again," Mark murmured.

Ian nodded.

They passed the one small smudge and made their way down the stairs. There, they paused.

"Back entrance," Ian mused.

"Let's try it."

They took the hallway that passed by the dining room, parlor, kitchen and pantry. At the rear door, Mark angled his lantern, directing the light on the doorknob.

"Yes, he left this way."

"I don't see…ah!" Ian murmured. Once again, the speck of blood was so small it might have gone unnoticed forever. "The back was locked, as well."

"The killer had the key," Mark said.

Ian opened the door. Mark lifted the lantern. A tiled trail led into a garden setting with white-painted wrought-iron furniture. A small fountain bubbled, the sound oddly cheerful. The men looked at each other and moved toward it. There were flecks of blood on the stonework.

"Well, here's where he cleaned his weapon," Ian said softly. "Then..."

"Then he continued on through the back," Mark said, wandering along a dirt path that wound between pruned oaks. He came to a dead end at a brick wall."

"All right, how did he scale this?" Ian demanded.

Mark turned to him. "He had an accomplice, someone who waited and tossed him a rope. He climbed to the top and leapt over the wall, landing on the walkway below. Here, in the rear of the house, there is very little street traffic. There are other upper-class homes, but at that time of night, most people would be sleeping. He leapt to the sidewalk, and then he and his accomplice slipped easily through any crowd, then headed to a safe place, because some of his garments must have been bloodied."

"A safe place or..." Ian murmured.

"A carriage," Mark said.

"A fine carriage, one that could move through the streets with little danger of being stopped by the police," Ian said. "I'm certain we'll discover this person if we can only discover where the bloody clothing was left."

Mark nodded and shrugged grimly. "Ian, the killer might well be concealing his deeds by riding away in a fine carriage, as you say. But do you really believe he would dare hold on to the bloody clothing? Why not dispose of it?"

"Because, when you dispose of something, it might be found," Ian said firmly. "I also believe…" He paused.

"What?" Mark asked.

"I have no real basis for this, but… I don't believe we're dealing with a madman, but rather a cold and calculating political assassin. Still, I think this person is convinced of his own superiority. His own righteousness. Therefore I believe he keeps whatever vest or cloak or other garment he uses to hide the knife while he makes good his escape. It's something he perhaps even gloats over. Why are you staring at me?" Ian asked. "Do you think my theory is ridiculous?"

Mark shook his head. "Not at all. But I was thinking that…all right, we know the killer is agile. Able to move in silence. Able to scale a wall with a rope."

"Yes."

"What we don't know is that the killer is a man. We might be looking for a woman."

"But Giles Brandon is—was—a large and powerful man."

"Which may be why we see the defensive wounds. He may have thought he had the power to wrest the weapon from his attacker. I'm not saying that we *are* looking for a woman. I'm just suggesting that a female killer may not be out of the question."

AFTER ELEANOR BRANDON screeched out her desperate curse, the entire castle went still, frozen in time. No one moved. It seemed as if no one even breathed.

Then again, it might have seemed that way to Ally

only because she herself was so stunned and unnerved by the curse directed against her.

She fought the chill that ran up her spine and spoke herself. "Mrs. Brandon, I am very sorry for your loss. I can only pray that God will bring you peace."

And then Brian Stirling had hold of the woman, his hands on her shoulders. He turned her to face him. "Eleanor, please, before God, none of us would have wished Giles dead," he said. "We're all sorry for your loss."

Eleanor Brandon was no longer a whirlwind, a shrieking harpy. She seemed to collapse into Brian's arms, shaking and sobbing. She slammed her hands weakly against his chest. "What will I do now, Lord Stirling? What will I do now?" She straightened suddenly. "You will have me arrested."

"Eleanor, I will not have you arrested." Brian looked up. Ally knew he was seeking Camille.

She hurried forward, followed by Lady Maggie.

"Come, Eleanor, let me take you upstairs. You must stay with us tonight. I'll get you some brandy."

Eleanor shook her head, looking at them both. "He wrote against the Crown. I know how you felt about the articles he wrote."

"This is Great Britain," Camille said, "where we are free to express our opinions. Giles was entitled to his beliefs. Now, come along, Eleanor. Please, let us help you."

The woman lifted her hand in a weak wave. "My... coachman."

"We'll see to him," Maggie assured her.

"Please, everyone," Brian said, turning to address the

crowd of elegantly clad guests who still stood in the foyer, silent, gaping. "For those who wish to stay on, the musicians will continue to play." With Camille and Maggie comforting the still-weeping Eleanor, he cut through the crowd and went straight to Lavinia. "If you're not leaving, my dear friend, I would cherish a dance."

"As if I would leave after such an offer," Lavinia responded teasingly. "I would love to dance."

As the two moved back toward the ballroom, Hunter did his part, bowing before another society widow and taking her hand. Lord Jamie also became a volunteer on the dance floor.

Ally didn't realize that she hadn't moved until Kat came to stand beside her. "Are you all right, dear?"

Ally smiled ruefully. "Let's see. I've just found out I'm engaged, my fiancé couldn't be bothered to appear for the announcement—perhaps *he* didn't know, either?—and now I've been cursed. Quite an interesting evening."

Kat laughed softly. "You forgot the part where **you** were held up by a highwayman, as well. Oh, Ally, please, don't let Eleanor's ravings become something real in your mind."

"That was quite a curse."

"Well, I don't believe in curses, so don't let this one play havoc with your mind. Meanwhile, you didn't get your gift yet from Hunter and me. So…" Kat reached into a pocket in her skirt and produced a jewel box. "Please, Ally, take it."

"Thank you," Ally said softly, taking the box and

opening it. The box contained a scarab, an incredible piece of workmanship, gold and jeweled and elegant. She estimated that it was worth a small fortune, and she shook her head. "I can't take this."

"Ally, Egyptology is what we do," Kat reminded her. "And it's not an artifact, it's a new piece that we commissioned. Hunter has seen to it that the real scarab is in the museum in Cairo. But though this is a copy, it is precise, and with the precious stones arranged as they are, it is supposed to be magical. It will deflect any threat." She smiled. "The original was given to Princess Netahula-re. It was said that her brother's wife attempted to murder her with poison. She didn't die, merely became sick, and her brother's wife was caught attempting to kill her, so *she* met a dire fate—a rather ghastly one—instead. So this scarab, like the original, will protect you. If there *is* such a thing as a curse—which, of course, I don't believe—now you've been protected. So all is well."

"I don't believe in curses, either, but I do thank you and Hunter with all my heart. But Kat, I truly need to speak with all of you. I had no idea what was really going on tonight, and—"

"Kat, there you are!" Hunter, a bit out of breath, found them in the doorway. "Oh, you gave her the scarab. Do you like it?"

"I love it. It's beautiful. It's too much."

"Nonsense. You've grown into a woman we all hold in great esteem," Hunter told her. He kissed her cheek, then caught his wife's hand. "Not to be rude in any way, but I've now danced with a dozen oversized and aging maids and madams, and I'd like one dance with my wife. Ally, you'll excuse us?"

"Yes, but—"

The two hurried away to the dance floor, Ally staring after them in frustration.

She lowered her head, thinking that perhaps tonight was simply not the right moment to try to talk to them and get them to understand. Somehow, though, she would have to convince them that they had done an excellent job with her education, so now she could not help but long to use it.

"My dear?"

She spun around. Lord Joseph Farrow, Earl of Warren, now her intended father-in-law, was by her side.

"You mustn't be worried by the ravings of a distraught lunatic," he said softly.

"I'm not worried," she told him. Logically, she knew she was telling the complete truth, yet there was still that little edge of fear playing along her spine.

But, she reminded herself, she had the scarab!

"Will you honor me with a last dance?" he inquired. "The hour has grown quite late, and I must be on my way."

"Of course," she murmured.

As they moved onto the floor, she realized there was a light of amusement in his eyes.

She looked up at him questioningly, and he smiled and said, "You knew nothing about any of this until it happened, I believe?"

She flushed. "How did you know?"

"The way your jaw dropped, my dear."

"I'm so sorry."

"Quite all right. But tell me, and tell me truthfully, are you dismayed or pleased to discover that you will one day be a countess, the wife of an earl?"

"I'm not marrying you, my lord," she teased. "And you appear quite fit and healthy, not to mention that I wish you the longest life possible."

"Well, thank you. But one generation must always give way to the next, and I admit to being quite grateful to have a son."

"You are scarcely a tottering old oak, my lord. You could remarry and have many sons if you so choose."

He lowered his head slightly, and then his eyes met hers. "I will never remarry. And you, my dear, have evaded my question. What do you think about this proposed union with my son?"

"Since I haven't met your son, I can scarcely have an opinion."

She was surprised that he didn't immediately tell her that his son was a man held by all in the highest esteem or extol his virtues in some manner.

"That's true. I had thought that one of your guardians would have explained this situation to you," Lord Farrow said.

"I believe they intended to, although not until today," Ally said. "And then, well…it seemed there was one interruption after another."

"Even without knowing my son, what are your feelings

about this marriage? After all, many lasses would marry a doddering imbecile in order to become a countess."

She smiled at that. "Am I honored to be considered worthy? Certainly. And do I deeply love my guardians and appreciate all they've done—and continue to do—for me? Yes."

"Charmingly said," Lord Farrow said, bowing his head slightly and offering her a very small smile of amusement. "Frankly, I was quite worried. It all has to do with a vow, you see, though I'm afraid I'm not free to speak about any of it, really."

Ally shook her head. "Whatever vows were made to care for me, I have been raised in a manner that will allow me to see my own way in the world. Your son certainly does not have to marry me."

"No, my dear, the future is sealed," he told her.

She stared at him, frowning. Then she realized the music had stopped. People were beginning to leave.

"But—"

She couldn't say more, as guests were walking past, offering congratulations, applauding the union.

"My dear, I must leave," Lord Farrow said. "No doubt we will speak again." Then, and gripping her hands, he kissed her cheek, then made his exit. She watched him go, then felt a touch on her shoulder. She turned to see Lady Lavinia standing there.

"Mark is quite gorgeous and noble," Lavinia told her. "What exquisite children you will have."

Andrew Harrington, walking up behind Lavinia, laughed. "Good heavens, Vinnie," he whispered, then shuddered playfully. "Sometimes the most gorgeous people have the most hideous children."

"Andrew, that's quite horrible," Lavinia told him.

"But true." He gave a roguish smile and took Ally's hands. "Forgive me. I am speaking with a mouth full of sour grapes. I would gladly be your suitor. Unfair, I say, that Lord Stirling has kept you all but under wraps these many years, only to allow us all a sight of such exquisite beauty, then announce that you are to marry."

"You're very kind," Ally murmured. She could see that the journalist, Thane Grier, was nearby, busily writing in his notebook.

"Not kind at all—baldly jealous," Andrew announced. "Ah, well…we will see what befalls, eh? Still, I'm but a lowly knight—you're being offered a future earl."

"My deepest desire in life, sir, is to be a person who stands upon her own merits and needs no titles nor another's grandeur to make a mark upon the world," she said.

"Bravo!"

It was Thane Grier who had spoken, as, pocketing his notebook, he hurried toward them. "So a humble man without so much as a 'sir' before his name might have had a chance?"

"Might have," Lavinia said sharply. "But Miss Grayson is now officially engaged to Mark Farrow."

"Engaged is not quite married," Thane said. Ally noted that he was nicely built, that his smile seemed genuine, and that his face was handsome. Then again, Andrew Harrington, with his wheat-colored hair, green eyes, superb stance and expertly tailored apparel was quite striking, as well.

And yet neither man could quite compare to the highwayman....

She started, stunned and alarmed by her own thought.

"Are you all right, dear?" Lavinia asked.

"Indeed. Quite," she replied quickly.

"Good heavens, you're not disturbed by that batty woman's curse, are you?" Andrew asked.

"She is far too sane and practical a young woman for such silliness," Thane said, watching her with admiration and a glint in his eyes, as if he understood something about her she didn't understand herself.

As they stood there, Shelby came up to stand before Ally.

"Your pardon," he said politely to the others. "Lord Stirling has suggested I take you home now, Miss Grayson. He fears the aunts will begin to worry."

"Yes, yes, I must go. Good night," she said, nodding to Thane, Andrew and Lavinia.

"Good night and God bless," Thane called after her.

As Shelby led her toward the door, he whispered, "Camille said you refused to stay for the night when this evening was planned, that you were determined to get home to the aunts. You can still stay, you know. Your bedroom always awaits."

"No, but thank you, and thank you for taking me home. When the aunts absolutely refused to attend, I knew I'd have to get back to them," Ally assured him.

It was not an easy process to leave. Many guests were still milling about on the castle steps, awaiting their carriages. Sir Angus spoke to her again, giving his congratulations. Lord Lionel Wittburg, looking both old and exhausted, also stopped her, wishing her health, happiness and long life. As Shelby at last helped her into the coach bearing Lord Stirling's coat of arms, she saw that another of Brian's men—one of the strong ones who often guarded the gate—was seated on the driver's bench. Lord Stirling was quite determined that no coach of his would be held up again.

Seated, while Shelby climbed up to take the reins, Ally looked back at the castle.

She felt the strangest sense of déjà vu.

There was the journalist, Thane Grier, standing just a few feet apart from the others at the door.

There was the sheriff, Sir Angus Cunningham.

Next to him stood Andrew Harrington, and next to him, Sir Lionel Wittburg.

The light from the doorway framed the threesome, shadows seeming to fall around them.

Ally thought she saw a woman...in black.

She reminded herself that there had been several women in black at the party. Widows in mourning, daughters who had lost fathers, mothers who had lost sons.

Eleanor Brandon had been in black.

Eleanor Brandon, newly made widow of Giles, whose husband's body was scarcely cold. She should have been resting, sedated, in her own home, but for some reason she had ordered her coachman to bring her to the castle.

She couldn't have been the woman standing next to Andrew Harrington's cousin that morning, could she?

The murder had not even been known at that point.

Ally gave herself a shake. She was seeing things. Eleanor Brandon had been taken up to bed. She would have been given plenty of brandy by now, and if she had remained as hysterical and upset as she had been, Brian Stirling would have called for a doctor.

But when she had danced with Sir Angus, she had been startled by another figure in black, one who had uncannily reminded her of the morning just past.

She sat back in the coach, then looked out the window again.

Imagined or real…

In the shadows stood a woman in black.

MARK POURED IAN A WHISKEY, which the detective accepted with thanks, then swallowed in a gulp. Smiling, Mark refilled the glass.

"The truth will come out," he assured his friend.

Ian took the second serving and walked to the handsome daybed in the parlor, perching on the end of it, cradling the glass between his hands. "Not by legal and customary means, I fear," he said.

"However it occurs, the truth will be known," Mark said determinedly.

Ian looked at him morosely. "What if you are caught?" he demanded.

"I will not be caught."

Ian shook his head. "Not even you are infallible, my friend."

"Then I'll have to move very swiftly." He took a sip of his own whiskey. "Three murders, all the same. Each man busy at his desk. Each man writing an opinion piece against the monarchy. No evidence of a break-in. As if the men were murdered by a ghost. We know better. In each case, there must have been a set of keys, either provided by someone in the household or stolen from them. Tomorrow afternoon, I'll go with you when you interview the housekeeper again." He hesitated. "Ian, not only do I think the victims knew their killer very well, I believe the killer is an anti-monarchist himself. He—or she, but for the sake of semantics, let's say he—believes killing his own allies is the best thing he can do to further his cause of toppling the government."

Before Ian could respond, the sound of a door opening and closing came from the front entry.

Joseph Farrow, doffing his cloak and trusting it to Jeeter's waiting hands, entered, thanking his valet as he did so.

He didn't appear at all startled when he saw Mark and Ian in the parlor. Ian stood immediately, nodding his head in respect.

"Well?" Joseph demanded, then caught himself. "Forgive me. Hello, Detective Douglas. I hope my son has made you welcome?"

"Of course," Ian murmured.

"We have a few theories, Father," Mark said, and explained.

"That's outrageous!" Joseph said. "Why would an anti-monarchist kill his own kind?"

"He's creating martyrs—and trying to cast the blame on the monarchy," Mark said.

Joseph poured himself a whiskey and paced the floor. "There were those who tried very hard to blame the whole Jack the Ripper horror on the monarchy," he said, shaking his head. "Ridiculous! The queen has endured such slander before and remained unbowed. They will not get away with this."

"No, Father, they will not," Mark assured him.

"So...?" Joseph queried.

Ian looked guiltily at Mark, then told Joseph, "Lord Farrow, I sincerely believe that the killer is a man of some means. I believe the only way he is escaping so easily is because he has a carriage awaiting him each time he commits one of his deadly deeds."

Joseph said, "There were many who believed the Ripper made his escape by carriage, and that is why no one saw him. Then again, the Ripper moved through neighborhoods where slaughterhouses were abundant, and it might well have seemed half the populace wore aprons covered in animal blood. In this instance..." He lowered his head for a moment, shaking it. "In this instance, Detective Douglas, I believe you may be right."

"So we must keep following every path until we find the right one," Mark murmured.

Ian Douglas set his glass back on the cherrywood brandy table. "I thank you for your hospitality. I will take my leave now."

"Thank you, Detective, for your aid," Joseph told him.

"It's my job," Ian said simply. Jeeter appeared, ready to show him out.

When he had gone, Joseph Farrow looked at his son. "You haven't asked yet about your engagement ball."

"I'm sorry. I'm sure it was an elegant occasion."

"Alexandra Grayson is quite charming, not to mention exquisite," Joseph said.

"I know."

"Of course you do. She had a meeting with the highwayman, after all," Joseph said, frowning.

"Father, I didn't know who was in the coach, I didn't see the coat of arms until we had stopped it. And the highwayman, to maintain his credibility, could hardly have ignored such a rich prize."

Joseph didn't look pacified. "Miss Grayson was hardly charmed by a fiancé who could not quite manage to make an appearance."

"There was nothing I could do."

"I think we should push forward with all haste to finalize this marriage."

"What?" Mark said, astounded.

"You will lose her otherwise," Joseph said softly.

"Father, you have told me about this vow you and Lord Stirling made between you, and though you know I find the entire concept ridiculous and outdated, I will honor it because I honor you. But I can hardly lose a woman who is mine only through the machinations of others."

Joseph turned away from him, staring at the fire. "I'm afraid her life may be in danger in the future. And though you've yet to really know her, I cannot tell you what a tragedy her loss would be."

"Father, why—"

"I can't tell you. You must simply believe me."

"Father—"

"I learned something from Angus Cunningham tonight, Mark. You have heard of Lady Rowenna? She is the daughter of Lord Carnarenfew."

"Yes, yes…she has land and a manor past the western forest area."

"She was nearly killed yesterday."

"How?"

"A bullet fired into her house."

Mark shook his head. "Perhaps a hunter was lost, misfired—"

"I believe it was an attempt to kill her. She is known to be an illegitimate grandchild of the queen's uncle."

"Father, I admit to being completely lost."

"Miss Grayson lives in a cottage in the woods. With three doting aunts and not even a guard dog."

"Father, I have agreed I will marry her."

"Very soon," Joseph said. "Unless you are blind, you must realize it will be no hardship."

Mark looked down. A hardship? Never. His encounter with the young woman in question had stayed with him all day. She hadn't been in any way what he had expected. She was strong, not a wife he would simply take and protect. She was opinionated. She was smart and sharp and…

He didn't see her accepting such a marriage easily.

A rueful smile curved his lips. "Father, why have you never remarried?" he asked softly.

"Why?" Joseph repeated with a frown. As usual, Mark saw his father's eyes grow soft at the mere memory of his mother. "I love her still, son. No other woman will ever be my wife."

"It would have been nice to be allowed that emotion myself," Mark said simply. "Meanwhile, we are in a very grim situation here."

"All the more reason this must happen quickly," Joseph said. "I'm sorry, son. The situation is far too dire to allow emotions to rule. My prayer is only for this to happen quickly and that Miss Grayson be safe. You are going to be an earl one day, yet you decided you must sign on in secrecy with the queen's private guard, must play detective, must risk your life...."

Joseph turned away. Mark stiffened. "Father, you served in the military."

"Yes, and I survived, praise God. If you're going to continue to risk your neck, I'd like to at least have a grandchild!"

"Well, that's rather straightforward," Mark murmured. "I will make sure that I...that I see Miss Grayson, that...she's kept safe. But don't you see, Father? The faster we solve these terrible crimes, the sooner everyone will be safe. Tomorrow morning, the news of Giles Brandon's death will be told in grisly detail in the papers, and the last article he wrote will run, as well. Would to God there was someone out there with the power of the pen who would suggest it is the anti-monarchists themselves who are behind these heinous murders."

"Would to God," Joseph said wearily. He started for

the stairs, then turned back. "Mark, forgive me. I am proud of you. I raised you to know your own mind. I…couldn't bear to lose you, that is all."

"You won't lose me, Father," Mark assured him.

Joseph went on up the stairs.

The clock over the fireplace began to chime.

It was already morning.

Jeeter came into the room. "Sir…I have acquired a first edition of the paper."

"Thank you, Jeeter."

Mark hurried across the room and accepted the paper. He could still smell the scent of the fresh ink.

As he had expected, the headline blazed with the murder of Giles Brandon. Halfway down, on the right-hand side, was Giles Brandon's last article.

But halfway down, on the left-hand side was another article. Its opening words seemed to blaze loudly, too.

Is the monarchy guilty? Or is a zealot at work, an anti-monarchist willing to commit the murders of his own friends and comrades just to topple the monarchy and enact a change in government?

Mark's mouth gaped open. Luckily he was near a chair, for he was able to sit instead of winding up on the floor.

Good God! He had just been saying they needed such a writer, and here…

He read the article. It was excellent, pointing out all the reasons why it was most unlikely that either the queen or some other member of the monarchy could be involved. The writer listed all the reasons why a deranged and passionate zealot might well be responsible. It was excellent. Of course, it had been written before anyone had known about the murder of Giles Brandon, but even based only on the two previous murders, it still made perfect sense, the words cleverly arranged, the arguments entirely persuasive.

He looked quickly for a byline.

A. *Anonymous.*

He folded the newspaper, rose and set it thoughtfully on the table by the newel post.

A. Anonymous.

Thank God for the pseudonym.

If the writer's real name ever became known, A. Anonymous would become a prime target for a grisly murder.

CHAPTER FIVE

"I'M JUST GOING FOR A WALK in the woods with my sketch pad, as I've done at least a thousand times over the years," Ally said, looking from one dear but alarmed face to another.

She smiled, shaking her head. "What on earth is the matter with you darlings this morning?" she demanded.

Violet, tall and very slim, clasped her hands together. "Ally, all those other times were *before* you were way-laid by the highwayman." Violet gazed at Merry, Merry gazed at Edith, and then they all gazed at her.

Ally realized suddenly that in the days since the ball, they had kept her extremely busy. Sunday there had been church, and then they'd asked the rector back to the house for dinner. Monday Violet had needed help with a gown. Tuesday Merry had needed assistance in the garden. Edith had asked her to help in the kitchen on Wednesday, and so on. There had been something that needed doing every day. And now it was Saturday again.

A week since the ball and her engagement to a man she had yet to see.

A week to remember her encounter with the highwayman. A week…and no real chance to have a conversation with any of her guardians.

A week in which she'd at least had a bit of time to write.

"The highwayman…please! Is that why you've kept me so busy? To keep me from going out? He is long gone."

"And after that, dear Ally became engaged," Merry said, smiling dreamily, as she had so often since Ally had come home from the party. "I still dream of the way you looked coming home. You could have been such a princess!"

"No, my darling, not a princess," Ally protested, but Merry was already waltzing about the room with an imaginary partner. Ally had to smile. She loved them all so much. Violet, the sternest of the three; Merry, ever-young at heart; and Edith, who held the scales between the two, sometimes as cheerful as Merry and sometimes stalwart in supporting Violet's far stricter tendencies. They had been waiting for her outside the front door when she had returned and flitted about like a threesome of oversize fairies, demanding to know every last detail. She had thanked them over and over again for the dress. They had insisted it was all Maggie's doing, but she could see the pleasure in their eyes when she told them how many compliments she had received on the gown.

She had described the castle, the dinner, the dancing—and the announcement that had so taken her by surprise, an announcement that had been no surprise to them. She had left out the part about Giles Brandon's wife coming in, screaming hysterically and cursing her. When they had pressed for more details, she had obliged at first, then told them, "No, not another word. It was a lovely party—except for one thing."

"And that was?" Violet asked, puzzled.

"You three were not there. And I determined last night I will never go to another party or event—no matter how kind my godparents are—unless you are there, as well."

"Oh, but, dear!" Violet protested.

"We're...we're...we're not...party types," Merry managed.

"Oh, no, no, no," Edith said.

"Then I am not, either," Ally said. "I never should have let you get away with it this time," she said sternly.

"Oh, but...we're not..." Violet tried again.

"If you dare say that you're not *society* and I *am,* I will refuse to go to the castle ever again! I'm an orphan. You raised me. You are my parents. Do you understand?"

Merry giggled. "We're all old women, dear."

"You are my family. I adore my godparents. They are wonderful people, and I am incredibly lucky to have them in my life. But *you* are my family. Are we understood?"

They looked at one another. "Of course, dear," they said in unison.

Her mind returning to the present, Ally said, "Please, I'm just going for a walk in the woods."

"You really mustn't," Violet argued.

"You're engaged now," Merry told her.

She stiffened. If she told them she didn't feel at all engaged and wasn't at all sure about going through with the marriage, they would simply stand there arguing until doomsday.

"Engaged," she murmured. The ring sat heavily upon her finger. "But not married," she said brightly.

"Oh, dear, what does that mean?" Merry asked Violet.

"Well, she's going through with the wedding," Violet said, then looked at Ally. "You *are* going through with the wedding, aren't you?"

"Oh! She must go through with the wedding!" Edith exclaimed, and looked worriedly at the others.

"Ally, dear," Violet said, "what did you mean—that you're not married yet?"

"It means I'm going for a walk in the woods," Ally said, grinning. "I love you all so much," she added, giving each of them a hug. Then, before anyone could stop her again, she slipped her cloak off the peg by the door and hurried out.

She nearly ran down the path from the house, pausing only when she was a good hundred feet away, then looking back with deep affection.

The cottage was storybook perfect, with a thatched

roof and a chimney that always seemed to trail a puff of smoke to somehow indicate the warmth to be found inside. Merry was an avid lover of flowers, so there were beautiful beds and little stone planters all around the entry. The aunts were quite elderly now, but still spry and cheerful and girlish in so many ways. Cocoa cured all ills, and if cocoa failed, there was tea and scones, everything fresh brewed and fresh baked. She had learned from her many tutors, but she had learned from the women, as well. They never sat still, or if they did, it was only to read or do needlework. They had taught her about industry, keeping busy, respecting the land, the virtues to be found in sweeping, and, most of all, they had taught her about unconditional love. She smiled, again thinking herself very lucky. Then her smile faded and her brow puckered, and she couldn't help but wonder *why?*

With a shake of her head, she turned again. Winding through stands of beautiful and ancient oaks, she followed her own well-worn path down to the stream that bubbled through the forest. There was an old layer of rock there that she had worn smooth over the years. It was situated next to the massive trunk of one of the old oaks that stood just at the water's edge. There she could doff shoes and stockings, dangle her feet and draw—or write.

She wondered what the newspaper had featured that day, but the aunts didn't get their papers until late in the afternoon, so it would be some time before she would be able to see it. She held her sketchbook on her lap as she crawled onto the rock and went through her ritual, slipping off the offending shoes and hose, testing the chill of the water with a toe, then leaning back against the oak, her pad clutched in her arms.

She closed her eyes, summoning the images she wanted to convey.

First…the village. That scene was the most important.

Unfortunately, thoughts of the engagement and her absent fiancé kept intruding.

The village…

The people gathered in the square. The cries…

Down with the monarchy!

Images passed quickly through her mind. Thane Grier, his pose casual as he watched what was going on.

Then Sir Angus Cunningham, trying to calm the crowd, and the woman…the veiled woman in black, crying out. Lord Wittburg at Sir Angus's side, and last, Sir Andrew Harrington. The crowd at last beginning to listen, starting to break up as Shelby began to drive the horses forward.

And then…

The highwayman.

"Dreaming of me?"

The question—suddenly spoken in a deep and amused masculine voice in the middle of the forest, where the only sounds should have been the bubbling of the water and the sweet song of the birds—was so startling that she jerked up and nearly lost her balance on the rock. As it was, her sketchbook flew out of her arms and her pencil came perilously close to being lost forever in the stream.

"You!" she gasped, stunned. Should she scream? Jump up? Run?

It was indeed him. He was dressed as he had been when he had held up the carriage: black breeches, unbleached poet's shirt, knee-high riding boots—and black silk mask. One foot was planted on the rock, his elbow upon his knee, and she had to wonder just how long he had been standing there, watching her.

"Yes, me," he said.

He rescued the pencil and set it and the sketchbook safely aside, then took a seat next to her on the rock.

She realized he was alone. And that he intended no harm. Apparently he had come to find her. She couldn't help but wonder if he had done so before during the past week.

"Is this a private rock?" he inquired.

"Actually, yes."

"Is it your land, then?" he asked.

"No. It belongs to Lord Stirling."

"Then we are both trespassing."

"Don't be ridiculous—I'm welcome on his land. You, however…"

He laughed, perfectly comfortable as he leaned against the oak. "Actually," he informed her, "this land does not belong to Lord Stirling."

"Indeed?"

He pointed to the trail. "Up to there…it is his. But where we sit right now…if I'm not mistaken, we are on land that belongs to Lord Farrow, Earl of Warren."

She stared back at him as coolly as she could, considering the fact that her heart was pounding too quickly, her blood flowing with a shimmering heat.

"Well, I believe Lord Farrow would welcome me and

allow me this position, while he would certainly send you packing. Or rather, have you arrested."

He shrugged. "Quite possibly." He stared at her, still deeply amused. She noted his eyes. Blue-gray, they had the ability to be light, to be dark, to appear cloaked in shadow. Mercurial, they changed within seconds, as swiftly as his moods.

"You are a fool, and what you're doing here is beyond me. You'll notice I'm carrying nothing more valuable than a sketchbook. Shouldn't you be out on the road somewhere, assaulting more innocents?"

"Dear Miss Grayson, please don't ever fool yourself that I assault only innocents," he said. "Actually, I rather like it here. And a hardworking highwayman does deserve a rest now and then."

"Not on my rock."

"We've established the fact that it's neither your rock nor mine," he said lazily.

She knew she should simply get up and walk away. He seemed to be carrying no weapons, and his horse was nowhere in sight.

He gazed her way, stretching out more comfortably, one hand behind his head. "I understand congratulations are in order."

"How do you know that?" she demanded sharply.

"I read."

"How commendable. You could certainly find real employment, then."

He shrugged, looking back to the water. "There was a whole page about you, Miss Grayson, second page of the paper. You came after news of a murder, an article that all but skewers the queen and another that defends her. An excellent article, really," he mused. His smile deepened. "The news of your engagement took precedence over the news that you were held up by the highwayman. Sad, but true."

"I told you that you were no more than petty riffraff," she informed him, and yet her mind was reeling.

An excellent article, really.

That? From a highwayman?

"So you will soon be Lady Farrow."

She didn't reply.

"Aren't you eager to become a countess?" he demanded dryly.

She stared at him. To her own surprise she said, "Did the article mention that the groom-to-be was not in attendance?"

"Yes, it did. Churlish of him, don't you think?"

She looked away, shaking her head. "To tell you the truth, it doesn't matter in the least."

"You were not hurt by him?"

"How on earth could I be hurt by someone I don't know? Indeed, I knew nothing about the engagement until it was announced."

"Brian...Camille...never told you?" he demanded, seeming quite startled.

"Brian? Camille? You're dreadfully familiar, you know," she told him.

"I beg your pardon. Allow me to rephrase. Neither Lord nor Lady Stirling ever told you what was to be your fate?"

She burst out laughing. "My fate?"

"Well, it *is* your fate, isn't it?"

She looked out at the water, determined not to share her personal feelings with an outlaw, no matter how charming.

"Fate is what we make of it, isn't it?" she murmured.

"They never told you," he said, dropping down beside her on the rock.

"Is this really any of your business?" she demanded.

He smiled, shrugged. She realized that their shoulders were touching as they sat side by side, and though she knew she should have sounded an alarm or at least run away the moment she saw him, she was actually quite pleased to be sitting as she was. Content. No, not content, actually. Exhilarated. She enjoyed arguing with him, and she didn't mind his proximity at all. For an outlaw, he had a rather seductive scent. Apparently his line of work did not prevent him from bathing or keeping his clothing clean.

"I am a student of human nature, and quite curious," he told her.

"It was simply one of those nights," she murmured. "They would have told me—if it hadn't been for you," she charged him, angry enough to jab his upper arm with her fist.

"I wasn't even there!" he protested, rubbing the spot where she had punched him.

"When we reached the castle, Shelby was in a state, and therefore Brian was in a state, so he rode out—and you are extremely lucky he didn't catch you, but mark my words, you had best be careful, he may still do so."

"Believe me," he said softly, but smiling still, "I never underestimate the Earl of Carlyle."

"Be sure that you don't."

"I am warned. So...still, no one told you?"

"Then I had to get ready for the event, and an Inspector Turner was in the kitchen, and by then, guests were arriving. So, thanks to you, the Earl of Warren—who seems to be an entirely decent man—got to see his prospective daughter-in-law gape and stare and probably look quite like an idiot when the grand engagement was announced."

"You don't sound pleased at the prospect of your marriage."

"I'm not."

"Why not? Most young women in your position would be thrilled by the opportunity to become a countess."

She waved a hand in the air. "It's hardly your business."

To her surprise, he caught her waving hand. She had forgotten the ring on her finger. His own hand was clad in a knit glove that left the fingertips free. She was surprised by her own lack of protest when he shifted his lazy position to sit up and study the ring.

"Nice," he told her.

She did snatch her hand away, then, though to her distress, she felt her cheeks reddening. "If you don't mind, I'd just as soon not discuss the situation with an outlaw."

"I've heard," he said, ignoring her words, "that this secret agreement was made between Lord Stirling and Lord Farrow years ago."

"Must you?" she objected.

"So all these years, you've been groomed to be the perfect countess. Voice like a lark, dances like an angel and so on."

She gritted her teeth. "Perhaps dancing wouldn't be such a bad occupation for you. Better than robbing carriages."

"What makes you think I can't dance, Miss Grayson?"

He leapt with swift agility to his feet. Elaborately, he bowed to her.

She stared at him, then started to laugh.

He straightened. "I am a dangerous outlaw, you know. You should not laugh at me."

"If I considered you dangerous, I'd be long gone by now."

"I see. You find me amusing?" He reached for her hand, drawing her to her feet despite herself. She was suddenly close—his scent was provocative—wondering at her own sanity. But he wasn't dangerous. Not to her. Somehow she knew it.

She smiled, not even protesting his hold. "Yes, I find you quite…diverting," she informed him.

"Then dance with me."

"There is no music."

"Hum."

"Don't be silly."

"Fine. I shall hum."

And he did, a quite passable Viennese waltz, and before she knew it, they were dancing swiftly through the copse. She felt the close contact of his body, and she thought she had never been so in tune with her partner's every movement. His hands were sure, and he led with confidence and strength, but never too much power. She loved his touch, the way they moved, the way the earth felt beneath her bare feet. The air seemed to rush around her with a fresh, clean sweetness. His thighs were hard, muscled, his whole body vital and alive.

She was laughing, finding it quite absurd, dancing in the forest with an outlaw. They were close, their faces nearly touching. His mouth was so very close to hers....

The reality of what she was doing suddenly frightened her. She wasn't at all certain she could agree to a marriage, not if she wished to live her own dream, but this behavior was certainly a dishonor to those who cared for her.

Her laughter faded. She pulled away. This was indeed absurd. She should be ashamed of herself.

"I can't do this," she said softly.

"Dance in the forest? Ah, that's right. You are an engaged woman."

"I owe nothing to Lord Farrow's son."

"Oh?"

"I don't even know him."

"Ah."

She shook her head. "You're a criminal," she informed him.

"But a criminal with a newspaper," he told her.

She forgot everything else. "Where?" she demanded.

He hesitated. "I'll bring it."

He disappeared down one of the trails, and she waited, uncertain, her heart thundering. His horse must be near.

He returned with the day's paper, and she snatched it from him with a delighted cry.

Last Sunday, the first piece by A. Anonymous had run. The paper had been just as he had described it, with the article about the murder of Giles Brandon and the opinion piece that had been Brandon's last.

And then there had been the defense of the monarchy, by A. Anonymous.

Today there was another article on the front page by A. Anonymous.

She avidly read the piece that reminded people again that the anti-monarchists themselves might well be responsible for the murders—which were, sadly, still unsolved. When she turned the page, she saw there was another mention of her impending marriage.

And after that…

An article about the highwayman. He had struck several carriages throughout the week, but instead of bringing down terrible rancor, he had enchanted an elderly noble woman. She had been delighted to discover that the ring he had taken had wound up in the hands of the Victorian Ladies Society for the Betterment of Our Sisters. She had paid a ransom for her ring, which had really been a donation, and thereby, financed a day's free meal in a churchyard.

"Good God, you're fast," he said as she turned pages.

She afforded him a quick glance. "I rarely had other children around. Reading became…my companion," she murmured. "You're being too modest, by the way. Your adventures are gaining popularity. This lady does not exactly say so, but I believe she is all but begging you to hold her up again."

He shrugged.

She had barely realized it when he sat down close beside her on her rock again. It seemed entirely natural. Their arms were side by side, and he was leaning in, studying the pages along with her. She was aware once more of his scent and the flush of heat he aroused in her. She straightened self-consciously.

"A. Anonymous," he muttered. "There's a dead man for you."

"What?" She frowned fiercely. "I thought you were a bandit, but a loyal British bandit who honored the queen."

"A. Anonymous's identity will be discovered. And once that happens, don't you think the anti-monarchists will put him on a murder list?"

"I think the man has every right to speak out. And you! You say you are the queen's man, even if a rogue. You should be applauding him."

"I'm simply saying that he'd best make sure his byline remains in the paper. Or perhaps, for his own good, he should cease writing."

"Perhaps he cannot do so. Perhaps he feels it necessary for such an article to be written and published, even if he must remain anonymous."

"The paper pays for such political essays," the highwayman pointed out.

"Maybe A. Anonymous is smart enough to have the checks sent to a post box."

"And don't you think the killers will know that? They will have their ways to discover the truth. Perhaps they'll get into the newspaper files somehow, find out where the checks are sent—and wait."

She felt her blood grow cold, and she shivered. He frowned instantly. "Are you cold? I have my cape...back with the horse," he said ruefully.

"No, no...I have a cape. There," she murmured, pointing to where it had fallen to the ground. He leapt to his feet, procured the cape and slipped it around her shoulders. As he did so, there was a moment of closeness that seemed incredibly sweet.

She drew away. "You speak about the danger to A. Anonymous, but what about yourself? Eventually someone will kill you."

"I can take care of myself."

"You're a criminal, for God's sake. And criminals who continue along a path such as yours are eventually undone."

Beneath the mask, his lips curled. "But I am not a common criminal, at least. I have had some training in etiquette."

"Indeed. And therefore there can be no earthly excuse for the road you have chosen."

She turned away from him, walking to the spot where she had left her stockings and shoes.

"Don't go," he said, suddenly very serious.

"I must. And don't...don't come here again. I've told you, Brian Stirling is a dangerous man."

"You don't believe it, but so am I."

"He is the Earl of Carlyle."

"And I am a thief."

"I can't be here with you," she said firmly. He was going to touch her again, she thought, her mind running foolishly to the thought that it was almost as if…as if she longed to slip back into his arms, feel the brush of his fingers, let him lift her chin…and place his lips upon hers.

"I have to go," she said.

"Wait!" he called.

Despite herself, she hesitated.

He came to the tree where she stood and set his palm upon it, leaning toward her. There was a sudden seriousness in his eyes that gave her pause.

"I must admit, I have had a passion—born of the direst need—for my…career as an outlaw. But if I weren't a criminal, my dear Miss Grayson, do you think you would have offered me a place, however slight, in your life?"

"In my life…?"

"We are moving ever forward, out of the Dark Ages," he said ruefully. "Would you have let me call upon you, do you think?"

She stared back at him. His smile was so wistful beneath his mask. Before anything could happen that might be her undoing, she needed to flee.

"Sadly, you are a criminal. And I am engaged."

"Perhaps…a few more words from you and I may atone for my sins."

"You tease me, and I am afraid I cannot play your game," she told him. Yet she set a hand upon his chest before she slipped past him, almost desperate to escape and return to the cottage.

He watched her go, wishing she would come back....

Angry she had stayed so long.

She had run off with the newspaper, he realized, and he couldn't help but smile. Such a little thing to give someone so much pleasure. Frowning, he realized she had left her sketchbook.

He should leave it. She would come back for it eventually.

Yet it might rain before she found the opportunity. And if he took it, he would have an opportunity to return it to her—as the highwayman, of course. Clasping the sketchbook, he hurried down the trail to his horse.

It was rather convenient that the cottage in the woods was not far from the hunting lodge his father kept, Mark thought wryly. And indeed, the stream actually was on his father's property.

He realized that he wasn't at all certain how he was feeling after his encounter with Miss Alexandra Grayson. Certainly she shouldn't be entertaining an outlaw in the forest—not when she was wearing an engagement ring.

And yet...

He was fascinated by the tawny fall of her hair, by the laughter in her eyes and by the keen eagerness with which she had read the paper. Even by her arguments. He wasn't even sure why he had been so insistent about all he said, except in part for the enjoyment of sparring with her. He'd applauded the article in the paper, which truly had been excellent. And it was true that he prayed for the poor fool who had written it, because it really would be quite easy for someone to bribe his way into the files, or maybe there was someone at the newspaper who was less than honest and would be ready to divulge the truth to the wrong party for a price.

He heard a whistle and reined in his horse, replying in kind. A moment later, Patrick came riding hard down the trail.

"Your father is at the lodge, looking for you," Patrick told him.

"Whatever for? I never explain my whereabouts."

"Apparently he assumed you were at the lodge, perhaps playing with one of what he calls your detecting gadgets, and he has promised your appearance at a luncheon."

"A luncheon?"

"At the museum."

"I had thought we should comb the trails again this afternoon—"

"Mark, give this one afternoon to your father. We will ride out as ourselves and report anything we see, I swear it. Trust your fellow bandits," Patrick said, grinning.

"All right. Watch the roads, though. I do want to know who is traveling where," Mark told him. Then, spurring his horse, he hurried on toward the lodge.

His father was at his desk, holding a long scarf, frowning as he lifted it and found it heavy.

"What is this?" he asked his son.

Mark walked over to the desk and picked up the long

knit scarf. He set it around his neck. Then he removed it and swung it, creating a whirring in the air.

"A backup weapon, Father."

Lord Farrow looked unhappy.

"Where did you learn to make this?"

"From a book."

"A book on warfare?"

"A book of stories about Sherlock Holmes. Arthur Conan Doyle is a very cunning man."

His father sighed. "When you're not out and about imitating his character, do you frequent the literary circles and drive the man crazy with questions?"

"Sometimes."

Joseph sighed. "I believe I am actually best off when I'm unaware of your exploits."

"Father, I remind you again, I serve the queen. You fought in the army, as I did. And now I believe I can serve in a better way. Would you have me do any less?"

"No," Joseph said after a moment. "I would that these wretched internal conflicts came to a halt." He sighed deeply. "A man must always do what he feels in his heart he must. But for today, perhaps you could play the role of my son. Can you come with me to the museum? We shall have to hurry."

"Yes."

"Yes?" Joseph said.

"Yes, I'll come with you."

Joseph smiled. "I hadn't expected so easy a victory. The carriage awaits. Pray, dress like a nobleman this once, eh?"

"I shall be impeccable," Mark promised. He started for his bedroom, then paused. "Are we going to lunch for a reason?"

"Indeed. You're to meet your fiancée."

"Today?"

"You should have met last week."

"Yes…but…"

"Is something wrong?"

"I…no. No, of course not. I'll get dressed quickly."

ALLY WAS STARTLED TO SEE Lord Stirling's carriage in the clearing in front of the cottage. She had known that they needed to discuss all that had happened, but she had assumed the Stirlings were busy with affairs of their own following all the fuss of the ball.

She looked back quickly, feeling a sense of panic that the highwayman might have followed her. She couldn't help but feel a quickening in her heart, desperate that he should not be caught by Brian Stirling.

There was no sign of him.

She hoped she looked at least somewhat presentable as she started toward the cottage.

She still had the newspaper and realized she had forgotten her sketchbook. She lamented her foolish exit from the encounter, and considered going back for it. She had just turned back when the door of the cottage opened.

Kat was standing there. "Ally?"

No time to run back.

Ally stuffed the newspaper into a pocket, straightened her skirt and returned along the trail to the house.

"Kat," she said with pleasure. "I saw that the Stirling carriage is here."

"Yes, I'm here with Camille. I was about to start combing the forest for you. We've come to collect you for lunch and an event."

"An event? Lunch?"

"A late lunch. There was a bit of a sudden furor, someone at the museum wanting Brian to speak at a small opening—and at all such things, there is a bit of fund-raising," Kat said. "Camille got it into her head that we should go, then take lunch in the café at the museum."

"That's a lovely idea. I adore the museum."

"We all do—and the café is newly decorated with several recently cataloged funerary containers. It's a lovely place to meet people."

"And a place to talk, I hope."

"Oh, yes, of course."

"We need to talk," Ally persisted softly.

"It will be a marvelous place for you to meet," Kat said airily.

"For...who to meet?" Ally asked.

"You and your fiancé, dear. Mark. The Earl of Warren's son. You will just adore him. He's quite handsome, terribly well read." She shook her head. "And customarily so responsible in every way. But if it was a matter of business, it was a matter of business, and I know that Joseph would not be the type to lie—even for his son—for the sake of expediency. Today, though it won't be quite like meeting at a magical ball, it will still be lovely."

Lovely? Ally thought in a moment of panic.

She winced and opened her mouth. She could start with Kat, tell her that she couldn't marry a stranger. Surely they would understand that.

Before she could speak, the door burst open. Brian Stirling strode out, carrying the day's paper. "Rubbish!" he roared irritably. "This article written by Giles Brandon...and yet the fellow had a way with words. He will sway those who can't see that even if they disagree with policy, they cannot go blaming murder on the queen."

"There's another article," Ally said, forgetting that she was not supposed to have seen the paper.

Luckily Brian didn't seem to notice. He was deep in thought over the situation.

"Yes, a valiant effort, a fine second piece by the author A. Anonymous. I pray no one ever discovers who he may be."

Ally took a deep breath. "Why is that?" she asked.

And he repeated the words the highwayman had so recently said.

"Because he'd be a dead man!"

CHAPTER SIX

BRIAN STIRLING, WARY OF THE highwayman, didn't ride inside the carriage but chose the seat next to Shelby. Hunter chose to ride behind the conveyance, also keeping an eye out for any disturbance along the way.

Once again the aunts begged off, promising that they would happily come along in a few days' time when the group set out on a mission to support Lady Maggie's passion, a day tending to the children in the East End. Ally had argued fiercely with them, as had Lady Camille, who could be extremely persuasive. But they hadn't planned on going out, they insisted, and good heavens, how could they get ready when they'd had no warning?

In the carriage, having at last given up, Ally remembered another frustration. "Camille, what about Eleanor Brandon? Where is she now? Poor woman. Has she no relatives? Her husband's body barely found...and she, alone with her coachman, coming to the castle because there was nothing else she could do to ease her pain."

Camille sighed softly. "She was much better the next morning. It must have been horrible for her to come home only to find that her husband was lying in the morgue. It's been a week, but I don't believe they will release his body for another few days. Shelby drove Eleanor home Sunday morning and spoke with the housekeeper, who has promised to stay with her all the time from now on."

"I feel sorry for the poor woman," Ally murmured.

"And not frightened by any curse?" Kat said.

"No, of course not," Ally replied.

She hesitated, looking out the window. She had almost forgotten about the curse, but now, despite herself, she felt a chill.

Impatiently, she forced all thoughts of curses away.

She had to do so, because this was her chance.

She was alone in the carriage with Camille and Kat. It was the perfect time to explain that although she sincerely appreciated their efforts, she didn't want to marry. Even if the man was noble and his father charming. It was time to tell them that she was grateful for the many tutors and lessons that had enabled her to learn so many things, but she had found a calling, and now, more than ever, she was certain she could make it on her own.

But how *could* she tell them when both a highwayman and a lord had echoed the same sentiment about A. Anonymous?

She drew a breath. Maybe they didn't need to know the whole truth but only the fact that she felt it was beyond archaic to enter into an arranged marriage.

"Camille, Kat..." she began.

It seemed they were destined to be interrupted. Before she could speak, the carriage jolted and began to slow.

"The village," Kat said.

"Another protest," Camille added.

"Naturally. The newspaper carried so much about the murder," Kat said.

"And that piece by Giles Brandon, damning the Crown..." Camille said.

"It's true, sadly. He had an amazing talent with words," Kat murmured.

"Yes, but...oh, people simply do not think!" Camille said.

"But there was another article in the paper, too," Ally said. "And another today, one that chastised those who would foolishly give in to persuasion without seeking facts."

"You read it?" Kat asked. "I thought the paper had only arrived just before we left?"

"I saw the headlines," Ally said quickly.

"Brian was quite upset," Camille said distractedly. "This is so ridiculous! Look at all the people, and this is such a small village."

Ally pulled back the curtain at the window. She was dismayed. There was an even larger crowd gathered than there had been the other day. As Camille had said, there were a lot of people for such a small village. Still, it was nearly six weeks since the first murder, two weeks since the second, one since the third, and the police were still desperately searching for the killer. Judging by the amount of people here, she could only believe this demonstration had been organized and people brought in from the surrounding countryside. Angus was once again on the steps of the brick building that housed the sheriff's office and the court, trying to speak. He roared in fury when a tomato came flying his way.

The carriage halted.

Brian Stirling hopped down from the driver's seat, and with Hunter striding angrily behind him, they approached the steps.

Before they could reach their destination, another man leapt up beside Angus.

"Cease! Have you all lost your senses?" he asked.

He was tall and young, and stood very straight, with rich dark hair and a strong-featured face, jaw set squarely, firmly sculpted high cheekbones, and eyes that seemed to assess and blaze, and had the ability to quell the crowd.

"Sir!" someone called out, but the voice seemed to quaver a bit. "Don't you realize that something must be done? There's been nothing yet, not a clue. The police allow these murders."

"They don't allow any such thing. There are special units who are desperately seeking the truth, day after day. And they will find it. Do you read the papers? Do you see what lies between the lines?" he demanded. "You are being manipulated. We are British, damn it! We are all allowed our political beliefs, to speak, feel and think as we choose. We are about to enter a glorious new century, and every day, with British ingenuity and technical prowess, we are making life better. But there are those out there who don't want to allow you your opinions. Good God, look at your queen. Look at the progress she has struggled to achieve for her people. I'm not trying to tell you that you should or shouldn't support the monarchy. I'm telling you to use your own minds. Yes, there has been another murder, and yes, it was terrible. But there is an article today warning that someone wants us all to jump to conclusions, to damn the police. Read that piece, which is so filled with intelligence the editors saw fit to set it on the front page. Isn't it just as likely that the murders are coldly and cunningly being committed to create martyrs for a cause? What better way to steer people to someone's devoutly desired outcome? Think about it. Look in all directions. Don't be herded like a flock of sheep. Use your minds, your God-given right to form your own opinions!"

Silence followed his powerful speech. And then it was as if the crowd began to melt. A man near the carriage simply threw down his sign. Murmurs rose, some still arguing that the queen must be behind the murders. But there were retorts now, and others muttering that they were sick of losing work. Someone else said clearly, "I don't believe it. I don't believe it now any more than I ever believed that the queen was behind the Jack the Ripper murders. It's true. We are being manipulated, herded about like sheep."

"Don't let yourselves be so used," came a voice. Brian had reached the steps.

"Lord Stirling," someone muttered.

"Indeed, as my esteemed friend has said, live your lives and use your minds. We are thinking men—and women. Protest, if you will, but think clearly and look at all possibilities before you cast out slanderous accusations," he said.

The crowd continued to disperse.

"Well, what do you think?" Camille asked, leaning forward, tapping Ally's knee.

"I think the crowd was quelled nicely," she said. And despite the fear that had so recently been instilled in her, she was feeling a keen sense of pride. *The man had told them all to read the article by A. Anonymous.* "Who is that man?"

Camille glanced at Kat, and Kat smiled and shrugged.

"Your fiancé, dear. That's Sir Mark Farrow."

"Sir...?"

"He was knighted for service in South Africa," Camille explained. "Ah, there, see? His father waits with their carriage, just over there."

Ally stared out the window again. She couldn't see the man. His back was to her. He, Brian, Hunter and his father were talking. As she watched, they split up, going to their prospective carriages.

"I'd thought they were in town," Camille murmured to Kat, as Ally let the curtain drop and returned her attention to her companions.

"They must have been at Lord Farrow's hunting lodge. The property borders yours, doesn't it?" Kat said.

"Yes, I believe so. We haven't any fences, of course.

I'd not know myself where our property ends and Lord Farrow's begins."

There was a tap at the window. Ally nearly jumped from her seat. She drew back the curtain.

"You are all quite all right?" Brian Stirling asked.

"Of course, my love," Camille said.

Brian smiled. Then he returned to his seat beside Shelby, while Hunter walked back to his horse. The carriage jerked, and they resumed their journey.

"So, Ally," Kat said, smiling wickedly. "What did you think? Isn't he quite something?"

"You are referring to Mark Farrow?" she said.

"Of course," Camille said. They were staring at her like a pair of very smug and well-pleased cats.

"He seems to be a…commendable person," she said.

"That's all?" Kat laughed.

"I still don't know him," Ally reminded them.

"But you will," Camille said.

"He's very handsome," Kat told her. "Of course, in my mind, no one is quite as charming and handsome as Hunter, but…"

"He's younger, appropriate for Ally," Camille reminded her.

Again the two of them gave her those cat-like smiles. *Now or never.*

"He does seem to be an excellent speaker. An intelligent man, as well—he reads the paper and gives credit where it is due," Ally began. "But…"

"But?" Camille asked, her smile replaced by a frown. Ally shook her head. "I—"

"Ally, he will be one of the foremost voices in the land," Camille told her softly.

"And he is no dandy, expecting others to do his fighting for him. He doesn't sit in any ivory tower, using his position to avoid doing anything with his life," Kat said.

"Brian and Lord Farrow have been friends for ages," Camille said. "And Brian knew that Lord Farrow's son would grow to be trustworthy, filled with a sense of responsibility. Even as a child, Mark had a keen sense of dignity and honor."

And are such bloodless traits why you fell in love with Brian Stirling? Ally longed to ask.

"Please, Camille," she said softly. "I know that you and Brian have given much thought to my welfare, especially considering the fact that you have your own family, and I was simply a child entrusted to Maggie and Jamie by a priest. I can never thank you enough, all of you, and—"

"Thank us?" Camille seemed truly puzzled.

"Thank us?" Kat repeated.

"We need no thanks," Camille said.

"We love you!" Kat assured her. "You have grown up to be everything one hopes for in a child."

"That is why it will be such a perfect union," Camille said.

"I'm sure he is quite wonderful—" Ally began, aware that a trace of irritation was slipping into her voice.

"Wait. You don't know him. It may amaze you to discover that he is indeed perfect. You can't possibly know until you meet him," Camille said.

"It's just that...I was thinking of a career," Ally managed at last.

"A career?" Camille said.

Ally had to smile. "Kat has a career. She is an artist. You, Camille, are an Egyptologist. I, too, was thinking of a career. Because," she added hastily, "I have been privileged to benefit from your concern and nurturing all these years. I have wanted nothing more than to grow up to be like you."

They both stared at her blankly.

"But I am married to Lord Stirling," Camille said at last.

"And if it weren't for Hunter, I'd not have my art," Kat said.

"You underestimate yourself, Kat," Ally said softly. "Your talent would have surfaced. I believe you would not have been able to stop it."

Again they stared at her.

At last Camille asked, "What career is in your mind?"

"I wish to write."

"To write," Kat repeated. She looked at Maggie. "But she can write as a man's wife." She looked at Ally again. "Many women keep diaries—"

"Not a diary. I want to see my work published."

Once again they stared at her.

"Still," Camille said, addressing Kat again, "a married woman may submit her work for publication."

"Yes, of course," Kat agreed. "Writing is most often done at a desk."

"Or on a rock," Ally murmured.

"Pardon?" Camille said.

"It is work most often done in the home," Kat said.

They both sat back, smiling again.

"There's no reason why it wouldn't work," Camille said.

"None at all," Kat agreed.

"You say Mark Farrow will be a powerful man," Ally said. "*Is* a powerful man," she amended, remembering the way he had spoken. "Such men sometimes do not want a wife who is interested—no, passionate about—a pursuit of her own."

Camille leaned forward. "We are not living in the Middle Ages. No one will drag you to the altar and force you to say your vows. But, Ally..." She paused, seeming distressed. "In these times, it seems more apparent than ever that you must have such a man in your life."

"Pardon?" Ally said.

Camille looked at Kat uncomfortably, and Ally had the distinct feeling that there was something they weren't telling her. And weren't going to tell her.

"We are in the age of Empire," Kat said lightly.

"But it's a dangerous world still," Camille said simply.

"Whatever are you talking about?" Ally pleaded.

"Don't you want...well, all the things a young woman usually wants?" Kat asked softly.

"A home, a husband...children?" Camille went on.

Ally hesitated, before answering carefully. "This may sound quite strange, but as I said before, I have learned from incredible women. Love is important. And respecting oneself. I feel...I feel I have the ability to...to create something important myself. As to the rest, I want what you have had. I want to love, as you love. And I want a husband who will look at me as Brian looks at you, Camille, as Hunter looks at you, Kat, and as Lord Jamie looks at Maggie."

They were both silent.

Then Maggie said, "But it wasn't always so, you see. We fell in love."

"You will surely fall in love with Mark," Kat assured her. "I was a fool once—Hunter stood before me, and I was blinded by someone I later realized would have sadly disappointed me within a few weeks' time. Love doesn't always just...appear. It begins slowly sometimes...with a word, a realization...a stirring sensation."

Ally hesitated. She had felt the stirring sensation that Kat spoke about...

For the highwayman. But she would *not* fall in love with a criminal.

"Meet Mark, at least," Camille implored her.

"Of course," Ally said, feeling the ring heavy on her finger. "But I feel I must say something to Brian, Jamie and Hunter about my own plans."

"No!" Kat protested.

"No, please. Not yet," Maggie begged.

"Do nothing until you have at least spoken with Mark," Camille said. "All I'm asking is that you give him a chance. Please?"

"As you wish," Ally murmured. She didn't like it, but at least she had spoken her mind to both Camille and

Kat, and if she knew the two of them, Maggie would soon know everything she had said.

So yes, she would meet Mark Farrow, the future Earl of Warren. But she was not going to give up on her dream.

MARK HEARD HIS FATHER'S SOFT groan the minute they made it up the steps to the museum.

And then he knew why.

Ian Douglas was standing just inside the door, waiting.

"Now?" Joseph said, a growl in his voice.

Ian reddened, then spoke in hushed tones. "Forgive me, Lord Warren. Were this not of such great importance…but the chief has been with the prime minister, and he believes we must speak with the housekeeper and Eleanor Brandon immediately."

"There is a large force involving sheriffs, the Metropolitan Police and the City of London police to deal with this crisis," Joseph reminded Ian.

Ian shuffled uncomfortably, looking around before speaking again. "I'm sorry, Lord Farrow. Apparently the queen herself believes that another mind must be brought to bear, such as…"

"Such as my son, who is here to meet his fiancée, a young lady he failed to meet last week at his own engagement party."

"Father, I believe we were to view the exhibition first, then go in to lunch," Mark said. "I must obey Ian's summons, but I can surely do so and return in time to dine."

Lord Farrow frowned at Ian. "He simply must be back in time for dessert and coffee."

"Yes, my lord," Ian said, and gulped. "I've horses waiting—faster than steering any conveyance through the city traffic," he said.

"Father, I *will* be back."

Mark turned and strode out with Ian. Handsome police horses were waiting for them, the reins held by an officer. Ian had chosen wisely, as there were various cart jams, a stalled automobile and other blockages on the street. On horseback, they quickly reached the town house where Giles Brandon had been killed.

Time had passed, but there were still officers in front of the residence, though Mark didn't believe it was necessary. The killer had done what he needed to do here. Eleanor was in no danger.

The front door was answered by the housekeeper. She was a bone-thin woman with wide brown eyes and a skeletal face. Her color appeared far too ashen for any living being.

"Hattie Simmons," Ian said, smiling kindly, offering the woman his hand. She was probably not accustomed to such courtesy, because she looked at Ian for several seconds before accepting the greeting. Ian was about to introduce Mark, but he shook his head, offering his hand, as well. "Mark, Miss Simmons," he said.

"Mrs. Brandon is in the parlor, waiting," Hattie said.

"Have you tea, by any chance?" Mark asked.

Ian frowned slightly then realized his intent. "I'll sit with Mrs. Brandon. Perhaps you can help Hattie with the tea," he said.

"A pleasure," Mark said.

"I am the housekeeper. I must do the tea," Hattie said.

"I used to help my mum with the tea," Mark said. "A task I enjoyed. Truly, you must have had a wretched day and night. Please, let me be of assistance."

She didn't answer nor show any emotion. She simply turned and began to walk toward the kitchen. Mark shrugged to Ian and followed Hattie as the two men parted.

In the kitchen, Hattie set a heavy pot on the stove. Mark saw where a serving tray waited, and set it on the table before taking a seat. Hattie reached into a bread box, looking for scones or muffins, anything to serve, he thought. Neither she nor Eleanor Brandon looked like the type of women who would remember to eat unless someone prodded them into it.

"Hattie—may I call you Hattie?"

"It's what everyone calls me," the woman said dourly.

"Hattie, I'm sorry to bring this all up, but you do know that we must talk, do you not?"

She nodded grimly, lips pursed.

"I want to make sure I understand everything fully, so I'll tell you what I've been told. You were out for the night because Mr. Brandon wanted the house empty. He wanted complete silence and privacy while he was working."

She gave him the same grim nod. "I have told my story to the other officers."

"I'm not actually an officer, Hattie. I want to listen to all you have to say and see if there isn't something we haven't done to solve these terrible crimes."

She inclined her head to the side and shrugged.

"When you returned in the morning, the house was locked?"

"The gate and the house," Hattie offered.

"Those muffins look absolutely delicious," Mark said. "May I?"

She might have been as skinny as a starved mare, but apparently she took pride in her baking. "They're two days old, sir. I wish I had something fresh to offer you," she said, bringing a muffin to him on a plate.

"I'm sure that your two-day-old muffins are far superior to many fresh ones," he assured her. Taking a bite, he extolled, "And I am right. Delicious."

She managed to flush despite her pallor. "Thank you."

"All right, Hattie, so you returned home from a night out—where were you, by the way?"

"I stayed with my friend Maude. She's the house-keeper for the Perrys, down the street, but she has her own little room with a private entrance."

He nodded, planning to have someone speak with Maude and the Perrys, just to certify the woman's words.

"So you came home, and you worked in the kitchen," he said.

"Yes. I didn't hear Mr. Brandon about. I knew sooner or later he would start bellowing for his tea. But I try never to disturb him first."

"I see."

She watched him, and he made a display of savoring her muffin. "Hattie, at what time did you go up to Mr. Brandon's office?"

"Around nine, I believe."

"Was his office door locked?"

"Yes, as always." She hesitated, looking at him, and then she began offering information. "At first, I didn't want to knock. So I went away. But then…" Again she hesitated. Her face began to pucker. "I went back and knocked. And he didn't yell. I knocked harder, then again and again. Still he didn't answer. I went down for my keys."

"You went down for your keys, you say. Where are they kept?"

She pointed. The household keys were on a ring that was hung on a clothes peg by the back door.

"So you got the keys and went up."

"Yes. I knocked again. I called his name. Then I opened the door."

Her face betrayed the horror she must have felt. "There was so much blood…." she said weakly.

"You knew he was dead?"

"Oh yes!"

"Did you touch him?"

She shook her head. "No. I didn't need to touch him." She stared at him. "You wouldn't have needed to touch him. You would have known, too. There was no way I could have saved him. That…that was obvious."

"So then?"

She swallowed hard. "I ran. I ran all the way to the police station. And an officer came back with me…but I didn't go back up. No…I couldn't go back up. I…I couldn't stay in the house."

"What did you do?"

"I went back to Maude's."

"Did a police officer escort you?"

She nodded vaguely. Then she stared at him. "I only came back this morning because of Mrs. Brandon. She needs me. She's a good woman, a kind woman." Hattie was silent for a second, but then her next words spilled out. "A truly fine woman." She crossed herself. "God knows, there's no man deserved what Mr. Brandon got, but...neither did *she* deserve what she was always getting from him."

"They didn't get along?"

Hattie sniffed. "I can't say they didn't get along. They didn't fight. He yelled. She stayed silent. He ordered her about. She did what he said. And that was that." Hattie smiled. "This was her house, you know. He was able to be a writer because of her money. Mrs. Brandon, she isn't even all that old. But she looks it. He wore her to the ground with his constant ranting and raving. He had her convinced he was the next best thing to our blessed Lord Christ and she was privileged to be in the same room as the likes of him."

Hattie definitely hadn't liked Giles Brandon. But Mrs. Brandon's money or not, it seemed Giles had been in control of it. Looking at Hattie, he was certain she hadn't been the one to wield the knife against the man. And yet, skinny as she was...there was a steely strength about her. He didn't suspect her, but he didn't want to exclude her, either.

"Hattie...when you go out during the day, shopping, running errands, do you take your keys with you?" he asked.

"Yes. Well, not if I'm out for Mrs. Brandon. I don't

need to be lugging that heavy chain with me when she's home. She can let me back in."

"Who else comes here, besides yourself, of course, and Mrs. Brandon?"

"Are you jesting, sir?"

"No, Hattie, I'm serious."

"I wouldn't know where to begin," Hattie said. "All manner of folk come here. Mr. Brandon held meetings here sometimes. He didn't just *write* against the monarchy, you know. He was involved in groups planning to bring the Crown crashing right down."

"How did you feel about that, Hattie?" he asked.

She lifted her hands, her gaze almost amused and very world weary. "What do I care, the likes of me, one way or the other? A woman such as me...well, there will be an old master or a new master. I work. I survive. It doesn't matter to me who is at the top of the list. I will always remain at the bottom."

He wasn't sure how to respond to that. "You're a fine housekeeper, Hattie. And that is an excellent talent."

She lowered her eyes. "Thank you," she said awkwardly. Then she shrugged. "Mrs. Brandon is...well, I will be here for her."

"That's good of you, Hattie," he said. He clasped both her hands. "That's very good of you. And remember what I've said—you are a talented woman."

She smiled, and right then, the water began to boil.

THE MUSEUM WAS FILLED WITH people. The new exhibition had just opened, and Camille—who so often had a hand in such events—had determined it wasn't going to be a day just for the elite. The doors were opened to the general public as well. She hoped the well-off would offer contributions, but part of the reason she wanted such a mixture of people was that she believed in the goodness of humanity. She wanted the privileged to see what their contributions could do for those who were not quite so blessed.

"The tearoom is downstairs," Camille said as they entered. "We should mingle for a while, then dine in an hour or so."

"Perfect," Ally said. "I'm quite anxious to see the exhibit." She was lying through her teeth, but she had no other choice.

"Ah, there are Maggie and Jamie, speaking with Lord Joseph Farrow. I don't see Mark with him. How very odd. Perhaps he's already in the exhibit halls," Camille said.

She started off toward the group. "Come along, Ally," Kat said softly, and followed Camille.

But Ally hesitated. Even from a distance, she could hear Lord Farrow say, "He's had to step out for a moment—running late, I fear. But he will be along."

He would be along? Despite herself, she felt a surge of anger. So the wondrous Mark Farrow still couldn't find the time to meet his fiancée! How insulting.

She wouldn't let herself dwell on that at the moment; she had to make use of it, and of her time here. She made certain her guardians were deeply involved in their conversation with Lord Farrow, then sidled along the wall and made her way back to the door—and instantly out through it. She didn't run, which would have called attention to herself, but she made her way quickly down the steps and to the street.

Luckily, she had been at the museum many times and had learned the surrounding streets quite well.

She didn't need to hire a hansom cab. She could reach her destination far more quickly on foot. The city was, as always, a hive of activity. She moved swiftly, threading her way through workers, businessmen on their way to banks, carriages, pushcarts, automobiles in a veritable sea of humanity.

As she walked, she lamented the fact she had left her sketchbook by the stream. She had written some excellent material in it, but she was very proud of the piece secreted in the pocket of her skirt, as well.

This morning, watching her fiancé on the steps of the sheriff's office, she had become more convinced than ever that she hadn't been wrong about the importance of what she was doing. She had been afraid before at times, confident sometimes, and then, at other times, certain she was lacking real talent with words. But though she was certain she had a tremendous amount still to learn, she was also convinced that it was imperative for her to keep turning in her essays. Because of this luncheon, she was getting a chance to send her work straight from the city, instead of trying to appear nonchalant while she mailed it from the village.

In fact, she realized, she had to thank Mark Farrow

for his apparent disinterest. Had the man been there, she might not have escaped the museum so easily.

She paused, admitting to herself that the man had been an excellent speaker. He did not rant or rave. He had a powerful voice, filled with both calmness and conviction.

He spoke with wisdom, from the heart. And he had the physical presence that allowed him to rivet the attention of the crowd.

Maybe he was a decent man and not just the idle son of a rich lord.

Deep in thought, she never once looked back, the idea of pursuit never entering her mind.

Rounding the final corner, Ally saw the post office. Walking inside, the hood of her cape over her head, she joined the line, and then finally approached the clerk at the counter. She gave him the folded letter from her pocket, paid to send it, then asked for all mail addressed to Olivia Cottage. An envelope was handed over to her; she thanked the man and hurried out.

She found an empty alcove in front of a shop door advertising the fact that it would soon be opening as "Madame LeDeveau's, Exquisite French Designs." There she ripped open the envelope. With awe, she saw the bank check it held. The amount was far from huge, but to Ally, it was amazing. A. Anonymous had been published twice. And paid. *Twice.* That meant she was capable of fulfilling a dream. The feeling of accomplishment was sweet, and for a moment she let herself savor it.

Then she started.

She looked at the time on her watch pendant, and her heart sank. She had been gone far longer than she had intended. She started to hurry back to the museum, once again never thinking to look behind her.

CHAPTER SEVEN

AFTER TEA, IAN AND MARK changed places.

Eleanor Brandon appeared sane that morning, though drained of all energy and emotion. She had barely eaten a morsel of food, and had scarcely sipped her tea.

"Eleanor," Mark said gently, "is there anything, anything at all you can tell us that would help us in any way?"

It was as if his words reached her from a great distance, and she had to struggle to focus on him. She smiled, but her smile was grim. "I have told my story over and over again. But I have heard the police sometimes ask you to come in and answer questions."

He shrugged. "I'm a good listener, that's all. I try to fit puzzle pieces together."

She studied him with skeptical eyes. "I see."

He wondered just what she saw. She smiled suddenly. "They asked me if my husband and I got along. Can you believe such a thing?"

"I'm afraid, Eleanor, that many a dead spouse winds up that way because love and hate are strongly linked."

"Do you think I could have done this?"

"No," he told her.

"I see. Then aren't you going to ask me if Giles had any enemies? Because of course he did. Rich, powerful enemies—enemies protected by the Crown."

"Eleanor, you can't make assumptions," he said quietly.

She laughed softly, a hoarse, dry sound. "Do I think that Victoria herself hopped down from her throne to slash my husband's throat? No. Do I think she wanted him dead? Yes. Of course the royals wanted him dead. Are they all so fine and pious? No." She leaned forward suddenly. "You're young. Perhaps you don't remember the Ripper killings well. There was speculation Prince Al-. bert was connected to it somehow, that it was a scheme concocted to keep people from knowing he was married to a commoner, a *Catholic*. How to get a prince out of such a situation? Why, murder the poor girl and a pack of prostitutes to make it all appear to be the work of a madman. How clever!"

"Eleanor, everyone knows the story, and it makes no sense. The woman with whom he was supposedly involved was a Catholic, yes. But she wasn't a prostitute. She worked in a tailor's shop."

Eleanor impatiently waved a hand in the air. "They

all start out with decent employment in the East End. And then they become prostitutes. Filthy, dirty old hags with no interest except for their next jigger of gin!"

"But the Ripper was killing sad old prostitutes, not lowly workers."

"Mary Kelly wasn't old. She was young. And still beautiful, so they said."

"And there was no doubt she was a prostitute."

"I believe the police knew who the killer was," she said firmly. "Just as they know who's doing these killings now."

"Eleanor—"

"You won't convince me that my husband wasn't killed by the Crown."

He sat back, unhappily certain that she would spout her accusations everywhere once she was feeling up to going out again. He was a firm believer in the right of every man and woman to hold an opinion, but...

"Eleanor, how can you discount the fact his death makes him a martyr to a cause? And," he added softly, "you do know that the police must investigate all possibilities, even..." He trailed off and looked at her sadly.

She stared at him, then gasped. "I'm still under suspicion?" she demanded. "But...I wasn't here!"

"The police have interviewed your sister. All alibis must be verified."

Her expression hardened. "My sister and I do not get along, but I know she would not lie. I was with her."

"Yes, she confirmed that you were at her house."

"She wasn't pleased about it. And I'd never have gone, except for the fact that..."

"Your husband wanted you out."

She flushed, lifting her chin. "You don't understand a genius like my husband's!"

"Eleanor, I am sorry to speak ill of the man you have so recently lost. But his genius came with a touch of cruelty, and I believe you know that."

She looked away, and he was certain she flushed slightly.

"Eleanor, where do you keep your keys to this house?" he asked.

She frowned. "I...sometimes, they are in my reticule, and sometimes they are on the dresser in my bedroom."

"A shared room?" he asked quietly.

Again her face took on a tinge of color. "We each had a bedroom—which is not at all uncommon," she informed him. "Giles often worked late at night. He needed freedom to come and go, without disturbing me."

"There were times, then, when anyone in the house might have had access to your keys?"

She shrugged.

"I understand your husband often entertained a group dedicated to the downfall of the monarchy."

"Yes."

"Did you often entertain those who were fiercely loyal to the queen?"

"Never!"

"Well, Eleanor," he said quietly, "it appears that the key to this house was stolen and copied. It seems likely someone took it while in the house. Since you never entertained any loyalists... I'm not telling you what to believe. I'm just saying you should think long and deeply." He paused, meeting her eyes, his expression firm. "And I swear to you, we *will* catch your husband's killer."

ALLY WAS AFRAID SHE WAS still breathing too hard and that the thunder of her heart would give her away, but the museum guard just gave her a friendly smile of acknowledgment and she easily slipped in with a group of schoolboys in uniform.

She stood at the rear of the group now, catching her breath and listening as their teacher gave a dissertation on the art of ancient burial rituals. Then she felt a tap on her shoulder and jumped, startled, before turning to find Sir Andrew Harrington standing there.

"Miss Grayson, there you are. I had heard you were here, but I have searched and searched, and all but despaired of finding you. I feared I wouldn't get a chance to do so much as say hello before that errant fiancé of yours finally arrived." He stepped up beside her. "Where have you been?" he asked. "I could add the words, 'all my life,' but that is such a sad and pathetic line."

She laughed. "We have met before, you know."

"Ah, but you were young, and what man would have dared face so many fierce guardians as give their protection to you? There are many besides myself who thought the time would come when we might gently press our suits. Who knew you would be introduced to society and affianced, all in one night?"

She had to smile. He was merely flattering her, which

she knew was his way. But he was attractive and charming, and she found herself enjoying his attentions. "Sir Harrington, I'm sure there are many young women who swoon at your mere presence."

He laughed and shrugged. "Well, perhaps not at my mere presence. But enough of that. Have you seen the new mummy? They've unwrapped it completely. Come along, I'll show you."

"It's not time to head down to the tearoom yet?" she asked anxiously, glancing at her watch locket.

"We have a minute," he told her.

With a hand very properly on her elbow, he led her into the next room. She immediately noticed that Thane Grier was there in his typical pose, leaning against the wall, his notepad out. He didn't seem to be paying attention to the exhibit, rather, he was watching the people who were there. As she walked into the room, he straightened. He couldn't miss the fact that she was escorted by Andrew, but he didn't seem to mind intruding. As he approached, she wondered what he intended to write.

"Miss Grayson."

They paused. Grier approached, offering his hand. "Good afternoon. I'm sorry to interrupt, but your engagement is newsworthy."

"Why would my engagement be big news?" she inquired.

Grier's smile deepened. "Surely you must be aware that Mark Farrow is considered—"

"The best catch in the realm, short of royalty," Andrew supplied dryly.

Ally frowned, but Thane Grier shrugged, as if he might not have put it in such terms, but Andrew had indeed expressed his meaning.

"I'm not sure what you want me to say, Mr. Grier," Ally murmured.

"Well, if I may ask, why do you think, out of all the women in Britain—in the world, even—you've been chosen for such an honor? You will certainly be an incredibly beautiful bride, but...you aren't titled. Indeed, you are an orphan."

She stared at him, aware that her every word might be skewed by him, and also aware that it was in terrible taste for him to question her so. But he was a journalist. He didn't care if he was rude.

"Legally, the Earl of Carlyle is my guardian," she said. "I'm sure this engagement is due to his friendship with Lord Farrow."

"Still..."

Grier was pressing for something, seeking something. A hidden meaning.

If there was one, however, she certainly didn't know what it was.

"I'm afraid I've given you the best reply I can," Ally said. "Perhaps you should pose your question to either Lord Stirling or Lord Farrow. Or to Mark Farrow himself."

"I have, but Mark Farrow has yet to reply."

"Then you'll have to wait, won't you."

"Look here, Grier," Andrew Harrington said. "It's one thing to ask Miss Grayson a question, quite another to hound her."

"I do apologize," Thane Grier said quickly.

"And I would tell you more, if I were able," Ally said.

Lord Lionel Wittburg somehow chose that moment to come upon them and rescue her. "Ah, there you are, Ally. Lady Camille was just looking for you."

"I'm on my way down to the tearoom," Ally said.

Thane Grier nodded respectfully in acknowledgment of Lord Wittburg. "Your Grace," he said.

Wittburg nodded in turn but had no interest in the journalist. "Writers," he said, adding, "They'll be the bane of all of us."

Ally didn't entirely agree, but she let him lead her away. They took the broad marble stairs down to the lower floor, where the tearoom was already filled with benefactors and common folk alike. "Lady Camille is at the table of honor, and there is your seat, next to hers."

Ally thanked him and hurried across the room, aware that she was being watched speculatively by almost all eyes in the room. Many a young woman who had been presented that year was staring at her—as were their mothers and guardians. She hadn't realized until just that moment that Mark Farrow truly was considered *la crème de la crème*.

Yet the man of the hour remained absent.

Certainly all those staring at her were aware that, despite her engagement, she was being left to attend this function alone.

She took the seat next to Camille, noting the chair to her right was empty. Brian was not next to Camille, but down the table, seated next to Lady Newburg, who, after the Stirlings, was probably the museum's largest benefactor.

"I'm sorry I'm late," Ally apologized.

"It's quite all right. Many people are still finding their way down," Camille assured her, squeezing her hand.

Lord Farrow was on the other side of Camille. He leaned over, saying, "I'm quite sure my son will be along any minute."

But Mark Farrow wasn't right along. A cucumber salad was served, and Brian, who had a long family history with the museum, stood up to give the welcoming speech. He was an excellent orator, and the room was filled with laughter and applause.

Then the director of antiquities, a serious little man, stood to talk. He was a dear fellow, but not an eloquent speaker. Ally found her mind wandering.

She wished she was seated by Kat, who was next to the author Arthur Conan Doyle, who was a dear friend of Kat's. Ally had thrived on every minute when she had been at a function where he was either a speaker or a guest. His real-life stories were always amusing, intriguing, even sometimes sad, but they never failed to hold her enthralled. She looked about and saw other dignitaries in the room, authors, statesmen, an actor she had seen on the stage, an opera star. There was a photographer there, as well, with an assistant to run around with his heavy equipment.

The director's voice seemed to drone on and on as a main course of white fish in a tomato variant of Florentine sauce was served.

And then cleared away.

Dessert was an apricot puff, and still he spoke.

Ally tried to pretend to be attentive. She glanced at Camille as coffee was poured and saw that Camille's eyes were sparkling. Both of them were surely thinking the same thing: If the man didn't make his point soon, the benefactors would be asking for their money back—with interest.

"Hello."

The sudden sound of the whisper at her ear was so startling that she nearly cried out. Luckily, she refrained, turning around instead.

Her fiancé had arrived at last.

He drew out the chair next to her, taking his place. Up close, she saw his face was handsome and strongly sculpted. His shoulders were broad, nicely filling out his fawn overcoat. His brocade waistcoat was flatteringly fitted, and his brown trousers were the height of fashion. His eyes...

Were disturbing. They were a mercurial blue, with a darker rim. There was something about him....

"I'm sorry, forgive me. I was detained on business," he whispered. "I'm Mark Farrow."

She was never tongue-tied, yet she was so at that minute. She nodded, and at last managed to say, "Hello. Pleasure."

What a ridiculous conversation. She was engaged to the man.

No, *that* fact was what was ridiculous!

The room suddenly burst into thunderous applause, and the director flushed and bowed, then bowed again.

Poor little man. He had no idea people were welcoming the end of his speech.

"Mark," Camille said, delighted. "You've made it at last."

"I do apologize. It was most pressing business. I was actually one of the first ones here," he continued, and then he smiled affectionately past Camille, at his father. "I'm afraid I was called away. But…Miss Grayson, perhaps I could show you the new exhibit?"

"I'd be delighted," Ally said.

He smiled, rose and pulled back her chair. "If you will all excuse us…?"

"Certainly," Camille murmured.

And so Ally rose, draped her cloak over her arm and allowed the stranger to whom she had been affianced to escort her out of the room.

He waved to several people, and said a word here or there to others, as they wended their way between the tables. Leaving the room, they were blinded by a flash.

The photographer hard at work, Ally thought dryly.

Thane Grier was there, as well, writing away. He offered Ally his usual rueful smile.

"Mark!" someone called, and Mark paused. Ally was surprised to see Arthur Conan Doyle heading for them, grinning broadly. "And dear Ally." The man's mustache teased her cheek as he gave her a kiss. "I have been greatly pleased by all I've heard, Mark. I tell you, some of those fellows, they don't see the truth when it stares them in the eye."

"Arthur, you're a brilliant man," Mark said, and Ally

decided she liked him a little bit, simply because his words seemed sincere and she so adored the man herself. "Actually, I'd like to probe your mind on a few subjects. Have you time this week?"

"Indeed, we will make arrangements."

"It will be my pleasure."

"Congratulations to the both of you," the author said; then, with a quick wave, he walked on.

"You know him well?" Ally asked.

"No better than you do, it appears," he said dryly.

"I think he's wonderful."

"Is he your favorite author?"

She hesitated. "Yes. I also admit to be in awe of the American, Poe."

"Indeed? He has a bit of a gruesome touch."

"I find him compelling."

"Actually, so do I. And such a sad life he led."

They had reached the stairs. Ally knew that others could have heard their words, and she was glad they had been so casual. As they reached the level where the new exhibit was being shown, she paused and looked back.

They had not been followed by either the journalist or the photographer.

She disentangled her arm. "May I speak frankly?" she asked.

"Please."

"You do not have to go through with this."

"I beg your pardon?"

"I understand, sir, that you are, shall we say, the very

top of the pyramid," Ally murmured. Those eyes of his! It was absurd, bizarre. They gave her a sense of déjà vu. As did his touch. She realized at that moment what she had been thinking: that his eyes were incredibly like the highwayman's. Ridiculous, she told herself. She had only seen the bandit in a mask. Still...these were his eyes.

The two men were of the same height and powerful build. And the voice...

No, it was impossible.

"I don't understand what is going on. In fact, I daresay there's not a soul in England who does. Apparently your father and Lord Stirling—whom I adore, please don't misunderstand—have entered into some kind of a medieval agreement. But you mustn't feel obliged. I am not a poor and defenseless orphan. I am quite capable of taking care of myself."

"Are you refusing to marry me?" he demanded.

"No, not actually refus—"

"Good. Come, then. Let us see the exhibit."

He started forward, but she didn't follow. She felt suddenly afraid. He turned, taking her arm and drawing her forward with him. "You must be well versed in Egyptology."

"I can't help but know something," she told him, swallowing both her fear and her impossible conclusions. "I have spent many nights at the castle, and its decoration is purely Egyptian. And of course, I've spent time at Kat's studios and—did you understand what I was saying at all?"

"That I don't have to marry you."

"Right."

"And I asked you if you were refusing."

"Refusing isn't my point."

"Good. Then the wedding plans shall proceed."

Once again he was off. He paused next to a large stone carved with hieroglyphs. "Can you read this?" he asked.

"'He who treads here threatens the wrath of Isis,'" she read quickly. "You know nothing about me," she told him.

He laughed suddenly. "I know all about you. Let's see... 'She has hair like spun gold, eyes that rival the sun, and her voice is a lark's.' Straight from the lips of Lord Stirling, and I can see that he hasn't lied."

"Thank you, that is quite charming, but, still, you don't really *know* me. And I don't know you at all."

"I am the only child of Lord Joseph Farrow, Earl of Warren. Is there more that you need to know?"

She frowned. The question was sharp—and annoying. Did he think his title made him such an incredible catch that nothing else would matter to her?

He was wrong. She had met him now, and she was sorry she had. She had admired him when he had spoken that morning. She had assumed him a thinking man, one who would want to hear what she had to say. But now...

"Actually, I have seen this exhibit already," she lied. "It has been a tremendous pleasure. I am so glad we've gotten to know each other," she continued, piling one falsehood upon another.

She didn't know why she was so ridiculously angry.

Maybe because he had seemed so like her highwayman, only to prove himself an elitist ass.

She started walking away from him, not caring where she was heading. In seconds, she had escaped him. At the moment, that was all that mattered.

"MISS GRAYSON!"

She didn't hear him.

No, she had heard him. She had simply chosen not to listen. Mark winced. He'd been a fool. He'd tried to change the tone of his voice just a shade. He'd worn his hair free. His clothing had been chosen for its tailoring—the farthest cry he could find from riding breeches, high boots and an unbleached shirt.

He'd wanted to be a different man. Apparently he had managed quite well. She liked the highwayman. She didn't like him.

He frowned. As she disappeared, something fell from the cloak still draped over her arm. He hurried forward and picked it up.

It was an envelope addressed to Olivia Cottage, at a nearby post office. He knew he should find her quickly and return it. He even started after her, intending to do exactly that. Then he stopped.

She had chosen to walk away from him. So be it. He tapped the envelope, pensive. Olivia Cottage? Perhaps it wasn't even her envelope. She had perhaps swept it up accidentally along with her cloak.

He opened the envelope and saw that it held a check written from the offices of the daily paper to Olivia Cottage. He shook his head, frowning. He'd never heard the name before, and he thought he'd known all the city's reporters. He started across the floor, irritated that he'd rushed so insanely from Giles Brandon's town house to the museum, just to be instantly spurned.

He came to a dead standstill.

A. Anonymous.

Olivia Cottage must be the real name of A. Anonymous, which meant that the person was in the museum somewhere.

And if the wrong person had found the check…

He shook his head wearily. The murders had to be stopped. But he was very afraid that before the killer could be caught, he would strike again.

And A. Anonymous, or Olivia Cottage, was a prime target for such a ruthless zealot, who surely must despise the person for making such cogent arguments as to the killer's own motives and identity.

The room suddenly felt frigidly cold.

What if Ally *hadn't* swept up the envelope by mistake?

What if *she* was A. Anonymous?

THANE GRIER, LOOKING WORN and sad, was seated on the steps when Ally dashed out.

He looked up, and for a moment, his eyes were naked, a sense of dejection visible on his face.

She was certain he could see the wild look and disillusionment on hers, as well.

They both started laughing.

He patted the stone step. "I know I'm a lowly journalist, but pray, join me. I'm sure you've found me annoying at times, but you appear in need of an escape. I promise I'll not grill you."

She hesitated, then shrugged. Someone might come out and see her in such an unladylike situation, but she didn't care. She joined him.

"What happened to your fiancé?" he asked, then lifted a hand and added quickly, "Sorry. I promised not to ask questions."

"Why do you look so depressed?" she asked.

He shook his head, then looked at her. "A. Anonymous," he said.

"Pardon?" she said, stunned.

"I'm supposed to be a journalist of note, but I was bounced to the second page by an anonymous essayist. And not just once but twice. And here I am today, reporting for the society page."

She smiled and assured him, "You're a journalist dealing in facts with a keen and objective eye. The editors had to be fair. Whatever their own political leanings, they had to print an opposing view to the piece by Giles Brandon, especially with news of his murder blaring from the front page. Maybe someone with wisdom decided it was a way to prevent an out-and-out civil war."

"We'll never have another civil war here," he said indignantly.

"You've seen how ugly it can get," she reminded him.

"Yes, I suppose. How do you know?"

"I watched you, the day Giles Brandon was killed and again this morning."

"Did you see the piece about your engagement?" he asked.

She laughed softly. "Actually, no. I never got that deeply into the paper."

"You see?" he demanded. "You were reading the essays."

"Sorry, it's just because... I mean, usually I read the newspaper front to back."

"I think you'd like the piece. I admit, I did comment on your fiancé's failure to appear at his own engagement party, but I did say it must have been a sad day for him, since I'd never seen a woman glow with such inner and outer beauty."

"That's lovely. Thank you."

He studied her, his lean, ascetic face at an angle, eyes curious. "I'm sorry—and this is off the record, I swear it—but why was such an engagement arranged?"

Ally sighed in exasperation. "I was not lying to you! If there's anything more than the fact that Lord Stirling and Lord Farrow are friends, I don't know what it is."

"Aren't you curious?"

"I've...been worried about other matters."

"Are you still unnerved after having been attacked by the highwayman?"

She smiled, shaking her head.

"Then...?"

"Life, I suppose."

"Life? As if you'll have anything to worry about in life. Do you know what Lord Farrow is worth?"

"Am I Lord Farrow? No, I do not know, nor do I care."

"But your fate is to marry his son."

"My fate, you say? My fate should be more than marriage."

He stared at her, then started to chuckle. "Are you going to become a suffragette?"

She frowned. "Women *should* have the vote. Consider that two of the longest-reigning monarchs, two who have had the most productive reigns, were women."

"So you are going to turn him down? Somehow escape the marriage?"

"It's not a matter of turning him down," she murmured uneasily.

"Ah…"

"What does that mean?"

"You're worried about Lord Stirling and what he will think. And do. You have spent your life residing on his property."

"My aunts are hardly lacking in ability. Had they chosen, they might have made a fortune in any large city. They are the finest seamstresses—" She broke off because he was chuckling again.

"Whoa, Miss Grayson, please. You need not preach to me. I never saw anyone work as hard as my mother. She taught us, she read to us—she gave me my love for the written word. She also scrubbed and cleaned, washed and ironed and cooked. I have never seen anyone work harder or be more deserving of respect. She held educated political opinions." He was silent for a moment. "And now she's gone. She did get to see my first article published, though."

"I'm very glad."

He smiled at her. "Do you know, whatever I wrote about you...it wasn't enough. You are truly lovely in every way." He offered her a handshake. "If ever you find a struggling journalist can be of assistance to you, please, don't hesitate to ask."

She shook his hand firmly. "Thank you," she told him, then stood, trying to smooth the wrinkles from her dress. "And if you should need help, please feel free to call upon me."

"If you happen to discover the identity of A. Anonymous, please...that would indeed help me."

She shrugged. "I'm sorry, but if there's ever anything else..."

"Your guardian is at the door," he said, and stood quickly.

She turned. Brian Stirling and Camille were exiting the museum, chatting with Maggie and Jamie, and Kat and Hunter. Brian was frowning, and Ally was certain he was looking for her. Maggie was the first to spot her. "Ah, there she is," she said, and waved.

"Go...go," Thane urged her.

She walked forward and asked smoothly, "Were you looking for me? I'm sorry. I felt the need for a bit of fresh air."

"Of course, of course. Mark is looking for you, too, dear," Maggie told her. "He's going to take his father's carriage and see you back to the cottage."

"Wonderful," Ally responded.

As she spoke, Mark Farrow appeared behind the others. "Ah, there you are, Ally."

She smiled, longing to tell him that she was Alexandra, or Miss Grayson. She managed not to speak.

"Shall we? My driver is right down the street. Do you mind a slight walk, or shall I ask him to come closer?"

"I walk quite well," she said coolly.

"So it seems," he said, and she was startled to realize that there was something angry in the words.

"Don't forget, the carriage will come for you Friday, Ally," Maggie called. "It's our day in the East End, remember?"

"Of course. I wouldn't miss it. And the aunts are coming, you know."

"Those dears. They only come when they think they can work," Maggie called back.

Mark Farrow had reached her. He offered his arm. She took it, thinking that his muscles felt cast from steel. She couldn't help remembering how she had admired him when he had spoken to the crowd that morning.

Sadly, he was not so refined when it came to more intimate conversation. She respected many members of the nobility, but not those who thought they were better than others due merely to an accident of birth.

She turned back. All six of her guardians were there, looking at her like doting parents, pleased and proud. Her heart sank.

They wanted this so badly. They seemed to believe they had created a future of pure bliss for her.

The next thing she knew, she was taking Mark's hand as he helped her into the carriage. He didn't sit next to her, but across from her. She heard the driver flick the reins and urge the horses to get moving.

Then she realized Mark Farrow was staring at her hard with those unusual eyes.

"Tell me, Miss Grayson," he said, and she regretted that she was not to have an opportunity to tell him that he must address her so, "what did you think of that papyrus?"

"Which papyrus?" she asked.

"The large one in the middle of the exhibit."

"Ah. Yes. A most unusual piece. Huge, isn't it?"

He smiled. "And the three sarcophagi that were exactly alike?"

"Uncanny, weren't they?"

"What did you think of the very different canopic jars that were on exhibit? Have you ever seen objects that are quite so unusual?"

"Never."

He leaned forward. "Miss Grayson, you're a liar. You never saw that exhibit at all."

"I beg your pardon!"

"And I don't believe that's the only thing you have lied about."

He reached into his pocket. "Is this yours?" he demanded.

To her horror, he produced the envelope containing the check made out to Olivia Cottage.

CHAPTER EIGHT

SHE STARED AT THE ENVELOPE and then managed to look him in the eyes. "Olivia Cottage? Why on earth would that be mine?"

"If fell from your cloak," he informed her.

She shrugged, looked toward the window and realized the curtain was drawn. She stared at him again. "I suggest you turn it over to one of the museum directors. I assume whoever lost it will be looking for it."

She stared straight at him.

He stared back.

She was certain she didn't blink or betray herself in any way. At last he returned the envelope to his pocket. "So...how did you manage to miss the entire exhibit?"

"I did not miss the entire exhibit. How did you manage to miss the entire luncheon?"

"You did miss the exhibit," he said. "And I had legitimate business." Was there the slightest defensive note in his voice?

"I do think this proposed marriage is something we need to discuss," she said.

"Because I was unavoidably detained?" he demanded in an irritated tone.

"Because I don't believe that we're compatible."

"Miss Grayson, I did my best to arrive today."

She waved a hand in the air. "You don't know me. This was arranged. Aren't you just a bit loath to go through with it?"

He leaned forward, suddenly intense. "I know my father, and I know Lord Stirling. If there were not a very sound reason for this, it would not be happening."

"Still," she said softly, very gently, "it is all very strange. I have now met your father. He seems to be a kind and admirable man. But do you obey him unquestioningly in all things?"

He sat back, and she realized he was curious. She was suddenly certain he didn't customarily follow any instruction without knowing the cause. She had decided that she almost hated him, but she was startled to feel differently toward him just now, because…because there suddenly seemed to be a difference in him.

His eyes met hers again. "Tell me, how have I offended you so seriously and so quickly?"

She shook her head. "No man should ever assume he is worth his weight in gold because he will inherit a title."

"Ah," he murmured, but there was a note of anger in his voice when he went on. "Do not ask me to apologize for my father. He is an exceptionally fine man."

"He is. But no son should expect the world because of the life his father has led."

"I see."

He was silent then, still watching her, and looking ever so slightly amused. Then he leaned forward and caught her hands, startling her. She felt the strength in his fingers, but his touch was gentle. "Pray, tell me, is there another? Is there someone you'd rather wed? Someone who stirs your heart?"

A highwayman, she thought. One with your eyes.

"No," she assured him after a moment. "There is no one. It's not a matter of wishing for someone else."

Oddly, even the way he touched her seemed familiar. She looked at his hands. He wore no gloves. His fingers were long, curling around hers. He was close, and she felt a sudden heat. Everything about him was uncannily close to the highwayman. She remembered the Alexander Dumas novel, *The Man in the Iron Mask*. Did he perhaps have a double riding through the countryside, holding up carriages in revenge against an aristocracy that had shunned him?

"Then give me a chance," he told her very softly. "Let this marriage go forward as planned. What have you to lose?" he asked her. "I do come with an exceptionally fine town house, though I admit that as of late I have been more customarily at my father's house. Mine is rather empty, you see. We possess a hunting lodge deep in the woods, should you miss the forest. Then there are the estates in the north. We have a castle, as old and strong as Brian Stirling's, though not, I admit, in such close proximity to London."

"You are speaking about possessions," she reminded him, but she felt herself smile slightly.

He shrugged. "It is good to have a place to live."

She had to laugh, and she found herself leaning toward him. "What will you get in return?" she asked him. "No dowry. Although," she added with a sigh, "I'm sure the godparents have arranged something. No title. No great lineage. In fact, all the country is surely wondering why you're marrying me."

"Perhaps I have been delighted to discover a beautiful spirit as well as a beautiful face. And your guardians do rave constantly about your achievements. There is nothing to soothe the soul like a talented musician."

"You can afford to hire all the musicians in the kingdom," she told him.

"Perhaps I'm more interested in intimate entertainment before a fire, in one musician for life, a song, if you will, with heart and feeling."

Something in his voice, deep and husky, triggered a quickening inside of her. Incredible!

And did he think her an idiot?

Ridiculous as the thought might be, she was suddenly certain he was indeed the highwayman. But why would he carry on such a masquerade? Surely this man had fortune aplenty without the need to rob carriages.

"Lovely sentiment," she murmured, staring at him.

Did he really think he had her fooled? That she could be so easily taken in by a mask?

Apparently he did.

"And you think any sentiment that falls from my lips must be false?" he queried.

"I don't know what I think at the moment. I've just met you. And I certainly can't begin to understand how you can imagine I could fulfill any dreams you may harbor, or why you're willing to go through with this."

"But I am," he said. That time, there was a note of steel in his voice. She frowned, puzzled. He was the highwayman. And as such, he'd conversed with her. Sat close. Danced with her. Talked with her.

She lowered her head quickly, realizing that her heart was soaring in a most bizarre fashion. She had begun to feel a totally morally wrong fascination with the highwayman, but there had been something in their exchanges that had simply...beguiled her. To realize that her intended and the highwayman were one and the same...

But what was going on?

"You seem to be a very busy man. I don't see how marriage can possibly fit into your schedule," she said, then turned toward the window.

"One makes it fit," he murmured.

She pushed open the drape, determined to look out, wishing they were at her home in the woods already, so afraid she was going to give herself away.

"What's wrong?" he asked.

She couldn't resist. She turned and looked at him, letting the curtain drop back over the windows. "I suppose I'm a little nervous. My encounter with the highwayman, you know."

He sat back. "I sincerely doubt he will attack *this* carriage."

"Oh? He is rather brave...or at least reckless. He attacked the Earl of Carlyle's carriage."

"But you were riding in it alone."

"He couldn't have known that."

"Maybe the rogue had been watching you."

"I think he is just a bit stupid."

"Stupid? The man has eluded all law enforcement—*and* the Earl of Carlyle."

She arched a brow. "It sounds as if you are defending him."

"Of course I'm not defending him!"

Ally looked down at her hands, determined not to betray herself. She was even more certain now that Mark Farrow and the highwayman were one and the same. What she couldn't begin to fathom was the reason for his dual identity.

She was sure she startled him when she suddenly reached for his hands. Pretending she was reaching out for strength, she carefully studied his fingers as she said, "He will be caught. Eventually. But until that time, he might well attack this carriage—oh! He already attacked this carriage, didn't he? I heard your father had been stopped and robbed. Afterward, the highwayman reportedly donated generously to several of the churches in the East End."

He didn't so much as bat an eye. He stared at her, and the only telltale sign of his interest was a slight twitch in his fingers. He sat back, drawing his hands with him. "I had forgotten," he murmured.

"How could you forget such an assault upon your own father?" she demanded.

He waved a hand in the air. "My father was not shaken. It seemed of little importance to him. I think he believed the man saw himself as some kind of modern-day Robin Hood."

"You are very unusual people," she murmured. "Perhaps your father was simply taken by surprise and handed over what the thief wanted. If the highwayman were to stop us now, we would have to give him anything he demanded."

"You think I cannot defend myself?" he asked.

She shrugged. "He is very able."

"I am a crack shot, Miss Grayson."

"He wields a bullwhip, like those you see in pictures from the Americas."

"I can take care of myself—and of you, my dear."

"I would hate to see you killed," she murmured.

"Well, thank you for not wishing me dead, at least."

"I'm warning you, he might well kill you if you fought him."

"Perhaps *I* would kill *him*."

She waved a patronizing hand in the air, aware she had gotten beneath his skin. Men—even the best of them—had their egos.

"Perhaps. But I see this conversation is distressing

you. I'm so sorry. I shouldn't have brought it up. It's just that…I believe I was very near where we are now when the Earl of Carlyle's carriage was stopped."

"You needn't fret," he said, and she thought he sounded quite irritated. "If we were stopped, it wouldn't be simply a matter of ability. I would die for you."

"How honorable. But if you *did* die for me, then I'd be left with that rogue." She offered him very wide eyes and a shiver.

"Miss Grayson, we will not be attacked."

"But—"

"Let's cease this conversation, shall we?" he demanded.

She *would* cease for the moment, she decided. With the curtain drawn back again, she looked out as they passed through the village and was glad to see that no protest was in evidence.

The carriage slowed as they came into an area of more traffic. Staring at the usual flow of village business, she was startled to see a woman in black standing before a storefront window.

Many women wore black, she told herself. Full mourning attire was hardly a rarity.

Yet there was something familiar about this woman.

"What is it?" Mark asked sharply, sliding across the carriage to sit next to her.

"I…nothing."

"No, it's something."

"It's silly."

"Tell me."

He was close. The pressure of his body was not...displeasing. Nor was his scent. And his face was right beside hers, tempting her to touch him.

"Well?" he demanded.

She lowered her head quickly. Proximity did not seem to be affecting him as it did her.

"I keep thinking I see a woman in black."

"A woman in black?"

"I told you...it was nothing."

"It drew your attention, so it was something."

"She was at the protest against the monarchy last week. I believe Sir Andrew Harrington's cousin, Elizabeth Prine, the widow of the second man who was murdered, was beside her. And then, just now...I seem to see a woman in black wherever I go."

"There are always women in black."

"I know."

"Still, you are amazingly observant."

She felt him studying her closely. Too closely. He couldn't possibly know what was going through her mind, she thought.

She let the curtain fall, but he remained next to her. She had thought it meant nothing to him that they sat so close. Then he asked softly, "Would marriage to me really be such a punishment?"

His unique gray-rimmed eyes were on her, far too intently. She almost felt as if she had been mesmerized. Then he moved his fingers to her cheeks and brushed over her flesh, exploring the contours of her face. She was startled to feel a rush of heat, excitement cascading along the length of her. She longed to reach out and touch him in return, and she had to remind herself that they had just met, and that, engaged or not, there were rules as to how she must behave.

"I barely know you," she whispered.

"But my intent is for you to know me very well," he replied, and there was a huskiness in his voice, a rueful teasing note. It seemed as if the entire carriage had filled with heat. She forgot that they were passing through the village, that they were at long last very nearly home. "I am not so terrible," he murmured, and he picked up her hand and brushed her fingers with the lightest kiss. There was something incredibly arousing in that small gesture. Once again, waves of electricity went sweeping through her.

"You barely know me," she managed, her eyes somehow riveted to his. "Perhaps *I* am terrible," she whispered.

He shook his head slowly, and she felt a wave of panic. She tried very hard to find a sense of logic and decorum. It was true that she barely knew him. She'd had three encounters with him…today, and twice as an outlaw, and she couldn't begin to understand why he was playing such an underhanded game….

He leaned closer. His mouth was perfectly formed, lips full, firm, sensual…

"We are engaged," he reminded her, the fingers of his right hand entwined with hers and those of his left winding into the hair at her nape, cradling her skull. His lips touched hers in a kiss that was taken but not coerced, seductive in its very strength and boldness, yet so slow and enticing that she never thought to protest. His mouth moved over hers, and she inhaled what seemed to be the essence of the man, in any costume. Never once did she hesitate. She felt the exotic caress of his lips and tongue, the kiss deepening while the heat within the carriage seemed to explode. The deep and persistent stroke of his tongue in her mouth was beyond her dreams of the erotic, and she found herself moving into his arms, her fingers falling on his chest not to push him away, but rather to feel the thud of his heart, the rise and fall of his breath....

Then, slowly, he pulled back, his fingers still entwined with hers, his eyes a shimmering silver. She realized the carriage had stopped.

She had lost her mind, she decided.

"Regretfully, we're here," he said huskily.

"Oh!" Self-consciously, she tried to smooth back the strands of her hair, tried to withdraw—not an easy task in the confines of the carriage. She touched her lips, which seemed different now. She was shaken. She was angry.

Angry that she had been so easily swept away by him.

"Then I must go in," she said, a little sharply.

"Why are you angry?" he asked.

"I'm not angry. I'm home. May we alight?"

"I am ever more convinced of the rightness of this marriage," he said softly.

"We shall see," she murmured, thinking to skim past him.

But he caught her. The feel of his hands upon her was nearly unbearable, it was so sensual.

"I am enchanted," he said, and she thought it sounded almost like a warning.

"And I am greatly uncomfortable remaining in this carriage," she said. "If you don't mind…"

"It's quite all right. We are engaged. There's no need for you to be mad."

"I don't know what you're talking about."

"You're not mad at me, you know. You're mad at yourself."

"I'm not mad at anyone."

He smiled, and the slow curving of his lips infuriated her. "Yes, you are. You didn't intend to respond to my kiss, but no matter how you try, you cannot find me repulsive."

"Perhaps I shall have to try kissing every man I fail to find repulsive."

His eyes narrowed. "We are engaged. The ring is on your finger."

"I can take it off." But in fact, she couldn't. It caught on her knuckle. "Oh, good heavens! May we get out of this carriage now?"

At last he moved, but she longed to slap him hard, for that cockiness was in his eyes, the same expression she had seen in the highwayman's gaze.

But he stepped down without further comment, turning not to assist her but to lift her to the ground.

"Thank you for the ride. I'm home and quite safe now."

She thought that at last, she could make her escape, but the aunts chose that moment to step outside.

"Oh," Edith cried, "it's Mark Farrow!"

Violet, nearly crashing into Edith in the doorway, was equally observant. "Mark! How lovely. You decided to see our Ally home."

Merry, sweeping out alongside Violet, had the presence to suggest, "You must come in for a spot of tea before your ride home."

"Oh, he's far too busy," Ally said quickly.

"Not at all. I would love a cup of tea," Mark said, and the glance he gave her was clear evidence of the delight he was feeling at her discomfort.

"But your coachman may be needed—"

"That gentleman might enjoy a spot of tea, as well," Violet said.

"Arthur?" Mark called easily, and the coachman, a large, broad-shouldered fellow with slightly graying hair and a quick smile, stepped down from the driver's seat. "Arthur, would you care for a cup of tea?"

Arthur swept off his livery hat and bowed his head. "Tea would be most lovely, sir." He turned to Violet. "If you don't mind, Mum."

"We have only a humble abode," Violet said, "but all visitors are welcome here."

Merry clasped her hands together. "Tea it is."

Ally barely suppressed a groan.

"Oh, this is lovely, lovely. Do come in." Edith beckoned.

So, despite her discomfort, Ally again felt the support

of Mark Farrow's arm as he led her into the cottage. There, at last, she managed to disentangle herself. "Darlings," she said firmly to the aunts. "You three must sit down and chat. I will bring the tea."

"Oh, no, dear. You must sit with your fiancé—" Merry began.

"We've already had the loveliest chat in the carriage. Now, you three must get to know him better."

She disappeared into the kitchen before any protest could be lodged. Once there, she seethed for several minutes before remembering she needed to set the water to boiling.

As she stood there, she found herself touching her lips again, and remembering. She didn't hate him at all, she knew. He was simply accustomed to being the one who was in control, of himself and of the world around him...

Even as a highwayman.

And *she* was supposed to marry him.

She bit her lip, listening to the chatter from the parlor. He laughed easily. He complimented the aunts on little things in the house. He seemed to have nothing but the best rapport with his coachman. She felt the strangest tremor take hold of her. She was going to become his wife. She had thought to fight against such an arrangement, but though her life had been sheltered, she had met men before, and she had never had such a feeling of magic as when he touched her....

"Ah, but he deserves all I can give in return," she said into the empty room, and she laughed suddenly, plotting.

Because she was quite certain she would see the high-wayman again. Very soon.

ON SUNDAY, MARK CHAFED. The service in the small church outside the village seemed endless, and the sermon, during which the rector strongly urged people to behave with temperance, was the perfect cure for sleeplessness.

From where he sat by his father's side, he could see that Violet, Merry and Edith were in their pew, with Ally there, as well, beside Violet. His heart quickened as he decided that when the service was over, he would insist they come to his father's house for luncheon.

At some point during the service he found himself staring at Ally. Taken unaware, color rushed to her cheeks and she looked away as soon as she noticed his attention.

When he rose for the final hymn, it was with every intention of heading straight to her, but as he walked down the aisle, he felt a tap on his shoulder.

He turned and, to his surprise, saw Detective Ian Douglas. The situation must be dire if the man had left the city to find him.

"May I speak with you?" Ian asked.

Mark saw that his father had gone on; he was greeting the sisters and Ally. Ally noticed him, then turned away. It seemed she despised his real self, despite that kiss.

And yet...

It was impossible to forget touching her. The feel of her lips beneath his. The supple warmth of her body...

"Mark?"

"Yes, I'm sorry. What is it, Ian? Not another murder?"

"A problem."

"With?"

"Lord Lionel Wittburg. Will you come with me?"

His father had turned. He saw Ian Douglas and rolled his eyes, but he nodded.

"Will you give me just a moment?" Mark asked Ian. At the other man's nod, he strode down the aisle and out the door, to where the others waited in the sun just beyond. With the eyes of the village upon him, he dared do no less than at least greet his bride-to-be.

She watched him approach with wary eyes.

"My dear," he greeted her. As he knew that, with the aunts about and his father there, she would not protest, he caught her hands, kissed both her cheeks, and then, as he met her eyes, teased her lips with the brush of a kiss, as well. He could almost feel her stiffen, but as he had expected, she stood still, if defiant—and she didn't make a single move to strike him, though he was sure she longed to. He might have charmed the aunties with his visit for tea, but she was still not impressed.

She withdrew her hands from his and said, nodding toward the church, "I gather you have someone waiting."

"I'm afraid I arranged a meeting with an old friend, though one look at you and I had quite forgotten."

Merry giggled delightedly at his words. "This is so wonderful!"

"Quite," Ally murmured dryly.

"Your father has just invited us to a lovely luncheon," Violet informed him.

"I hope to return soon and join you," Mark said.

"You are always so busy," Edith said, shaking her head.

"Well, when they are married, Ally will have the dear boy all night every night, and they will not have to miss each other."

"Merry!" Violet said, shocked.

"What?" Merry protested. "I merely said when they're married, they will...oh!" She blushed and fell silent.

"You'd best go. Your friend looks quite nervous," Ally advised him. "He looks like a policeman. Is he?"

Mark was startled. Ian, who'd moved to stand at the top of the steps, was dressed in a simple suit.

"Yes, actually, he is a detective. How did you know?"

"His suit," Ally told him. "Neat, but serviceable, not extravagant, and he has a weary look about him, yet one of a quiet dignity. And his shoes. They are firm leather, not fancy kid. They are made for walking."

"Very observant," Joseph said. Mark stared at her.

She shrugged. "I am a tremendous fan of Arthur Conan Doyle."

"And of Poe," Mark murmured.

"The one teases our fears while the other teaches us something of life," Ally said. She smiled and walked past him, heading back toward the church—and Ian.

Mark followed.

Ally extended a hand. "I am Alexandra Grayson. It is a pleasure, Detective."

Ian flushed a deep red but quickly took her hand. "Miss Grayson, the pleasure is mine."

"I understand you and Mark are old friends."

"Yes."

"Are you here in pursuit of the highwayman?"

"No, but many fine officers *are* seeking that villain."

"I see."

"We are all going to lunch at Lord Farrow's lodge. Perhaps you'll accompany us."

"I'm afraid that..."

"Ian and I are dining closer to the city, as he must be back by nightfall," Mark said.

"Yes, yes, that's right."

"I see," Ally told him, and smiled. "Well, then, you must be going."

"I'm afraid so," Mark said.

"Then I mustn't detain you. It has been a pleasure."

A moment later, their goodbyes said, she turned away.

"Forgive me, dearest, but I must have a final kiss," Mark told her, and drew her back, brushing her lips with a kiss. Dear God, the scent of her. Clean and sweet and...

And strong. She was out of his arms in a heartbeat, her mouth tight. He was certain she longed to wipe his kiss from her lips.

"Detective, again, it was a pleasure. I look forward to getting to know you," Ally said, and then she was gone.

Ian watched as she walked back to the others. He kept staring, not moving.

"Ian!" Mark said sharply.

"What? Oh, yes. The business at hand."

They rode out to Lionel Wittburg's manor, west on the forest road toward London. As they traveled, Ian explained that he'd received a call from Lord Wittburg's valet. The man had been very upset as he explained that Lord Wittburg had not risen in days, had simply lain there raving that the queen had killed his friend Hudson Porter. He had become like a madman, even refusing to eat.

Mark had known the man and his valet, Keaton, since he himself was a child. Keaton greeted them eagerly, begging them to follow him to Lord Wittburg's chambers.

The room was vast, with a massive bed set apart on a dais, and the rest of the space set up for receiving.

Lionel was in the bed, staring up at the ceiling.

Mark rushed to the man's bedside.

He touched Wittburg's flesh, and it was cold and clammy. The man didn't seem to see them as he ranted. "It's happening again. There is a conspiracy. All men are blind. All men see what they want to see. I believe it happened. I believe… Dead women. So many, and now it is dead men. Dead men in a row. All lined up."

"Lord Wittburg," Mark said sharply. He glanced at Keaton. "Have you called a doctor?"

"He saw the doctor last week, and he prescribed pills. Lord Wittburg was having trouble sleeping."

Mark looked at the drug vials and shook his head. "Opiates. Too strong. His pulse is weak. Ian, help me. Let's get him up."

"Get him up?" Keaton said. "But…he is ill. Perhaps if he slept more…"

"If he sleeps more, he may not wake up. Do you have coffee?"

"Of course," Keaton said, indignant at the suggestion that the household might lack such an important commodity.

"Make some. Ian, help me, please."

Wittburg was a very large man. He was also dead weight. But with Ian on the opposite side, Mark managed to force him out of bed.

"Now what?" Ian asked, struggling beneath the weight of the man.

"Keep walking him."

As they walked, Lord Lionel Wittburg continued to rave on in the same manner as before. "Sins of the fathers. Always sins of the fathers. History shows us. Cain and Abel. It's happening again. So many dead, and all life, they say, is precious. Some don't believe that. Some believe life is more precious for the highborn. What is one dead prostitute, eh? A prostitute will die of liver disease in time. The gin will kill her. Perhaps a knife is more merciful. The killings were sick…sick. But the knife was swift. Dear God! There must have been moments of such terror. Still, cut. Cut! A throat is slit. The blood rushes out. The prostitutes were slain so. The antimonarchists were slain so. Ah, Hudson. How we debated. How you attacked, how I defended, and never once did we let debate ruin the foundation of our friendship. They said you were bitter, but I knew you were not.

You did not expect consideration after sleeping with the lieutenant's wife! Slit, slit...throat cut. Prostitutes. Men with minds."

"What on earth is he talking about?" Ian asked.

"He was, as you know, close friends with the first man killed, Hudson Porter. They served together in the war. Wittburg is a keenly intelligent man. Hudson Porter was a student and lover of history."

"But he's talking about the Ripper murders, and those are long past."

"I'm afraid he's connecting them to the monarchy."

"But he supports the monarchy."

"But even he has been swayed, so it seems," Mark said.

Just then Keaton returned with a silver tray bearing an urn of coffee.

"Let's get Lord Lionel into the chair before the fire," Mark said.

As they did so, Keaton poured coffee, which Mark then lifted to Lord Wittburg's lips, forcing the man to drink.

Lord Wittburg choked and coughed, then seemed to start. He stared at Mark, as if noticing him for the first time. "A man like your father," he murmured. "If only the world had more of his ilk...." He frowned. "When did you come?"

"Just moments ago. Lord Wittburg, you're taking far too many medications," Mark told him.

"I wanted to sleep."

"I don't mean to insult your physician, but these will give you delusions, Lord Wittburg."

The man glanced at his valet, who was looking on anxiously. He smiled after a moment. "I'm all right now, Keaton."

"May I...dispose of these, my lord?" the valet asked, indicating the drug vials.

Lord Wittburg smiled. "I fought in India and Africa. I took down the fiercest Thugees. And yet I let myself fall prey to ghosts. Yes, Keaton. You are a good man. I am grateful for your care. Get rid of them."

"Keaton called you?" Wittburg said to Mark.

"He called Ian, knowing you were upset about the murder of Hudson Porter, and that Ian was one of the key men working on the case," Mark explained.

"I thank you both for coming. And I believe I will have more coffee. You may tell Keaton I will dine now, as well."

"We will stay awhile," Mark assured him.

They joined Wittburg for a meal, served there in the lord's chambers. As they dined, Wittburg once again spoke with sanity, talking about horses, the races, the museum—anything but the social climate.

At last, feeling assured that Wittburg was in a better state of mind, Mark indicated to Ian that they could leave, but as they readied themselves to go, Lord Wittburg called Mark back, beckoning him close, so he could whisper.

"You do not know how history repeats itself, dear boy. You do not know the half of it."

At first Mark thought the man was raving again, but then he looked into Lord Wittburg's eyes and knew he was not.

The older man clenched Mark's hand tightly. "Find out the truth about your marriage, Mark Farrow. Then you will understand. Find out the truth about the woman who would be your wife."

CHAPTER NINE

ALLY HAD NOT BEEN EAGER to spend her day at Lord Farrow's hunting lodge, though she liked the man very much. She was anxious to get back home and out to the stream to search for her sketchbook.

But when she arrived at the lodge, she was thrilled to discover that Lord Farrow had a guest. Arthur Conan Doyle was there, sitting outside, watching the hounds romp.

She greeted him with pleasure.

A middle-aged man, he was solid, not too tall, with a face that was showing signs of both age and sorrow. She knew he suffered because of his wife's illness. He traveled to Europe and to Egypt, often when the weather was bad, as a physician trying to find a way to help her.

Louisa was a sweet and gentle woman, and very strong in her way. She loved the man she called Conan, and their children, Kingsley and Mary. She was ill, however, and seldom went out with her husband now.

Seeing Ally, he rose and greeted her like an old friend, giving her a hug.

"I see you know the woman who will soon be my daughter-in-law," Joseph Farrow said.

"Yes, we met through Lady Kat, who is a dear friend of mine."

The aunts were staring with a bit of wonder.

Lord Farrow introduced them one by one. The author was charming to each of them in turn.

Lunch was served by a man named Bertram, who apparently both ran the stables and managed the house quite efficiently. The aunts insisted on helping with the meal, and Ally assisted, as well. Everything was soon taken to a table on the terrace behind the house.

There was a third man present when they brought out the food. Sir Andrew Harrington stood the moment the women appeared, as did Doyle and Lord Farrow.

"How lovely to have a lunch served by such beauties," Sir Andrew said.

"Sir Andrew. What a surprise," Ally said. "What brings you here?"

"I'm often in the area. I have family about, you know. I was in church and heard that Lord Farrow was having a Sunday luncheon, and he is never rude enough to turn a hungry man away," Harrington said.

"You are always welcome," Lord Farrow said. "And I must present—"

"Violet, Merry and Edith," Sir Andrew said, smiling

and elegantly kissing the aunts' hands, which of course caused Merry to giggle.

"Charmed," she assured him.

"A pleasure," Edith said.

"Certainly," Violet agreed.

Sir Andrew joined them, and the talk was casual, the meal lovely. Sir Andrew told the sisters that he had seen their designs and had found none superior, anywhere.

The aunts were incapable of simply being guests, Ally realized, as the meal was eaten and coffee served. Lord Farrow assured them that two women from the village came in during the week to keep the premises clean, but after coffee, they insisted on helping to clear the table.

When that was done, Lord Farrow offered them all a tour of his stables, but both Doyle and Ally refused. She liked Andrew Harrington very much, but she wanted time alone with the author.

As soon as the others were gone, Doyle leaned toward Ally and said, "Goodness, my dear. What lovely fortune has befallen you."

She hesitated and said, "I don't really wish to marry."

"What?"

"Well, I do. One day."

"You dislike Mark Farrow? I assure you, he's a most honorable man."

"One who disappears frequently."

Smiling, Doyle wagged a finger at her. "I have been mocked, and I have been believed, but I have never been so thoroughly questioned as by that young man."

"I beg your pardon?"

"He's a smart fellow. Those who seek answers in science are sometimes brilliant, sometimes near insane. Those who look at the facts alone will make more discoveries than any other men."

"I'm still not following."

"I have made a very good living off the fictional Sherlock but in fact he was based on a Doctor Bell, a brilliant man, one of my professors. Holmes is fiction but the makeup of his character is not. Mark thrives on listening. Observing and then knitting all the facts together. It is mathematics, in a way, add up what is known and come to a conclusion." He hesitated and leaned toward her. "He asked me here today. If he is not here, it is for a very good reason."

Ally frowned. "He went to lunch with a detective friend. Ian Douglas."

"Ah."

"And what does that mean?"

"It means he is searching for a killer."

"But he is not a detective."

"No. He is the son of the Earl of Warren."

"But—"

"I think, if he could, Mark would be in his element running the force. But he has responsibilities he cannot abdicate. And, with his position, he can delve into nooks and crannies where a regular officer might not be able to go. Give the man a chance, Ally."

She hesitated. "There is something I suspect. But you must swear you will keep this secret between us."

He arched a brow.

"I think Mark Farrow is the highwayman."

He sat back, trying to mask his thoughts.

"You *know* he is the highwayman!" she exclaimed.

"Hush," he warned. "I *know* nothing."

"But—"

"If he is the highwayman, there is very good reason for it. Please believe that," Arthur Conan Doyle implored. "And hush. The aunts are coming back."

In moments the rest of the part was by their side.

"Ally, what beautiful horses. You should see them," Violet said. "But then, I suppose you will have many chances in the future."

"She will see them soon," Lord Farrow said. "How interesting that you two have such a friendship," he said, nodding toward Ally and Doyle. "You and my son have much in common," he told her.

"Would that I were your son," Sir Andrew teased gallantly.

"You, Sir Andrew, have been a fine soldier. You need be no one else," Lord Farrow said.

"Well spoken, as ever," Sir Andrew said.

"This has been the loveliest day," Violet said, "but I fear we must go back, though I had hoped to wait until Mark had returned."

"The forest at night is quite dark," Edith said.

"I can certainly see you home," Sir Andrew offered.

"Bertram will escort them," Joseph Farrow said.

They chatted for a few minutes longer, but Mark Farrow still did not appear. Ally was not sorry—she had enjoyed her moments alone with Arthur Conan Doyle.

And it was fun, as well, to be teased by Sir Andrew and his open flattery.

Arthur Conan Doyle hugged her warmly again when they left.

"You are welcome to call upon me at any time," he told her after helping her into the aunts' carriage.

She smiled and thanked him.

"Indeed, my life, too, is at your service," Sir Andrew assured her before mounting his horse.

Then she settled into her seat next to Edith, and Violet was clicking to the horse and lifting the reins.

Lord Joseph Farrow watched Ally intently and waved as they drove away.

Ally thought she would never sleep that night, and indeed, she lay awake for hours.

What, exactly, was her fiancé doing in his clandestine life?

MARK KNEW FROM THE MOMENT he stepped into the newspaper offices that every eye in the place was on him. The female typists and clerks flushed, nodded, then began gossiping behind his back.

The men, he realized, did the same.

A man with ink smeared on the elbows of his jacket led Mark to the office of Victor Quayle, the managing editor. He'd met Quayle on a number of occasions, but the man was still startled to see him, dropping the sheet he had been reading and nearly swallowing his pipe.

"Good Lord! Lord Farrow."

"Please, Victor. It's Mark."

Victor Quayle, balding young, shook his hand strenuously. "What brings you here?" He frowned. "I believe our reporting of your engagement was quite straightforward. If you were not at your own party. I can hardly blame my reporter for stating the truth."

Mark shook his head. "I've come because I'm concerned. And because I found this at the museum yesterday." He produced the envelope addressed to Olivia Cottage.

Victor seemed puzzled. "We mailed this out to a freelancer," he explained.

"Your freelancer must have been at the museum."

Victor shrugged. "I suppose."

"Who is Olivia Cottage?" Mark asked.

Victor hesitated. "I…can't say."

"I know it's expedient for you to keep certain sources secret, but I believe this is the identity of your columnist A. Anonymous," Mark said. He turned, making certain the door to the editor's office was closed. "I fear for her— or him. I seek the truth only to see that the writer is protected."

Victor shook his head, looking tired. "Would you like something? The coffee here is dreadful, but it does help keep one up."

"No, thank you. Please, Victor. I swear to you, I'm seeking nothing but a way to help this person."

"Of course. You are a Monarchist," Victor murmured.

"I'd help the anti-monarchists, as well—had I a clue as to where the killer might strike next."

"Dreadful, isn't it?" Victor asked. He looked a bit guilty. "My feelings on the situation are of no account. I have to print what's going on with the mood of the country."

"You run an excellent paper," Mark said. "And I am seeking only to keep people alive."

Victor sighed. "I'd help you if I could."

"What do you mean?"

Victor laughed dryly. "I don't know the identity of A. Anonymous—or Olivia Cottage, which is merely another false identity. When I tell you I can't say, I mean just that. I don't know who the person is. The article came to me, along with a request for any payment should we publish it, to be mailed to the post office, addressed to Olivia Cottage. The post office in question is quite near the museum. I'm grateful you've returned this. I can mail it out again. Though…"

"Though…" Mark prodded.

Victor shrugged. "I assume the person must not be in a dire financial condition or they would never be so negligent with a payment."

"Have you received anything new from this Olivia Cottage?"

"Not yet," Mark said. He smiled. "But I am hoping."

"I don't wish to ask you to betray anyone, but will you let me know if you're going to publish another article by this person?"

"Yes, I can do that."

Mark thanked him, asked about his family, and left. As he departed, he brushed by Thane Grier. "Good afternoon," he said, studying the journalist.

Grier seemed surprised to see him there. "Is anything wro—"

"Nothing at all."

"You didn't come about the article I wrote?"

Mark laughed. "You're a journalist, writing the truth. Why would I have a problem?"

"I did mention your absence from your own engagement party."

"And it is true. I wasn't there," Mark said.

"If you've read today's paper...there's a small piece about you and Miss Grayson at the museum. It's quite positive."

"Thank you." Staring at him, Mark frowned. "You were doing far more serious pieces than the social calendar before."

"Indeed," Grier muttered, then said swiftly, "This is not my preferred topic, I admit, but there are many reporters and only so much news. I did write the article on Giles Brandon's murder."

"Yes, I read it. Well done. No sensationalism."

Thane Grier shrugged. "Sometimes they prefer sensationalism."

"I think you've done well. I prefer my news to be just that. An opinion piece is just that—an opinion. The news itself should never be slanted."

"Mention that to Victor next time you're in," Grier murmured. "Sorry...I just... Oh! Allow me to offer my personal congratulations on your engagement. I am seldom in such awe of a young woman who appears on the social pages."

"Thank you," Mark told him.

"She has a fine mind," Grier said.

Mark nodded, and they made their goodbyes. As he left the office, Mark realized that the reporter had said something very true.

A fine mind...

Bright, sharp, witty.

All in lovely wrapping.

Thane Grier's words had struck at the essence of the truth. He might have been drawn in by beautiful appearance.

He had been seduced by a fine mind.

HER SKETCHBOOK WAS NOWHERE to be found.

Although Ally searched high and low, she couldn't find the sketchbook in which she did so much of her writing.

Deeply disturbed and exhausted, she crawled atop the rock.

The highwayman hadn't come, either.

A chill slipped through her bones as she contemplated the conundrum she was facing. Yesterday, in the carriage, she was certain she had convincingly denied ever seeing the envelope addressed to Olivia Cottage. But Mark Farrow was the highwayman.

And if her book wasn't here...

If the highwayman—Mark!—had found it, then sooner or later, her denial yesterday would mean nothing.

MARK'S ORIGINAL INTENT HAD been to ride out as soon as he had asked what questions he could at the newspaper offices.

But while riding out to his father's hunting lodge, he realized he could use his time better by first stopping to make another call that was both necessary and very important.

Elizabeth Harrington Prine was a woman of approximately forty, and still quite beautiful. She was tall, and moved with an elegance that drew the eye as much as did her appearance. She opened her own front door and seem quite startled to see Mark, but she recovered quickly.

"Mark!" she said. "Do come in. I apologize. I haven't been receiving visitors lately."

"I beg you to forgive the intrusion when you are still in mourning."

"You're not intruding. As you must know, when Jack was…killed, there were police about everywhere. The house was trampled. And then…friends try. They want to help you with funeral arrangements, they bring food, and you must keep up a facade of coping. Finally, when the activity is over, you have time to grieve alone."

"Elizabeth, I'm very sorry for your loss."

She studied his face with her bright green eyes. "I believe those words from you, Mark. You never dragged down a man because his beliefs were different from your own. However, before you come in, I must warn you— if I ever find out that the monarchy was involved in this wretched business, well, I will end up hanged myself, because I will seek revenge."

"I don't believe any such thing will come to pass, Elizabeth."

She offered a dry smile as she led him into the parlor. Her house was on the outskirts of the village. From here he could head for his father's lodge in the woods—and to the little cottage where he could confront Ally as the highwayman. Meanwhile, he had decided after his conversations with Eleanor Brandon and the housekeeper that it might be of importance to find out more about Elizabeth's whereabouts when Jack Prine had been murdered. Hudson Porter, the first anti-monarchist killed, had not been married. Tomorrow he would make a point of speaking with the man's housekeeper.

"Will you have some tea?"

"Thank you, no, Elizabeth."

"I didn't think this was a social call."

"Elizabeth, you weren't here the night he was killed, were you?"

She shook her head. "I was in London. We were invited to a party. Jack wouldn't come. He was convinced it was necessary for him to work. But he encouraged me to go."

"And what about your housekeeper?"

"My woman works only during the day." Elizabeth hesitated. "She found him in the morning, when she arrived. I had stayed at the town house in Kensington."

"I understand there was no sign of a break-in."

"No," she said.

"That would mean that Jack quite possibly knew his killer."

Elizabeth suddenly sat very straight. "You're suggesting he was killed by another anti-monarchist—just as that piece in the paper suggested."

"Elizabeth, would he have invited a monarchist in?"

She nodded. "Of course, if he knew the man. I know you have your opinions and are still decent to a man even when his differ from yours. God knows, Jack was still *friends* with many a man who supported the monarchy. Good heavens, Lord Lionel Wittburg was very close with Hudson Porter, and he was the first to be killed. And I know that Lord Wittburg was terribly distressed."

"Elizabeth, how many people have keys to your home?"

She had been cooperative, but now she stiffened. "My husband kept keys, naturally. I have keys, as does my housekeeper."

"Where are they left?"

"I don't have a habit of leaving my keys about."

"But where are they kept?"

She sighed. "In my dresser drawer."

"What about your housekeeper? May I speak with her today?"

Somehow she managed to sit even more stiffly. "I'm afraid I gave her the afternoon off."

"That's all right. I can come back." He rose. "Elizabeth, I'm sorry. I am trying to find the truth."

Elizabeth rose, as well. "You should be looking in the right places, then."

"And where would those places be?"

She stared at him with angry eyes. "You might start with the Crown!"

He left the house, warning her to lock the door behind him. He heard the bolt click shut. But then, just as he was about to start down the walk, he was suddenly certain he heard something else.

Voices.

Either Elizabeth had lied and the housekeeper was there, or…

Or the widow was entertaining someone else.

Darling Ally,
We've headed over to the Morton house. Mr. and Mrs. Morton both have the fever, and her sister is on the way, but Father Carroll said they must have some help in the meantime. Edith has made soup, and we have packed up a few other things. I'm afraid we'll be very late. Please make yourself something to eat, and lock up and don't let anyone in. Take the greatest care, darling. We love you. The Aunties.

Ally had to smile. She knew Violet always did the writing, but she never signed her name. She always signed "The Aunties."

That they were gone for the evening didn't disturb her. They were always bustling about the neighborhood, taking care of a baby for an ailing mother, feeding a family that was having difficulty. They were the dearest women in the world. She thought often that although she'd had her few wild moments as a child, she had generally been well behaved. Not because any punishment would be fierce, but because she couldn't bear the disappointment in their eyes when she hurt them in any way.

"Clever," she murmured aloud to herself. "I shall have to remember that when I become a parent."

She made herself tea and found one of the aunties had left stew simmering over the fire, so she fixed herself a bowl, picked up one of her favorite novels by Defoe and sat before the fire. But words that usually held her spellbound suddenly swam before her eyes.

If, as she suspected, the highwayman *had* discovered her sketchbook, at some point he would read it.

And what if he had not discovered it? Judging by the way Mark had behaved in the carriage, he had not, or at least he had not read it yet.

What if someone else had taken it?

A chill swept down her spine.

The fire seemed to be crackling low. There was still no electricity in the cottage, and it suddenly seemed the oil lamps cast eerie shadows around the small room.

Don't be ridiculous, she chastised herself. It was certainly her imagination at work, making the normal events of an evening seem strange.

Even so, she set down her bowl, filled with a sense of unease.

She stood up restlessly and paced, heading first to the front door. It was securely bolted.

She quickly went through the house, parlor, dining area, all the bedrooms, and assured herself that the windows were closed and locked.

She was being silly. She had lived here her whole life. Half the time they neglected to lock the doors at all.

Still, no reason not to be safe.

As she walked back along the hallway, on her way to check the kitchen and back door, she heard a sudden thump against the wall in the front. She stood dead still, her blood seeming to congeal.

She waited.

Nothing.

After a moment she forced herself to hurry along the hallway and into the kitchen. As she reached it and started toward the back door, she saw the knob start to move.

For a moment, her breath caught.

She rushed forward and saw that the bolt was indeed engaged. But the round brass knob was still moving, twisting, as some unseen hand tested it.

She stood silent, staring.

Then the movement stopped, and fear swept through her, followed by a greater fury. Whoever was out there had determined he was not entering that way and had gone off to find another.

She silently took one of the chairs from the table, lifting it so it would not scrape and give away her position to listening ears, and settled it by the back door, under the knob. Then she looked wildly about for a weapon. There was definitely not a gun to be found in the house. There were, however, sewing shears aplenty.

But as she started to race through to the sewing room, she saw the iron fireplace poker. She ran to the hearth, picked it up and tested it in her hands, a sturdy-enough weapon. She glanced across the parlor.

There might be no electricity in the cottage, but the aunties had been pleased when Lord Stirling had insisted they needed a phone. They still considered it to be a new-fangled invention, but the queen had decided that she liked the telephone, and that had been enough for many, though there were still not that many places one could call.

Ally hesitated, thinking of the noise when she cranked the line, but she headed toward it, anyway. Ginny, the local operator, would answer. And Ginny could get through to the sheriff, Sir Angus Cunningham, and Brian. But the castle was far beyond the village, and there was no way Brian could arrive quickly. Still, so long as Ginny was able to reach someone…

Ally made a mad sprint for the phone. She vigorously cranked it….

And there was nothing. No sound at all.

Ally realized that whoever was outside had cut the wires.

She stood very still again, listening, her heart thundering so loudly that at first she wasn't able to hear anything else. Then…

Something. A scraping sound. From the direction of Merry's bedroom. Holding the poker tightly in her hands, she crept along the hallway. Slipping into the bedroom, she heard someone working at the window latch.

Then nothing again.

She barely dared to breathe.

In the distance, there was a clicking sound.

Now the intruder was trying the latch at the sewing-room window.

She hurried out of Merry's room and down the hall, tiptoeing as she entered the sewing room. She inched silently along the wall, her back flat against it, and waited. She wished she dared jerk aside the curtain and see who was trying so desperately to gain entrance. She wanted to know the face of her enemy.

She couldn't. She dared not warn the intruder she even knew he was there. She was afraid he might be armed. Even if he wasn't, he could slip back into the darkness of the night far too quickly, and she would then be exposed, while the intruder remained hidden. She couldn't give away her one advantage, the element of surprise.

Suddenly there was a snapping sound. She realized the invader had managed to slip the latch.

There was movement behind the curtain, a seemingly massive body pushing the fabric aside and trying to crawl through the window.

Ally didn't dare wait. She threw herself against the intruder, swinging the poker with all her might.

As she moved, she heard her name.

"Ally!" The cry came from the front of the cottage. Then it seemed to move closer. "Ally!"

The person she had attacked let out a grunt of pain. She screamed as hands pushed against the fabric and managed to grab her wrist.

An Important Message from the Editors

Dear Reader,

Because you've chosen to read one of our fine novels, we'd like to say "thank you!" And, as a **special** way to thank you, we're offering you a choice of <u>two more</u> of the books you love so well **plus** an exciting Mystery Gift to send you — absolutely <u>FREE</u>!

Please enjoy them with our compliments...

Pam Powers

Lift here

Peel off seal and place inside...

What's Your Reading Pleasure...
ROMANCE? *OR* SUSPENSE?

Do you prefer spine-tingling page turners OR heart-stirring stories about love and relationships? Tell us which books you enjoy – and you'll get 2 FREE "ROMANCE" BOOKS or 2 FREE "SUSPENSE" BOOKS with no obligation to purchase anything.

Choose "ROMANCE" and get **2 FREE BOOKS** that will fuel your imagination with intensely moving stories about life, love and relationships.

FREE!

Choose "SUSPENSE" and you'll get **2 FREE BOOKS** that will thrill you with a spine-tingling blend of suspense and mystery.

FREE!

Whichever category you select, your 2 free books have a combined cover price of $11.98 or more in the U.S. and $13.98 or more in Canada.

And remember... just for accepting the Editor's Free Gift Offer, we'll send you 2 books and a gift, ABSOLUTELY FREE!

YOURS FREE! *We'll send you a fabulous surprise gift absolutely FREE, just for trying "Romance" or "Suspense"!*

® and ™ are trademarks owned and used by the trademark owner and/or its licensee.

Order online at
www.FreeBooksandGift.com

▼ DETACH AND MAIL CARD TODAY! ▼

Yes!

I have placed my Editor's "Thank You" seal in the space provided at right. Please send me 2 free books, which I have selected, and a fabulous mystery gift. I understand I am under no obligation to purchase any books, as explained on the back of this card.

PLACE
FREE GIFT
SEAL
HERE

ROMANCE
193 MDL EE4Y   393 MDL EE5N

SUSPENSE
192 MDL EE5C   392 MDL EE5Y

FIRST NAME	LAST NAME

ADDRESS

APT.#	CITY

STATE/PROV.	ZIP/POSTAL CODE

Thank You!

The Reader Service — Here's How It Works:

Accepting your 2 free books and gift places you under no obligation to buy anything. You may keep the books and gift and return the shipping statement marked "cancel." If you do not cancel, about a month later we'll send you 3 additional books and bill you just $5.24 each in the U.S., or $5.74 each in Canada, plus 25¢ shipping & handling per book and applicable taxes if any.* That's the complete price and — compared to cover prices starting from $5.99 each in the U.S. and $6.99 each in Canada — it's quite a bargain! You may cancel at any time, but if you choose to continue, every month we'll send you 3 more books, which you may either purchase at the discount price or return to us and cancel your subscription.

*Terms and prices subject to change without notice. Sales tax applicable in N.Y. Canadian residents will be charged applicable provincial taxes and GST.

"Ally!" She heard her name being called again.

Then came the thundering of footsteps nearing the window, and a deep muttered curse came from the figure caught in the drape. Suddenly her wrist was released.

The curtain wafted in the night breeze.

Then it began to move again, was jerked aside.

She lifted the poker, ready to swing.

CHAPTER TEN

"ALLY!" MARK CALLED.

"Oh, God," she breathed.

He stared at her. Despite what had just happened, she wasn't in a state of panic. She stood, her hair cascading around her face, pale and taut, but ready to do battle, a poker raised high in defense, eyes narrowed.

He was glad she had decided not to strike. After all, he was a masked man, half inside a window.

She dropped the poker when she recognized him, and he spared a moment to realize in irritation that she seemed perfectly willing to trust a highwayman with her safety.

"You're all right?" he demanded quickly.

"Yes."

"Keep your guard up. I'm going after him."

He damned the situation. Arriving at last, he had barely dismounted in the small yard in front of the cottage when he had seen the dark figure sneaking around the back. He didn't know if he had been seen, didn't know if Ally had been alerted in any way. So he'd shouted fiercely for her, allowing the intruder a chance to escape. Still, it might not be too late to find him.

Cursing beneath his breath, he tore into the woods, in the direction in which he thought he had seen the figure escaping. There were a few broken branches at first; a path he thought he could follow. But in the forest, the darkness became complete, thick enough to easily swallow a man up. There were a million hiding places.

A million places from which to attack, as well.

Although he didn't think whoever had been trying to gain entry was still around. The culprit had failed, then run.

Better to run and live to fight again another day.

Disgusted, furious with himself, he walked back toward the house.

He approached the window first, certain Ally would still be on guard. "It's me," he called. She swept back the curtain. He caught hold of the window frame and jumped inside.

She was still holding the poker. Her eyes held a wild look, but her breathing was growing slower.

"Did you...?"

"No."

He reached for the poker. "It's all right. You can put this down now."

They were in near darkness, the light that softly bathed them coming from the lamps in the hall. He touched her face and took the poker from her. "He's gone."

They were in the aunts' workroom, he realized. Dressmakers' dummies stood in eerie silence, draped in various pieces of apparel. He took her arm, leading her toward the hall and then down to the parlor, where he set her down on the sofa.

She rose instantly. "The window—" she began.

"I'll take care of it. Wouldn't want any criminal types getting in."

She stared at him, then started to laugh. "You're a highwayman," she reminded him.

"But I don't break into *houses*," he informed her.

He left her then, hurrying back to the sewing room. The intruder had bent the latch. He could repair it, using the blade of his knife and a fair amount of pressure, but it had been weakened. What was worse was the fact that none of the windows in the place was invulnerable. He found a stout wooden beam—part of a stand for a mannequin, he imagined—and he used it to wedge the window shut. No one would be breaking in again that way unless they actually shattered the window.

Still, the cottage wasn't safe.

Back in the parlor, he noticed the phone. "Why didn't you call for help?"

"The line has been cut."

"Stay here," he said.

She lifted her hands, smiling again. "I have nowhere to go." But she stood as he started toward the front door.

"Where are you going?" he asked with a frown.

"With you."

"Ally, whoever it was, he was after you, not me. I'm just going to see about the phone connection. I'll be right back. Please, stay inside. And lock the door when I'm gone."

It didn't take him long to discover that the phone connection had indeed been severed. When she opened the door to let him back in, he felt a rising sense of anxiety he had not imagined possible. He paced the parlor.

"You cannot stay here. I'll... You'll ride with me. Lord Farrow is in residence at his lodge tonight. You'll be safe with him."

"No," she said firmly.

"No? Ally, are you mad? Someone tried to get in here, most likely to kill you."

"Perhaps it was just someone who was desperate," she said. "Someone who saw the aunts leave, perhaps, and thought the cottage was empty."

He stared at her, and she flushed. "Why would I suddenly be in danger?" she demanded.

"Why indeed?" he murmured. "The reason doesn't matter now. You can't stay here."

"I have to stay here. Don't you see? The aunts will come back, and we don't know that they won't be in danger, too."

He stared at her, clenching his teeth tightly. But she was right. Someone out there was ruthless. There was no question about it. And he couldn't put her aunts in danger. Still, it nagged at him that she had almost certainly lied to him. She was quite probably Olivia Cottage, also known as A. Anonymous, and since three grown, able-bodied men had had their throats slit...

He sat down. "We'll wait."

"*We'll* wait?"

"Do you really want me to leave right now?" he asked her.

"How will I explain you to the aunts?"

"Where did they go?"

"To the Mortons' house, to help out. The Mortons are ill."

"Then we must wait for them to return, then leave. None of you can come back to this house tonight."

"And where shall we spend the night?"

"At Lord Farrow's."

She sighed. "This is...bizarre. It's probably because of Mark Farrow."

"What?" he demanded.

"Well, I am no one, and I have nothing. I've lived my life in these woods in no danger. But now, I am suddenly engaged to Mark Farrow, and you see what has happened."

She had seldom appeared more beautiful to him than she did then, seated on the sofa in a simple skirt and white blouse, hair free and wild, eyes serious in the firelight.

"I think this may go beyond your engagement to Mark Farrow," he told her, trying not to sound irritated.

Could she possibly suspect that he and Mark were one and the same?

"And why else would someone be seeking to harm me?" she asked.

"I don't know. Perhaps you should tell me."

"You're an outlaw," she reminded him.

No, she didn't know. Couldn't know!

He let out a sigh of frustration, wondering if he should tell her the truth. Never, since she was clearly not being honest with him.

"None of that matters. You can no longer stay here."

"As I said, I will not leave until they have returned."

"Perhaps you should pack a few things and be ready to leave once they arrive."

"And you're going to wait? And greet them? If the poor dears see you, they'll have heart palpitations on the spot."

He started to pace, ignoring her as if she hadn't spoken.

"Must you?" she demanded.

"Must I what?"

"Prowl so. Will you please sit down?"

He was startled when she patted the place by her side. "Sit, please. You're making me nervous."

He frowned, then sat. He was stunned when she leaned against his shoulder. "I am so tired," she murmured.

He couldn't resist, despite the peril of the night and the very real concern he felt for her safety. He leaned back, setting a hand upon her hair and head, urging her to rest her head on his knee. "Rest, then...rest for now. How long do you think the aunts will be?"

"Their note said they would return late," she murmured, practically curling onto his lap. Her hair spread over him. She was warm against his legs. He had to force himself to focus on something other than the instant reaction of his body to the nearness of this woman.

He set a hand on her hair again, smoothing it back. I am in love, he thought, even though he knew everything she had ever said was sensible. He barely knew her. And yet he knew all he needed to know. She was promised to him. *Him?* She lay so trustingly, so intimately against him, though as far as she knew, she was promised to another man.

He'd never wanted anything so much in his life. But...wanting her so much, he could force nothing. Indeed, with her there, he barely dared to breathe.

She stirred.

His body stirred in response.

Could she tell? He could not give himself away.

He swallowed hard. "How much later do you think they will be?"

"I don't know the time now."

"It's close to ten."

"Probably another hour...two hours."

He might well combust by then. He forced himself to concentrate. "Do you know where you struck the fellow with your poker?"

"In the curtain," she replied ruefully.

"Did you catch his face?"

"I don't believe so, and he still had strength in his arms, enough to grab my wrist. I believe I must have struck him in the torso."

"I wish you'd caught him in the legs."

"I'm dreadfully sorry," she snapped.

He had to laugh. "No, you were quite wonderful, actually. You did not cower in a corner, nor did you run out into the danger, screaming madly for help. You attacked him before he had a chance to attack you. But...it might be possible to notice someone limping, you see."

"Oh? Is there a tavern where all criminals go for their nightcaps? Where you might imbibe and watch for a limping intruder?"

"I doubt the man was your run-of-the mill criminal, Ally."

"The longer I think on this, the more I'm certain he was just some poor fellow who saw what he thought was an empty cottage in the woods and was seeking only food and a few trinkets to steal."

"That's not the truth, and you know it."

Her fingers moved upon his knee as she adjusted herself to look at him. His body quickened, but he forced himself to calmly meet her eyes. She smiled suddenly.

"What?"

"This is insane. You're an outlaw," she said softly. "Yet here I am, so trusting, all but in your arms. You held up my carriage, behaved abominably, and yet...I trust you," she whispered, her eyes huge, her voice low and sensual.

His jaw locked for a moment. He forced it to work. "You're engaged."

"So they say."

"There is a ring on your finger."

"Yes, a rather lovely one. But with effort I can surely remove it."

"You need to marry Mark Farrow."

"Oh? Have you suddenly turned into my guardian?"

"Your life is in danger. You are not thinking clearly."

She reached up and lightly stroked his chin. "At least you're a noble outlaw," she said.

Those fingers on his flesh. Her eyes...

He suddenly set her upright. There was still the possibility that the intruder might come back, perhaps with reinforcements.

"Ally—"

"I don't know what it is about you," she said, watching him as he got up and stood before the fire. Then she sighed, running her hand over the place at her side where he had so recently sat. "Even if I am to marry Mark Farrow, I am not married yet, am I?"

"What are you saying?" he demanded, afraid his tone was far too fierce.

She smiled. It was a beautiful, sad, wistful smile. "I am saying I may well have to marry the man, but I am a modern woman. My life is my own. And I am not married yet."

"Are you propositioning me, Miss Grayson?" he demanded. He couldn't help but feel his temper start to rise. If she didn't know...

Every possessive bone in his body started to ache.

"Never," she said.

He breathed a sigh of relief.

"I would never put it so," she whispered. "I have just found that…well, I am about to enter a life I did not seek, a marriage I did not wish. But before that time, I am a free woman."

Damn her! She had to know, surely. She was doing this just to torture him. He had to say something.

But he had no chance to reply. He heard the approaching sound of wheels turning, a horse's hooves thudding.

"They're here," he said.

She leapt to her feet. "You have to go."

He stood still. "No."

"What? How on earth shall I explain you?" she demanded, looking wild again. "Good heavens, they said they'd be late!"

"Imagine."

"Go! You've got to leave."

"No. Who is driving them home?"

"No one. Violet always drives the rockaway coach."

He nodded and started toward the door. She all but threw herself against him. "No!"

"There is no help for it."

He stepped outside, calling, "Please, don't be afraid."

Despite his words, Violet screamed. Merry, at her side, let out a choking sound. Edith, in the rear, appeared to swoon.

"Darlings, it's all right!" Ally cried.

She rushed to help a now-disheveled Edith find her feet. He strode forward, thinking Violet the staunchest of the three.

"Madam, I am so sorry to upset you."

"It's him. It's the highwayman," Merry breathed.

"But not at all a dangerous man, I swear. However, there *was* someone dangerous here tonight, trying to break into the cottage and almost succeeding," he said quickly.

"What?" Merry gasped.

Edith nearly swooned again. Ally steadied her.

"Listen, please...the highwayman helped me," Ally explained desperately. "He drove the intruder off when he was nearly in the cottage."

"The point is," Mark put in, "you can't stay here."

That created a furor and one of the most curious conversations Mark had ever heard.

"Can't stay here?" Violet echoed.

"But where will we go?" Merry demanded.

"We can't just leave everything," Edith managed in a whisper.

"We must," Merry said.

"Of course we must," Violet said. "We cannot allow Ally to be in any danger whatsoever."

"No, no, of course not," Merry said.

"He's a *highwayman*," Edith wailed.

"He rescued Ally," Violet said. "That is all that matters. Therefore, we will not turn you in, young man!"

"The point is," Mark said, "you need to pack a few things. And then I will ride with you as far as Lord Farrow's lodge."

"Lord Farrow's lodge?" Violet said.

"You don't have to stay there forever. But the lodge is close, and it is safe."

Violet stared at him long and hard. She wagged a finger at him. "You must change your evil ways, young man."

"Lord Farrow might well demand your arrest!" Ally said.

"I will leave you before he sees me," Mark assured her.

"Come, come, don't dawdle, sisters," Violet said. "Ally, have you anything packed?"

"Not yet."

"Then we all must move. Hurry along," Violet ordered.

Ally arched a brow and stared at him with a stern frown. He shrugged. There was nothing else he could have done. He would never allow them to travel through the forest alone. Not with Ally, certainly not that night. And now…never.

"You don't even have a dog," he muttered as Violet walked past him.

She lifted her chin. "We've had watchdogs in the past," she snapped. "But when one loses a fine companion, it is not easily replaced."

With that, she walked past him, into the house. Shrugging, Ally followed, still lending a hand to Edith, who seemed about to pass out again after she merely looked his way.

The sisters were efficient. It didn't take them even thirty minutes to pack up what belongings they needed for the night. He loaded the rockaway coach for them, then mounted his horse. Violet again took the reins, and Ally sat with Edith.

The lantern set above the driver's perch cast light before them as they traveled. Their horse plodded slowly but surely through the night. Of course, what might have been a quick ride seemed endless.

They encountered no one.

When at last they approached his father's lodge, they could see light burning from within. Bertram, his father's burly factotum, emerged from the house at the sound of their approach. Jeeter followed, and his father came behind Jeeter.

"I must leave you now," Mark murmured, and, spurring his horse, he turned to ride back down the drive, knowing his father would allow no harm to come to any of them.

Ally explained the night's events to Lord Farrow, who immediately asked Jeeter and Bertrum to help with their belongings, then led them inside. "What happened to the intruder? How did you scare him off?" Lord Farrow demanded.

"Oh, dear, you cannot imagine," Merry began, but Ally nudged her warningly and spoke over her.

"A…friend happened by," she said. Could Lord Farrow possibly know about his son's double life?

The highwayman had ridden away the second he knew they had been seen approaching the lodge.

"A friend," she repeated. "He escorted us this far and saw we were safe, but he had…pressing business and could not wait."

"We do apologize for intruding," Violet said.

But Lord Farrow was far too gracious to allow for any apologies.

"My dears, Miss Grayson is to be my daughter-in-law. You are like my sisters. You are more than welcome here. I am merely concerned about what has happened and how to keep it from happening again." He frowned. "The wedding must be held as soon as arrangements can be made."

"What?" Ally gasped, then caught herself as she realized the truth of her feelings.

She was going to marry him. Because she was falling in love with him, already was in love with him, even if she felt unable to be wholly honest with him. But then, how dare he lie to her so?

Yet he had managed to be there tonight in the nick of time. Yes, she had fought the intruder, but would she have won?

Fear began to seep into her soul. Had she been marked for murder? Why? Did someone else suspect that she was A. Anonymous?

"The wedding must take place very soon," Lord Farrow said quietly, looking at her with steady eyes.

"We must have time to plan," she insisted.

"Safety must come before the niceties," Lord Farrow said. "But that can all be discussed tomorrow. We've guest rooms down the hall, quite spacious. In fact, you can each have your own room—"

"No, no, please. We are best together tonight," Ally said.

"All in one bed?" Lord Farrow asked. "You needn't be so crushed."

"I'll sleep with Edith, and Merry and Violet can be together. I think we all feel we need some loving company tonight," Ally said.

He smiled at her. She felt a rush of affection for the man. Maybe it was because she knew he honestly liked her.

How comforting to think of having him for her father-in-law.

On the other hand, how disturbing to think of having a husband.

"I will ride first watch," Bertram said.

Lord Farrow nodded. "Set the lads and ladies loose, as well."

"The lads and ladies?" Violet asked.

"Wolfhounds," Lord Farrow said. "Marvelous creatures. Large as tigers, loyal to the core, and exceptional guard dogs."

"Oh, yes, we had a wonderful wolfhound once, remember, Ally?" Merry asked.

"Yes, but I was young."

"Perhaps we should have such a dog again," Violet murmured.

"I'll see to it," Lord Farrow told her. "And now, to bed. It's quite lucky I was here tonight. Angus would have definitely seen to you in the village, but there is space here, and we are almost family. Is there anything you would like? Tea?"

"A shot of whiskey," Edith said.

They all stared at her in stunned silence for a minute.

Lord Farrow shrugged and grinned. "A shot of whiskey it is. And, if you think you can possibly remain awake a bit longer, I'll have Sir Angus Cunningham out here as quickly as possible. He is the sheriff, and he must know what has happened immediately."

"I suppose we must speak with the sheriff, yes," Violet said.

"Indeed," Merry agreed, and she looked at Edith. "So you must go slowly with that whiskey."

MARK AWOKE TO THE SOUND of a snort and the feel of a soft, wet muzzle against his cheek. He opened his eyes, looked up and groaned. Galloway, one of his finest Arab-mix steeds, was standing above him, curious and eager to wake him.

He sat up, pulling straw from his hair, yet dryly thinking he had slept rather well for bedding down in the stable.

Then, before he could rise, he heard the soft sound of paws. A second later, the hounds were on him, letting out a bark and a whimper here and there, and all but laving him to death with poking noses and kisses.

"Excuse me," he protested, using the back of the largest, Malcolm, to rise at last. He patted the four heads of the giant animals madly wagging their tails, and when Cara would have risen on her hind legs—and even at his height, she stood an inch above him—he commanded, "Down! Ah, good girl," he praised her when she obeyed. Then he looked around. "Father, where are you? I'm sure you're finding this quite amusing."

In hunting attire—tan jodhpurs, jacket and high black boots—Lord Farrow appeared. "Ah, you *are* here. I thought I might find you nearby."

Mark dusted straw from himself. "What else could I have done?" he asked ruefully.

Joseph grew grave. "Nothing. This was quite disturbing news. It's possible some lost fool decided the sisters' cottage might make a decent refuge, but you don't believe that, do you?"

Mark shook his head. "I want Ally staying here. And the aunts must stay, as well."

"The aunts will refuse. You know that. I had Sir Angus out last night. He went to search the cottage. He has sent men to secure the windows with braces, so even if someone shatters the glass, they will not be able to get in. I will send a pair of the hounds with them. And you might find out if a few of your friends are available to take night watch."

"Yes, we can share hours," Mark murmured.

"May I make a suggestion?"

"Please."

"The wedding has been intended for many years. Unless you have decided it is not something you can agree to—and, in truth, you are not beholden to keep my word—I strenuously suggest your marriage take place this Saturday."

"That allows little time for planning. I had thought you and the Stirlings wished for a magnificent affair."

"Which is not necessary," Joseph said, waving a hand in the air.

"No, not in my mind. Miss Grayson, however, might object."

"Well, we shall see. Are you intending to come in?" Joseph asked.

Mark shook his head. "Bertram will allow me his stable room to bathe and dress. I must make a trip into the city."

"Are you getting any closer to the truth?" his father asked.

"I'm not close to the truth, but I have been able to eliminate some possibilities. I am certain some who are under suspicion are not involved. So..."

"I understand. But if you intend to see your way through to this wedding by Saturday, I suggest you spend some time with Ally."

"Indeed. It's just that this morning, I must pore over some of the records Ian has obtained."

"As you see fit."

"Father?"

"Yes?"

"Lionel Wittburg was in a sad state yesterday."

"Ah. So that was why Detective Douglas was at the church?"

"Yes."

"How is Lord Wittburg now?"

"Much better, I believe."

"Good."

"But he said something curious. I will go through with the wedding, Father, as you long ago promised I would. But if I am to do so, you must tell me the truth."

"The truth? I made a vow to Lord Stirling."

"Father, that isn't the only reason. You must tell exactly

why it is so important that Ally Grayson is married to *me*."

Joseph stood very still. "There are secrets some men have taken to their graves, son," he said softly after a moment.

"But there are men alive who still know those secrets. Lionel Wittburg knows something."

"What did the old fool say?"

"Nothing. But I am asking *you*. Father. I need the truth."

Joseph fell silent. "We will talk later," he said at last. "When you are not called to duty in the city."

He turned and strode back toward the house. Mark watched his father go. At least it seemed Joseph meant to talk to him at last. He was suddenly very sorry it was necessary for him to head back to the city.

"OH, DEAR, WE CAN'T JUST STAY here endlessly," Violet said.

"I'm sure we'll be safe at the cottage," Edith said.

They were seated around the breakfast table. Ally was amazed by the beauty of this place, which was considered a mere hunting lodge. There was a grand salon, the breakfast room—with windows that overlooked the rear lawn and the forest—the enormous kitchen, a formal dining room, a large parlor, a library and the plentiful bedrooms. In Lord Farrow's father's and grandfather's day—and even before, he had said—the Earls of Warren had come here often with large parties of friends to hunt, so the size had been necessary. The current Lord Farrow loved to come here because of the peace and beauty of the countryside, but sadly, he admitted, his business kept him in London most of the time.

"If you must return to the cottage, I will send a pair of the dogs," Lord Farrow said. "But, Ally, I'm afraid you must remain here as my guest."

"But if we have the dogs—"

"I don't believe your aunts are really in any danger. I believe you are," he told her.

"You must stay here, then," Violet said firmly.

"I can't have you going off alone," Ally said firmly.

Lord Farrow cleared his throat. "We have decided the wedding will take place this Saturday," he said.

Ally gasped. "So soon?"

"It seems prudent," Lord Farrow said.

"I—I—" Ally stuttered.

"Yes, it must be this Saturday. Oh, Ally, that will be wonderful. You will never need to fear anything again," Merry said brightly.

"I'm not afraid right now. I'm angry, and I'm worried about you three being alone," she said firmly.

"Ally," Violet said, and winced. "I'm sorry to say this, but…I believe we will be fine by ourselves, especially with the beautiful hounds Lord Farrow so graciously intends to lend us. It is more than likely you have become the target of some insanely jealous person. You will be safest here, while we will be safe in our little domain."

"But—"

"Ally, for now, please?" Edith asked softly.

She lifted her hands. There was an inkling of truth in what they were saying. She no longer believed it was because she was engaged to Mark Farrow that she was suddenly a target. It had occurred to her that she might have been followed to the post office in London.

Perhaps someone—someone deadly—knew that she was A. Anonymous.

"Please, don't look so stricken, dear," Edith begged.

"You'll be with us all day on Friday. We'll be fitting your wedding gown for the last alterations. Oh, you will be so beautiful," Merry promised.

Ally tried to smile, but inside she felt a small sense of heartbreak. She loved them so dearly. She had loved growing up in the woods. She suddenly realized that not only was she supposed to marry a man who was all but a stranger to her, but she would be leaving behind her childhood, all she had loved so much for so long.

"I have a wonderful library," Lord Farrow told her.

"There you are, Ally. A wonderful library," Violet said.

She nodded. She wouldn't bring them fear or worry or put them into danger for anything in the world. "As you wish, my darlings," she told them.

Still, when their coach was packed up again and Bertram set out to escort them through the forest, the younger set of hounds, Cally and Oz, running about them, she felt that sense of poignancy again. She hugged them fiercely one by one.

Merry was going to cry.

"Friday, then, my love," Violet said, forcing cheer into her tone.

"Friday, then," Ally agreed.

"Come, I shall show you to the library, Ally," Lord Farrow said. "Don't worry—we shall know if anyone is remotely near. Wolfhounds are amazing guard dogs. You may read to your heart's content. I have new volumes, and a collection that goes back hundreds of years. And there's a typewriter on the desk in the library, should you wish to use it. If you need me, I will be in my office, which adjoins my bedroom."

She nodded, still feeling lost. Yet the library, in a loft on the second floor, was stunning in its size and scope.

"Those...over there," Lord Farrow said, pointing. "Be very careful with them. They are actual missives written during the Crusades," he told her. "There is an original edition of Chaucer, as well."

"I will be very careful."

"I know you will."

He left her there.

For a moment she stared at the volumes, entranced.

But then her eyes fell upon the typewriter.

They did not have one in the little cottage. To her own dismay, she ignored the volumes of historical importance and made straight for the desk.

There was paper by the typewriter. She quickly slid it into the carriage, then stared at the keys.

In a moment she began to type, her soul seeming to take flight as her fingers flew.

CHAPTER ELEVEN

IN THE POLICE OFFICE, Mark pored over the various lists Ian had acquired and compared them to the ones he had made up of carriages and personages waylaid by the highwayman.

"So do you think Lionel Wittburg might be involved in any way?" Ian asked, sitting on the corner of his own desk.

"Lord Wittburg is definitely having difficulties with the situation, but…"

"And what of the man who would have broken into the cottage?" Ian asked. "Are these events related, do you think?" Mark had started to tell Ian about the events at the cottage the minute he had arrived, but thanks to modern communication, Ian already knew. He had spoken with Sir Angus Cunningham on the telephone.

Mark pointed at one of the lists before him. "This is the information about visitors at Giles Brandon's town house obtained from Eleanor and the housekeeper?"

"Yes."

"Wittburg did visit him. And Sir Andrew Cunningham was there, as well. He escorted his cousin Elizabeth Prine, who lost her own husband to the killer, to visit Eleanor."

Ian shrugged. "Well, the two women are friends."

"True. And here—Lionel attended one of the meetings at Brandon's house."

"I was quite surprised to see that. It was after the death of Hudson Porter. The list of visitors to his house is there—I acquired it from the housekeeper on Friday. Now, each of the women who answered my questions made certain to warn me that she was afraid she would not remember the names of everyone who had visited."

"Hmm," Mark murmured, studying the lists side by side. He looked up. "But even if they have forgotten someone, I see several names that are in common."

"Of course. They were all involved in the same movement."

Mark shook his head. "But...Lord Lionel Wittburg?"

"Would such a man, titled, close to the queen, really seek to tear down the monarchy?"

"Perhaps if he were going mad, or were on a vendetta," Mark said.

"The writer—Thane Grier. He attended events at all three houses."

"He's a journalist. He covers such events."

"The highwayman has yet to accost any of these men."

"A journalist wouldn't have a fine carriage."

"Lionel Wittburg has a very fine carriage. So does Sir Andrew Cunningham."

"But that alone—"

"No. Alone, it means nothing," Ian agreed.

"I think it's possible that more than one man is responsible for these murders."

"Yes, I agree," Ian said.

"Not one of the homes showed signs of forced entry. The wives and housekeepers were gone. Either the killers had a key or the victim let him in. With forced entry, the killer had access by one of these methods."

"We're questioning everyone," Ian said. "But people do lie to the police."

"As soon as possible, the highwayman will stop Lord Wittburg and Sir Andrew," Mark told Ian, and rose. Ian looked worried and depressed. Mark set a hand on his shoulder. "Don't look so weary, friend. We will find the answers."

Mark left him and hurried to O'Flannery's. It was Monday afternoon, the time when the highwayman and his band regularly met for a meat pie and ale. When he arrived, he saw that Patrick, Thomas and Geoff were already seated. Flo had served them their ale; his pint was already in place.

He waved to Flo as he took his seat, and she nodded, ready to see that their food was prepared. "Well?" Patrick asked quietly.

"I need help—as Mark Farrow," he said, looking from face to face.

"Oh?" Geoff said.

"Someone attempted to break into the cottage where Ally Grayson lives with her aunts," he told them.

"Attempted?" Thomas demanded.

"I arrived in time to scare him off, though I'm ashamed to say I didn't apprehend him."

"So what help do you need?" Patrick asked.

"I would like us to take turns watching the cottage at night."

Patrick groaned. "We're to…stare at a cottage in the woods all night?"

"Well, if Alexandra is there…" Thomas murmured, grinning.

Mark shook his head. "She's staying with my father at the lodge."

"Oh?" Geoff said.

"So we are to watch three elderly women in the woods," Patrick said.

"Why would someone attack your future bride?" Geoff asked.

Mark shook his head. He thought he knew why, but he wasn't about to say so. Not even to these, his closest friends.

"So when do we meet to ride out again?" Patrick asked.

"I need to discover a bit more about the schedules of certain men," Mark said. He fell silent; Flo was coming with their meals.

"Piping hot. I've seen to it," Flo announced cheerfully.

She lowered her voice. "Such a strange mood in here. It's as if people are waiting to hear about another murder. It's been a quiet week, thank God. Not even the highwayman and his band have struck of late."

"What is the political mood?" Mark asked.

"How strange. That young journalist, Thane Grier, was in here just an hour ago, asking the exact same question."

"Does he come here often?" Mark asked.

"He likes to watch people," Flo said.

"He *is* a journalist," Patrick said.

"Yes," Mark agreed, and made a mental note. He thanked Flo. When she was gone, he said, "Patrick, will you take tonight? Geoff, Tuesday, Thomas, Wednesday. I will take Thursday night. We'll see where we are at that point. And then…"

"And then?" Patrick asked.

"I'm being married on Saturday at Castle Carlyle. I hope you will all attend."

ALLY INTENDED TO SEARCH the stables for signs of Mark's secret life that afternoon. Unfortunately, just as she set out to do so, Mark Farrow made his return.

"Going riding, are you?" he asked.

"Yes, I had thought to," she lied.

"Alone?"

"I—yes."

"Dangerous indeed," he informed her. "But if you are eager to ride, I will certainly accompany you."

"But you've just returned. You must be weary from…whatever it is you do all day."

"It's not so late. I'm happy to ride with you. Although," he noted, "you're hardly properly attired."

She was wearing a simple day dress. She had ridden often enough on the old pony the aunties kept, but... She flushed and decided honesty would not work against her. "I'm accustomed to climbing up bareback."

"In bloomers?"

"I'm afraid so."

"These are hot-blooded horses, Miss Grayson. They're not slow and plodding."

"I'm quite capable."

"I'm sure you are, but...ride with me?"

She hesitated. Then he reached down a hand, and she met his eyes and accepted it. He easily lifted her to sit before him in the saddle. His arms around her, he tightened his knees, and they were quickly riding hard over the lawn that led to the road.

She might have felt precarious, but his arms around her gave her confidence that he would never let her fall. He moved as one with the horse.

Easy for a bandit, she thought.

She had to admit that the ride was exhilarating. The wind whipped through her hair and stung her cheeks. The smell of the day was clean and fresh. The afternoon was waning, but a beautiful pink light remained. She felt strangely comfortable with Mark, braced against his chest, seated between his thighs. For long moments she let the arousing sensations race through her in time with the smooth gallop of his steed.

He reined in at last beside a brook. After leaping from

the saddle, he reached for her. He set her down, then patted the horse. "This is Galloway. He's a fine fellow."

"A very fine fellow," she agreed.

As the horse lowered its head to graze, Mark met her eyes. "The wedding is to be this Saturday."

"So I understand."

"You are willing?"

"Are you?"

"I have always been willing."

She paused, smiling, lowering her head. "I have decided that there is little I can do but go through with it. However, you must be warned."

"Oh?"

"I don't intend to follow orders."

"What made you assume I intend to give them?"

She lifted a hand in the air. "Certain aspects of my life must remain…my life."

"As it should be."

She hesitated, feeling a surge of mischief. "I lied to you the other day."

"Already? We're not even married yet."

"You asked me if there was someone in my life."

"Yes?"

"Well…"

"Who is he?"

"It doesn't matter. Just someone who intrigued me."

"Really? I would be greatly distressed, had I not shared your kiss," he told her.

Again, she waved a hand in the air. "A kiss?" she said dismissively.

He led the horse back to her, standing very close. She felt her knees tremble and her will weaken. No. She would not falter.

"You're so experienced?" he inquired.

"Would that stop the wedding?"

"No."

"You are...quite the modern thinker."

"What matters is after the wedding," he said. There was an edge to his voice, no matter how pleasantly he spoke.

"Then, we are fine."

"I wouldn't want to bore you with my past."

She was stunned by the surge of jealousy his casual words created in her heart.

"Thank God," she managed to murmur. "I'm afraid that day could go to night, and night to day again," she murmured.

"So...who is this rival?" he inquired, standing nearly against her.

"Someone totally inappropriate," she assured him.

"Sad," he commiserated. "But you will do the honorable thing and obey your godparents."

"Just as you are doing, obeying your father."

"You're quite mistaken," he told her.

"I am?"

If he came any closer, she thought, he would be standing on her feet. "I'm looking forward to this marriage. It may have been just a kiss, but a kiss can promise so much."

"Really?" she murmured. "Forgive me, but I was not quite so impressed."

"Then I must try again."

"I—I—"

There was no opportunity to say more. He dropped the horse's reins, and suddenly his arms were around her. And this kiss was not a simple thing. It was all consuming, filled with fire and passion. She was pressed hard against the length of him, feeling the promise of which he had spoken.

She felt the pressure of his mouth, the heat of his tongue in her mouth, sending liquid fire rushing through her, her lungs, her abdomen...lower. She could feel herself melting into his very being, felt his fingers on her face, her neck, sifting through her hair, on her breast, her waist, her hips....

She wanted to feel more of him, not just his touch. She wanted to reach out, feel the power in his muscles, brush her fingers against his naked flesh....

He released her suddenly. She swayed and nearly fell. He had already turned away, seeking the horse's reins. "I don't think it will be so bad," he said casually.

She fought the soaring rise of her temper. "May we return?"

"Your every wish is my command, Alexandra."

He set her atop the horse and leapt up behind her. They returned to the stables at the same fierce pace at which they had left. He rode past the stables and set her down before the lodge. "Thank you for the lovely ride," she said curtly.

"No," he said huskily from behind her. "I thank *you* for the lovely ride."

He was laughing at her, she was certain. And yet, she was going to marry the man. And her decision had nothing to do with honor.

Rather…all she could think of was his touch. Was this feeling, this thing like desperation, falling in love? Was love a simple hunger, a need…?

She lifted her chin. She was going to marry him. She might well be falling in love.

But she wasn't going to make it easy for him.

"WHOA!"

The coachman reined the elegant carriage bearing Lord Lionel Wittburg to a halt. Patrick rode up alongside the man, taking care to see he was disarmed even as he tried to draw out his pistol. Thomas stood by to assist Patrick; Geoff reined in by Mark.

Mark dismounted, throwing open the door to the carriage. Lord Wittburg was also in the process of reaching for his sidearm.

The last thing Mark wanted to do was hurt the elderly gentleman, but neither did he wish to be shot himself.

"Stop, my Lord. I wish no injury to you," he ordered.

He realized, watching Wittburg's expressions change, that he didn't wish for a gun battle, either, but his pride was at stake.

"My lord, if you will just be so good as to step down from the carriage?" he suggested.

Stiffly, with the utmost dignity, Wittburg did so. The minute he was clear of the carriage, Mark nodded to Geoff and stepped inside himself.

It was a fine though aging coach, and it did not take Mark long to search. He found a cloak, but the black garment showed no signs of blood. There were boots in the compartment, as well, but they appeared to have no trace upon them of anything but dirt.

"Does he carry that much treasure?" Geoff called from outside. Mark knew the men were less comfortable holding a gun on Lord Wittburg than on any other person they had stopped.

"He carries nothing of value," he called out in reply, as if disgusted. But he went over the compartment again, searched the cloak inch by inch, studied the boots once more.

At last he emerged.

"He carries nothing," he complained, jumping atop his horse.

"His watch and bob are fine enough," Thomas pointed out.

"'Tis not worth it," Mark said with a shake of his head.

Wittburg never lost his dignity. "You will hang," he assured Mark.

He'd heard the words often enough. Still, from Wittburg's lips…

"Perhaps," he said. "You may resume your journey, your Lordship."

Wittburg frowned, staring at him. "You are stealing nothing?"

"Don't make me change my mind."

At last Lionel Wittburg returned to his coach. He almost slipped on the step. Mark leapt down in time to keep him from a nasty fall.

Wittburg jerked his arm free. "I cannot thank you. I will not thank a criminal," he said. Then he was back in the coach, slamming the door.

"Go!" Patrick thundered to the driver.

"East and west," Mark said when the carriage had started off down the trail. They split, disappearing into the woods, just in time to avoid the shots Lord Wittburg fired from the window of the carriage.

BEING THE GUEST OF Lord Farrow was not difficult in the least. He was charming and private, and allowed Ally the same privacy.

When he announced that he needed to go into London on business, he seemed pleased to accept her company when she asked if she might come along.

In the carriage, however, he seemed disturbed. "I shouldn't have brought you. I must attend to business while I am there, and I am worried about your safety."

"You needn't be. I intend to shop and stay on the main streets, where there will be an abundance of people," she assured him.

Lord Wittburg hopped out near Big Ben, telling Bertram to attend to Miss Grayson. The big man nodded, patient and ready to do whatever was asked of him. Ally asked to be let off near the museum and suggested they meet at the same spot in two hours. She noticed the man kept a book on his seat, and she had to smile. No wonder he was patient. While he was waiting, he read.

She walked through one door of the museum.

And out another. Once again, she was determined on reaching the post office. Today, though, she couldn't help but wonder if she had been followed before, so she was careful. She skirted in and out of several shops, buying a few pieces of lace for the aunties, a couple of sachets and a small reticule.

If she hadn't lost her check, she might have bought the charming little muff she saw in one shop. But she had, and there was no safe way to retrieve it.

When she finally reached the post office, to mail her latest article, she discovered that her check had been mailed back to her. She decided that Mark must have returned it to the newspaper. She worried that he might be following her, and she looked around quickly. She saw no one suspicious. Outside, she started along the street and realized she was heading toward the newspaper offices. She had often gone just to stare at the building, dreaming that she might one day write for the paper, though what she really aspired to was becoming a novelist, spinning tales like Arthur Conan Doyle or the Brontë sisters—or even Poe. She had been surprised to recognize her own passion and ability when she had set her hand to essays.

She was standing on the sidewalk when she heard her name called.

"Miss Grayson!"

Turning around, she saw Thane Grier. He looked handsome and cheerful in a striped jacket, black trousers and tan waistcoat. He seemed happier than when she had seen him last.

"How are you?" he asked.

"Well, thank you. And you?"

"Couldn't be better." He lowered his voice and laughed softly. "A. Anonymous has not been writing every day."

"Ah, so the front page is yours again."

"Yes. Would you like to come up? It's not at all glamorous, but perhaps…?"

"I would love to!"

"Then you shall."

He showed her where the papers were stacked for the vendors, where the presses were, and then dozens and dozens of offices. Phones were in constant use, salesmen worked to make their living by selling advertising space, and scores of people sat at desks arranged in rows, typing, or leafing through huge tomes, verifying facts. She was flushed but pleased at the opportunity to meet the managing editor, and especially gratified when he said they were always eager to get outside pieces, such as those that had been written by A. Anonymous.

Ally did not want to overstay her welcome and tried to hurry out, but as she reached the door, he called her back. "Your wedding will be featured on page one, you know."

She smiled, unwilling to tell him that it was scheduled to take place on Saturday. She didn't know what plans were in effect or whether secrecy was involved.

After all, she was only the bride.

Thane walked her back down to the street. "May I buy you tea?" he asked.

She was flushed and excited, and ready to accept, but she realized she had used up all the time she had asked Bertram to allow her. "I'm sorry. I would honestly love to have tea with you, but I'm here with Lord Farrow, and I must return."

He smiled at her, a strange smile. "We should really talk," he told her.

She inclined her head. "We *have* been talking, have we not?"

"I shall talk, you must listen. You must be careful, you know."

"Why do you say so?"

"Did you know your proposed groom was in these offices just yesterday?"

"Was he?" She tried to sound casual. "What was he doing?"

"I don't know. I couldn't hear. But he was speaking with the managing editor. And he gave him an envelope."

"Maybe he's started writing," she said.

His eyes studied her gravely.

"Thank you. Sincerely. I've dreamed forever of being where I was today," she said when he made no reply to her speculation.

"I see. So *you* write."

"Good heavens, what an imagination you have."

"Mark Farrow was not delivering an envelope on your behalf?"

"Absolutely not," she assured him. "But thank you again. I have had a wonderful time."

"Strange, but delightful."

"What's that?"

"That you should find the offices of the newspaper so fascinating—that you have dreamed of entering them."

"I love to read."

"I see."

He didn't see. He was suspicious. And she didn't know what to say.

"Thank you again, but now I must hurry."

She shook his hand, turned and fled.

She hurried along several streets, rounded a corner, and then went into the museum through the rear entrance, then out the other side. As she had known he would be, Bertram was waiting.

Lord Farrow had apparently finished his business quickly, and he had somehow known how to find Bertram. He was already in the carriage. "I was beginning to fear I had really cast you into danger," he told her.

"Am I late? I'm so sorry."

"You are late by no more than a few minutes. I am just becoming…well, recent events lead one to unwarranted concern. Your timing was fine, my dear. So, was your shopping successful?"

Yes, successful. She now had her check in hand.

And another essay would soon be delivered.

In addition, she was almost certain she hadn't been followed to the post office.

The day continued to be a pleasant one, despite the fact Mark Farrow unnerved her by managing to return home by dinnertime. He seemed somewhat distracted, however, though he was polite throughout the meal.

When they had finished dining, she feigned exhaustion, which seemed to be fine with both men. She realized they were anxious to speak alone, a feat they intended to accomplish by "retiring" for brandy and cigars.

Seeing the two men headed into Lord Farrow's private chambers, followed by Bertram with a tray, Ally eschewed her first idea of escaping to the bedroom. She slipped outside and headed for the stables instead.

But where to start?

She glanced at the tack room and, across from it, Bertram's private quarters. That might well be the best place to look.

The door was open. She slipped in. Bertram seemed to be a man of few needs. There were shelves with books, a cabinet with liquor and a fireplace in the outer of the two rooms. One closet. Ally went through it quickly but discovered nothing other than clothing that clearly belonged to the large man. His bedroom was sparsely furnished, offering a bed, a chest of drawers and a bedside table. Quickly, she went through the drawers, feeling like the worst busybody in the world. There was a small water closet, offering nothing but soap and towels.

She quickly left the room, closing the door behind her. The wolfhounds were at her heels, wagging their giant tails, as she came out. "Good girl, good boy," she murmured, patting their heads. She felt comfortable, knowing she was safe from intruders with the dogs at her side.

But what she was actually frightened of was someone

from the house finding her prying, and the dogs would be no help on that score.

She glanced toward the lodge, saw no one and hurried over to the tack room. There she found rows of neatly hung bridles, sawhorses with saddles, and cans of polish and other accoutrements. She left the tack room and looked up to the hayloft. There was a ladder. She glanced back once, then scrambled up the ladder.

She found nothing but hay and more hay.

Frustrated, she sat on a bale. It was hard beneath her. Startled, she stood quickly. The hay was nothing but a facade. She groped about and found she could lift a portion of it. The hay masked a trunk. Inside the trunk were black cloaks and boots.

And black silk masks.

In a frenzy, she looked further.

Her sketchbook was not there.

She went dead still then, hearing voices. Her heart thundered. She crept toward the edge of the loft and looked down.

"There are many men working on the case, and it is a two-way street, Father. Ian takes whatever suggestions I offer and sends officers out on the street to investigate them. He is quite a clever man. You know as well as I do that Lord Wittburg would have been horrified at the arrival of a police officer. He would never have allowed Ian into his chambers."

"It's a dangerous game you're playing, that much I know very well," Lord Farrow said. "What frightens me is that despite all that is being done—and I do not doubt

Ian has men covering the streets, following every lead—it seems no one is any closer to the truth than before."

What were they doing in the stables? she wondered. Why couldn't they have stayed in the house with their brandies and cigars?

And how on earth was she going to get back inside?

"What are you doing, prowling about out here?" Mark said suddenly.

Ally nearly gasped, then realized he was talking to the dogs. She heard a woof of pleasure. Mark must be patting one of them on the head.

A moment later she breathed a sigh of relief. "I'm to bed, then, son. I have to leave very early for the city tomorrow morning. I'll ride in. Bertram will stay here. We'll not leave Miss Grayson alone at any time."

"Thank you, Father."

Their voices continued, but she no longer heard what they said. She assumed they were heading back to the house. Carefully, though, she waited.

At last she decided enough time had gone by. Looking over the ledge, she saw no one. With all the speed she could summon, she hurried down the ladder.

The hounds were waiting. "Traitors!" she told the pair. They only, good-naturedly, woofed anew, nudging her for affection. "All right, all right," she murmured, and stroked them both, looking about to see if the Farrow men or Bertram might still be about.

Seeing no one, she sprinted for the lodge and slipped inside.

The house was quiet. She started through the parlor.

"My dear Miss Grayson."

She froze. Mark Farrow stepped from the shadows, where he had been seated on the divan.

She could see nothing of his face in the dim light.

"Mark..." she murmured.

"Ally. I thought you had gone to bed."

"I needed a breath of fresh air."

"I see."

"It's a lovely night."

"Indeed."

"Well...good night."

"Good night. Oh!" he said suddenly.

"Yes?"

"My father and I will both be out on business most of the day tomorrow. But Bertram will be here, working the grounds. Please, don't go walking or riding anywhere alone. You'll be safe here."

"Of course," she said, then turned and hurried toward the hall.

"Ally?"

She froze, then turned back slowly. He still stood in the shadows.

"There's something in your hair."

"My hair?"

She touched it and winced.

Hay.

"A twig," she murmured. "Thank you...I've got it. Good night," she said again, firmly.

She turned. If he called her again, what would she do? Or say?

But he didn't call her back, though she felt his presence...his eyes...as she walked away.

He was watching her all the while.

CHAPTER TWELVE

ALLY HAD TO ADMIT THAT she loved the lodge. She would always love the cottage in the woods, and it would forever be home to her, but the lodge was something special. For one thing, there was electricity, which meant there was always light to read by. Her room offered an elaborate bath, with a deep sunken tub, and there was always wonderfully hot water in which to bathe.

Alone when she woke, she found it gratifying to think she had the entire place to herself for an entire day. She would have time to indulge in a leisurely meal, time to explore the loft again and look for her sketchbook, and time to spend in the library—with no chance that prying eyes might want to see what she was typing.

Though she did miss the aunts scurrying about, she couldn't help but luxuriate in her solitude. And she had been gone longer before, she reminded herself, when she had stayed at the castle.

But this time…

This time she was about to marry Mark Farrow. So this time, she was gone…forever.

Not wanting to brood, she finished her meal of fruit, eggs and muffins, and hurried outside. She had to discover where Bertram was before she could really begin to explore, but that proved to be easy. He was busy pruning a hedge in front of the lodge.

She started toward the stables, then hesitated, deciding to return to the house for a scarf so she could tie up her freshly washed hair and keep from accumulating the telltale hay that had so nearly given her away the night before.

She entered the parlor and walked down the hall, slipping into the bedroom that had so quickly become her own. She walked to the dresser, opened the top drawer, then caught sight of movement in the mirror.

She nearly screamed.

In the reflection, she saw the highwayman. He was seated comfortably on her bed, mask in place, booted legs stretched out on the quilt.

She spun around.

"What in God's name are you doing here? Are you insane?" she demanded, all the while knowing he lived there, but not about to give him the satisfaction of knowing she had discovered his secret identity.

"Shh," he said quickly, rising and walking swiftly toward her. "You would not betray me, would you?"

Oh, but this was sweet.

"Never," she told him solemnly.

"They are gone for the day?" he asked.

"Who?"

"Lord Farrow and his son."

She nodded. "Yes, yes, they're gone," she said, sounding distressed. "But this is insane. You shouldn't be here. Bertram is guarding the house. And the dogs—how did you get past the dogs?"

"I've managed to befriend them. The best dog can be slowly won over with the right offerings of scraps and bones. I've been through this area many times, and I have made use of it. The Farrows are not often in residence here, you know."

"You're still in danger here."

"Why?"

"Bertram is just outside."

"But he would never simply enter the house with you here, Ally. He would knock. He would only burst in if you were to scream or to call for help. Do you intend to scream?"

She shook her head.

He was wearing boots, black riding breeches and an unbleached poet's shirt, open at the neck. She noticed that he'd tossed his cape over a chair by the fire. His riding crop and pistol were there, as well. He'd certainly been thorough about creating the pretense.

"I told you," she said softly. "I would never betray you."

He smiled beneath the mask. "Yet you are to marry on Saturday."

"How do you know that?" she asked.

"It's in the newspaper. Lord Stirling called in the announcement, apparently."

"I see."

"You intend to go through with it?" he asked.

"A matter of honor," she told him.

"And do you know the man? Do you think you will be able to spend a lifetime with him? What is he like?"

Oh, she was going to enjoy this, she thought.

"He's extremely arrogant."

"Hardly sounds like a good match."

"Abrasive."

"Really?"

"A man controlled by his own ego."

"Appalling."

She smiled, allowing her hand to fall upon his chest. She was glad of the quick little intake of breath that followed. She slid her fingers up to the bare skin at his throat, then down, flicking open one of the buttons of the shirt. Her fingers teased against the flesh of his chest.

"I am to marry such a man on Saturday...."

"Yes?"

"And so, though I fear for your life, I cannot say I am not glad you are here. With me. Alone."

Again his breath quickened.

She rose on the balls of her feet, her fingers gliding back to his face. She cupped his strong jaw, and slowly set her mouth against his, her tongue sliding over his lips, pressing between them.

As she had expected, she was quickly swept into his

arms. She felt the firm pressure of his fingers spanning the small of her back, bringing her flush against him, felt his fingers in her hair, raking through it, cupping her skull. She felt the thrust of his tongue, an erotic sensation that filled her to the depths of her soul.

She wondered briefly just what revenge she might be taking. She was where she wanted to be. And yet...

He shifted, breaking the touch. "You're to be married," he reminded her.

"I am not married yet."

"No?"

"And since we have been given such sweet time, I would spend it with you," she whispered.

She had not known exactly how far she meant to take her charade before telling the truth. But she had first discovered her fascination with this man when he was in his highwayman's disguise, and she wouldn't resist the chance to explore further.

But she would stop, reveal what she knew. She would....

Then his mouth found hers once again. The pressure of his lips was vital and demanding, and she hungered for that touch, for the caress of his tongue, for his hands upon her and hers on him. She laid her palm on his cheek, played her fingers down his skin and slid her hand against his shirt, loosening more of the delicate pearl buttons. She was scarcely aware when he lifted her, when he eased them down together on the softness of the quilt, his weight half atop her. She felt the heat and strength of his hips and thighs, and fire seemed to ripple along his skin. His eyes, gleaming blue-gray through the slits in the mask, were on her. And then he touched her.

He ran a finger over the soft wet swell of her lower lip. His fingers fell to the buttons of her bodice, and she caught her breath and simply stared at him as he progressed slowly, button by button. He laid his palm on her breast, over the sheer material of her silk shift, and sensation seemed to rip through her. She closed her eyes, and his mouth found hers again, with an ever greater passion. Then he moved against her with a sweet, barely leashed savagery, hands sliding down her breasts, midriff, to her hips, his lips and tongue running riot over her throat, then teasing her flesh through the silk, settling upon her nipple in an erotic frenzy. The lightest graze of his teeth sent new fire lapping at her senses. She had no idea when or how he had undone the waistband of her day skirt, how he had tugged the fabric lower, out of his way. She knew only the feel of his hands, burning, gentle, firm...stroking over her hips, over her buttocks. She hadn't realized she was all but tearing at his shirt herself, only that it was suddenly gone, and then his naked chest was against her, against the silk, and even that barrier was too great.

He rose, sweeping away both the skirt and the petticoat beneath it. He caught her feet, removing her delicate shoes, and his fingers slid along her thighs, finding her garters, slowly rolling down her hose, letting them waft to the floor like puffs of cloud. She closed her eyes, realizing on some distant plane that she had taken this too far, yet in the wave of euphoria that had seized her, not caring. When he was beside her again, she realized he was completely naked, bare and blazing, and his hands were on the hem of the shift, and it was meant to disappear, as well.

She opened her mouth at last to form some sound, to speak, to protest...to cry out that this was merely revenge, that it should not go so far.

She never spoke, for he kissed her again. Kissed her with the hard flesh of his body and muscle playing against her, with his hands everywhere, stroking, holding, seeking. The stroke of his tongue seemed to penetrate her very being, and then he left her mouth and it was not imaginary but real, for his lips fell upon her flesh everywhere. She shivered and trembled. She was gold and she burned. She felt the intimacy of his mouth on her abdomen, laving teasing circles there, drawn to the line of her hip, back again, then lower. She touched his flesh, and it was alive. Beneath his skin, muscles flexed and eased, so alive. His fingers skimmed down her hip, slid between her thighs. He touched her, and she gasped just as her lips were once again claimed by the overwhelming passion of his kiss.

She writhed, her fingers threading into his hair, clawing his back. His mouth moved swiftly, lightly touching her throat, her breast...her stomach, thighs...and between. The intimacy was stunning, shocking. She cried out, rocking to elude him...arching to know more of him. The searing sweetness he created seemed to bubble and boil deep within her, radiate to her limbs, constrict and release, then rise, blind her mind and eyes, fill her to a point of near madness...and explode with a volatile, violent pleasure that was ecstasy, insanity....

She was still reeling when she felt the pressure of his body. He held her in his arms, his lips finding hers, fierce and hard, and then...his body was on her. His powerful thighs were between hers, the length of him against her. She felt the tip of his erection first, and then movement, full, thick, good, a pressure that filled a craving and yet cut like a knife.

He cradled her gently, moved slowly. She tightened around him, and he eased her with his touch. She began to cry out, and again his kiss silenced her, the caress of his tongue easing the seconds of sharp torture that came...and then became something else, something painfully pleasurable. Time ticked by and she was aware of nothing but the scent and feel of him, the hardness of him against her, within her. Each nuance of his flesh. Each thrust and ebb, like a tide, like a storm. His body was both thunder and lightning, the rub of flesh against naked flesh ever more erotic, his touch exquisite. Sensation, the rush to completion, built as every thrust grew harder, filling her further. It was impossible, this craving, this desperate wanting, needing. Her breath, too, was thunder, her pulse an avalanche. Her heart careened out of control. Her center, where he thrust and stroked so intimately...

The world took flight. Nothing was real. Only his flesh. Only the firm and searing control of his body...out of control....

Again the shattering burst of climax. The taut craning of the man in the mask…

The world reeled around her. The sense of being filled, draped with honey…warm, so warm, and yet…

He eased to her side. She was stunned. And with their lovemaking over, the splendor known, the ecstasy reached, she was suddenly afraid of what she had done. What if he didn't believe…?

She didn't dare open her eyes. For the longest time she hid in his arms as he smoothed tangles from the wildness of her hair.

He shifted slightly. Unwilling, she opened her eyes.

He was taking off the mask.

"No…wait…"

But the mask was off, and he was staring at her.

"I knew who you were," she whispered.

"I know," he told her.

Startled, she sat up. "You did not!"

"I did." He smiled.

"You're lying." Suddenly feeling her nakedness, she reached for the wrinkled quilt, drawing it to her breast. "You're a liar. Your ego cannot bear the fact that I might have wanted someone else."

"So this was all to teach me a lesson?"

"Not exactly, though you certainly deserved such a lesson."

"You wanted to torment me. Well, I'm sorry, but I knew. There was, after all, that little matter of the fact that you were in the stables, up in the loft, last night."

"You did not see me there."

"No, but the dogs betrayed you. And then you came into the house covered in hay. You eavesdropped on my conversation with my father."

"I was not eavesdropping," she said indignantly. "I was stuck there."

"You might have made your presence known."

"So your father knows of your secret life. Is he a criminal, as well?" she asked, ignoring his point.

"My father? A criminal?"

He stared at her, and he had never looked more the son of an earl. Then he smiled, started to laugh and reached for her. She drew back, suddenly furious. He'd managed to turn the tables again. She had meant to play him, but it seemed that he had played her, instead.

"What? You've developed a sudden shyness?"

"I've discovered that I prefer an outlaw!"

"Why are you angry? You were intent on making me furious, making me believe you would happily bed a highwayman before me."

"Making you *think?* It was the truth."

He stood, natural and easy in his nakedness. Rippled muscle from head to toe, and totally unaware of the effect he had on her body or her mind.

"Ally—"

"I'd prefer to be alone."

"Ally, come now. The joke has been on both of us."

"This is all a joke?"

He sighed. "Forgive me, then. Will it make you feel better if I tell you that at first I wasn't certain, that you did torture me quite effectively while I was wondering whether you did or didn't know?"

The sudden clanging of a bell caused her to jump and him to frown. "It's the telephone," he informed her. He reached for the quilt. "May I?"

"No!"

But the quilt was gone even as the words left her mouth. He wrapped it about himself and left the room.

Suddenly freezing and deeply dismayed, she raced into the bathroom, locking the door behind her. She filled the tub with hot water and sank into it gratefully, shaking. How she hated him.

How she loved him....

There was a tapping on the door. "Ally?"

"Go away!"

To her amazement, he did. She waited, hunched in the water, certain he would return. She was angry, and she wanted to remain angry.

She wanted him to talk to her. She wanted to understand everything.

She wanted to love him for the man he was, the way she had grown to love the strange nobility and the mind of an outlaw.

But he didn't return. She was sore, she realized, and she let the water ease her muscles. Her thoughts remained at frantic odds with one another as the water grew slowly cold. At last she rose. She hesitated before going out to the bedroom, but he wasn't there. She dressed quickly, with fumbling fingers.

When she ventured out to the parlor, he was waiting.

He was the son of the earl this time, decked in a fine brocade waistcoat and a handsome tweed jacket, britches and riding boots. He stood before the fire, her sketchbook in his hands.

And he was reading.

"Give that to me!" she demanded, starting toward him.

He snapped the book shut. When he stared at her then, he was a total stranger.

"You are an idiot," he told her.

She stood rigidly still, fury bubbling inside her.

"I beg your pardon?" she demanded icily.

"You went back to the post office."

"Back?"

"You wore a far more dangerous mask than I ever did, Ally Grayson," he accused her. "Why do you think you were nearly assaulted at the cottage? Do you think these people are playing games? Perhaps I should take you to the morgue with me. Maybe seeing a man with his throat slit would force some sense into you."

"What are you talking about?"

"A. Anonymous. I was a fool to believe you when you denied the envelope was yours. And now...good God. You've written another essay."

"I write excellent essays," she informed him regally.

"You will get yourself killed."

She narrowed her eyes. "I see. As if a *highwayman* might not get himself shot one day."

"That's entirely different."

"It is? How? You apparently feel there is a strong reason to masquerade and risk your life stopping carriages.

Perhaps I see an equal reason to risk my life stating what seems to me to be of importance."

"A. Anonymous is inviting a murderer in!"

"A. Anonymous writes so that people will *think*."

"You're all but begging for your throat to be sliced."

"I write what I see, what others should see," she said with dignity.

"You went to the post office—again. After the cottage was nearly breached."

"I was not followed."

"Oh? The telephone call that just came was from Scotland Yard. You were seen."

"You had me followed? How dare you?"

He shook his head. "I did not have you followed. I had Ian send a man to watch the post office. And you were seen."

"Well, obviously, if you told the police…"

"You were followed from the museum. You might well have been followed again. But what does that matter? You were seen once, you could be seen again."

"Would you stop behaving as if what I did was a criminal act? It's what *you've* been doing that is illegal."

He stood very still, staring at her.

"It stops now."

She shook her head fiercely. "No."

"You are about to become my wife."

"I will not stop writing."

"I don't intend to marry a corpse."

She was startled by the shiver that seized her. She had never seen him so fiercely cold and unyielding.

She said softly, "I don't know you. I don't know you at all. But as I have said all along, you are not obligated to go through with the marriage."

She spun around and returned to her bedroom, closing and then locking the door. But it didn't matter. He made no attempt to enter.

In a few minutes she heard the front door slam. She knew he had left.

For a while longer she remained where she was. Finally she stood. She no longer needed to search the hayloft. She was alone in the magnificent lodge. She could avail herself of the library. She could read the magnificent books. She could write....

Yes, she could write. She had the right to express herself. She would not stop at the dictate of a man, not even the man intended to be her husband.

She walked out of her room and went to the library. The hounds were in, she realized. When she sat at the desk, Malcolm came up to her and whined, then settled at her feet. Cara trotted in behind him and curled up on the Persian rug in the center of the room.

Ally slid a paper into the typewriter.

No words came.

She was stunned and leaned her arms on the machine, bending her head over them...

And then she cried.

But not for long. She straightened, smoothed her hair back, stared at the typewriter and began to put her thoughts into words.

The world is changing. Each day we see new technology. Man himself longs to stay the same, and yet, in this changing world, we must make changes. Men go off to war as soldiers—always a new war awaits as we strive to maintain out empire—but women who feel they must fight are forced to defy what is known as the standard and find a disguise in which to approach the battlefield.

Whether we face a war in Asia, Africa, Europe or farther afield, this much is certain. Every man—and woman—living must at some time wage a battle within him—or herself. Far too often, we will wear disguises in life. In fact we must wear disguises, because it is often that facade that allows us to achieve that which we seek.

To love is to see beneath the mask while suffering no change in feeling.

She sat back. This was not what she should be sending to the newspaper!

She stared at what she had written and started to rip it from the typewriter, intending to crumple it up.

Then she hesitated, struck by a thought.

The anti-monarchists were certain the monarchists were responsible for the murders.

The monarchists were certain the anti-monarchists were guilty, an idea she had helped to perpetuate.

But...

Emotion, not logic, tended to rule the world. Passions on a grand scale held sway in politics.

What if they had all been wrong?

What if murder had been committed not because of politics but because of a far more personal passion? She had never felt emotion or sensation so deeply as now—because—honesty forced her to admit—she had never known such intense feelings before Mark had entered her world.

She could suddenly understand feelings of hatred, anger, all tied in with love and longing, and the hurt that could come only when emotions were deeply felt.

She hesitated; then her fingers found flight.

She might be wrong, or she might have been wrong the first time. It didn't matter. She was stating her opinions, not insisting on them as fact. She was offering her thoughts for discussion, so that others might delve into their own minds.

Right or wrong, her intent was to make people think.

THAT EVENING, LORD FARROW returned home before his son. Ally was grateful. She greeted him warmly but told him that she had to go home.

"It isn't safe," he protested.

She smiled. "I'm certain Mark has either a friend or a policeman watching the cottage through the night," she said, and his face betrayed the fact she was right. "And we have the loan of your dogs. They are excellent defenders. I will be safe, as will my aunts. I must go home."

"But...in a few days' time, *this* will be your home." He paused, frowning. "Have you decided not to marry my son?"

"If he wants me *as I am*, I will gladly marry your son. But tonight, please, I need to go home."

Lord Farrow was not happy, and she knew he didn't understand.

"We shall visit your aunts tomorrow."

"I can't stay here," she insisted.

"We'll talk in the morning," he said.

In bed that night, Ally tossed and turned. She realized Lord Farrow was intent on keeping her safe. He was never going to let her stay at the cottage.

When she awoke in the morning, Mark was still absent.

THE HOME WHERE HUDSON PORTER, dear old army comrade and good friend of Lord Lionel Wittburg, had lived was perhaps a mile closer to London than the village. As Ian had assured him, the housekeeper was still working there daily, awaiting the arrival of the man's only relatives from Boston. Mark arrived early.

"Mrs. Barker," he said, greeting her at the door.

She nodded. She had known he was coming and made a little bowing motion to him, as if she wasn't quite certain what she should do in his presence.

"Tea, sir? My lord, uh…Your Grace."

"No, thank you. Let's just sit and talk, shall we?"

Maybe he should have opted for tea. The woman, as slender and bony as Hattie, the Brandon housekeeper, reminded him of a bee ready to take flight.

"You live in the house?" he asked.

She nodded, looking toward the window.

"Why weren't you here the night Hudson Porter was killed?"

"The police have been here," she murmured.

"Yes, I know."

She lifted her hands in a shrug. "He gave me the night off."

"Why?"

"He...he wanted to work. Undisturbed."

"And what did you do with the night?"

"I...I stayed with a friend."

"Who is the friend?"

"Linda Good."

"And where does she live?"

"Near the village." She met his eyes quickly, then looked away again. "I...sir...Your Grace...my lord...I have been through this so many times. I came home to find Mr. Porter upstairs. His throat slit. It was horrible. I—I don't think I can do this anymore. He is buried now. We need to let him rest."

The woman's nervousness was apparent. He wondered why. Ian Douglas would certainly have had her alibi corroborated.

Still...

"Where are your keys kept?" he asked her.

She pointed. As there had been at the Brandon house, there was a hook near the door.

"Will you show me, please, where the murder occurred?"

She nodded, as if glad to have something to do at last. She led him up the stairs.

The room bore a striking resemblance to that in which Giles Brandon had died. Bookshelves lined the walls; the desk sat dead center. One door. One way in, one way out.

"Thank you. You can leave me," he told her.

She hovered.

"It's fine," he said pointedly, staring at her.

At last, reluctantly, she left.

Mark began to go through the desk. He knew the police had done so already, and at first he found nothing. Then, looking at the man's calendar for the night on which he had been killed, he found a notation that seemed strange.

Mrs. Barker off?

Why the question mark if he had determined to give the woman the night off himself?

He stared at the calendar, thinking it had to make sense somehow.

Then his mind drifted. He was tired, having spent most of the night riding aimlessly, tension knotted in his belly.

She had captivated him from the first moment. Her smile, her quick mind, the sound of her laughter, the scent of her perfume, all had ensorcelled him. It had been the most incredible thing in the world to discover that such a woman, beautiful in every way, was destined to be his bride. Even the game they had played—knowing, not knowing, the teasing and the taunting... They were both headstrong, prone to temper, and even the glitter of challenge in her eyes was something he had come to love....

But how could she? How could she continue to test

the brutal hands of a murderer? She had been caught, and not only was she not in the least remorseful, she was defiant. She would throw over not only a life of security, a title, position, but *him* in pursuit of an elusive dream. And there was the rub. He had been falling in love and had thought she had been doing so, as well, that the personalities of the earl's son and the highwayman would become one, and they would laugh in latter years over their first meeting. There had been nothing like touching her, being with her, making love to her, feeling the heat and the fury, the passion and...

He sensed that the housekeeper had returned. That she was standing at the door. He rose, smiling at her.

"Sir...you have Mr. Porter's calendar," she murmured.

"Yes, I do. I'm taking it in to Scotland Yard. It will be returned to Mr. Porter's relatives when they arrive."

As he left, he felt that she was far more nervous than she should have been, and he was angry with himself for being too distracted to think clearly about the murders.

Damn Ally! She was wrong.... She couldn't risk her own life so carelessly because...

Because she had become a part of him.

He determined to ride back to the lodge. He wasn't certain if he could bring himself to apologize, but he had to see her. Talk to her.

Touch her.

Outside, on the dirt road, reaching for Galloway's reins, he felt a sudden sense of urgency.

God, yes. He had to get back to her.

CHAPTER THIRTEEN

LORD FARROW NEVER FALTERED. Though his son was absent with no explanation, Joseph did his best and remained polite and considerate, pretending it was quite natural for his son to disappear now and then.

Of course, since Mark was the highwayman, it *was* natural.

Over eggs she asked him, "You know your son is the highwayman?"

He stared at her, then nodded. "And *you* know because you were in the hayloft."

She flushed. "Lord Farrow—why?"

He let out a sigh. "It's not my place to tell you. Mark must do so. But rest assured, it is a secret that must be kept. Not even Brian Stirling is aware. Believe me, he would not harm any man or woman."

She was silent, knowing he would tell her nothing more. She asked, "Are you going into the city today?"

"I need to, yes. But I promised I would take you to see your aunts first."

"Actually, I would like to go back to the museum and spend some time with Lady Camille."

"Do you know she is working?" he asked, surprised.

"Yes, she will be there. As the exhibition has just opened, she will be in for several days to assure herself all is in order."

"I worry—"

"You mustn't worry so much. In London, the streets are busy. The museum is guarded, and I know everyone there. I shall be quite safe. I can't spend my life hidden away."

"I wish Mark were here," Joseph murmured.

"I'll be fine," she said firmly.

When they arrived in London, she bade him a good day and went into the museum. Camille was working, and she was surprised but pleased to see Ally. "What are you doing here, when you are to be married in just a few days' time?" she queried.

Ally smiled. "Camille, what *should* I be doing? The wedding is at your residence, I'm certain my aunts are working hard on the dress, and…it's all really out of my hands."

"I had hoped that…"

"That I might be getting to know Mark?" Ally asked. "Well, he isn't about. Don't let me disturb you. You must do your work."

"Ally, I heard about what happened at the cottage the other night. Please, be careful."

"I shall be very careful."

She smiled, and left Camille's office, hurried through the exhibits and out to the street. When she would have headed toward the post office, she changed course instead, walking straight to the offices of the newspaper.

Thanks to Thane Grier, she knew her way about and headed for the editorial offices, hoping he would be there. To her relief, he was.

He nearly spilled his tea as he fumbled to his feet, startled to see her. "Miss Grayson."

"Good morning."

"Wel-welcome."

"Thank you."

"What are you doing here?"

"I wanted to read some old articles. Would that be possible?"

He arched his brows. "Yes…if you've the patience of a saint. You must go through many, many papers to find anything specific."

"I don't wish to go back terribly far. I want to read everything I can on the murders of Hudson Porter, Jack Prine and Giles Brandon."

Grier's brows hiked up.

"Indulge me?" she said softly.

He lifted his arms. "I'll help you."

"I don't want to take you away from your work."

"I've been staring at the same two words for quite some time now," he told her. "A break will do me good."

Thane led her to the newspaper's morgue and introduced her to the clerk there, a cheerful lady in her early sixties who was happy to steer them in the right direction. The room seemed huge; there were boxes of files everywhere. The woman, however, knew where everything was, at least by date, and since they were seeking relatively recent news, it was not so difficult a task. Between the three of them, they soon had an array of papers on a desk, and Mrs. Easton, the clerk, went on about her business.

"What exactly are you looking for?" Thane asked. "I could be of more help if you would enlighten me."

"I don't know. I'm reading between the lines."

"Don't tell me you're trying to discover who the murderer might be?"

She shrugged.

"There's no evidence in the files," he told her.

She hesitated. "Do you remember the Ripper case?"

"I was young, but who can forget it?"

"There were all manner of theories put about."

"There still are."

"True. But from everything I've read, it's most likely those murders were committed by a deranged individual with not a trace of the complex elements people want to afford the current killer, such as thinking he might be in some way attached to the Crown."

Thane frowned, shaking his head. "You've lost me already."

"What if the murders had nothing to do with the present situation?"

"You mean the uproar over the monarchy?"

"I do. What if the murders were a cover-up?"

"For what?"

"I don't know. That's why I'd like to read all the papers."

"All right, let's read."

Time ticked by. Thane looked up at Ally. "For a moment I thought I was on to something."

"Oh?"

"Insane housekeepers," he said with a sigh.

"But...?"

"Then I remembered Hattie—Giles Brandon's housekeeper. She is barely skin and bones. I don't think she could have successfully wielded a weapon against him."

"Perhaps she wasn't working alone," Ally said.

"How does an insane housekeeper coerce someone into working with them?" Thane asked.

She lifted her hands. "I don't know."

He hesitated, staring at her. "I wish you worked here," he said softly.

She flushed. "Thank you."

His mouth twisted slightly. "What we should do is find out the truth about you."

She laughed. "Oh, Thane! There is no truth about me."

He sat back in his chair, stretching. "Ally—if I may—you are an incredible woman. I can't believe any man, titled or no, would give up a chance to spend his life with you—once he knew you."

"That's very sweet."

"No, no, listen. The key is that the man know you. But your engagement to Farrow was set years ago. Lord Farrow couldn't possibly have known you would grow up to be such a beauty, a woman of kindness and intelligence—"

"Thane, please believe me—"

"Why pledge your son—when you're the Earl of Warren—to an orphan foundling simply because your dear friend has decided to become godparent to the child? Perhaps if you had been Brian's child from an affair..."

"I am not Brian's child."

"How do you know?"

"Camille. If I were Brian's child, if he had been involved in an affair before marriage, neither of them would have denied me. They are fierce in their sense of right and wrong, and Camille, even as his legitimate wife, would have demanded all the earl's children be raised in his house."

"Maybe Camille doesn't know." Thane looked perplexed, as if her reasoning made sense. "Still...there is something," he insisted.

"I don't know. My memories begin in the woods, and that's all I can say," she told him. "Back to work."

"Studying the case, yes," he murmured.

After a while, he looked at her again. "You're still getting married on Saturday?"

"It's the plan," she murmured.

"I've not been invited."

She looked up at him. "Well, it's my wedding, so you're invited."

"Thank you."

Suddenly Ally realized that time was slipping away. In fact, she had stayed far too long. She had to get back. She rose, and Thane instantly did the same. "Thane, I must leave, but thank you so much."

"Will you come back?" he asked her.

"I hope so. I'm sure you think that I can't possibly be useful, that I'm just playing at all this, but...thank you. Thank you so much."

"It's my pleasure. I am happy to indulge you at any time."

Smiling, she hurried out, wondering if the essay she had left on the clerk's desk had made its way to the editor yet, and if her latest piece would see print in the morning's paper.

Thane watched her leave.

Then he followed.

BY THE TIME HE REACHED the museum, Mark was afraid he had grown so distraught he might well be acting like a madman.

But he had arrived at the lodge to find no one in residence. Since Bertram wasn't about and only the hounds were keeping guard duty, he forced himself to be reasonable. His father usually had business in London; he had, in fact, only remained at the lodge so long rather than return to the town house in order that Ally might stay with them there, in safety.

If his father had allowed Bertram to take him in the carriage, rather than riding on his own, it had to mean that Ally was with him.

By the time he reached the city, much of the day had gone by. And in London, even knowing his father would be found in the Houses of Parliament, actually reaching Lord Joseph Farrow was no easy task. He didn't find his father, but he did at last realize Bertram would have the carriage waiting, and when he found Bertram, he was directed to the museum.

At the museum, he had a moment's peace when he found Camille. "Yes, Ally is here. She is about in the museum somewhere."

The museum was vast. But no one had seen Ally in hours.

In the end, as dusk began to fall and it came close to closing time, he knew she had only used the museum as an excuse to roam the city, something that he, coming to know her so well, knew he should have realized earlier. It wasn't that she intentionally lied. She simply believed in herself so strongly that she would humor others, so they, too, would believe she was safe, since she certainly believed she was in no danger herself.

He went back to Camille's office.

"Camille, if she returns, hold her. Under lock and key if necessary," he said, and then he left the museum, thinking he would begin looking for her at the post office. She simply didn't understand the danger she had cast herself into if others knew she was writing as A. Anonymous, he thought in frustration.

LONDON WAS ALWAYS BUSY. Ally loved it and considered it a wonderful city. And yet, to her amazement, when she turned the corner, heading down the street to the museum entrance, it suddenly seemed very empty.

She could hear music from various pubs and restaurants. From distant streets came the clip-clop of horses' hooves. But darkness was falling.

A streetlight flickered...and died. The shadows seemed to grow darker...deeper.

She hurried forward, trying to reassure herself. Businesses were still open. Workers were sipping their pints behind the doors of pubs.

Then she heard the sound of the carriage approaching.

She turned back to look.

It was a grand carriage, moving slowly down the street. Because of the shadows, she couldn't see the driver.

Odd that it was moving so slowly.

She looked forward, quickening her pace again.

The carriage drew abreast of her.

And stopped.

"Alexandra!"

The sound of her name, called in a husky tone, sent shivers racing down her spine. She started to run.

The carriage moved again, drew past her, then stopped.

The door opened. A man stepped out. A big man.

"Alexandra!"

The voice was deep, rough. All she saw was the huge figure, a black cape swirling around it. She started to run, aware of footsteps behind her. She screamed as she felt a heavy hand clutch her shoulder.

"Stop!"

She was swung around—and found herself staring into the face of Lord Lionel Wittburg.

"Lord Wittburg!" He was flushed, his eyes wild. She fought his hand. He was old, but he was still powerful. She remembered that he had been a military man. He had never lost the physique or the strength of a hardened soldier.

"Come with me. You must. *Now.*"

"Lord Wittburg, you have to let me go—I'm expected at the museum."

"No, you must come with me."

She gasped as he reached for her, lifting her. She slammed her fists against his chest, but he was like a stone wall, half carrying, half dragging her toward the carriage.

Suddenly she was ripped from Wittburg's hold and fell to the road as Wittburg let out a fierce bellow. Ally was aware of a second man in the street. Wittburg was like a man gone mad, swinging his fists. But the second man ducked, rose and sent a jab flying.

Lord Lionel Wittburg went down, a soft gasp escaping his lungs.

"Ally!"

It was Mark. Impossible…but real.

He came to her, helping her to her feet. There was the thunder of more footsteps, people streaming from the museum and nearby pubs, and from the carriage, a man jumping down to the street.

Mark was holding her close. She could hear his heart beating. She looked at him, but he was staring at Lord

Wittburg. The man's coachman was at his side by then. Mark left her and went to hunker down next to Wittburg. He stared at the coachman. "What was he doing?"

Wittburg groaned and opened his eyes. He clutched Mark by the lapels. "The truth...she has to know the truth. Tell her the truth."

"Lord Wittburg, for the love of God, what truth?" Mark asked urgently.

Lord Wittburg's eyes closed again.

Mark looked up at the crowd that was now beginning to surround them. "Someone, call an ambulance!"

LORD LIONEL WITTBURG was going to live; Mark had only knocked him out with his sound jab to the jaw.

But what happened after was chaos. The streets were filled with people. An ambulance took Lord Wittburg, his coachman at his side, to the hospital. The police spoke with Mark and Ally. Camille arrived on the scene, then Brian, and then Lord Farrow.

Lord Wittburg's carriage was impounded by the police, to be held until the situation was cleared up. Ally insisted that the elderly gentleman had simply wanted to speak with her, not cause her harm, but he had not seemed himself, and yes, he had frightened her.

Finally they wound up back in Camille's office. Hunter, whose office was next to Camille's, joined them, as well.

Everyone was sweetly concerned about Ally, who kept insisting she was fine.

"I had thought you were staying in the museum," Camille told her.

There was silence, with everyone staring at her.

"Where were you?" Mark asked quietly.

She was afraid to reply.

"Ally?" he persisted.

"I was looking in shop windows," she said. It wasn't really a lie. She *had* looked in several.

"It's obvious you are in danger," Mark said. "Why are you so determined to provoke it? And the shops are long closed."

"I...tarried too long," she said. She was seated, drinking tea laced with whiskey. Camille sat near her. The men all stood, staring at her.

"Ally," Brian said, "it's not like you to cause so much concern to those who love you."

Those words hurt the most.

"Forgive me," she said simply. "I'm truly sorry."

"If you're so sorry, perhaps you could consider telling the truth," Mark said.

She stared at him. Again there was silence in the room.

"I was at the newspaper office," she said flatly.

"Why?" Hunter demanded.

"I was going through old articles," she said.

Her answer seemed to baffle everyone but Mark, who continued to stare at her. She decided to change the subject. "What happened tonight is sad, not dire," she told them. "Lord Wittburg needs your concern, not me. I think the poor man is losing his mind."

"All right, we're solving nothing here," Brian said. "We all need to go home, have dinner and get some rest."

The look Mark was giving her was chilling. "I think... I think I should return to my aunts."

"The cottage in the woods? No. Would you risk their lives?" Camille asked.

"You will come back to the lodge," Mark said.

She started to shake her head. The others, she knew, would acquiesce to him—she was about to become his wife, after all. They didn't know everything she did, not how things stood between them.

She was startled when he came to her, drawing her to her feet. "Don't come with me because I have demanded it. Come with me because I am asking you to do it. Because you care that it is so important to me." She was stunned by the heat and depth of emotion in his words, and by the cloud of passion in his eyes.

She found she couldn't speak, so she simply nodded.

"Tomorrow we will, I hope, find a sane explanation for all of this," Brian said pragmatically.

As it was so late by then, Lord Farrow suggested that they spend the night at the town house, and it was agreed. Ally protested that she had no possessions there, but as Kat and Hunter lived in the city, Hunter promised to see that clothing and toiletries were sent over for her disposal.

Mark rode in the carriage, his horse tied behind. At the town house, Ally met another of Lord Farrow's servants, a charming man named Jeeter, who greeted them at the door. He didn't cluck over her like a mother hen, but he was efficient, starting a meal, drawing a bath and serving brandy all at once, so it seemed. Ally found herself in another elegantly appointed room, and while she bathed away the dirt and grime of the city, a messenger arrived with fresh clothing. As she lay at her ease in the tub, she was aware of the faint sound of voices below: Mark and his father. She closed her eyes.

Mark had said nothing about Lord Wittburg's words when he had accosted her. She, too, had remained silent, realizing Mark had probably decided to speak to his father alone. He had been so angry with her because she had gone to the newspaper....

And yet...

He had been there in her defense, appearing miraculously, when she had been in trouble. And then he had come to her, *asking* her to stay with him....

She was in love with him. No matter his name or person. If she could just...learn to understand him.

No. If she could just somehow convince him that he must love her as she was.

WITH ALLY UPSTAIRS and Jeeter doing his best to create an impromptu meal, Mark faced his father in the parlor.

"This situation cannot go any further. Lionel Wittburg was absolutely convinced he had to speak with Ally. And when he looked at me, he told me that I had to tell her the truth. What truth, Father? I must know what's going on. And why, in God's name, would you not trust me?" The last he asked with a certain amount of anguish.

Then he was sorry, when he saw how weary Joseph Farrow looked as he sank into the leather chair by the fire, shaking his head. "I was sworn to secrecy."

"Father—"

"Yes, I know. And I trust you. I have always trusted you. You know that. But some secrets are meant to be taken to the grave."

"Not when they are putting others in peril."

Joseph was silent again for a moment. "Brian Stirling and I agreed that you and Alexandra would be promised to each other because...the queen requested that it be so."

"The queen?"

Joseph leaned back. Mark took the chair opposite him, waiting for his father to talk. At last Joseph looked at him. "To many a tale, there is a grain of truth. This all came about when you were young and Ally only a child. It all goes back to the Ripper."

"The Ripper?" Mark said, astounded.

"I swear to you, the man the police believed to be Jack the Ripper is dead. Have you never wondered why the investigation stopped soon after the death of Mary Kelly?"

"The investigation didn't exactly stop," Mark said. But his father was right. He had been young at the time. Still, many of those involved had alluded to the fact that the never-identified man popularly known as Jack the Ripper was dead.

His father exhaled. "There were many who tried to create a link between the murders and the Crown."

"You're not going to tell me that the Crown was involved?" Mark demanded. "And how do you know all this?"

"Because Lady Maggie was nearly killed by the murderer. Thank God the killer lost his own life instead. I don't know all the details of those horrid times. I have never asked Maggie or James to explain everything. There is no absolute proof, no way to truly close the books. But the man died near the cottage where Ally grew up. Despite the rumors, there was no Ripper conspiracy involving the Crown, but the theory was born because Prince Eddie did, in fact, go through a form of marriage with a Catholic girl named Annie. As you know, the prince was ultimately destroyed by syphilis. And Annie…was not well. And, of course, a Catholic marriage wasn't legal."

Mark stared at his father. "You're telling me that the rumored child of this affair is…Ally?"

Joseph nodded. "She had to be protected, you see," he said softly. "As I was trusted, so I am now entrusting this information to you. But the truth can never be known." He sighed softly. "Haven't you seen how fanatical people can be when ideas of right and wrong are involved? How men can allow their concept of a greater good to lead them to heinous murder? There are those who fear—as they have done through the centuries—that a Catholic connection to the royal bloodline would be dangerous. There is no reason for us to allow the truth of Ally's lineage, to be made public. She should live a life unburdened by the fears and sins of the past. No one must know. But she is the queen's grandchild. A brilliant young woman, and a beauty. She must never be endangered by her position or wounded by her illegitimacy. No one must know. That was the queen's request."

"There are obviously others who know the truth. Lionel Wittburg, for one. And I would have been in a far better position to understand and protect Ally if *I* had known the truth, as well."

"I'm sorry. I gave my word, and I do not give my word lightly."

Mark lowered his head. His father's story was fantastic. He found the entire situation almost impossible to believe. He shook his head. "So Lord Wittburg...none of his...wandering has to do with anything current? In his mind he has seen the state of affairs now and confused it with something that happened in the past? He is combining the two—suspecting the monarchy might have been involved then and so might be involved now?"

"I don't know," Joseph said. "I just don't know."

Mark stood and walked to the hearth, gazing at the flames. "We held him up the other day, you know. He must not have reported the incident to the police, because I have neither seen nor heard a mention of it. I searched his carriage. Not a spot of blood. Ian remains convinced the murderer has escaped each crime scene in a carriage. I believe he is right. But...I went to see Hudson Porter's housekeeper today, and she was behaving very strangely."

"So we are no closer to the truth?"

Mark shrugged. "I feel we *are* closer, but we are missing something. When I spoke with the woman today, I actually found myself thinking it might be a conspiracy of housekeepers. But these men were killed by someone with strength. And then there is Ally. Was the cottage in the woods attacked because she has suddenly been deemed a danger due to current events, or because some- one has become aware of her birth? Or are the two con- nected in some way? Were some too quick to assume that, since the victims were anti-monarchists, the Crown was involved? Were others too willing to think martyrs to a cause would make it all the more meaningful? Draw- ing attention to the past forces one to see that what seems obvious is not always the truth."

Joseph was frowning at him.

"What?"

"You're not concerned...about Ally's identity."

"Only if it puts her in danger." Mark shook his head. "I don't care who her parents were. Ally matters to me."

Joseph smiled slowly. "You two should marry and leave the country. Go to a distant hilltop in America, find a place in Australia. Get away from all this. Let others sort it out."

"We can't do that," Mark said. "We can't spend the rest of our lives looking over our shoulders, wondering."

He fell silent, seeing Ally appear at the top of the stairs. Joseph followed his son's gaze, saw her there and stood.

"Ally, you look refreshed and lovely," he said cheer- fully.

Mark could see her face, and he knew she was aware that she had been the topic of conversation. But he could see in her eyes the determination to play along with his father's light approach.

"This is a beautiful home," she said, coming down the

stairs. "And my accommodations are quite lovely. You are ever the gracious host, Lord Farrow."

"Let's see if Jeeter has concocted a meal for us, shall we?" the older man asked, offering his arm to escort her into the dining room.

Mid-meal, Joseph asked Ally if she was dismayed that the planning of her wedding was not in her own hands.

Ally laughed and told him, "Castle Carlyle is as fine a place as one could hope for. The aunts would be brokenhearted if they could not put their talents into a dress. I am not at all dismayed. The vows are what two people share. The rest is for others, and if it makes them happy to plan, then that makes me happy, as well."

When the meal was finished, Joseph stated that he was retiring. Ally wished both men good night and preceded Joseph up the stairs.

Mark followed more slowly, taking a brandy upstairs with him. He knew he would not sleep. It didn't torment him in the least, knowing Ally's background. He was not dismayed at the illegitimate circumstances of her birth, nor was he impressed that she had a connection to royalty. Truth was not always as important as it should have been, though he knew that the perception of truth could be damning.

It had been a long day. He drew a bath, sipped the brandy and tried to keep his head from spinning.

Monarchists.

Anti-monarchists.

Housekeepers.

Jack the Ripper.

Conspiracy theories.

The true identity of Jack the Ripper remained unknown. Even those convinced they knew the truth were not *absolutely* certain. But most of those with access to the facts tended to agree that the heinous killer had not been a prince gone insane, nor even a guardian of that prince. He had been a deranged individual, most probably a man unknown outside his small world.

Where did that get him?

Perhaps the murders now were not on a grand scale. Perhaps...

Perhaps the political angle was but a facade to hide something far more mundane.

He rose and dried himself off.

Ally.

He was frightened for her.

He hesitated, then donned breeches and stepped out into the hallway. He walked the few steps to her door. It wasn't locked. He entered.

She wore a simple white cotton gown sent over by Lady Kat, hair clean and loose on the pillows, provocative as she slept in shadow. He strode to the bed, looking down. He saw that her eyes were open, watching him.

After a moment, she offered him a rueful smile. "It is your father's house," she reminded him softly.

"I ask no man, my father included, to forgive me for taking what is mine—what I love," he added very softly, and stretched out beside her. She turned toward him, lips curving softly, sensually, into a small smile.

"Do you?" she asked softly.

"Love you? Yes. How absurd, some might say. Love cannot be so easy or so quick. Yet I say, damn them all. Do I love you? Yes. Do you vex me? Indeed."

She reached out, her elegant fingers falling lightly on his face, tracing his flesh with a touch so light and provocative that he strained from the soul to feel it more fully.

"I love you, too," she said. "And actually, it's quite annoying, because you have that noble arrogance, or perhaps it's simply a *male* arrogance."

"Perhaps we could sort some of it out over the next forty or fifty years?" he inquired, setting his fingers against her lips to silence her.

He was startled when she sat up, drawing the white gown over her head, tossing it aside. In the moonlight and shadow, her body gleamed—throat, shoulders, breasts like a perfect sculpture. Her hair gleamed with a strange brilliance, a cape that didn't cover but teased. She leaned against him and took the initiative, naked breasts pressing against his chest, strands of golden hair teasing his bare flesh as her face hovered above his for a moment. Then her lips lowered and brushed his with their caress.

The very essence of his being seemed to tremble and tighten. He fought to stay still, to allow her to tease… touch…and taste. She eased her body against him, moved her body sinuously along his. Her actions were instinctive. He prayed that this was truly more than mere passion, that she trusted him, that their battles were tempered by the emotions that lay beneath.

Thought left him, fading into oblivion as pure sensation began to take flight. Her lips nuzzled his chest; her teeth lightly danced against his nakedness. Her fingers moved down the length of him, caught at the waistband of his hastily donned pants, urged them open, slid lower....

He swept her into his arms, discarding the hateful barrier of clothing. He caught sight of her face in the moonlight and crushed her to him, his lips not tender then, but avid, tormented. He touched her in turn, hands rounding every curve. Her fingers curled around his buttocks, and she pressed him back in return, her touch sliding tauntingly along his erection at first, then growing more forceful, sliding, gripping. He pressed her back against the mattress, eager to taste her flesh. She returned his onslaught, sliding against him again, lower and lower...the hot sluicing of her tongue bringing thunder into his heart, his veins, pumping into his every extremity.

Their lovemaking was fierce, desperate...tender. The world became nothing but the need to reach a pinnacle, then the need to drift down. And then the need rose again. He could not cease touching her, nor aching for her lips....

Again and again, shadow and darkness gently cradled the most explosive climaxes...and returned them again to that place of sanity where the slightest touch was a treasure. Even as exhaustion came, they lay together and, in silence, treasured the feel of flesh against flesh.

They spoke no more that night, both silently agreed that there were moments that must be treasured and never questioned.

CHAPTER FOURTEEN

THEY WERE AT BREAKFAST when the telephone rang.

Lord Farrow jumped, rolled his eyes and apologized. "I just cannot accustom myself to that racket."

Jeeter came into the breakfast room, looking at Mark. "It is Detective Douglas," he said.

Mark excused himself and disappeared. When he returned, he appeared to be troubled.

"Well?" Joseph asked.

"I don't believe it," Mark said. He stared at his father. "They searched Lord Wittburg's carriage. They found a black cape encrusted with what they believe to be blood. And blood spots around the carriage."

Joseph stared at his son in stunned silence. "*Lionel?*"

Ally shook her head. "No."

"I find it impossible to believe myself. He could not

have gone so insane. He is not an agile man—and his coachman denies ever picking up Lord Wittburg anywhere near any of the murder scenes."

"Lord Wittburg was distressed, Mark. He was not making sense. But I don't believe he meant me harm," Ally insisted.

"He remains in the hospital," Mark said. He ignored his breakfast, seemingly distracted as he said, "I have to go in. Father—"

"I have nothing urgent today. I think we will take Ally to see the aunts."

Ally nodded, wishing rather desperately that she could go with Mark. Something was very wrong. She refused to believe what seemed to be so apparently the truth.

"Mark, could...could the police perhaps have...do you think...?"

"That the police falsified the evidence or put it there? I don't believe that, either," Mark said. "Forgive me. I have to go."

His father nodded. Mark rose to leave just as Jeeter walked in with the newspaper. Mark paused, taking the paper. Ally was certain he had taken it to see if the news of Lionel Wittburg's impending arrest might be in it.

She was stunned when he stared at her, a veil of pure silver heating his gaze to something so venomous that she shrank back in her chair.

"It appears that A. Anonymous is writing again," he said, his voice sharp and penetrating. "We'll talk later."

He cast the paper on the table and strode out. Ally longed to snatch it up, but Lord Farrow had already reached for it. "The fellow's essays are quite good. Whatever caused such a snap in Mark's temper?" Lord Farrow murmured. "Nothing on Lord Wittburg," he murmured gratefully. "Very interesting opinion piece, though. Suggesting there might be a different motive entirely for the crimes."

His head was bowed as he read.

Ally had no more taste for breakfast. "Excuse me, I'll just get ready to leave," she murmured, and fled the table. How she longed to be elsewhere. But she knew, on that day particularly, Lord Farrow would not let her out of his sight.

Upstairs, she paced the bedroom. Mark was furious again. She ached as she thought how very close they had grown...how he could whisper he loved her...then go off like a flare. She had done nothing wrong, she told herself. In fact, had it not been for him, she would not even have written such an essay.

She must have paced and seethed longer than she knew. A tap at the door sounded, and she heard Lord Farrow ask, "Ally? Are you ready?"

"Yes, yes, of course."

She tried very hard to think of casual conversation as they traveled from London deep into the woods. Her efforts, however, proved unnecessary. Lord Farrow seemed to have sunk into a deep retrospection himself. After the first half hour, she was grateful when they seemed to have settled into a comfortable silence.

She was startled to see a man seated on the porch of the cottage, whittling a stick.

He seemed equally startled to see the carriage and stood as they rode up.

"Patrick," Lord Farrow said. "Good to see you."

Ally stared at the man. He was a tall redhead who flushed as he looked at her and offered a rueful smile along with his hand. "Patrick MacIver, Miss Grayson."

"Patrick is one of Mark's good friends, my dear."

She laughed suddenly, knowing they had met. "A highwayman, I believe?"

Patrick paled and stared at Lord Farrow.

"It's all right, Patrick."

The red-haired man shrugged. "We have met," he murmured.

She squared her shoulders; this man deserved no blame. "I assume you are here because you're guarding my aunts. Thank you."

He relaxed, color returning to his cheeks, and his smile became warm and very real. "I have been so honored. There are three of us entrusted with the task, and what we had thought no more than duty has become pure pleasure. They appear so sweet, yet they are cunning. They knew us immediately. I'm quite willing to bet we've all gained a full stone in weight, and we will have handsome new waistcoats for the wedding."

Ally didn't get a chance to reply. The sisters had heard the carriage arrive. Violet came out first, her arms flying in the air before she wrapped them around Ally. Merry was behind her, and Edith behind Merry. The two wolfhounds bounded out after the sisters, cutting the air with their deep baying, massive tails wagging with a frenzy that might well have knocked some-one over.

Then, of course, there had to be tea.

But when Ally went in with the aunts, Lord Farrow stayed outside with Patrick, and she knew her soon-to-be father-in-law was telling the other man about the latest events. She refrained from ruining the aunts' pleasure by telling them anything. They were chatting about her dress, telling her how beautiful it was, then insisting she not see it until it was time to dress on Saturday morning.

"It's not going to be quite the affair that was always intended," Merry said, shaking her head a bit sadly.

"But magnificent still," Edith said.

"Very fine," Violet said sagely.

Ally laughed and hugged all three. "If you darlings are there, it will be all I could want."

"Oh, but Lord Stirling must be there—to give you away," Merry said, eyes wide.

"Of course I want the guardians there, as well. But quite seriously, my loves…you are my life."

"Oh," Merry said, and she started to sniffle.

"Don't you go crying," Violet warned sternly, then drew out her own handkerchief.

Edith let out a sob.

"Oh, please, please," Ally said, gathering them in an awkward hug once again.

"But…we're losing our baby."

"You'll never lose me. *Never*," she vowed.

The kettle began to whistle. "Tea," Violet said, composing herself.

"The scones are in the bread box, dear," Merry told Ally. "Goodness, we will be so busy in the next two days. Tomorrow we have Lady Maggie's charity event, and Saturday I suppose it would be best if we all returned to the castle after we're finished in London tomorrow. I hope that will suit Lord Farrow. But how else can we fit everything in?"

"I should be ashamed," Ally said. "I had all but forgotten tomorrow."

"Good heavens, child," Violet said sternly. "Don't be ridiculous. You've so much going on. In fact, you should not go at all."

"I must go. I've gone every year for...well, as long as I can remember," Ally said.

"We'll ask Mark," Edith said.

"No. We will ask no one. It is Lady Maggie's event, and I will be there."

"But your wedding is the next day," Edith said.

"And what do I have to do but attend?" Ally said, and laughed. "Everything has been taken care of for me."

The aunts looked at one another skeptically.

"Well..." said Violet, and the other two echoed her.

"It is decided," Ally told them firmly.

"Then perhaps Lord Farrow will not mind transporting some of the food we've prepared," Merry murmured.

"Lord Stirling will send his carriage in the morning, as always," Edith reminded her.

Ally suddenly noticed all of the boxes and containers around the kitchen. The aunts had certainly been industrious. The poor in the East End would receive not just sustenance; they would receive deliciousness. She laughed suddenly and hugged them all again, one by one. "You will never, never, ever lose me," she promised them. "No child was ever so lucky," she swore. Then she drew back when she heard Merry sniff again.

"Tea. And we must make Bertram come in, as well. If we don't go get him, he will read atop the driver's box and forget he needs to eat," Ally said.

Violet set her hands on her hips. "I will make sure he comes in."

Ally smiled.

Bertram didn't stand a chance.

MARK SAT IN IAN'S OFFICE, aware he was still steaming and that every few seconds he clenched his teeth so hard that the clicking could be heard all across London. The paper lay across Ian's desk, and the other man was bent over it, reading.

What did he have to do to make her realize the danger she kept putting herself in?

"Excellent article," Ian said, looking up from the paper. "Except, of course, we now know that, sad as it may seem, Lord Lionel is guilty of murder. Poor soul. He lost his mind somewhere."

Mark had to wonder then if he wasn't angry about the article in part because Ally had somehow come to the same conclusion that had plagued his own mind. *What if they had all been missing the forest for the trees?*

"You've spoken to Lord Wittburg at the hospital, I imagine?" Mark said.

"Of course. He denies everything."

"I think he is telling the truth."

"Mark, we found the evidence."

Mark shook his head firmly. "I stopped his carriage just the other day. There was no cloak, no blood. The evidence was put into that carriage sometime later."

Ian stiffened. "Mark, we may not solve every crime, but I'd swear by any of my officers!"

"I'm not suggesting your officers did anything."

"Well then…?"

"There was mass chaos on the street. A throng appeared in response to the fracas."

"All right. How did whoever happened to be holding this evidence know that Lord Wittburg's carriage would be there?" Ian asked.

Mark stood. "I need to see Lionel."

Ian shook his head. "Mark, you don't want it to be him."

"No. I can't believe it is him. I need to talk to him."

"Of course," Ian said with a sigh. "Do you want me with you?"

"Indeed. I want you to hear what I hear. But I also want you to get your men busy checking on bank records."

"Bank records?" Ian said.

Mark tapped the newspaper. "You said it was an excellent article. It suggests maybe we are looking at grand motives when perhaps it is all part of something more personal. Find out who benefited from the death of each man. We know, from the housekeeper, that Eleanor

Brandon *apparently* adored her husband. But he remained rude to her. I don't know anything about the relationship between Jack and Elizabeth Prine."

"Hudson Porter wasn't married," Ian said. "And what are you thinking? That these women conspired together to kill their husbands?"

"Someone else was involved, someone who perhaps did want to boost the cause of the anti-monarchists. But I think it would be expedient to discover who gained financially from these deaths."

"Giles Brandon's money came from his wife."

"And maybe she wanted it back. Maybe I'm going off on a tangent. But before we hang Lord Wittburg, I'd like to be certain we know the truth."

THE AFTERNOON WAS LOVELY, and even in her agitated state, Ally enjoyed herself tremendously.

As she prepared to gather up the remains of the tea, the largest hound-on-loan, Sylvester, bounded to the door.

"What is it, boy?" she asked. "Nature calling?"

She opened the door for him and stepped outside. He began to bark, then ran off toward one of the trails. She followed him, then stopped, certain she heard a rustling in the forest ahead.

"Sylvester!" she called.

The dog didn't return.

"Sylvester!" she called again. By then the female was out, and Lord Farrow was by her side. He turned back toward the cottage, tense. "Patrick!"

Patrick appeared instantly.

"You're armed?" Lord Farrow asked.

Patrick nodded, lifting the edge of his jacket to show his gun. Lord Farrow nodded, and the two of them started down the trail, following the female hound, Millicent. Ally started to follow, as well.

"Go back to the cottage," Lord Farrow told her.

"But—"

"Please. Bertram will not leave you, nor the aunts," he assured her.

She stood tensely, allowing them to go. She nearly started, suddenly aware that someone was at her shoulder. She turned. Bertram.

"Miss...it would be better if you were in the cottage. It might be nothing, but..."

She sighed and walked back into the cottage. The aunts were still picking up, unaware of anything wrong. "Would you get that jar of jam, dear?" Merry asked.

"Of course," she said. She helped in the kitchen, listening, tense.

Minutes later, the door to the cottage opened and the hounds rushed in, bumping furniture out of place as they did so. Lord Farrow and Patrick followed, talking casually to each other.

Ally stared at Lord Farrow.

"I think I'd love another cup of tea, if one is available. Violet?" he said.

In frustration, Ally stared at him, then at Patrick, who shrugged. She let out a breath of frustration, knowing she was just going to have to wait.

LORD WITTBURG SEEMED to have gone terribly downhill.

Mark could easily understand why. He was being treated in a facility where the criminally insane were kept.

The smell was horrid. And though he had been brought to a private—albeit barred—room, the strange screams and cries of the demented were all too audible.

Mark sat by his bedside. Lord Wittburg opened tired eyes to him. He half managed a smile.

"Mark."

"Lord Wittburg."

He wasn't unaware of his surroundings, Mark thought, as the older man shook his head. "That I have come to this."

"Lord Wittburg—"

"I murdered no one, Mark."

"Your Grace, I know you did not."

The elderly man took his hand and squeezed it. "I believe you," he whispered, little substance to his voice. "I shall need an excellent legal defense."

"Lord Wittburg—"

"Those things were put into my carriage," he said, his voice still weak but filled with anger.

"By whom?" Ian couldn't help but demand from the doorway.

Mark leaned low. "Your Grace, did anyone know you would be searching for Ally near the museum?"

Lord Wittburg didn't answer. His eyes had closed. Mark thought he had drifted off.

"I saw the fellow from the paper. He was on the street," Lord Wittburg said suddenly.

"Which fellow?" Mark asked.

"Grier. Thane Grier."

"Anyone else?" Mark asked.

Wittburg exhaled. "I'd been at the club."

"Yes?"

"Talking with Doyle. The author chap. Arthur Conan Doyle. Sad fellow. His wife is quite sick."

"Who else was there?" Mark asked.

"Oh...the usual. Sir Angus Cunningham had come in, that was not so usual. But Sir Andrew Harrington had invited him for tea...so much happening these days."

"Anyone else?"

"The usual." Eyes closed again, Lord Wittburg smiled. "No women, though. The men... they were talking about the changing world. But the club is still a sanctuary! No women."

"Lord Wittburg, can you think of anything else? Why were you so determined to speak with Ally?"

His eyes flew open. "She needs to know. To safeguard herself."

"I will safeguard her," Mark promised.

Wittburg's eyes closed again.

"Lord Wittburg?" Mark said.

There was no reply. The man's eyes stayed closed.

The orderly who had brought them in gently tapped Mark on the shoulder. "Sir, he has been sedated. I don't believe he'll wake again for hours."

Mark nodded and rose. He and Ian walked out together.

"So now...what? Arthur Conan Doyle has decided to experiment before he writes, so he set out to commit murder and plant evidence?" Ian asked wearily.

"Amusing, my friend, amusing."

"What has this to do with your earlier theory—housekeepers gone mad?" Ian asked.

"No women, he said. I think it's interesting that the fact was a topic of conversation," Mark told him.

"Thane Grier tends to be about whenever something has happened," Ian said.

"He's a journalist. It's his job to keep his ears open and appear at any newsworthy happening," Mark mused.

"I'm sad to say that we've nothing as yet," Ian said. "Nothing that will help Lord Wittburg."

"Get those bank records for me. And the men's wills," Mark said.

On the street, he paused. "Ian, I think we should pay a visit to Eleanor Brandon again."

"She was devastated by her husband's death, Mark."

"Let's see if she remains devastated."

Ian let out a deep sigh. "All right."

NEITHER ELEANOR BRANDON nor her housekeeper, Hattie, was pleased by another visit.

Tea was not offered. In fact, Hattie was loath to invite them in. Ian insisted.

Eleanor met them in the parlor. She was in black, and wore it well. She was far calmer than she had appeared before.

"Why are you back? You should be searching for my husband's killer," she said, her tone hostile.

Ian looked to Mark.

"Eleanor, we've been concerned. We've come to find out how you're doing. Are you having any difficulties, financial or otherwise?"

"No. If you've come to help me...just leave. What I need now is peace in my own home."

"Of course, of course," Mark told her. "Well, then, we'll be going."

Ian stared at him. He shrugged.

Outside the house, Ian stared at him as if he'd lost his mind. "You made us go there for that?"

"I think her pretense of being so hysterical when she burst into Lord Stirling's party for Ally was very well acted."

"How can you know that?"

"I don't know it. I think it. We need to speak with her sister."

Again Ian sighed. "I verified the alibi, Mark."

"I want more."

"It's a long ride."

"So we'll take a long ride."

WHEN THEY WERE LEAVING, Lord Farrow conferred with Patrick. Ally heard the latter say someone named Thomas would be coming, and that Geoff would soon follow, so he could let Mark know he need not worry, because between the three of them, they would not leave the cottage or the aunts alone.

Since Ally knew for a fact then that Patrick was one

of the highwaymen, she was certain that Geoff and Thomas finished out the foursome. After going through another round of hugs with the aunts, she went to Patrick and thanked him sincerely. He assured her gallantly that he was more than pleased to be of service.

In the carriage with Lord Farrow, she demanded, "Well? What did you find in the forest?"

"Nothing...and something."

"Lord Farrow!"

"Someone was there. I'm almost certain. They reached the road, though, and disappeared. I'm sorry we were too late, but I'm grateful to see my hounds know their duty, and now there will be two men guarding your aunts at all times."

"I'm very grateful," Ally murmured.

He shook his head, smiling suddenly. "With all that is going on, sometimes it's hard to see, but there are decent people in the world. They don't expect your gratitude for doing the right thing."

"Still, I *am* grateful."

When they reached the lodge, Ally discovered that Lord Farrow could cook, and he was happy for her assistance. He wanted Bertram tending to the stables and the horses, because they would be leaving again early in the morning. As he set a meat pie into the oven, Lord Farrow explained that he'd learned his skills in the military.

She dined with him alone, and he suggested an early night. She was exhausted and glad to comply. But once in bed, she didn't sleep.

She waited.

IT WAS EVENING WHEN they reached the home of Marianne York, sister to Eleanor Brandon. Miss York, a thin and prune-faced spinster, possessed a tart attitude and sniffed at the fact another London detective had come to see her.

"I wish I could tell you otherwise," she said with another sniff. "Eleanor was here. Not by invitation, but she *is* my sister, and she arrived. I warned her about marrying Giles Brandon. Throws her out of her own house, he does, just because he's writing."

"I'm curious. Your relationship is…not warm," Mark said pleasantly. "There are wonderful hotels in London where she might have spent a night."

"On what?" Marianne sneered.

Ian cleared his throat. He indicated the parlor, which was handsomely appointed. "Not to be indelicate, but…it's my understanding your father left you two well set."

Marianne's snort was loud. "I have my money, and that's a fact. Eleanor, that silly goose, put everything into Giles Brandon's name when she married him. I told her she was a fool. She told me I was a dried-up spinster. But I live well enough on my own. She lived in torment. Oh, don't tell me she was so ready to be browbeaten by his *genius*. She seethed. She was miserable, barely able to stand it when she was forced by circumstance to seek hospitality from me. But still, she knew I would be obliged to let her in."

"Well, thank you. Thank you for speaking with us," Mark said.

It was late. When they reached the street, they prepared to head in opposite directions. Mounting Galloway, Mark looked at Ian. "I think we really do need to look at things a bit more deeply, don't you agree? Perhaps pay a visit to Elizabeth Harrington Prine tomorrow?"

Ian gave his deepest sigh of the day. "Poor Sir Andrew will be quite distressed to discover his kin being questioned," he said with a shake of his head.

"Poor Lord Lionel might well hang," Mark reminded him.

Ian nodded. "I should have the records you requested by tomorrow. And yes, we'll visit Elizabeth."

Mark was certain his father would have chosen to ride to the lodge from the cottage in the woods. Weary, he headed Galloway for home.

Malcolm and Cara bounded out to meet him when he arrived. Bertram came from the stables, ready to take his horse. Exhausted, Mark thanked Bertram and headed into the house.

It was late, and the lodge was quiet. He was certain both his father and Ally had gone to bed.

He started for his room, then hesitated and slipped down the hall to hers. This time she was sleeping. He stood over the bed for several seconds, then lay down beside her. Her breathing was easy and deep.

He drew her into his arms and held her.

ALLY WOKE ALONE, AND YET…

She had the distinct impression that Mark had been there. She studied the bedding, the indentation in the pillow next to hers. She smiled. Then her smile became a frown.

How dare he go into such a fury over her article? He had plenty of explaining to do himself. For one thing, she was certain he had discovered the meaning behind Lionel Wittburg's words to her that evening, but he hadn't shared the information with her.

She hoped to accost him at breakfast.

But after dressing and finding Lord Farrow at the breakfast table with his coffee, she was in for deep disappointment. "Mark is off already, I'm afraid," he told her.

"Indeed."

Lord Farrow set his hand on hers. "It's important, or else he wouldn't leave you."

"Of course," she murmured, hoping he didn't hear the sarcasm in her voice.

"At any rate, I'm ready when you are."

"A sip of coffee, my lord, and I am ready, too," she returned.

Despite the distance from the lodge to the East End, they arrived in plenty of time. There were booths set up to provide food, and chairs arrayed for the events, everything located in the churchyard.

Ally knew that Maggie had received fierce criticism from many quarters for some of her unorthodox activities.

Maggie spoke to prostitutes about disease, and she handed out condoms. She was an entertaining speaker, explaining to her audience that thousands of years ago, the ancient Egyptians—without even understanding why—had learned that condoms made from linen or animal organs had prevented disease. Ally always watched Maggie, who was impatient with propriety when it stood in the way of health, with amusement. She was such a lady, yet facts about disease tripped off her tongue so easily.

Maggie ignored the outraged letters she received. She spoke with passion, assuring those who would condemn her that more starving mouths in the East End served no purpose. And since she was Lady Maggie, she prevailed.

Ally found herself assigned to the children's area. The elite of London had donated all manner of items, and poor wives with families, as well as prostitutes raising the off-spring of unknown fathers, came to her. Diapers, booties, blankets and clothing—including last season's no-longer-fashionable hats and shoes—were available for the needy. Ally also had soap, towels and a bathing tin that a lad kept emptying and refilling, since sometimes she couldn't bear to put a truly filthy urchin into new clothing.

After four straight hours on her feet, she had to admit she was glad when Merry came to tell her to take a break and that was that.

"But you're still working," Ally protested.

"Oh, no, dear. I just had a lovely tea break with Lady Maggie and the Reverend. Those two do go on, but how he loves and admires her. Slip around the corner there, and you'll find a sheltered little garden. Someone will bring your tea right along."

And so, glad for a chance to sit, Ally washed her

hands and wiped them on her apron, then started for the garden. She stopped near the entrance, seeing that Thane Grier was there, interviewing Maggie. They both paused, seeing her in return, and waved. She waved back and hurried on to a table.

She was barely seated when Thane joined her.

"Hello. Quite a day."

"It always is," she told him.

"That was your essay in the paper yesterday, wasn't it?" he asked her bluntly.

She gaped, taken off guard.

He lifted a hand. "You don't have to reply—you rather accidentally gave me the answer. But don't worry. Your secret is safe with me."

"I don't know what to say."

He grinned. "I've come to say thank you."

"For what?"

"I think you got me on to something."

"Oh?"

"I've started doing some silent investigating."

He was a handsome man, younger than she had thought him at first, and he seemed honestly grateful to her. She smiled and nodded, urging him on.

"Well," he said, looking around and lowering his voice, "Giles and Eleanor Brandon did not get along well at all. In public she worshiped the man. She allowed him to hold all kinds of meetings in the house. She had to. When they were married, she put all her assets into his name. Now that he's dead, she has everything back."

"Still, what does that prove?" Ally asked.

"It *proves* nothing. But greed is among the top motives for murder, and has been throughout history. Elizabeth Prine didn't have any money—until she married Jack Prine."

"And she inherited what he had?" Ally said.

He nodded. "Exactly."

"But Hudson Porter wasn't married," Ally pointed out.

Thane grinned. "Ah-ha! And there lies my great discovery."

"He was married?"

Thane shook his head. "No, though he does have relatives coming from America. But guess what?"

"Tell me!"

"The housekeeper was left a hefty sum." He sat back, staring at her smugly.

"That still doesn't prove anything."

His smile faded slightly. "No, but the fact that these three women have inherited vast sums is very suspicious, don't you think?"

She nodded. "But..."

"These women all know one another. Two of them socialized. And all had a reason to get rid of a man."

"Still, I don't believe any of them had the strength to kill a man like Giles Brandon. And you still have no proof of a conspiracy. Many people know one another but never conspire to commit murder."

"We have to find the evidence that these three did."

"We?"

"You started me on this."

"Yes, but I hardly have the freedom of movement to be an investigative reporter," she informed him.

He grinned at her. "I have taken the liberty of delivering a number of older articles to Lady Stirling for delivery to you. You see, I don't believe for a minute that Lord Wittburg is guilty of murder, though you will note, when you have a chance, I did an excellent write-up about his strange assault on you, his subsequent arrest and the discovery of damning evidence in his carriage."

"I don't believe he's guilty, either. I think he just wanted to talk to me. I do believe that we—or someone—must find the truth. If he is convicted of murder, I will be at fault."

"Never at fault—those who are evil are at fault," he told her gravely.

She smiled. "I haven't heard about any protests in the street lately—protests such as the one we saw in the village."

"The furor seems to be dying down," he agreed. "Well, until next time. If there is a next time."

Ally gazed at him. "This is quite incredible. An entire nation might be brought to its knees because a few women wished their husbands gone."

"A chilling thought, indeed," he agreed. Then he said, "So tomorrow is the day."

"Yes."

He shook his head in admiration. "Yet here, today, the bride tends to filthy, unwashed children, and the lady of the castle helps her dear friend educate prostitutes."

"What should I be doing?" she inquired, shrugging.

"Is there to be a honeymoon?"

"Am I being interviewed now?" she asked.

"Yes. If it's all right."

"I don't believe we're taking a honeymoon now. Perhaps in the future."

"Where is the bridegroom?" he asked. "Stupid question. Even I know where the bridegroom is."

Ally frowned. "You do?"

"Of course. He often works with Detective Douglas." He stared at her. "He was instrumental in bringing in the Sheffield killer several months ago. You didn't know?"

"It must have slipped my mind," Ally murmured dryly.

"Well, be prepared, you mustn't expect the usual with your soon-to-be husband."

"And he must learn not to expect the usual with me. Sadly, it's time I get back to my duties. Thane, it's been wonderful to see you. And I will see you tomorrow."

"Of course. And don't forget your envelope. Study those articles. Though I guess you'll be a bit busy. Still, when you get a chance..."

"I'll get a chance. I promise," Ally assured him.

She had quite overstayed her tea time, she was certain. Thoughtful, she returned to her position.

ELIZABETH PRINE, REGAL in her widow's weeds, greeted Mark politely and formally, but with a puckered brow. "How are you? Have you come about my husband again? Of course you have. You would not have the poor taste to make a social call on a recently bereaved woman."

"Elizabeth, we need help," he told her. "May I come in?"

She hesitated slightly. "Of course."

"Elizabeth, I honestly believe someone in the political movement you and Jack embraced is responsible for these killings."

"Mark," she said softly, forgetting decorum. "That's what you wish to believe."

"How could anyone else have obtained the keys?"

"My housekeeper must have been negligent."

"Eleanor Brandon's housekeeper isn't the negligent type in the least."

"I'm happy for Eleanor Brandon."

"Here's the thing—the murders are connected. The men were killed in the same manner."

"They are anti-monarchists. So why look to another anti-monarchist!"

"Elizabeth, the killer knew your husband."

She sighed. "Mark, I wish I could help."

"Were you and Jack...I am sorry to ask, but were you and Jack having any marital difficulties?"

"Mark Farrow!"

"I have to ask, Elizabeth."

"From what I understand," she said sharply, "they have found the killer in Lord Lionel Wittburg. Oh, yes, a supporter of the Crown," she said angrily. "You are here, tormenting me, when it seems that, however great a man he may once have been, he has snapped. Mark, please, I am so weary."

He hesitated. "Really, Elizabeth?" he asked very softly. "There's been a suggestion that...you've been seeing someone."

She gasped, then rose in indignation.

But not quickly enough, he thought. "How dare you!"

"I dare because I am looking for a murderer."

"Get out of my house, Mark. And don't come back. I don't care how esteemed your position is."

"Thank you for your hospitality, Elizabeth," he said. He walked to the door, aware she was following him. "By the way, where's your housekeeper today?"

"Gone. If you must know, I fired her after Jack's death. Now, get out!"

"One last thing, Elizabeth. Witnesses have put you with a man."

It was a lie. But it struck home, and it struck hard. Despite her desperate play at dignity, he saw that the color had completely drained from her face.

She slammed the door behind him.

He didn't know if her lover was inside with her or not.

But he now knew the housekeeper had quite probably been fired immediately after the murder—and that Elizabeth Prine had been concealing her lover in the house when he had visited with Ian Douglas.

He had taken a stab in the dark, followed a hunch and succeeded.

And he had largely done it, he had to admit, because of Ally's article. Husbands and wives, and the dramas between them. Love and hate. The very thin lines...

Some spouses might seek to rid themselves of a partner because of money, one of the oldest motives for crime.

Others might kill for love, for hate. Kill for the freedom to be with another.

He turned away from the house. He had to convince Ian to set men to watch the house as quickly as possible.

Something else had been evident today, as well.

Elizabeth Prine had started to pack. The little knickknacks that had adorned the house were no longer there.

She was planning to flee.

CHAPTER FIFTEEN

ALLY HAD FORGOTTEN THAT SHE and the aunts were going straight to Castle Carlyle. After a very long but productive day, she joined Camille and the aunts in the Stirlings' carriage, while Brian rode behind, and they made their way home.

The chatter along the way was exuberant. The aunts found it absolutely delightful that Lord and Lady Stirling, and Sir Hunter and Lady Kat MacDonald, had all pooled their resources for such a wonderful day of charity. Camille, amused, reminded them that there had been a time when royal children were required to ritually bathe the feet of the poor and the ailing in the church. Merry decided such an ordeal was perhaps better left in the past—she had smelled a few feet during the day.

Despite the excitement, both Merry and Edith were nodding off by the time they neared the castle, a head bobbing upon each of Violet's shoulders as they traveled. Ally, seated next to Camille, was ready to nod off herself. At the castle, she stepped wearily out of the carriage and helped the aunts down. Camille came last, offering her a large envelope.

"Thane Grier asked me to deliver this to you," Camille told her.

"What is it, dear?" Violet asked.

"Oh, just some old articles. He's a nice man, and we have talked about how I love to read."

"How nice," Edith said, stifling a yawn.

Camille looked at her with a brow arched questioningly. Ally merely smiled, and headed for the entry.

"Good heavens, but we all need baths," Violet murmured, wiping at a smudge on her hand.

"Yes, let me get you up to your rooms. It is late, so I'll have tea brought to you all, so you can fall straight into bed once you've bathed," Camille assured her.

"You are such a dear," Violet told her.

"Ever thoughtful," Edith added.

"An amazing woman," Merry finished.

Ally couldn't help but smile at her. "Ditto," she said softly.

Camille shook her head, smiling. "It will be a busy day tomorrow," she said. "The caterers will arrive early, there will be musicians running about everywhere...and there will be a bride to dress."

"Lovely!" Violet said.

"So lovely," Edith agreed.

"Absolutely lovely," Merry said with a huge sniff.

"Please, darlings, don't start crying!" Ally kissed them one by one, saw Brian's amusement as he came in behind them, and obeyed his little wave warning her to escape quickly so they could better deal with the aunts.

She ran up the stairs, finding solitude and peace in the room she had known so long and so well. Egyptian art stared at her as she leaned against the door. She closed her eyes. She told herself that she would surely be back here, just as she would surely return to the cottage in the woods. But for a moment she felt like the aunts—ready to burst into tears.

She moved away from the door. Violet was right. They had all worked very hard, they were filthy, and they needed baths.

She ran very hot water and sank into the tub, a sigh of pleasure escaping her. Then her eyes flew open.

Tomorrow was her wedding.

She felt a sudden sense of panic.

She had fallen in love with him, she reminded herself. And the thought of sleeping beside him night after night was full of wonder, excitement, almost awe, but...

But she wouldn't have a chance to talk to him before the wedding now. And if he still didn't understand her need to be herself...

She jumped out of the bathtub, wondering at her own mind. Then she remembered the envelope.

Dripping, she ran back into the bedroom and found the envelope. Chilled, she ran back and slid back into the tub, holding the papers above the surface. She could let the heat ease her weary muscles as she read.

There were pictures with many of the articles. Some dated back several years. Most were about various meetings of anti-monarchy societies. Another was about Lord Wittburg paying to see Hudson Porter released from jail when he had been arrested for disorderly conduct. One reported on Jack Prine's wedding to Elizabeth Harrington and referred to a meeting of opposite poles. Andrew Harrington was in the accompanying picture. The wedding had taken place in the village, and Sir Angus Cunningham was there, too, standing proudly by the side of the groom. When she looked closely, she could see that Thane Grier had been in attendance, as well.

She replaced the articles in the envelope, careful not to get them wet, and set it aside. Then she leaned back.

What if murders of convenience could conveniently serve another cause?

Who would have spoken to whom first? And in whose mind had the original scheme been concocted? Had it come out of a chance meeting?

She didn't know. She sank beneath the surface, eager to wash her hair. Thoughts seemed to go crashing through her head. She realized she was too tired to make sense of them, and when she had thoroughly scrubbed, she rose, toweled herself dry, found a nightgown, finished drying her hair the best she could before the fire, and sank into her bed.

A bust of Nefertiti stared at her with painted ebony

eyes. She turned off the lamp at her bedside, ignoring the Egyptian goddess.

She was going to be married in the morning.

IAN DOUGLAS HAD BEEN excited when Mark had talked with him, and had understood the avenue down which Mark thought they should go. Yes, he would arrange for officers to watch the house. It was outside his jurisdiction, but he could find some off-duty men. He could speak with Sheriff Cunningham, as well.

"I think it's time to use only men you trust implicitly," Mark said.

Ian groaned, but said, "I believe you're right." He hesitated. "I've looked at those financial records, as you suggested."

"And?"

"On Jack Prine's death, Elizabeth inherited everything. On Giles Brandon's death, his estate reverted back into his wife's name. And Hudson Porter's housekeeper received a large inheritance in the will. Still...this is so...well, we'll see. If Elizabeth *has* taken a lover.... Even so, such an act may be immoral, but it's not illegal."

"Depending on who that lover proves to be," Mark pointed out.

"You should get home. You've tomorrow to think of."

"Tomorrow?"

"Your wedding."

"Good God, yes!" Mark said. He bade Ian goodnight and rode home. The trip seemed very long. When he reached the house, he hailed Bertram and handed over the horse. He rushed in, hurried along the hall and pushed open the door to her room.

It was empty.

For a moment, panic seized him. Then he winced. Of course she wasn't here. She was at Castle Carlyle.

His heart was thundering. He returned to the main room of the lodge and helped himself to a brandy, feeling ridiculous. How very strange. Just a few weeks ago she had been no more than a vague promise he had made. And now...

She was everything.

She was even his reason for being the man he must be. No harm must ever come to her. He couldn't imagine life without her.

How did he stop her from being so defiant, so determined, so...dangerous to herself?

"I marry her," he murmured to the fire. "It's the best I can do."

SOMEONE WAS WATCHING the house. He should have known it was inevitable once he had seen Mark Farrow return that day. Damn the man. His life had been made before his birth. He would inherit land, wealth, a title. Everything. Why did he have to meddle in the business of others, imagine himself a great detective, pit his mind against the criminal masses?

Farrow should die!

He shook his head irritably and knew he would rather not face Farrow. He had killed men unaware, when he had been armed and they had not. How was he to find Farrow without a weapon?

That was a worry for a later time.

He watched the man on duty; he was in plainclothes and followed the same route, up and down the walk.

The back entry.

The man wasn't watching the back.

It didn't improve his temper to have to climb through the trees and over the wall. To creep, all but on his stomach, to the back of the house.

He'd kept the full set of keys, so he had no difficulty gaining entry. The house was quiet. She was upstairs.

As he walked through the parlor, he saw the signs of her packing. All the shelves, tabletops and cabinets had been emptied.

He stood dead still. Mark Farrow had been in the house today. He had seen this. He would have known that Elizabeth was planning to leave.

He took a deep breath. How could she have been so stupid?

He looked toward the top of the stairs, then began to walk up them, feeling for the sheath at his ankle. When he reached the bedroom, she was waiting. Her hair was down, and she was propped against the pillow. A lamp burned at her side.

"Mark Farrow was here again today."

"Yes. I took care of him," she replied.

"Oh? How?"

"I was absolutely brilliant, I was indignant—I was regal!"

"He suspects you've been having an affair."

She hesitated. "He can't prove anything."

He moved toward her, smiling. When he reached her bedside, he doused the lamp. She made a purring sound. He lay down beside her. "Roll to your side," he whispered huskily.

"However you want it," she murmured, and obliged.

He drew the blade from the sheath.

He wished he dared to do it differently. He wished he could see her face. She thought he had done it all for her. That he hadn't been able to bear life without her.

But he couldn't afford for her to scream.

He was good. She was waiting—for a different touch.

He delivered the knife delicately to her throat, so that it was there before she ever knew what had happened.

Then he used force. And ripped.

The only sound that escaped her was a gurgling as the blood soaked into the sheets and pillow.

He didn't wait for her to die. He carefully wiped the knife on the sheets, then walked at his leisure down the stairs. He didn't relish the thought of escaping through the rear, crawling through the grass, hopping the fence.

Ah well, some things were necessary.

And his carriage awaited.

It was going to be a busy night.

"OH!" VIOLET CRIED.

"Dear Lord!" Merry said.

"Oh!" Edith repeated.

Ally was so grateful to them. She felt as if she were

moving in a fog. The castle was alive with people every-where, but Camille had arrived at her room early, in the best of spirits, to assure her that everything would be brought to her and that she mustn't be seen.

And then it was time to start.

Croissants reached the room shortly, accompanied by steaming coffee.

Then came the aunts, followed by Kat, Maggie and Camille. It was a large room, but...

First, her hair. Violet was a magician with the curling iron. Her nails were filed and tinted. Her toenails were tended likewise. The excitement grew downstairs, and eventually Camille was needed, then Maggie, then Kat. She was left with the aunts when it came time to don the dress, which had been waiting in an empty room down the hall.

Hose and delicate undergarments first. The corset. The dress...exquisite with thousands upon thousands of beaded pearls. Once she was in it, she wasn't certain she would be able to breathe. A touch of last-minute makeup, a dab of perfume, the shoes, the train, and then the tiara with the veil.

At last she was complete, feeling like a bird stuffed and ornamented for a feast. By then Camille, Maggie and Kat were back, dressed in their own finery for the occasion, beautiful as ever. The aunts looked lovely, too. The six of them surrounded her, three on each side, and Camille, called for the full-length mirror.

She didn't know herself. The sweep of her hair made her appear older and wiser. The gown gave her an hour-glass figure. She seemed taller—the heels on the shoes, no doubt. The touch of blush on her cheeks, her eyes brilliant, showing no trace of the fear that was suddenly coursing through her system....

"I told you off-white would be perfect," Violet said.

"My dear sister, that's a soft beige," Merry protested.

"It's off-white," Violet insisted.

"You're both wrong. It's pearl," Edith announced.

"It's beautiful, whatever you call it," Ally assured them, rushing to embrace them.

"Be careful. You'll wrinkle," Violet protested, then embraced her. "Let it wrinkle!"

"Since there are six of us," Maggie said wryly, "it will be very wrinkled. Kisses on the cheek, no crushing hugs."

So the kisses began. But even the aunts were wearing lip color, and soon Ally's cheeks were bright red. Violet sighed, but it was Kat who laughed and did her makeup over again. Camille picked up her pendant watch and gasped. "It's time!"

"Do you think I actually have a groom?" Ally asked. They all fell silent, staring at her in horror. "It's just that Mark Farrow does have a tendency to be late, or absent altogether."

"He's here. I saw him arrive," Kat said.

There was a tap at the door. Ally's heart leapt. For one dreadful second she thought she might be sick. Camille threw the door open. Brian Stirling, excessively handsome, was waiting to escort her down the stairs.

"Ally?" he asked.

She nodded, striding forward to accept his arm. Then

she panicked. She hadn't thought twice about the ridiculous curse Eleanor Brandon had cast on her in days, but it suddenly seemed to hang like a pall upon her.

"The scarab!" she gasped.

"What?" Camille demanded.

"The scarab."

"Ah," Kat said, understanding. "In the jewelry box, Ally? Where shall we pin it?"

"It doesn't exactly go, does it?" Camille commented.

"But it's such a beautiful piece," Maggie said.

"I have to wear it," Ally begged.

"In the bodice, slip it in the bodice," Kat suggested, the deed following the words.

In moments the women had disappeared down the stairs and she was on Brian's arm.

The wedding march was already playing.

"I'm going to trip down the stairs," Ally murmured.

"No, you're not," Brian assured her. "I will not let you fall."

The music continued to play. She saw that the castle was draped in elegant white-and-silver banners. There were people everywhere, all dressed magnificently. As they walked, flashbulbs flared, some with a puff of smoke.

She swept through the massive medieval entry on Brian's arm, and then on to the ballroom. Her heart skipped a beat. Yes, Mark had actually made it to his own wedding, and on time. Even through the veil, she could see him: the man she had admired on the steps at the courthouse, calming the crowd; the man she had fallen in love with when he had accosted the carriage; the man with whom she had danced by the stream in the woods...the man she loved in the darkness, in nothing at all.

He was clad now, elegantly so. He wore a brocade waistcoat and an elegant frock coat, reminiscent of an earlier time. He was tall, his dark hair gleaming, his face strong and striking. And his eyes...

She trembled as they moved forward to join him. Patrick was standing as his best man, and there were others aligned behind him. Maggie, her first "godparent," stood by her side and took the bouquet from her hands, as Brian handed her over to Mark when the priest demanded, "Who gives this woman over to marriage?"

Those who loved her were close, she knew. The aunties were right in the front, like three mothers of the bride.

It was a dream; it was a blur. She felt as if she were moving through a fantasy. She was dimly aware of the aunties sniffling. Merry, she thought, was the loudest sobber. Edith was the one who consoled her, her words audible. "There, there. They make a fine couple."

Someone hushed them.

The priest droned on.

Love, honor and obey. How could she vow before God to do such a thing? Would God understand a little white lie?

After all, she *did* love him.

She held the silver-gray touch of Mark's eyes through it all, somehow said the right things at the right time.

Felt the touch of his hand on hers.

And sighed when he kissed her.

The roar of applause was like the roar of the surf, and the taste and scent and feel of him suddenly quelled her panic, the reality of the man making everything all right. Music played again, and they walked out of the great hall, though she had no idea where they were going, especially when they walked outside. There she discovered that everyone had been invited, not just the gentry, but the maids and blacksmiths, chefs...anyone who served in either household, or lived close enough to attend. The wishes shouted to her were sincere and excited.

She felt the scarab against her breast, and she smiled in return.

She had been insane to feel such foreboding. It had happened just as it was supposed to. It was a dream. She had met him; she loved him; she had married him.

Encouraged, she threw the bouquet. It was caught by a farmer's daughter, who cried out her delight. Tables were set in the giant courtyard, more were set up inside the castle. Musicians played throughout the castle and the grounds.

"Champagne?" Mark asked, handing her a flute.

"To souls united," Patrick cried. "And a better toast than that. To Ally, a true lady for such a man as Mark." Ally had to laugh when she heard him whisper to one of his friends, "I told you I intended to be decent."

Those moments were magical. Mark could not have been more handsome or charming. His father could not have been more welcoming.

Her first dance with her husband wound up being barefoot on the lawn, and they both smiled, remembering a different dance in the forest.

She swept by the aunts with their damp eyes.

"She's so gorgeous in off-white."

"Beige."

"Pearl."

The music filled the air, her veins, her soul. She was loathe to be parted from Mark, even to dance with his father. But there was so much more to the wedding, so many people. Mark, of course, danced with each of the aunts, as well as Maggie, Camille and Kat, and she danced with Brian, Jamie and Hunter…and what seemed like a million other men, Sir Angus, Sir Andrew, Lord This and Lord That whom she had not met before. Theodore, the chef, all dressed up for the occasion. Thane Grier, who hadn't dared ask her, but whom she had drawn from the crowd.

Patrick, Thomas and Geoff…

The priest!

Detective Ian Douglas.

"Detective!"

"I'm sorry."

"But you were invited. You are a very good friend of Mark's."

"Yes."

She stared at him. "You're not here because of that, are you?"

He swallowed hard.

"What's happened?"

He shook his head.

"I insist that you tell me."

"I don't want the word out yet."

She shook her head. "I can be trusted, Detective Douglas."

He winced and swallowed again. "Elizabeth Prine was found dead in her bed just a few hours ago," he said.

She missed a step and nearly stumbled.

"Elizabeth Prine. Jack Prine's widow?"

"Yes."

She felt the scarab against her flesh. "There's more, isn't there?" she demanded.

He nodded.

"Tell me. You are going to take Mark with you soon, on our wedding day. Tell me all that has happened."

"I...we...we don't want any of it known yet."

"I understand that," she said, trying for patience.

"Eleanor Brandon..."

"Dead?"

"She will be. She is unconscious. The blood loss was terrible."

They whirled to a waltz.

The dream had become a nightmare.

"What about her housekeeper?" she demanded quickly.

He looked at her with narrowed eyes.

"Don't be ridiculous. Mark never betrays a confidence," she said bitterly. "I know what I know from the newspapers."

"The housekeeper..." He paused, shuddering. "She must have been very easy to kill," he said softly.

"Hudson Porter wasn't married. His housekeeper...?"

"Yes."

"They're all dead?"

Mark came up behind Ian and tapped him on the shoulder. His expression was grim. "Damn it, Ian, what are you saying to my wife?"

She forced a smile for Ian and slid into Mark's arms, forcing him around the floor with her, her head tilted back. "He is telling me the truth—something you seem loathe to do."

"This is none of your business, Ally."

She gasped.

He shook his head fiercely. "You're clever, Ally. You write with a wicked edge. But don't you see? This is a madman. He butchered four women in one night. Well, Eleanor Brandon is still hanging on, but most likely she'll die before she can so much as mouth her killer's name. Ally, you have to stay out of this, and you have to stop writing. Do you understand?"

"You're going to casually leave your own wedding in a matter of minutes, aren't you?" she asked pleasantly.

"Ally, I *will* be back."

"I'm sure you will—at some point. But if I am to be so excluded, you must not count on the fact that I will be waiting."

"Ally—"

"Why did Lionel Wittburg say what he did when he was lying in the street?" she demanded fiercely.

"It doesn't matter."

"Yes, it does. And why were you and the others masquerading as highwaymen?"

"That should have been obvious," he said coldly. "To one with your talent for ferreting out the possibilities."

"The killer escapes in a carriage, so you stop carriages to search for evidence meanwhile poor Lord Wittburg lies in a hospital, his only crime trying to tell me what you would not."

"I did not know then."

"Does Brian know you will soon be leaving?" she demanded. He didn't answer, but from his eyes, she could tell that Brian knew. She felt ill. The whole world, it seemed, had accepted the fact that he would go, would always go. And she understood that. What she couldn't bear was being treated like a crystalline figure that couldn't be moved because it might break. He acknowledged her talent, yet he was unwilling for her to exercise it.

"We are to head to the carriage, as if we are escaping for our wedding night," he told her.

"How convenient that we've already had one," she murmured icily.

"Ally, good God, surely you must see the enormity of this. This man will stop at nothing to hide the truth."

"I do see the enormity."

"Then forgive me," he asked her.

A cry went up in the courtyard. The Farrow carriage, gaily festooned, the two black carriage horses feathered in white, rolled into view.

"It's our cue," he said softly. His eyes were on hers, steel-gray and thunderclouds. She longed for the man she had known so recently, the one who had asked rather than demanded.

But she turned, waving to the crowd, lightly running toward the carriage with her hand in Mark's. Bertram had the step down, and Mark helped her inside, sweeping up her train.

She looked back, forced a smile and waved. Edith and Merry, with Violet between them, were clinging together, sobbing.

"I love you, darlings," she called cheerfully, then sank back into the carriage, ripping the tiara from her head, sending the pins flying in her fury.

"Was the act carried out as you wished?" she demanded as the carriage started down the path to the great gates of the castle.

"Ally," he said, his voice pained.

"Where am I going?" she demanded coldly, willing herself not to show emotion. "It's all an act, isn't it? Everything in your life is an act. Marrying a stranger is part of scene five."

"Ally," he said evenly, "four people were murdered in a single night, and the killer slipped away, his crimes not even discovered for hours. Should we mind so terribly that our lives of privilege are being briefly disrupted?"

She was even further infuriated. He didn't understand at all that she wanted only to be respected and included.

"I didn't want a life of privilege," she told him. "I merely want my life to be my own. Once I had freedom. Now I do not."

"Ally, you are hardly in a prison."

"I'm not?"

"If you are, I did not create it."

She stared at him, incredulous that he could say such a thing.

"Your prison was created by your birth."

She shook her head, fighting tears. "It was created when you came into my life."

She waved a hand angrily when he would have spoken. "I beg of you, if you must talk, answer my question. Where am I going?" she demanded icily. "All your friends are back at the castle."

He looked away, as if he no longer cared. "They won't be," he said.

"Good God, can you not even answer one question? Where am I going?"

Silence was her only answer. They had barely cleared the gates when the carriage jerked to a halt. She heard the sound of horses' hooves clicking up the road beside them.

"I will be back as soon as possible," he said, and exited the carriage. She leaned out, seeing that Patrick, Thomas, Geoff and Ian were there, mounted and leading Mark's horse. In a swift movement, he had leapt atop it.

The carriage jerked again.

She still didn't know where she was going.

She burst into tears.

THEY VISITED THE MURDER scenes in order of closeness, which took them to Elizabeth Prine's house first. The coroner was on site, and there were police officers guarding the house, but it was not roped off, and the officers in the front were in plainclothes. They were trying to keep the events quiet until they could at least get an understanding of what had happened themselves, hoping to get a jump on the killer.

It didn't take long to ascertain that the killer had a key and had come in the back.

The body of Elizabeth Prine told them much, much more. She hadn't just known her killer; she had expected him. Mark was sorry to realize he had been right about the affair.

His discovery of that fact might well have been what set off the murder spree. He made a detailed examination of the room, the house and the grounds, but he was certain the one aspect that mattered was the one that was first evident: Elizabeth's lover had been her murderer. And from the beginning, Ian had been right about the killer's mode of escape; out to a back road, where he was picked up by some conveyance before whatever blood had spilled on him might be witnessed by a casual passerby.

While questioning the officer who had been on duty watching the house, Mark found that theory to be the only one possible—the officer had watched the door and the house all night. No one had entered from the front. He was adamant about that fact.

There was nothing different at the Porter house, except that the housekeeper, slain in her bed, had probably not expected company. It was doubtful, however, that she had heard the killer. If she had been lucky, she had been dead before she even realized he was there.

Their last stop was the Brandon house. Again the housekeeper had been caught in her sleep. Again the entry had been with a key. He tracked the killer's every step. The housekeeper had been killed first. The man had entered silently, his intent lethal. After the housekeeper had been dispatched in her lower-floor room, he had mounted the stairs. It occurred to Mark that they needed to speak with the maid Elizabeth had fired. She might have information *and* she might be in danger.

But apparently Eleanor Brandon had been fore-warned. There were signs of struggle in the bedroom. She had been left, Ian told him, on the bed, and he was sure the killer had assumed she was dying, choking on her own blood, when he had left. It had been one of the duty officers—accustomed to watching the house since the murder of Giles Brandon—who had noticed the lights didn't go on in the morning. She was alive now because he had kicked in the front door, sounded the alarm and taken her to the hospital.

At last they went to the hospital. Eleanor Brandon lay on the bed, as white as a sheet—except for the crimson stitching at her throat. She had defensive wounds on her arms.

"Much like her husband," Ian said.

Mark nodded. "What are the chances she will awaken?" he asked the doctor.

The man shook his head. "One in a hundred, but we will do our best."

By the time they left the hospital, it was late. Patrick, Thomas and Geoff, who had waited outside, leaning against a retaining wall, straightened when they reappeared.

"There's nothing we can do now," Mark said. "It's late. Tomorrow, however, I think our best use of time will be to ride again."

"As highwaymen?"

"The women were involved. They were a part of the murders. They didn't wield the knife, but they allowed it to happen. Maybe the killer was promised part of the financial reward. The killer, in turn, had his own purpose. Once again, we know he escaped the scene in his coach, which waits in the back streets, so there are at least two men involved—a driver and lookout, and the killer. The cloak found in Lord Wittburg's coach was real, but it was placed there to cast blame. If the killer hadn't feared Elizabeth Prine had betrayed him… In any case, the night Lord Wittburg accosted Ally, he had been at the club. He saw Arthur Conan Doyle, Sir Andrew Harrington, and the sheriff, Sir Angus Cunningham. He also saw the journalist Thane Grier on the street. We can discount Doyle, because he wasn't involved in any of the business that took place at the houses, or in the ranks of the anti-monarchists." He offered them a grim smile. "We can also discount him because I know he is incapable of this kind of butchery. Read his work and you will agree. But in all the lists, Harrington and Cunningham have appeared again and again. And the journalist has appeared many times at the right place."

"Sir Angus is the sheriff," Ian said almost angrily.

"Yes, but at this point, I don't think his status can sway us from looking into the possibility that he is involved."

"Sir Angus involved...in something this heinous!" Ian was incredulous.

"I didn't say it must be Sir Angus, only that it could be. How long do you think you can hide the news of the murders, keep them out of the newspapers?"

Ian shook his head. "The longer we hide the truth, the longer it appears we are trying to abet a conspiracy."

"Then I suggest you inform the newspapers yourself. Soon. Let your men go over the scenes one more time, seeking any evidence. Then let the information out."

Ian nodded glumly. "I can only imagine the sermons in the churches across the land tomorrow."

ALLY WAS SURPRISED BUT PLEASED to realize she was being taken into the city. The carriage arrived at last at Lord Farrow's townhome.

Bertram, looking sheepish, helped her down. "Jeeter will be inside to help you with whatever you may require, Lady Farrow," he murmured, his eyes not quite meeting hers. "And you needn't be afraid. I will be standing guard."

"Thank you, Bertram. I am not afraid, but I am grateful for your protection," she told him.

"Lord Joseph intends to stay at his club this evening, leaving the house for your convenience," he told her.

Ah, yes, she was a newlywed, after all.

"None but your guardians know your destination this evening."

"Thank you." None knew? Anyone could recognize the carriage. Now, however, it was safely off the street, beneath the porte cochere.

Inside, she greeted Jeeter, but she longed to escape everyone. She hurried upstairs to the room that had been hers before and found it had been well prepared. She stood in front of the dresser mirror for a moment. Her hair tumbled about her shoulders, and she was in definite disarray. She had set off so differently that morning.

She started to undo the tiny buttons on the bodice of the gown, then hesitated, frowning. There was a strange mark on the delicate beauty of the sleeve.

A red mark....

She nearly ripped the elegant gown in her haste to be free of it. Yes, there was a smudge of what appeared to be blood on the sleeve. There was another on the back of the gown, where a man would have set his hand while leading her in a waltz.

Her blood seemed to congeal.

Anyone might have cut himself. Shaving, of course, or cooking, gardening...

Committing a murder?

CHAPTER SIXTEEN

MARK HAD NO IDEA WHAT to expect when he reached home that night. When last he saw her, Ally had been furious, yet what bride would not be? He wondered, staring at the entry, if he hadn't assumed too much. He didn't think that being the son of the very eminent Lord Joseph Farrow had ever caused him to consider himself important. He had spent most of his youth fighting against such an image, doing his duty for the Empire, never shirking the responsibility of taking his place in the front lines. Two guiding aspects had caused him to set out on the life he now led: a true empathy with the aging Queen Victoria, and a real friendship with and appreciation for Arthur Conan Doyle. Fans had avidly fallen in love with his sleuth, Sherlock Holmes, a fact that had startled Doyle, whose interest lay in creating what he considered more important literature. He'd been distraught when the public had decried Holmes' fictional death, while in his real life, his wife sickened. But in private circles, he never tired of speaking about the importance of observation, his years studying with Dr. Joseph Bell, and how his methods could serve the police.

It was true, though, that being Lord Joseph Farrow's son and heir had aided him in his investigations, allowing him through doors that might not be opened to others.

Had he since deluded himself regarding his own importance? Might he have let others handle the situation while he remained at his own wedding party? Was he living with the illusion that he was the only man clever enough to solve these latest crimes? And had he let his ego drive him to put a wedge between himself and his new bride?

He winced. Surely that was not true. It was just that he had become so involved in this case. Perhaps, before he had met Alexandra Grayson, he had imagined she would be sheltered, weak and sweet, and yes, perhaps grateful to marry into such an illustrious family.

His own life had included several affairs, none hurtful to either party, the longest being with a renowned actress who relished the public's suspicions that she was having an affair with Mark Farrow but never sought marriage. He had cared for her; but he hadn't loved her. Knowing he had agreed to honor his father's word, he had imagined he would be a decent-enough husband. In all honesty, he couldn't say that he had expected himself to be a faithful one. He'd agreed to an arranged marriage, but he had never thought he could fall in love with his prospective bride.

His wife.

He had never expected that on his wedding night, his bride might be angry enough to escape him, and it was with fear of just such an eventuality that he entered the house. Even when Jeeter told him that his lady had long since retired, he mounted the stairs with his heart pounding with a fear he had never felt in the worst of battles.

Yet when he opened the door, miraculously, she was there.

A fire burned, providing the only light in the room. It cast enough of a glow to show him the form in the bed, far more enticing than he'd dared hope. The covers were drawn low, and she was clad in white silk that skimmed over her curves like a second skin, causing his flesh to burn, his body to quicken.

He expelled his breath in relief as he quietly entered the room and shut the door. Heart in his throat, he began to divest himself of the wedding finery he still wore, cuff links and studs, coat, waistcoat, shirt.

He closed his eyes for a moment as he stood before the mirror, remembering the vast amounts of blood he had encountered that day, and he suddenly felt it had covered him, flesh and soul, and he could not go to her in such a way. He let himself out of the room, determined to bathe elsewhere.

In his own quarters, he found himself making haste. Shedding the remnants of his wedding attire, he sank into the tub while it was still filling. For a moment he savored the warmth, but only for a moment. He found soap and a washcloth, mocking himself as he scrubbed, for he was suddenly as industrious as Lady MacBeth, desperate to rid himself of the stench of death and the evil that too often bloomed in the hearts of men.

So intent was he on his thoughts, he didn't hear the outer door to his chambers open, nor did he hear the door to his bath open seconds later. He was scrubbing furiously at his hands when he looked up at last.

And there she was, in her flimsy covering of sheer white silk, the sweep of her glorious wheat-gold hair around her shoulders and falling down her back. She was as stunningly lovely as an angel, but her smile hinted of something far more carnal and erotic. He paused, startled, mesmerized. She seemed to glide to take a seat at the side of the massive clawed tub. He didn't politely wait for her to speak, nor did he remain silent in clever resolve to hear her mind; he simply could not find his own tongue.

"So you're back," she said very softly.

He swallowed, aware that the water would do little to hide the reaction the mere sound of her voice could evoke.

"You knew I would return as soon as possible."

"Of course," she whispered, and leaned toward him.

He was amazed the furious woman he had left had become this goddess of seduction on his return. As she neared him, wafting the scent of soap, perfume and her own intoxicating self in his direction, he felt an inner trembling of gratitude as he moved eagerly to accept her kiss....

He was stunned when he felt the tip of a knife blade against his jugular vein.

She leaned back, eyes as sharp as golden daggers, hand steady on the hilt. He gritted his teeth, furious with her—and with himself.

"What is this greeting?" he asked her icily.

"A lesson," she informed him.

"Really? And what would you have me learn? That I have welcomed a venomous snake into my home?" he demanded.

She arched a brow. "The first lesson, sir, is that you are as vulnerable as any man—or woman. I cannot live my life ever under guard. Guard her. See that she goes nowhere."

His eyes narrowed. "As you see, we are all under threat at all times."

"Second, you have not married an idiot."

"I haven't? Odd that you should raise that subject now."

"Be careful what you say while I hold the knife."

Despite her words and the dagger at his throat, he was finding it difficult to concentrate. Steam had dampened the silk. It rested provocatively over her breasts, so close to him, outlining every nuance of her form.

"What is it you want—my love?" he asked smoothly.

"I am not a possession. I am not to be carried here or there without thought or question—without *opinion*. Believe it or not, sir, I was not distressed that you should be called away on our wedding day. I might mention, however, that most brides would be so. I was angry— no, far too gentle a word. I was *furious* that you could not see fit to explain the circumstances to me yourself, that you did not ask for any thought of mine, not even as to the place where I was to be taken while you strutted about being the great Mark Farrow."

"Go on."

"This is where you offer an apology," she informed him.

He smiled. "I will not apologize for considering your safety the most important factor in my decisions."

"My safety? I have not been taken off guard. I am not the one with a knife against my throat."

"There is one thing I have learned about such a situation that you, apparently, have not," he informed her.

"And that is?"

"Always know when an opponent does not mean to use a weapon."

In a flash of motion, he caught her wrist, his fingers a vise around it. The knife flew across the bathroom floor, thudding against the wall. He tugged, and she lost her balance. With a little cry, she wound up on top of him in the bathtub.

She had been the embodiment of an angel; now he was wrestling with a hellcat. Muttering curses, she struggled against his hold on her. His arm around her midriff held her tightly against him. Water was still streaming into the tub from the faucet, and now it was spilling in waves upon the floor as she struggled. He sat halfway up, pinning her hard against him, long enough to turn off the water. She was as strong as a demon, but at last he managed to still her flailing arms. He could feel her fury; it emanated from her with a searing heat far greater than that of the water. She was rigid, soaked and at his mercy, and she knew it.

"I'm delighted to see you, too, my love," he whispered against the dampness of her ear. Tendrils of hair teased his face. She was undoubtedly aware of his complete arousal, since she was locked so tightly against his body. She dared not move.

He was startled when she ignored his gibe and said, "I will not be able to bear it if you don't learn that you can speak to me, if you don't trust me, if you don't…offer me the truth."

"What truth would you have of me?" he demanded.

"For a start, what did Lionel Wittburg mean about me?"

He hesitated, then sighed. He wanted to hold her more tightly and tenderly than ever, but she remained stiff and hostile in his arms.

"It's complicated," he murmured.

"Apparently we have time," she responded.

He took a deep breath, easing his hold on her. *No one must know,* his father had said. But Ally had a right to know. And since he couldn't help but be afraid that the current circumstances might somehow involve her past, he felt strongly that she had to be forewarned. "You have heard the Jack the Ripper conspiracy theories?" he asked quietly.

"Of course." She twisted in his arms, managing to

face him closely, a frown puckering her forehead, her eyes not so much hostile as puzzled. "I can't believe that the monarchy was involved."

He shook his head. "No. But often, grains of truth are at the root of fantastic stories."

"What can any of this have to do with me? I certainly don't believe in any conspiracy theories involving the government. And such rumors can't matter now, so many years later."

"The rumors regarding Prince Albert Victor, Duke of Clarence, known as Eddie, had a grain of truth."

"I don't believe—"

"He was no murderer, Ally. But he did fall in love, apparently, and he married illegally. A woman named Annie. And they bore a child. Eddie was desperately sick, and circumstances might well have made poor Annie mad. Certainly she was ill, and ultimately she died. The Crown was in danger then, and Eddie was not surrounded by the best of advisers—or even friends, I imagine."

"So…?"

He found he had to take another breath. "You're the child," he said quietly.

She shook her head. "The…child?"

"The daughter of Prince Eddie and his beloved Annie."

She shook her head; he had known she would deny his words. "That's…preposterous!"

He didn't reply. She struggled once more against his hold. "That was a rumor…just a story. Nothing more.

If that was the lever used to force you to marry an orphan, I'm truly sorry."

He didn't try to argue.

"Please...let me up," she begged.

He released her at last, then helped her to find her footing, dripping on the already wet tile, her silken finery totally drenched and revealing. He rose behind her, quickly seeking towels. Shivering, she took the towel he offered and fled.

Wrapping his own towel around his waist, he followed.

She had headed for "her" room, her private space, as close as she could come to having something of hers here in his father's house. She didn't try to shut him out; she simply stood before the fire, shaking.

He went to her, turning her to face him, stripping away the soaking silk, wrapping her in the towel.

"It's not true," she insisted.

"I don't know if it is or isn't," he told her. "It's the story my father was told. I only know that I don't care."

Her eyes sought his, filled with pleading and naked emotion that stirred him. His every thought one of tenderness and love, he wrapped her in his arms, lifting her, holding her, sitting with her in the stuffed armchair before the fire. She continued to shake, lost somewhere in her own mind, and he spoke again. "I only know I love you."

She didn't reply, but she twisted in his arms and wrapped her own arms around him. Her lips, parted and damp, rose to his. He joined her in the kiss, salty with a hint of tears, and as he desperately tried to reassure her, the kiss became passionate. Locked tightly, fiercely, in that embrace, he strove to be all she needed, to show her the truth of his love. She returned every emotion in kind, and he forgot where they had begun, or even why. This was his wedding night, and he was deeply, desperately, in love with his wife.

He rose and carried her to the bed, the towels falling away unnoticed. He kissed the flesh of her throat and shoulders with infinite tenderness and need, worshiping her curves and the silken expanse of her skin. Her fingers played across his chest, kneaded his back, danced along his spine. Her lips found his throat, the place where his pulse beat, where so recently she had held the knife, and he feared the loss of her touch far more than the steel of any blade. He cupped the fullness of her breast with his palm, feeling his own erection springing anew, feeling the pulse there of his blood and hunger, augmented by the delicate touch of her fingers, erotic and tantalizing, then a firmer stroke…creating insanity. He buried his face against her throat, breathed in the clean scent and dampness of her hair, felt as if he were dying there. Spurred to an erotic fever, he drew her away and tended with ardor to her breasts, midriff, belly. His fingers stroked to her kneecaps, drew a pattern up the length of her spine. He buried himself between the sleek length of her legs, and teased and savored, feeling her drive him to ever greater madness with each arch and nuance of movement, every gasp that escaped her lips.

And then he found himself forced back, while she ran

the liquid fire of her tongue over him, down his torso, her hair teasing his flesh when she landed that exotic liquid caress upon the pulse of his sex.

He ceased to breathe.

He used the power of his hands to draw her up, lift her atop him, down on him. He thrust deeply, watched her arch, savored the sleek beauty of her breasts, her hair flying around her in a cascade of fire-tipped gold. And then he rolled, with her still locked to him, and thrust in an ever-frantic frenzy until he felt the gasp and sudden tension that seized her. Only then did he allow his own climax.

When he fell beside her, he instantly cradled her close and held her there, assuring her, "I love you, Ally. You. The girl I first met in the forest, who defied all convention. I love you."

"I love you, Mark. I love you, too," she whispered, her fingers curled on his chest.

All through the night, he felt the need to let her know just how much he loved her.

She didn't seem to mind.

In fact, she seemed to feel the need to let him know, as well.

It was very late Sunday when they awoke. At first, when Ally opened her eyes, she was certain he would be gone again.

But he wasn't. He was at her side, leaning on one elbow, doing nothing but watching her. She smiled slowly. She loved the look of him naked.

"I believe there is a tray with tea and sustenance just beyond the door," he told her. "Shall I retrieve it?"

"Yes, please," she replied.

He rose, secured one of the towels from the floor and wrapped it around himself before opening the door. He brought the tray in, setting it at the foot of the bed. Ally hadn't realized how ravenous she was.

"Jeeter, ever the perfect valet," Mark murmured. "No toast to grow cold, just biscuits and jam, hard boiled eggs."

Ally sat up as well, carefully, lest she upset the tray. She delicately poured the tea, preparing a cup for each of them. Mark arranged plates with biscuits. "Butter?" he inquired.

"Yes, please."

"Sugar?"

"Cream only."

"Jam?"

"Thank you."

Once they were perched just a bit precariously with plates and teacups and saucers before them on the bed, she grew serious. "Mark...could such a thing be true?" she asked him.

"Ally, as I said, I don't know, and I really don't care."

"But—"

"Does it matter to you?" he asked. "You were raised by the aunts. No one could love you more. And as for all your guardians..."

"But did they love me only out of loyalty to the Crown?" she asked.

"Ally, I don't believe anyone was ever asked to give you their love. Perhaps, at first, they felt a fierce need to protect you. But look back. You dishonor some very fine people to doubt they cared with all their hearts."

She lowered her head, then smiled. "Thank you."

"Pardon?"

"Thank you for giving them back to me," she said softly. Then she shook the wild mass of her hair, determined to similarly shake off the strange feeling such a revelation had given her. Could it be true? She still didn't know. And she was trying desperately to feel as Mark did: that it didn't matter.

"Tell me about yesterday," she begged.

He looked at her and smiled, lashes sweeping his eyes for a minute. "I married a very wanton creature," he told her.

"Perhaps," she murmured primly. "Mark, please. What happened when you left?"

He stiffened, shaking his head. "It was horrible."

"I'm not afraid of horrible," she said.

"Ally, I've not seen anything like this…ever, perhaps. It's not just the brutality of the crimes, the blood…"

"The killer is so cold-blooded and calculating," she finished.

He looked at her and nodded. "I saw that A. Anonymous has begun to suspect there might be a more personal aspect to the murders. Something that lies beneath the attempt to rock the governmental structure of Britain."

She nodded. "But…if the women were involved… they're dead now."

"Eleanor Brandon is barely hanging on to life. Or

was. I don't know what has happened this morning. The newspaper is conspicuously absent from this tray, so I'm assuming Jeeter has determined we will at least have breakfast in peace."

"If she lives, it's probable she will go to trial. And hang for conspiracy in her husband's murder."

"God knows what a jury will decide. Her physician does not feel she has much of a chance. There are men guarding her bedside, however. If she does regain consciousness, she will certainly give us the name of the killer. I hardly think she will be willing to hang for a man who tried to kill *her*, as well."

"Do you suppose the killer could have been Sir Angus Cunningham?" she asked him.

He stared at her, stunned, and in that moment, his eyes betrayed him.

"What makes you suggest Sir Angus?" he demanded.

She shrugged. "I read, remember," she told him. She hesitated, then added, "I've gone through a number of old newspaper articles."

"Oh? And how did you obtain them?" When she didn't answer, his face hardened. "Thane Grier?"

She didn't reply.

"Ally, he is under suspicion, as well," he said.

"I believe he is driven, that he is determined to make a name for himself. But he's not a killer."

"Ally, how can you possibly be so certain?"

"I'm not certain, of course," she murmured, looking down.

"Stay away from him," Mark said firmly.

She didn't reply.

"Ally…"

"Mark…"

"Stay away from him!"

She looked at him, arching a brow. "The killer is bold. And growing more so, evidently. If his intent was to portray the monarchy as ruthless, he has betrayed his own goal by killing the women. The world will know there must have been another agenda."

"Conspirators turn on one another all the time," he reminded her.

"Historically speaking, yes."

"What's obvious may not always be what turns out to be the truth," he said.

"And the truth, you believe, is that for the women, at least, making the monarchy appear to be cold-blooded and ruthless was only a bonus in addition to their real motive, which was to rid themselves of men they loathed in order to obtain their money."

"The killer was having an affair with Elizabeth Prine. I imagine the plot was hatched while they mused in each other's arms. It was a dangerous plot to begin with—having that many people involved. Afraid Elizabeth might betray him, he decided she had to die. But if she died, one of the other women might have been terrified and ready to tell the truth. Thus…"

"A bloodbath," she murmured.

"So…in all your reading, what else have you determined?" he asked her.

"I believe you should be watching Sir Andrew Harrington," she said.

Again Mark started, shaking his head.

"Instead of being angry," she asked, "why don't you speak to me?"

He shook his head. "Ally..." He sighed. "Perhaps we should be watching Andrew Harrington. There is of course more than one person out there who should be observed. And I remain afraid that you may be in danger."

"Because of the break-in at the cottage?"

"That and...many reasons. Perhaps someone else—other than Lionel Wittburg—knows who you are. Or what if someone doesn't know you may be a hidden royal but *does* know you're A. Anonymous? I'm not asking you to spend your life obeying my dictates—although, you did promise to love, honor and *obey*—I'm asking you to take care with your life until this killer is caught."

She reached out, nearly disturbing the tea tray, to touch his face. "I *am* careful, Mark. As you are."

He caught her hand. "Ally, you lived sheltered in a cottage in the woods. You walked where you would when you would. You can't go back to that again. Not now."

She didn't want to reply. "Finished with your tea?" she asked softly.

When he nodded, she removed the dishes and the tray, and quite literally jumped on him. Later, much later, she rose and bathed while he returned to his own room to do the same.

She knew, of course, that he would be leaving again, and she didn't know when he would be back.

She hadn't made any promises, however, as to what *she* would do.

Dressed, she sat at the vanity and brushed her hair. When he returned, she told him, "It's strange."

"What's strange?" he asked.

"You were off with Ian. I was on my way here." She set the brush down and turned to stare at him. "And all the while, the killer was enjoying our wedding feast."

As she had expected, he frowned. "What are you talking about?"

"I danced with the man," she told him.

"Ally…"

Rising, she strode to the corner of the room and picked up her wedding dress, then brought it to him. "There can, of course, be other explanations. But this man set out to kill four people. He succeeded in three instances, and Eleanor is barely alive. Perhaps someone fought back at some point and he sustained a small wound." She laid the dress out on the bed, pointing to the smudges. "Or perhaps someone injured himself cutting an apple. As I said, there could be dozens of explanations. But someone had a wound that was fresh enough to reopen while he was dancing with me at our wedding."

He stared at her, then back at the dress. She was startled when he suddenly drew her close, his grasp violent, almost hurtful.

His fingers threaded into her hair; his eyes met hers.

"Good God, Ally…."

"Mark..."

He shook his head, and she saw fury in the silver of his eyes. "This man is beyond despicable. He is insane...yet he walks around as if he were completely normal! He dared to come to our wedding, to dance with you, hold you...touch you. Sweet Jesus. If I find him, he will not live to hang. I swear it!"

"Mark!" she cried, distressed. "Mark, you can't take justice into your own hands!" she told him. "Of course," she added hastily, "you must defend yourself at all costs, but you must not be the aggressor. I am sorry I showed you this."

He swallowed; she knew he was fighting to control his emotions. "It is frightening to realize that we must look at the list of your dance partners."

"I believe that we can exclude the local folk," she murmured, and looked at him. "And the list would also include those closest to us, above reproach, your best friends, my guardians. But that leaves us with a long list, including Sir Andrew, Sir Angus..."

"And Thane Grier."

"And Thane Grier," she admitted.

He lowered his head.

"This gets us nowhere. I am sorry I spoke."

"Never be sorry for any truth you speak to me, Ally, and I swear to you, I will try very hard to tell you what is on my mind and explain my actions. It's just that...so much is so ugly that I don't want to..."

She leaned her head upon his shoulder. "I'm not afraid of that," she said softly.

"Sometimes *I* am," he told her.

"I must be a real part of your life, Mark. Not someone who makes you wretched, as I did yesterday, but a true companion."

He lifted her chin. "I love you, Ally."

"I know," she assured him. And then she stepped back. "I'm assuming," she said, "that the highwayman is about to ride again?"

"Oh? And why?" he asked.

"Well, Lord Wittburg was all but condemned for the bloody cloak that was found in his carriage. Therefore, I'm assuming the killer did not escape the murder scenes without some evidence. If the killer knew enough to plant the cloak in Lord Wittburg's possession, he was aware that someone suspected—or knew—that a carriage was the only way to escape the scene undetected. Therefore, given what happened Friday night, there is surely a new blood-stained cloak to be discovered."

He watched her and sighed.

"So the highwayman *is* to ride again," she said softly.

"Yes."

"I understand," she said.

"But not today," he told her.

"Oh? Then what is your intent for today?"

"To love my wife," he said softly, and he drew her close.

CHAPTER SEVENTEEN

SUNDAY WAS HERS, and it was a fantasy, a dream come true.

She discovered that Lord Farrow's townhome offered a cellar with billiards and a dart board, and she was quite talented at both. She and Mark played, they laughed, they wound up in each other's arms.

Jeeter discreetly arranged a delicious candlelit dinner, with a specially selected French wine, a delicate shrimp appetizer, and tender steaks that all but melted in the mouth.

Then there was the night. She had never so much as begun to imagine that she could love someone so fiercely, so desperately, so passionately. Every moment with Mark saw her fall more deeply in love. And every moment made her realize that his words were indeed true. Miraculously, wonderfully, he loved her, too. Nothing else seemed to matter.

She knew, however, that he would be gone when she awoke on Monday.

And he was.

She gratefully remembered her thought from the day before, that she hadn't made him any promises regarding her own behavior.

After she bathed and dressed, she went downstairs to find Jeeter, and asked him for the newspaper, which he seemed loath to give her, but he eventually brought it to her in the dining room along with her coffee.

The news of the murders blazed across the front page. The article, though not emphasizing the violence and horror, made no attempt to disguise it.

She was glad to see that the byline belonged to Thane Grier.

When she had finished eating, she explored upstairs. She felt like a snoop, opening so many doors, but she was certain Lord Farrow would have a typewriter in his townhome as well as the lodge.

She was right. She found it in his study.

She spent an hour working as A. Anonymous and then began to think out her exit from the premises.

She slipped downstairs in silence, certain Jeeter had known what she was about and hoping he would assume she was still at work. Bertram, she knew, would be guarding the house, ensuring that no one got in without his tacit permission.

She doubted he was afraid that she might be trying to get *out*.

The house was fenced and gated, but a discreet evaluation of the small backyard revealed an oak with a trunk that could be skimmed and a few low branches, giving her an opportunity to slip over the wall into the next yard.

She didn't know the neighbors, but no one seemed to be watching their yard, so it was easy enough to quickly race through the yard and exit via the open carriage gateway. On the street, she looked back to assure herself that Bertram was still guarding Lord Farrow's house and hadn't noticed her. Then she hurried down the street, delighted to see a streetcar conveniently coming her way.

She headed for the newspaper offices, hoping to find Thane.

She realized that she was using him for her own ends again, but he had gained, as well. She refused to believe he could be guilty of murder, and counted on the fact that he was so worried about his own byline that he would never share the suggestions and information that she gave him.

She saw him as she entered the offices she was coming to know well. He saw her, too, and rose quickly. She surreptitiously dropped the envelope she had brought, addressed to the managing editor, onto one of the desks she passed before he reached her.

He took her hands and smiled. "Ally! I had not expected to see you today. Did you read Sunday's paper? I admit it was the social page, but I did a smashing job covering your wedding."

"Sometimes the news *should* be pleasant," she said.

Then, since she hadn't read it, she quickly went on, "Your article this morning was excellent," she told him.

His smile faded. "Grim, I'm afraid."

"Very well done. Facts without flinching, and yet also without sensationalism."

"Thank you." He frowned. "What are you doing here? You're a new bride. Surely you have more pleasant pursuits."

"Mark had business," she said quickly. "The marriage was rushed forward, you know. We certainly intend to take a honeymoon soon, but for now, can you take some time to talk to me?"

He glanced around and laughed softly. "Today I can do anything. This morning's articles have sold more papers in one day than in...well, forever. We've even outsold the initial coverage of the murders, when everyone was screaming about the monarchy. Let's have coffee. I know a perfect spot."

He led her to a lovely little café with private booths, where they ordered small demitasses of café au lait, the newest trend imported from France. He folded his hands on the table. "So, Ally, what do you want from me?"

She arched a brow, and he smiled and went on. "You know, I could have fallen madly in love with you. Not only are you absolutely beautiful, you have a keen mind, a wonderful asset for the wife of an up-and-coming journalist." He lifted a hand when she looked uncomfortable. "Fear not. My feelings have turned to simple admiration and respect. Still, you've just married Mark Farrow. What are you doing here with me?"

"These murders must be solved," she said.

He sipped his coffee. "Ally, there are dozens of police officers on this case. Not to mention your husband. I report news, I don't create it."

"Do you have a carriage, Thane?"

He frowned, watching her. His answer came slowly. "No, I'm sorry. Why, do you need one?"

She shook her head. "No, no—not really," she added hastily. "I was just curious."

"I'm sorry."

"I read the articles you gave me."

He laughed. "You must have been a highly entertaining bride!"

She flushed.

"Oh, God, I'm sorry again. That was highly inappropriate. Forgive me."

"I had a bit of time alone since Friday," she told him. "I believe we are down to two men," she told him gravely. "It's hard for me to credit, but from everything I have read about the anti-monarchists and their meetings—and the relationships of people and places—either Sir Andrew Harrington or Sir Angus Cunningham is a murderer."

He inhaled sharply, staring at her.

"You gave me the articles," she reminded him.

"Sir Andrew is adored in drawing rooms across London," he reminded her. "And Sir Angus...he's a sheriff and a war hero."

She nodded. "Both men fought for our great Empire in foreign wars. They might well have found some reason for resenting the Queen and the monarchy, although the murders were not exclusively political."

He nodded. "Go on."

"All right. Sir Angus was at many public meetings, perhaps to keep the peace. That is an excuse, at any rate. As sheriff, he can easily go many places and with good reason."

"All right."

"And Sir Andrew is charming, smooth. He's welcome anywhere. He was also Elizabeth Prine's cousin." She shrugged. "First cousin, I believe, which would make one suspect—"

"Sir Angus," Thane supplied. "But not necessarily. William III and Queen Mary were first cousins. And take a look at Sir Angus and then at Sir Andrew. With which man would you be having an affair?"

"Neither intrigues me," she told him, and smiled, thinking of the only man who *did* intrigue her. Then, because she liked him, she said, "Truly, had I not been promised and in love...I would have chosen you over either."

"Truly? You have absolutely restored my faith in myself," he told her, grinning. "But..." He shook his head. "It's still possible neither man is our killer. We could be speaking of a man who has served time in the military and become accustomed to killing. After all, in war, one kills the enemy and it is not considered murder."

"Which raises another point. Whoever he is, he will be feeling as if he is the conqueror of the world. He has eluded all attempts to capture him. He was probably at my wedding, the social event of the season." She refrained from mentioning the blood she had discovered on her gown. "He will grow very cocky, too sure of himself. And that is when he will make mistakes."

"If he makes mistakes, he can be caught at last," Thane said.

She leaned forward. "Perhaps we can find a way to make sure that he makes a mistake."

IT WAS A FRUITLESS DAY.

Though they haunted the appropriate routes, neither Sir Angus Cunningham nor Sir Andrew Harrington traveled by carriage that day.

As the afternoon waned, they retired to the stables at Lord Farrow's lodge. While Thomas, Geoff and Patrick joined Lord Farrow for supper, Mark slipped into the village. He found Sir Angus in his office, where they gravely discussed the murders.

If Sir Angus was guilty, he gave no sign.

During the conversation, Mark did learn that Sir Andrew and several others had been discussing a game of tennis when they were observed lunching at the club in London.

He managed to extricate himself, telling Sir Angus he was eager to return to his bride.

Back at his father's lodge, he dismounted and brought Galloway into the stables, where he remembered he still had Ally's sketchbook in his saddlebag, though he'd yet to look at it.

Sitting on a bale of hay, he wrestled momentarily with

his conscience. He should, in good faith, hand it back to her unopened.

In fact, setting it aside, he made that determination.

But he couldn't resist.

He returned to the bale of hay, picked up the book and opened it.

He was surprised to find a sketch of him in it. Masked. Her ability to capture the essence of her subject startled him. He knew why she had so quickly recognized him. She exactly captured his eyes.

He smiled, feeling a surge of warmth.

He turned the page, expecting more sketches.

He found words instead.

Reading, he found he was not prying into further essays. She had been writing a story. It was quite arresting, drawing the reader along a dark path of adventure and danger. The story took place in a temple in Egypt, and the eerie quality of tombs and treasures came through. That was only natural, he thought. She had spent many of her days at Castle Carlyle, surrounded by Egyptian artifacts. And how often must she have listened to tales told by Sir Hunter and Lady Kat?

She'd never been to Egypt, he was certain. And yet he felt as if he were seeing ancient sights firsthand as he read.

He was surprised to find himself sorely disappointed when he turned to find the next page only half written.

Rising, he returned the book to the saddlebag, then went into the lodge to join his father and the others. He would find something to eat, listen to whatever advice or wisdom his father might have for the day, and hurry home. Tomorrow would be another long day, as would the one after and the one after....

Until the killer was caught.

What if he was wrong? What if he was seeking the solution among the gentry when the killer was an ordinary working man?

He wasn't wrong. He had carefully weighed the facts and the evidence. More, he couldn't afford to be wrong.

THANE STARED AT HER, shaking his head.

"You're insane," he said.

At least, Ally thought, he hadn't said she was an idiot. "I'm not."

"You're a daredevil, at the least. And I'm not," he told her.

"I tell you, it can work."

"What about your husband?"

"I admit he might have a little difficulty with the plan at first. And he will have a lot of difficulty with the fact I came to see you first. But...I hope he will see it can work, as well."

"And if he doesn't? I am not a handsome sight with both my eyes blackened," Thane assured her.

"Mark is a reasonable man," she reassured him, hoping she was right.

He gazed at her skeptically, but she knew that she had him hooked. She said, trying not to sound nervous, "I have to get back."

"My God, I must return, as well. And convince my editor I have been in pursuit of the story of the year."

"You have been," she assured him.

They walked back to the newspaper offices together; then Ally hurried on, anxious to catch the streetcar. She chafed as she had to wait. She had gotten one so easily that morning! The day was gone, darkness already upon them. She tried to tell herself it was most likely Mark would not return until very late. And yet, because she might well be caught slipping in—which would surely enrage him and ruin any chance of speaking rationally— she felt as if the minutes she waited were interminable.

At last the conveyance came. She realized it was not nearly as full as she had expected, that it had grown late indeed, and industrious bankers and other workers in busy central London had already reached their homes.

She disembarked down the long block from the Kensington house and started walking briskly. She glanced up at the elegant homes of merchants, gentry and nobility. Drapes were drawn. Soft light emanated from windows, illuminating the lives of those within.

A man passed her on the street, tipping his hat in acknowledgment. She smiled in return. The block seemed amazingly long.

She paused suddenly, certain she was being followed.

She spun quickly, then felt like a fool as a couple politely acknowledged her and swept past.

Her heart was thundering. She watched as the couple entered a home.

She took a breath, feeling a ridiculous sense of relief.

Again she heard footsteps.

She paused and looked back.

Nothing.

She chided herself, reminding herself that she was going to have to do one of two things: either walk blithely past Bertram or slip through the neighbor's yard again, up the tree and back inside.

There was no way Bertram would refrain from telling Mark that she had been out. And she didn't want him to know. Not until she told him. The tree it was.

Once again she thought she heard footfalls coming from behind her. She spun around without missing a beat.

There was nothing there, just shadows falling on the walk between the streetlamps.

A dog barked, and she jumped.

She felt a shiver. The street was rich with foliage. Handsome bushes adorned the small yards fronting many of the houses.

Anyone could be hiding there.

She turned again, determined to hurry.

It was then she realized that a carriage had rounded the street corner behind her. She heard the clip-clop of hooves and turned to look. A handsome pair of perfectly matched black horses drew the vehicle. The coachman wore a low black hat and cape.

The carriage slowed.

She started to walk again, knowing it was drawing nearer, slowing at a rate that would bring it to a stop when it came up beside her.

She started to run.

MARK HAD CALLED THE town house from the lodge.

After several tries—the operator had connected him

first to a tailor and then to a millinery shop—he had reached Jeeter, who assured him that Lady Alexandra was upstairs and had seemed to be enjoying a leisurely day.

He had decided not to bother her but had spent some time telling his father all he knew and all he had surmised. He was gratified when Joseph listened somberly, then sadly agreed that they might well be looking at a man they had previously accepted as a friend as a murderer. A monster.

"An ordinary man would not have the resources this killer seems able to call upon easily," Joseph had told him. "Eleanor Brandon is guarded in her hospital bed?"

"Of course."

"And Lord Lionel Wittburg is an innocent man."

"Yes, but he is still being watched. His mind remains somewhat unhinged."

"Perhaps you and Ally should see him together."

"Perhaps," Mark agreed. "We'll move into my town house this week, Father, and give your home back."

Joseph grinned. "I like the lodge. Take your time. I don't like to intrude on newlyweds, but should duty call me back to town, I would simply ask you to forgive me and return home."

After the call, Mark had ridden Galloway back into the city, slowing his pace by the time he reached the outskirts, not wanting to cripple his favorite horse. The closer he got to home, though, the more eager he was to reach Ally.

At last he reached his father's street.

There was a carriage in the road ahead of him. A large, fine carriage, one he didn't believe he had seen before.

There was a woman walking—no, running—on the sidewalk.

As he watched, he saw a man leap from the carriage, carrying something in his hand.

Something that glinted in the moonlight.

Like a knife.

ALLY LOOKED BACK as she ran.

A man had emerged from the carriage. In the shadows, she could see nothing about him.

Except that he was carrying something.

Something that glinted in the glow of the streetlamps.

Wicked images flickered through her mind.

Eleanor Brandon ranting, raving, in black widow's weeds. Eleanor Brandon acting the part of the bereaved widow, cursing her.

Eleanor Brandon as she must be now, supine in her hospital bed, stitches closing the fine crimson line that slashed her throat....

She ran hard.

"Stop!"

Ally heard the thunder of the command, knew someone else was on the street. Mark. She recognized his voice. She half turned, trying to see.

As she turned, the figure that had descended from the carriage plowed into her. They fell to the ground together, the man sprawled on top of her.

She twisted, screaming in panic.

She had a chance to see the face of the man just as Mark ripped him from atop her.

"Thane!" she cried out.

"Let me go!" he shouted to Mark. "What is the matter with you people?" he demanded.

His eyes were bulging in fear, but since Mark had him in a hammerlock around the throat, that was understandable.

"Where's the knife?" Mark demanded harshly.

"What knife?" Thane asked when Mark eased the pressure on his windpipe.

"It glinted in the light. I saw it."

But even as Mark spoke, Ally saw what Thane had carried. It was an office envelope, and what had been glinting was the small steel clasp that had held it shut. She picked it up off the ground and held it out toward Mark in explanation.

The coachman had leapt down by now, but he was keeping his distance. "Mr. Grier?" he called nervously. "Is everything all right?"

"Yes, fine," Thane called. "I *am* fine, am I not?" he asked Mark tentatively. When Mark didn't release him, he begged, "Please, I am unarmed."

Mark slowly allowed him to straighten. "Start explaining."

Thane tried to adjust his severely rumpled clothing. "I was merely trying to bring some additional clippings to Ally," he said indignantly. He glared at her.

The glare said, *Help!*

"Thane, thank you," she murmured, looking past him

to Mark, who was not any less suspicious. The glance he gave her shot daggers. She looked at Thane again. "You told me you didn't have a carriage," she said.

"I don't."

"Then…"

"It belongs to my editor," he said indignantly. "It's on loan, because he believes that I'm on to the story of the century."

"And are you?" Mark asked.

"Well…" Thane said, and he looked at Ally.

"We…we need to have a discussion," she murmured.

Mark stared at her, then pulled open Thane's jacket, patted his ribs and down to his calves.

"Don't move," Mark warned. He turned toward the carriage. The nervous coachman stepped away.

Mark disappeared into the carriage.

"Has he lost his mind?" Thane whispered to Ally.

She shook her head. A moment later, Mark reappeared.

"Perhaps we should go inside?" Ally suggested. She could see that a curtain had been drawn back in the window of the house nearest where they were standing.

"All right," Mark said. He lifted a hand, his eyes still filled with suspicion as he stared at Thane Grier.

Thane nodded. "Pull up over there, please. In front of Lord Farrow's," he called to the coachman.

Ally hadn't realized until then just how Mark had arrived. He gave a whistle, and Galloway came trotting up. She wondered why she felt a moment's resentment for the fact that even the horse was so obedient.

Mark started toward the house. Bertram had realized by then that something was going on down the street. He appeared in front of the house, and his eyes widened when he saw Ally.

"My…" He fell silent, his eyes on Mark. "I swear, sir, I was watching the house all the while."

"Don't worry, Bertram. I did not ask you to make sure my wife didn't skim over the back wall," he said. "That *is* how you left, isn't it, my love?"

"You climbed a wall to leave?" Thane asked her, and she knew he was amused and a bit admiring all in one. Then Mark looked at him, and his small smile faded instantly.

Mark glared at Ally.

"I'm sorry, Bertram," she murmured, and hurried past him toward the door. Thane and Mark followed.

Jeeter appeared when he heard the door. He, too, stared at Ally, stunned. "I…"

"Never mind, Jeeter," Mark said. "Shall we sit in the library?" He indicated the door to the handsomely appointed den, where the shelves were lined with books and the huge chairs were bound in soft brown leather.

Ally preceded them. She heard Jeeter ask, "Shall I bring tea?"

"Do you have whiskey?" Thane asked.

"Of course," Jeeter said.

"I think I'll be needing one," Thane said. "If that's all right?"

"Yes, me, too," Ally said.

Mark glowered but said nothing. Jeeter went off to prepare drinks.

Mark perched on the edge of a large desk. Ally nervously took one of the chairs facing it, while Thane sat in the other.

"Well?" Mark said.

"I went to the newspaper office," Ally told him.

"I believe I expressly suggested that you both stay home and avoid Mr. Grier."

"I never said I wouldn't leave," Ally reminded him. She cleared her throat uneasily. "You made a point of telling me I'm not a prisoner."

"Does your cohort know someone tried to break into the cottage when you were still living with your aunts?" he asked.

Thane stared at her. "No!" he said. "Why?"

"I don't know," Ally murmured, then stood. "Mark, this is ridiculous."

A tap at the door informed them that Jeeter had arrived with the drinks. Ally hated whiskey, but she swallowed the alcohol down in a single toss. She knew Mark was watching her closely.

Jeeter had barely delivered the other glasses. "Would you like another, my lady?" he asked.

"Yes," Ally said.

"No," Mark told him firmly.

She stared at him, frowning. Jeeter might be willing to bend over backward to make her happy, but not when it meant going against Mark. Stone-faced, the butler left, closing the door behind him once again.

Mark folded his arms across his chest.

Thane Grier was staring at him. "You thought I was the killer!" he said.

"You were chasing my wife down a dark street."

Thane shook his head. "You thought *I* could be capable of…"

"Someone has been capable."

"Why me?"

"You had opportunity. You knew all the players involved. You wrote about various anti-monarchy gatherings."

"That's my *job*," Thane said. He stared at Mark, totally disheartened. "I swear to you…I could never… never…"

"Ally?" Mark said.

She sighed, looking down. "Mark." She managed his name, but then she had to take another deep breath. "I wrote another essay."

She could see how the mere arching of his brow could be quelling. She couldn't look at him. She chose to pace before the shelves of books.

"A. Anonymous has made an impact," she said firmly. She paused and stared at him. "And I'm proud of my essays," she added softly. "But…I never sought to do what I have ended up doing. I intend to keep writing, but my dream is to write fiction," she said, trying to keep her voice from faltering. "But we're going to let word slip out that A. Anonymous is Thane Grier."

Mark frowned. His eyes left hers and were riveted on Thane.

Thane gulped. "It was Ally's idea."

"It's a likely death sentence," Mark informed Thane.

"Not if you're watching him to see what happens after the word gets out," Ally said.

"I'm willing to do it," Thane said quietly.

"Even knowing the killer will most probably come after you?"

"That's what we're hoping," Thane said.

Mark stared at Ally.

"We can set something up to capture him," she said.

"I know how to arrange a trap," Mark said irritably.

"Good, because I'm not at all sure," Ally murmured.

"Tell me, what will tomorrow's essay suggest?" Mark asked.

"It begins with the way people are all too ready to jump to conclusions and see whatever they want to see in a situation," she said. She took a breath and looked at Thane. "Then it moves on to the fact that far too often, our lives are masquerades. That we all wear masks. It delves into the lives of Jack and Elizabeth Prine, and it was simple greed, along with her desire to be with her lover, that led to such tragedy." She hesitated. "Then it suggests that the author knows more than is being written, and that someone's position in society should never preclude taking a long look when they fall suspect to heinous deeds."

Mark stared at Ally, then turned to Thane. "You're really willing to be the sacrificial goat in all this? Any man who has been knighted, any noble in the country, will be ready to hang you."

Thane went a shade paler but nodded.

Mark turned to Ally again. "I'm sorry, I haven't read this essay word for word, but I remain lost. How is this going to trap anyone?" He gazed sharply at Thane. "And how does this promote your career?"

"When it's all over, Thane will have the story. And it will be revealed that the essay was written to draw the killer out," Ally said.

"All right. That explains the man's foolishness in going along with such a scheme. But what makes you think you can get the killer to strike at a time and place where he can be caught—before Thane's throat is slit?" he added pleasantly.

Again Thane paled.

"There's still one problem involved, as I see it," Ally said. "Letting the suggestion slip that Thane is A. Anonymous."

"Easy enough," Mark murmured, and she was surprised and pleased that he seemed to be going along with her plan. "I have lunch at the club. Perhaps play tennis with someone. Maybe even confide in Angus and Andrew. Separately, of course."

She hesitated. "While you're confiding that information, you can also tell them that Thane intends to interview me. At the cottage. It will make a lovely story, my growing up with the aunts, then marrying a future earl. The road is where you expected to catch the killer, right?"

Mark was staring at her. "You won't be at the cottage," he said quietly.

"I'll have to be there. It will have to be just as it's supposed to be. I don't believe Thane will be assaulted on the way to the cottage, because he'll be expected. His absence would be too quickly noted."

"It might work," Mark said. "I could drive out with the two of you, then leave you to talk."

"An excellent solution," Thane said. "And, I am grateful to say, a safe one."

"But we're not doing it," Mark said.

"Right. Bad idea," Thane agreed.

"Why?" Ally demanded.

"Because I don't want you involved in this."

"What?"

"Ally, it was a long shot, after all," Thane said.

But Ally seemed not to hear him. Tight-lipped and tense, she was staring at Mark. "Excuse me?"

"You're expecting me to arrive with the two of you and then ride away. When Thane leaves, I'm to follow him at a distance, which would leave you alone in the cottage."

Her eyes narrowed. "I can walk into the newspaper offices tomorrow and proudly announce that *I'm* A. Anonymous."

Mark slid off the desk. "Not if you're tied up in the bedroom," he assured her.

"I really think I should leave," Thane said. "I have to get the carriage back within the hour."

Ally stood in front of Mark, her arms crossed over her chest, in the same rigid stance he had adopted where he stood just inches from her. "That story is going out tomorrow," she told him softly.

"Looks like you will be tied up all day."

"Will you chain me down forever?"

"If I have to."

"Mark, *please*."

"Time is ticking by here," Thane murmured.

"What about the aunts?" Mark demanded. "Have you lost all concern for them?"

"Don't be ridiculous. We'll see they're safely at Castle Carlyle."

Mark shook his head with a sigh. "You're forgetting one thing."

"What?" Ally demanded.

"Sir Angus Cunningham is the sheriff."

"Yes?" Ally said with a frown.

"If he chose, he could ride to the cottage, guns blazing, and when you were both dead, he could claim Thane was the killer and you were a tragic victim in the gun battle Thane started."

"I don't even own a gun!" Thane protested.

"That wouldn't matter. You would be found with one," Mark said.

"He has a point," Thane told Ally.

"Look," Ally said, "something has to be done. We can't allow this killer to go unpunished. Mark, you think the cottage was under attack because of—" she paused, glancing at Thane, then continued "—because of who I am, or possibly because the killer thought I was A. Anonymous, because he had followed me to or from the post office. Maybe the best thing to do is let Thane off the hook. You can tell your friends, in total confidence, that you're afraid your new bride may be the essayist."

His hands went to his hips. He moved a step closer, staring down at her in anger. "Have you completely lost your mind?"

"I really do need to go," Thane said.

Ally placed a hand on her husband's chest. "Mark, that essay will go out tomorrow, one way or another. And you suspect someone may know I'm the writer, anyway. If you really want to keep me safe, you're going to have to use me as bait."

He caught her hand, pushing it aside. "You will not do anything more," he said heatedly. "I mean it, Ally. Nothing."

"The essay will go out—"

"And I will have a plan!" he snapped, exiting the library. She heard the front door slam.

Thane let out a long breath. "That went, um...well." She glared at him.

"Well, he didn't kill me." He rose. "Ally...when you're ready, when he's ready...whenever, just tell me what you want me to do."

"Thank you, Thane."

She remained in the library, watching him leave. Then she bit her lower lip, thinking she really needed a second whiskey.

CHAPTER EIGHTEEN

As THANE GRIER LEFT the house, eager to reach the borrowed carriage and return it to the newspaper offices, he found Mark Farrow standing in the drive, staring at the now fully risen moon.

Farrow looked at him. "She just manipulated us both, you know."

"But...she didn't know I would come by," Thane protested.

"Yes, that was convenient for her," Mark murmured dryly.

"But..."

"If you hadn't arrived, she still would have used your name. She would have had me thinking that yes, by God, that would work, if you were willing. And she would have done all that just so she could turn it around and make me realize anew that she might well be in danger herself already," Mark told him.

"Do you think it's true?"

"I know someone tried to break into the cottage when she was there alone. Someone who might have known the aunts were out. At that time, the killer seemed to want to be discreet. Now...I don't think the man would hesitate to kill all four of them. I think it has become all too easy for him."

"How does such a man go about his day-to-day business, without giving himself away?" Thane asked.

Mark shook his head. "I don't know. I suppose that...eventually, he would show himself." He stared at Thane. "But how much more can happen before then?"

"Do you have a plan?" Thane asked.

Mark Farrow smiled grimly. "It's forming," he said.

"As I told Ally, I am willing to do whatever you would have me do," Thane said, and he tried not to shudder as he spoke.

Mark Farrow set a hand on his shoulder. "I will let you know."

Thane nodded, and at last made his way to the carriage.

ALLY WAS STILL SEATED IN the den when Mark returned to the house. She was cradling a second glass of whiskey.

She sipped it as she watched him enter the room.

"Intriguing," he said.

"That would be...?"

"You, drinking liquid courage."

"It's wretched stuff," she informed him.

"You're ready to be the bait to catch one of the most heinous murderers the country has known—but you need whiskey when you are planning to twist me around your finger."

She flushed. "I...no! I would never...well, I was afraid you wouldn't be happy."

He went to her, kneeling down beside the chair, taking the whiskey glass from her hand. "Do you really have the intention of writing fiction rather than essays so controversial they may get you killed?"

"It is what I have always wanted to do," she said.

"Come on." He rose, catching her hands, drawing her with him. Her eyes met his with weary skepticism.

"Where?" she whispered.

"To supper and to bed," he announced.

"You're...not really..."

"Going to tie you to the bed?"

"You did mention it."

"No, my love. Supper, then bed," he assured her.

THEY HAD EATEN AND BARELY reached the top of the stairs when they heard the telephone ringing. Mark paused, leaving her at the bedroom door, apologizing, but not wanting Jeeter to be left with the dilemma of whether or not to disturb him for a call.

Ally went into the bedroom and changed into a simple cotton nightgown. She brushed her hair while she waited. Mark didn't return. Sitting at her dressing table, she picked up the scarab Kat had given her and that she had been so determined to wear at her wedding.

The curse-nullifying scarab. What a beautiful piece. And how sad and silly any fear she might have had. Eleanor Brandon had been a fake, an excellent actress. Sadly, she had paid dearly for her willingness to conspire in her husband's death.

Still, she loved the scarab, and who knew, maybe it *had* been a lucky piece.

At last there was a tap on the bedroom door. She jumped when it sounded, then laughed at herself and, on a whim, pinned the scarab to her gown.

"My lady?" Jeeter called softly.

She threw the door open, heedless of the nightgown, which was certainly decent enough.

"What is it?" she asked.

"I wasn't certain if you had gone to sleep." He smiled sheepishly.

"It's fine. What is it?"

"Mr. Farrow was…called out."

She sighed. "Called out by whom and for what reason?"

He looked very uncomfortable, as if he didn't want to reply.

"Jeeter?"

"The carriage bearing Mr. Grier never returned to the newspaper. He had borrowed it strictly to come here, so of course they called."

Ally inhaled sharply, feeling cold. If something had happened to Thane Grier, it would be her fault.

Worse. If something happened to Mark...

"Bertram has gone with him," Jeeter said gently, and she wondered if he had the ability to read her mind or if she had given so much away through her expression.

"Thank you," she told him.

"And don't you worry, my lady, I won't be leaving."

"Thank you," she said again with a smile. "I won't worry with you here."

He left her. She closed the door and paced. She lay down. She got up.

She wasn't going to sleep until Mark returned. At length she remembered the envelope Thane had brought with him that afternoon.

She rose, slipped out of her bedroom barefoot and hurried down the stairs. She didn't see Jeeter in the parlor and went into the den. She undid the offending clasp and dumped the contents onto the desk. These articles were similar to those she had already seen. Events, parties. Meetings, statements put out by different anti-monarchy societies. One by one she went through them, trying to find a mention that either Sir Angus or Sir Andrew was an anti-monarchist. Both men had been knighted, so the motive couldn't be that one of them had been overlooked for an honor.

Sometimes there were pictures—photographs or sketches—sometimes not.

She found herself pausing at an article with a sketch. Frowning, she studied it, then gasped. It was an anonymous article about the injustice of property and title laws. The article rambled on, but it was the sketch that was intriguing. It had been done perhaps two years back.

And the unidentified woman in the drawing could easily be Elizabeth Prine.

A man stood at her side, consoling her.

Sir Andrew?

Or Sir Angus, without his muttonchops and facial hair.

She let out a sigh of frustration, unsure, and shoved the articles away. Then she drew them back and started going through them again. One had nothing to do with the anti-monarchists. It concerned a fund-raiser being held at the church. There was a sketch with that article, as well. Flowers bloomed everywhere, and women were wearing their loveliest hats. The past rector of the church, Father Mason, was shown speaking to the crowd. And up front...a woman who appeared to be Elizabeth Prine.

There was a man on either side of her. Ally studied it hard, frustrated that it was only a sketch. Was one man her husband? No, once again, it looked like it might have been Sir Angus Cunningham without his facial hair. And the other man...Elizabeth's cousin. Sir Andrew Harrington.

She sighed and whispered aloud to herself, "So... would you have an affair with your dashing but too-closely-related first cousin or an older man of distinguished accomplishments?"

As she pondered the question, she heard the sound of a thump just outside the front door.

She froze.

Dead still, she listened.

She thought she heard movement from upstairs. Silently, she stood. After several seconds, she made her way to the door of the den. She started to call out for Jeeter, but something inside warned her to keep quiet.

She dashed across the parlor, through the dining room, glancing into the kitchen and the breakfast room and beyond. Jeeter wasn't downstairs.

Was he upstairs?

What had caused the thump?

She walked across the parlor to the telephone, ruing the fact that using it would be so loud that if anyone *were* in the house, they would certainly know her location immediately.

More sounds from upstairs. And they seemed to be coming from the bedroom where she should have been sleeping.

She heard another sound from just outside the front door.

In agony, she hesitated. She couldn't attempt to use the phone. If there was an intruder in the house, he would surely be on her before she could so much as reach an operator.

If the phone lines hadn't already been cut.

She moved to the front entryway and saw that the door was ajar.

It had not been opened with a key but had been pried open.

With a knife?

Movement upstairs again...

A soft moaning sound from the front.

Where in God's name was Jeeter?

She was terrified of the answer.

The sounds coming from upstairs were suddenly hair-raising. Muffled thumps, again and again.

She closed her hand around the doorknob, praying the hinges were well oiled, and stepped outside.

And found the source of the moaning.

MARK'S CALL TO IAN DOUGLAS had set a massive search into action.

He and Bertram had taken the streets near his own area, while officers combed all of London.

They were near King's Cross Station when a uniformed officer rode up to them. "My lord!" he called to Mark. "The carriage has been found! By Hyde Park. Follow me."

A quick race through the night brought them to Hyde Park and the carriage. Ian Douglas had arrived first, and he stood by the open door to the conveyance.

"Empty," he told Mark.

"Grier?" Mark demanded.

"There's no sign of him," Ian said.

Frustrated, Mark stared at the carriage. He had

searched it thoroughly just hours ago. He shook his head in frustration.

"You've looked inside?"

Ian nodded. "I found nothing."

Mark strode toward the open door and stepped inside. The compartment held nothing. No driver. No sign of Thane Grier. No damning evidence. He turned to step down, then paused.

There was blood on the seat. Not the massive spill that would have resulted from a slit throat. Rather, a smudge that might have come from an injury.

There was shouting from outside. Mark hopped down from the carriage and saw one of the officers waving to Ian from the side of the road where thick bushes overgrew the walk.

"There's a body, sir," an officer called.

Ian and Mark started to run. A man lay on the ground, facedown. Ian felt for a pulse. He shook his head, then moved to turn the body over.

A pool of still-warm blood lay beneath the body.

The man's eyes were wide in death, staring sightlessly at whatever horror had assailed him.

Ian rose. "Search the park," he said.

"Already in progress. You've seen this man?" Ian asked.

"It's the coachman I saw today," he told Ian.

The coachman dead, Thane Grier gone. A spot of blood on the seat of the carriage.

Mark turned, heading quickly for his house. Bertram followed him.

"Where are you going?" Ian called after him.

"My house! Send whatever officers you can spare."

He leapt up on Galloway and nudged the animal, verbally urging him into a gallop.

"THANE!" ALLY CRIED, dropping down beside the man who lay prone, an arm outstretched, as if he were trying to reach the doorknob. "Thane?" She touched him; he wasn't dead. He was warm, and she could see that he was breathing shallowly. She rolled him onto his back and lifted his head.

His eyes fluttered, then closed again.

There was a huge gash on his forehead. She knew she had to get help. She eased his head back down. As she did so, his eyes fluttered open, then widened.

She realized suddenly that the light spilling from the house had grown brighter as the door opened wider. She started to turn.

Suddenly burly arms were around her, a rag shoved against her face. She struggled to avoid it, smelling the drug on the cloth.

She clawed at her captor's arms, then remembered the scarab pin she had secured to her gown. With desperate, trembling fingers, she reached for it, fighting the alternating waves of nausea and blackness that threatened to overwhelm her.

She clasped hold of the pin.

Near falling, she aimed as best as she could, directing the point toward what she hoped was her attacker's eye.

A harsh bellow erupted from the man. For an instant, his hold eased. Desperately fighting for consciousness, Ally rammed her foot backward with all her might.

The man fell back, and she started to run, desperate to reach the street.

But even as she ran, she saw another figure standing there, masked by the shadows of the night.

Wearing a black cloak.

She turned and fled toward the back of the house. She reached the tree, but she could hear her pursuers closing in. She gulped in fresh air and climbed as fast as she could.

She dropped down into the neighbor's yard, dashing toward the door, where she pounded on the wood and tried to scream.

There was a thump and a curse as her attacker followed.

She pounded hard on the door. "Help!"

She'd all but lost her voice, but anyone inside must have heard the pounding.

"Help!"

He was almost on her. There was nothing left but to run for the street and pray to elude the man in the cloak.

She screamed and ran, but her prayer went unanswered.

He was there. She fought fiercely as he caught her, and she recognized the eyes she had seen so many times before, filled with charm and laughter.

She opened her mouth to scream again.

This time, there was no escaping the drugged cloth.

There was no fighting the overwhelming blackness.

MARK RODE UP IN FRONT OF the house and dismounted instantly. His heart sank. The front door was standing wide open.

He rushed toward it, noticing that the bushes at the front entry had been flattened. Ducking down to the step, he found a drop of blood.

Bertram was behind him.

"Someone was here," Mark said.

"No one's here now," Bertram said.

A man in a cap, a nightshirt and slippers was on the road. Mark vaguely recognized him as one of the neighbors. "I heard screaming, pounding! I came down as fast as I could but... There was a carriage, but he drove away."

"Which way?" Mark demanded.

The man pointed, but Mark was suddenly certain he knew which way the carriage was headed.

"Sir," he told the befuddled man in the nightcap, "my father's valet is in the house. Alive or dead, I don't know. Please find him and get him help. Bertram, call my father's lodge. Get him out on the road with any help he can find. Tell Ian's officers to follow as quickly as they can."

With that, he leapt back into the saddle and headed in pursuit.

ALLY WAS STARTLED TO AWAKEN, finding herself still alive, even though she felt so sick that she almost wished she had stayed unconscious. She could feel the terrible swaying and jolting of the carriage, moving far too quickly through the night. She had no idea how long she had been unconscious or why she was still alive. She was aware that she was half on a seat and half on the floor—and she was slamming against a set of legs on one side and a body on the other. She very carefully opened her eyes a fraction.

It was Thane's body on one side.

And on the other side...

"Bloody bitch! She's blinded me," she heard.

It was the deep voice of a man she had known for years.

The sheriff, Sir Angus Cunningham.

She suddenly realized what she would have discovered had she studied the articles—and the sketches—longer.

There were two killers.

For some reason they had all assumed that the coachman was a servant of the murderer, not his true partner in crime. They had been wrong.

She shrieked aloud as fingers tore into her hair, wrenching her head up.

She expected the slash of the knife then and there, but he had just wanted to see her face.

She was pleased to realize she had half blinded him. His left eye was a closed slit, surrounded by swollen flesh. He was scratched and bruised.

"How does it feel? I should put *your* eye out!" he thundered.

She did her best to stare at him with scorn instead of fear, but the truth was that she was filled with total terror.

But he hadn't killed her yet. He was holding off. It must be part of his plan. He must think he could still hide what he was doing.

"What did you do to Thane? And where are you taking us—and why?" she asked, playing for time. The longer she kept him talking, the longer she stayed alive. And the longer she stayed alive, the more time Mark would have to come after her, to save her.

"To the cottage in the woods, of course."

Something far beyond the sense of panic that had already seized her settled in. *The aunts!*

"Who would have thought," he murmured, "that the charming child who grew up in the woods could become such a deadly and wretched enemy. *A. Anonymous.*" He practically spat the name.

"You followed me," she said.

"From the fund-raiser. You were oblivious to everything around you. I even read the envelope. I'll bet not even your oh-so-clever husband understands the meaning of the name Olivia Cottage." He snorted. "'I live in a cottage.'"

"I suppose it's clever if it affords you so much amusement. I couldn't think of anything else."

"It doesn't matter now how clever you thought you were."

"Well, *you're* extremely clever. It took me forever to realize it wasn't you *or* Sir Andrew but both of you."

"But, my dear, it's *neither* of us, don't you see?" He smiled grotesquely. "It's the handsome young newspaperman who will slit your throat at the cottage. He's in love with you, you see, but you're married and can never be his, so you must die. But the pathetic young man did love you, and your death will send him over the edge. He'll shoot himself in remorse. Your husband will arrive, of course. He'll despise himself for having trusted the reporter. Who knows? He may complete the evening and shoot himself, as well."

He still held her hair in a death grip, and she had no choice but to keep staring up at him. "Mark Farrow will never kill himself. And you're a fool. He knows it's you—and Sir Andrew."

Sir Angus shook his head. "If he knew," he said softly, "I'd be under arrest now."

"You will be by tomorrow," she promised.

He shook his head, studying her, at last easing his hold, then finally releasing her and sitting back calmly. From the way he acted, they might have been carrying on an ordinary conversation.

"You know, Ally, despite what you've done to me, I'm sorry. You were always the most beautiful, inquisitive, fascinating child." He laughed dryly. "Always destined for something good. Beloved by Lord Stirling. Secretly engaged to Mark Farrow. Did you think I could be so close and not learn the truth about you?" he asked.

She felt a new whisper of fear tease her spine.

"What truth are you talking about?" she responded.

"Even before you became such an ungodly nuisance, I was afraid that I might have to...take care of you, my dear."

"You might have to take care of me?"

"I never had proof, of course, but I studied the situation up and down. I knew all about Maggie's work in the East End and how close she came to being a victim of the man I *know* they believe was the Ripper. So your sick, addled father was innocent. And then you had to be hidden from the monarchy. Much better that you should die before the truth about you could come out."

She felt ill, but she forced herself to shrug. "*If* that is the truth, your logic is flawed. If I were being hidden *from* the monarchy, it wouldn't make much sense to hide me under the protection of Lord Stirling."

He shook his head, seeming confused, on the defensive. She wondered if he was perhaps feeling the beginnings of a trap closing in and was now fighting simply for self-preservation.

"Save my life and you may not hang," she said.

"I'm sorry, really I am—or I would be if you hadn't

maimed me—but I'm afraid you simply must die," he returned.

"If you and Andrew hadn't killed the women, you might have gotten away with it," she said. "Poor Lord Wittburg would have gone to trial."

"Yes, I know. You might even have been spared, since, quite frankly, you were like an ace in the hole. Quite opportune, Lord Wittburg going a bit crazy the way he did. What was he so desperate to tell you? Did he know about your birth, as well? I wasn't there to hear. Andrew was the one to think of that bit of genius, stuffing the bloody cloak into the old man's carriage. He must have moved like wildfire to get it done without being noticed."

"What was that?" Ally asked.

"What?" He looked around frantically. She saw the bottle of medicinal ether beside him on the seat. She needed to distract him so she could get hold of it. Though even if she could knock him out, she would still have to deal with the driver.

Andrew.

"Listen," Ally said.

"I hear nothing," he said, but he was listening.

"Hoofbeats," she said.

To her astonishment, she realized that there really were hoofbeats. She had lied at first, but now…yes!

Someone was coming.

HE HAD NEVER RACED A HORSE so fast in his life, but Mark was heedless of what he was doing to Galloway, mindless of the low hanging branches that sometimes caught his face. He could only pray that the murderers thought they could make it to their destination before they were caught. His heart thundered as he wondered how long they had thought he would be fooled by their ruse to get him out of the house. Did they really think he would believe that Thane Grier had killed the driver, then gone back for Ally?

He rode at such speed, it was amazing time could go so slowly....

And then, at last, he saw it.

It was still a fair distance ahead of him. He spurred Galloway to an even greater burst of speed. Amazingly, the horse seemed to share his reserves of desperate energy.

As they came nearer their quarry, Sir Andrew, driving in his black cape and low brimmed hat, looked back. He slapped the reins on the lathered flanks of the carriage horses with a vengeance, then reached for his sidearm.

Mark was forced to pull back for a minute; Sir Andrew was a crack shot.

But he had almost caught up to the carriage.

Gunfire exploded. The bullet barely missed him. He felt the wind of it, passing his cheek.

He spurred Galloway around to the other side of the careening vehicle. This time, he was ready. At the speed they were going, even he might miss with a pistol.

There was greater leeway for error with a whip.

He snaked it out with an expert crack. The lash fastened around Sir Andrew's neck. He gave a garbled cry as Mark jerked and pulled him from the driver's bench to the ground.

Mark couldn't afford the time to discover if the man was alive or dead. The horses were still racing at a break-neck pace. He forced Galloway closer, at last capturing one of the flying reins. Determined not to give himself away, he kept from crying "Whoa!" to the madly gal-loping animals.

He needed to get inside the carriage.

At last it began to slow and he saw his chance.

He threw himself from Galloway to the carriage, man-aging to grasp the upper rim of the coach itself.

For a moment his legs dangled precariously, and he thought his arms would snap.

Then he gained a foothold.

"WHAT IN GOD'S NAME?" Sir Angus thundered suddenly.

Something was thumping against the carriage.

He drew his gun and fired wildly. Then he aimed again.

Desperately, Ally grabbed for the bottle of ether.

He cried out, losing aim, grabbing for her.

Her fingers just barely twined around the bottle. She felt her hair being wrenched hard. She fought the pain, managing to twist the bottle top.

The scent of chloroform instantly made her dizzy. She had only seconds, she knew....

She threw the contents into Sir Angus's face.

His gun went off, the shot wild again. She could only pray it hadn't hit Mark.

If it was Mark...

She knew it was Mark.

She knew it....

Even when the drug splashed back into her own face and the world went black.

A SHOT CRACKED, SO CLOSE that the bullet sliced by his sleeve. Another shot shattered through the roof of the coach.

The horses had slowed further, and he was able to get the door open. His heart leapt into his throat.

There were three of them.

Thane Grier.

Sir Angus, his powerful bulk blocking the door.

And Ally, slumped beside him on the floor.

He could smell the sweet, sickening scent of ether. He held his breath as the first wave of dizziness seized him. The carriage was still rolling. He threw Sir Angus's body from it, still trying not to breathe as he reached for Ally. He picked her up and leapt out of the carriage, which rolled onward for another thirty feet. One of the terrified horses whinnied as the animals came to a halt at last.

He set Ally carefully on the side of the road. As he did, he realized he heard the sounds of other hoofbeats, approaching from ahead.

The first rider to reach him was his father, with Brian Stirling at his side.

"The carriage! Get Thane Grier out. The thing is full of ether."

Brian dismounted and ran to do as asked. His father knelt by his side.

"Son...?"

"She's breathing," Mark said. "She has a pulse."

Brian Stirling returned, carrying Thane Grier's limp body. "The castle is the closest place to take them," he said.

By then Bertram, with several mounted officers, had reached them. Brian handed Grier up to one of them and gave orders to ride for the castle. Forgetting everything else, Mark tenderly cradled Ally in his arms and returned to the sweating, panting Galloway.

"One more ride, boy. One more fast ride."

Again it seemed that no matter how fast they ran, it could not be fast enough. And yet finally they reached the castle.

Shelby had the gate open. Camille was waiting on the steps. The aunts were behind her, anxious, yet calm when the men burst into the grand entry, carrying their burdens. "Bring Ally to her room, and...Mr. Grier, is it?...to the one beside it. Do you know what has caused this?" Shelby asked.

"Ether," Mark said briefly.

"Then they will come out of it," Camille said.

He heard a soft sob. Merry. He forced himself to ignore the aunts as he headed for the stairs, anxious to set Ally down and assess the damage himself.

"She *will* come out of it," Camille said firmly, and she called to Molly the maid, begging her to see to Mr. Grier while they waited for the doctor, who had already been called.

Mark burst into Ally's room and set her down on the bed. He checked her pulse again, and it was strong. He laid his ear close to her chest, and felt the rise and fall of her breath. He looked anxiously up at Camille, his heart in his throat. She offered a smile.

He realized that the three aunts had followed them in, silent, clinging to one another.

It was Merry who stepped forward. "She will live. Our Ally is a precious princess, and she will live."

He trembled with fear. Her gown was ripped, muddied. Her hair was tangled with leaves and twigs. She had never appeared more beautiful to him, as she lay so silent and pale on the bed. Shaking, he touched her lips with the whisper of his own.

Her eyelids flickered. They opened to his. She almost smiled.

Her eyes closed again.

He fell by the side of the bed on his knees, thanking God.

Yes, she would live.

HER EYES OPENED. At first, she couldn't quite focus. Then she knew where she was, and that she was alive, though she could have been forgiven for thinking she was lying in some Egyptian tomb, because she was surrounded by busts and urns and papyri. She exhaled, smiling. She was in her room at the castle.

A second later she saw his face, his rugged, terribly handsome face. "For a moment I thought I'd traveled on to meet the long-gone pharaohs," she whispered.

"No. You're in the castle. Not our castle, I'm afraid, though we do have one, you know." He caught her hand and kissed it.

"She's awake!" Ally heard someone say. She looked around. It was still a bit painful, and she learned quickly that quick movement made her dizzy. There they were. Violet, Merry and Edith. And then she saw Maggie, Camille and Kat.

Ally smiled and turned to the aunties first. Her godmothers would understand.

"I dreamed of you the whole time," she whispered. "You were the most darling fairies, flitting about, watching over me."

"Fairies? Good heavens. We're solid Englishwomen," Violet said indignantly.

"Ally has always had the most wonderful imagination," Merry said.

"She's teasing us," Edith said, and, brushing past Mark, hugged Ally fiercely.

"Hugs all around," Ally said, and even Violet giggled as Ally somehow managed to hug and kiss all three together, then offer the same to Maggie, Kat and Camille. With sighs of relief, the six women left the room one by one, Camille assuring Mark that tea would come soon, now that Ally was awake.

Ally clutched Mark suddenly. "You—you're not injured? Were you shot?"

He shook his head. "You saved me."

She managed a smile. "And you saved me." She frowned. "How? What happened to Sir Andrew? And Angus? And Thane!"

"Thane is conscious and enjoying all kinds of attention next door. Sir Andrew is dead."

"How?"

"His neck was broken. A fall from the driver's seat of the carriage at a fast speed."

She nodded and exhaled, then grasped him again. "Jeeter?"

"They only knocked him out. It was expedient, I guess. He's going to be all right. I haven't actually seen him. Our next-door neighbor—the ambassador from Sweden, I now know—awoke and went to tend to him. He had the presence of mind to let the police know he'd found him and was taking him to the hospital. He called and said Jeeter will be fine. Of course, he's going to be distressed, certain he failed us. It will not be an easy task for us to convince him that Sir Angus and Sir Andrew were a lethal pair."

"What about Sir Angus?" she asked.

"He will hang—if he lives."

"What happened?"

"I did not madly seek revenge, though..." He cleared

his throat and explained, "When he started to come to, apparently he attacked one of Ian's officers. Ian was forced to drag him off. Sir Angus went for Ian, and one of the officers shot him."

"Where is he now?" she asked.

"In the prison ward at the hospital. It's doubtful he'll pull through."

She nodded. She couldn't feel sorrow. Angus had been a sheriff, sworn to uphold the law. Instead he had abused it and stolen others' lives.

"It will be all right," he said softly.

Again she nodded. Then she realized that she was no longer wearing the torn white gown but a soft gold one. Had it been hers? She didn't remember it.

"Lady Maggie," he said softly, noticing her quizzical look.

"Ah," she murmured. She shook her head. "So they *were* taking care of me. I did imagine fairies fluttering about." She frowned. "Mark, it's so horrible, if I really understand all that happened."

He inhaled. "As we've pieced it together, it seems that something happened to Sir Andrew when he was in the service."

"And Angus?" she asked.

He nodded. "In the creation of our Empire, there have been many soldiers who thought the Crown had betrayed them, sending them out to fight without enough men or weapons. Though he was knighted, Andrew suffered from a slowly simmering hatred. So he used his charm, made friends with many among the nobility, and gained a firm foothold in society. There he continued to nurture his hatred of the monarchy, a hatred that others shared, due to the times we live in. Many people feel that the government needs vast reform, and wonder if Victoria and her family are an expensive liability rather than a diplomatic asset. Apparently Sir Andrew also had a longstanding lust for his cousin Elizabeth, so he conveniently befriended her husband, who shared his hatred of the monarchy. As well, Jack had money, and as Andrew tended to need more than he had—playing tennis, lunching and drinking at the club, filling his wardrobe— this idea began to grow in his mind. As for Sir Angus, it seems that Andrew was instrumental in getting Angus the job, and, sensing a malleable mind, converted him to the anti-monarchy point of view. I believe Angus is the sort of man who wants more power, and he was ready to believe that power would be his if he could bring about a new world order. They committed murder for two reasons—financial reward and the accomplishment of their political goals. When he was afraid that Elizabeth might betray him, Andrew let expediency override whatever feelings he had for her. If they killed the women, they killed their accomplices, who might have become witnesses against them or given them away in some inadvertent manner."

"Poor Lord Wittburg could have died for their crimes." Ally looked at him intently. "I don't understand what happened today. Our plan seemed so fool-proof."

"It seems Sir Angus wasn't in the village today. He had come into the newspaper office on the pretext of advertising a festival in the village. He'd followed you to the post office earlier and knew something of your secret identity. Today, to him, was a stroke of luck. He was able to reach Sir Andrew at the club, and they began to plan."

"I see," she murmured.

"I can only be grateful he didn't kill you in London." She was startled by the tremor in his voice.

"They thought if they killed Thane and me at the cottage, you would believe that Thane had killed me out of jealousy, then himself out of remorse." She hesitated. "And he knew, Sir Angus knew...about me. I think he would have killed me even if I weren't A. Anonymous. You were supposed to die, as well. I suppose Thane, in his ardent desire to protect the queen, was supposed to have killed all the others, as well." She swallowed hard, shivering.

He caught her hand tightly. "They never would have succeeded. I knew exactly what had happened the minute we found the coachman, who, I am sorry to say, died in this tragedy, as well." And yet...just a few more minutes. They were close, so close.

"I bought time."

"Pardon?"

She smiled, holding his hand, leaning back. "The night that Eleanor put on the bereaved act and cursed me, Kat gave me a gift. A scarab pin. I stabbed Angus in the eye with it."

"We wondered what had happened to him. Bright girl," he told her.

She smiled. "Sometimes." She reached out to him. "Very bright boy," she teased.

He leaned forward and kissed her again. He tried to be gentle, still worried about the effects of the drug and the attack.

But…

Ally would have her way, and so he scooped her into his arms and lay down beside her.

THE QUEEN WANTED TO MEET Ally and Thane, the journalist whose final article on the murders had put everything into perspective and calmed the mood of the entire nation!

Mark escorted them to their audience in the outer chamber of Victoria's personal quarters.

It was evident she had a fondness for Mark. And he was absolutely charming to her.

The queen studied Ally carefully and with affection, Ally thought, and yet with a terrible sadness.

Thane was in ecstasy. Especially when Victoria said they must have tea.

"What now, Mark?" the queen demanded imperiously. "Will you be able to settle in to being a happy newlywed?"

"Yes," Mark said, and Ally thought there was far more

to the simple exchange than the words said. "I believe so. My wife seems to have a taste for Egyptian adventure. I believe we will head out on next season's expedition with our dear friends the Stirlings and the MacDonalds. Lord Jamie and Lady Maggie just may be convinced to go, as well."

"Lovely," the queen said, obviously pleased. She sighed deeply. "I will think of you. And after that, Mark?"

"After that, Your Highness, I will return and serve the Crown as best I may."

"You're married now," she reminded him.

"Yes, but to a most remarkable wife. One with whom I do believe I will be able to share all my thoughts, dreams, desires—and adventures." He smiled at Ally. She took his hand, and she squeezed it.

"An excellent stroke of luck," the queen said. "And you, Mr. Grier, will go on to a remarkable career as a journalist, I'm quite certain."

He nodded, blushing.

Shortly afterward tea was finished and the audience was over. The three of them rose, and one of the queen's ladies showed them out.

"Buckingham Palace," Thane said as they walked out the gates. "And I was a guest."

"You deserve to shine before royalty," Ally told him, grinning.

"Shine and return to work," he said wryly.

"Indeed," Mark said, and he looked down at Ally,

smiling. He offered Thane his hand then. "Well, we're off for the week."

"Where are you going?"

"North. Ally needs to see the family castle."

"Enjoy yourselves. Don't forget me," Thane warned them.

"Never," Ally promised.

They parted ways. Thane was already thinking of the piece he would do on the Farrows when they headed off on their voyage to Egypt.

He paused, looking back as the two headed off together, hand in hand, smiling at each other every few steps.

He sighed softly.

"And they lived happily ever after," he said aloud.

Then, with a smile, he headed off down the street for work.

Harlequin® Historical
Historical Romantic Adventure!

Loyalty...or love?

LORD GREVILLE'S CAPTIVE

Nicola Cornick

He had previously come to Grafton Manor to be betrothed to the beautiful Lady Anne—but that promise was broken with the onset of the English Civil War. Now Lord Greville has returned as an enemy, besieging the manor and holding its lady prisoner.

His devotion to his cause is swayed by his desire for Anne—he will have the lady, and her heart.

Yet Anne has a secret that must be kept from him at all costs....

On sale December 2006.
Available wherever Harlequin books are sold.

REQUEST YOUR
FREE BOOKS!

2 FREE NOVELS
FROM THE ROMANCE/SUSPENSE
COLLECTION PLUS 2 FREE GIFTS!

BOB206

SHANNON DRAKE

77033   WICKED   ___ $7.50 U.S. ___ $8.99 CAN.
                  (limited quantities available)

TOTAL AMOUNT $ _____
POSTAGE & HANDLING $ _____
($1.00 FOR 1 BOOK, 50¢ for each additional)
APPLICABLE TAXES* $ _____
TOTAL PAYABLE $ _____
          (check or money order—please do not send cash)

To order, complete this form and send it, along with a check or money
order for the total above, payable to HQN Books, to: **In the U.S.:**
3010 Walden Avenue, P.O. Box 9077, Buffalo, NY 14269-9077;
In Canada: P.O. Box 636, Fort Erie, Ontario, L2A 5X3.

Name: _____
Address: _____ City: _____
State/Prov.: _____ Zip/Postal Code: _____
Account Number (if applicable): _____

075 CSAS

*New York residents remit applicable sales taxes.
*Canadian residents remit applicable GST and provincial taxes.

HQN™

We *are* romance™